Philip José Farmer's Celebrated and Fantastic
RIVERWORLD

Where 36 billion people—everyone who ever lived, from Karl Marx to Tom Mix to Joan of Arc—are thrown together on the steep banks of a giant River, flowing through the barren clif. of an unknown planet to a final, icy sea . . .

Where adventurers in boats and dirigibles seek the headwaters, the home of the mysterious Ethicals, the unseen creators of the "dark design" . . .

"ONE OF THE MOST IMAGINATIVE WORLDS IN SCIENCE FICTION!"

Advance *Booklist*

Other books in the Riverworld Series:
To Your Scattered Bodies Go
The Fabulous Riverboat

THE DARK DESIGN

THE THIRD VOLUME IN
THE *RIVERWORLD* SERIES

PHILIP JOSÉ FARMER

A BERKLEY BOOK
published by
BERKLEY PUBLISHING CORPORATION

Though some of the names in The Riverworld Series are fictional, the characters are or were real. You may not be mentioned, but you're here.

*To Sam Long and my godson David,
son of Doctor Docter*

And still the Weaver plies his loom, whose warp
     and woof is wretched Man
Weaving th' unpattern'd dark design, so dark we
     doubt it owns a plan.
      —*The Kasîdah of Hâjî Abdû al-Yazdi*

"Sentence first—verdict afterwards."
      —*Alice in Wonderland*

Foreword

THE BOOK AT HAND IS VOLUME III OF THE RIVERWORLD SERIES. Originally, it was to be the conclusion of a trilogy. However, the Ms. was more than 400,000 words long. Published under one cover, it would be too heavy and unwieldy for the reader.

Therefore, the publisher and myself decided to cut it into two. Volume IV, *The Magic Labyrinth*, will follow this book. It will definitely conclude this phase of the series, explain all the mysteries set forth in the first three volumes, tie up all ends in a knot, Gordian or otherwise.

Any novels about the Riverworld after volume IV are not to be considered as part of the mainstream of the series. These will be the "sidestream," stories not directly concerned with mystery and the quests of the first three. My decision to write these is based on my belief—and that of many others—that the Riverworld concept is too big to compress within four volumes. After all, we have a planet on which a single river, or a very long and narrow sea, runs for 16,090,000 kilometers, or about 10,000,000 miles. More than thirty-six billion people live along its banks, human beings who existed from the Old Stone Age through the first part of the Electronic Age.

There is not room in the first four volumes to chronicle many events which might interest the reader. For instance, the resurrectees were not distributed along The River according to the chronological sequence in which they had been born on Earth. There was a considerable mixture of races and nationalities from different centuries. Take as an example one of the many thousands of blocs along the banks. This would be in an area ten kilometers long, and the people comprising it would be 60 percent 3rd-century A.D. Chinese, 39 percent 17th-century A.D. Russians, and 1 percent men and women from anywhere and anytime.

How would these people manage to form a viable state from anarchy? How would they succeed, or fail, in their efforts to get along with each other and to form a body which could defend itself against hostile states? What problems would they have?

In the book at hand, Jack London, Tom Mix, Nur ed-din el-Musafir, and Peter Jairus Frigate sail on the *Razzle Dazzle II* up The

River. There is considerable characterization of Frigate and Nur in volumes III and IV. However, there was not enough space to fully develop the characters of the others. So, the "sidestream" stories will give me scope to do this.

These will also relate how the crew of the *Razzle Dazzle* meet some major and minor representatives of various fields of human endeavor. These should include da Vinci, Rousseau, Karl Marx, Rameses II, Nietzsche, Bakunin, Alcibiades, Eddy, Ben Jonson, Li Po, Nichiren Daishonin, Asoka, an Ice Age cavewife, Joan of Arc, Gilgamesh, Edwin Booth, Faust et al.

It's been apparent to some that Peter Jairus Frigate remarkably resembles the author. It is true that I am the basis for that character, but Frigate has approximately the similarity to me that David Copperfield has to Charles Dickens. The author's physical and psychic features are only a springboard for propelling reality into that parareality—fiction.

I apologize to the readers for the cliffhanger endings of the first three volumes. The structure of the series was such that I could not emulate that of Isaac Asimov's Foundation series. In these each volume *seemed* to have a definite conclusion, the mystery seemingly solved, only to reveal in the sequel that the previous ending was false or misleading.

I hope to finish the series, volumes I through V (or possibly VI), before it's my time to lie down and rest while waiting to board the fabulous riverboat.

—PHILIP JOSÉ FARMER

1

DREAMS HAUNTED THE RIVERWORLD.

Sleep, night's Pandora, was even more generous than on Earth. There, it had been this for you and that for your neighbor. Tomorrow, that for you and this for next door.

Here in this endless valley, along these unceasing Riverbanks, she dumped her treasure chest, showering everybody with all gifts: terror and pleasure, memory and anticipation, mystery and revelation.

Billions stirred, muttered, groaned, whimpered, laughed, cried out, swam to wakefulness, sank back again.

Mighty engines battered the walls, and things wriggled out through the holes. Often, they did not retreat but stayed, phantoms who refused to fade at cockcrow.

Also, for some reason, dreams recurred more frequently than on the mother planet. The actors of the nocturnal Theater of the Absurd insisted on return engagements, performances which they, not the patrons, commanded. The attendees were powerless to jeer or applaud, to throw eggs and cabbages or walk out, to chatter with their seatmates or doze.

Among this captive audience was Richard Francis Burton.

FOG, GREY AND SWIRLING, FORMED THE STAGE AND THE BACKDROP. Burton stood in the pit like an Elizabethan too poor to afford a seat. Above him were thirteen figures, all in chairs which floated in the mist. One of them faced the others, who were arranged in a semicircle. That man was the protagonist—himself.

There was a fourteenth person there, though it stood in the wings and could be seen only by the Burton in the pit. It was a black, menacing shape which, now and then, chuckled hollowly.

A not quite similar scene had happened before, once in reality and many times in dreams, though who could be sure which was which? There he was, the man who'd died seven hundred and seventy times in a vain effort to elude his pursuers. And there sat the twelve who called themselves the Ethicals.

Six were men; six, women. Except for two, all had deeply tanned or heavily pigmented skins and black or dark brown hair. The eyes of two men and a woman had slight epicanthic folds, which made him think that they were Eurasians. That is, they were if they had originated on Earth.

Only two of the twelve had been named during the brief inquisition—Loga and Thanabur. Neither name seemed to be of any language he knew, and he knew at least a hundred. However, languages change, and it was possible that they might be from the fifty-second century A.D. One of their agents had told them that he came from that time. But Spruce had been under threat of torture and might have been lying.

Loga was one of the few with comparatively pale skins. Since he was sitting and there was (and had been) nothing material to measure him against, he could be short or tall. His body was thick and muscular, and his chest was matted with red hair. The hair on his head was fox-red. He had irregular and strong features: a prominent, deeply clefted chin; a massive jaw; a large and aquiline nose; thick pale-yellow eyebrows; wide, full lips; and dark green eyes.

The other light-skinned man, Thanabur, was obviously the leader. His physique and face were so much like Loga's that they could be brothers. His hair, however, was dark brown. One eye was green, though a rare leaf-green.

The other eye had startled Burton when Thanabur had first turned his face toward him. Instead of the green mate he had expected, he saw a jewel. It looked like an enormous blue diamond, a flashing, multifaceted precious stone set in his eye socket.

He felt uneasy whenever that jewel was turned on him. What was its purpose? What did it see in him that a living eye could not see?

Of the twelve, only three had spoken: Loga, Thanabur, and a slim but full-breasted blonde with large blue eyes. From the manner in which she and Loga spoke to each other, Burton thought that they could be husband and wife.

Watching them offstage, Burton noted again that just above the heads of each, his other self included, was a globe. They whirled, were of many changing colors, and extended six-sided arms, green, blue, black, and white. Then the arms would shrink into the globe, only to be replaced by others.

Burton tried to correlate the rotating spheres and the mutation in the arms with the personalities of the three and of himself, with their physical appearances, with the tones of their voices, with the meanings of their words, with their emotional attitudes. He failed to find any significant linkages.

When the first, the real, scene had taken place, he had not seen his own aura.

The spoken lines were not quite the same as during the actual event. It was as if the Dream-Maker had rewritten the scene.

Loga, the red-haired man, said, "We had a number of agents looking for you. They were a pitifully small number, considering the thirty-six billion, six million, nine thousand, six hundred and thirty-seven candidates that are living along The River."

"Candidates for what?" the Burton on the stage said.

In the first performance, he had not uttered that line.

"That's for us to know and you to find out," Loga said.

Loga flashed teeth that seemed inhumanly white. He said, "We had no idea that you were escaping us by suicide. The years went by. There were other things for us to do, so we pulled all agents from the Burton Case, as we called it, except for some stationed at both ends of The River. Somehow, you had knowledge of the polar tower. We found out how later."

Burton, the watcher, thought, *But you didn't find out from X.*

He tried to get nearer to the actors so he could look at them more closely. Which one was the Ethical who had awakened him in the preressurection place? Which one had visited him during a stormy, lightning-racked night? Who was it that had told him that he must help him? Who was the renegade whom Burton knew only as X?

He struggled against the wet, cold mists, as ethereal yet as strong as the magic chains which had bound the monster wolf Fenrir until Ragnarok, the doom of the gods.

Loga said, "We would have caught you, anyway. You see, every space in the restoration bubble—the place where you unaccountably awakened during the preresurrection phase—has an automatic counter. Any candidate who has a higher than average number of deaths is a subject for study sooner or later. Usually later, since we're short-handed.

"We had no idea it was you who had racked up the staggering number of seven hundred and seventy-seven deaths. Your space in the PR bubble was empty when we looked at it during our statistical investigation. The two technicians who had seen you when you woke up in the PR chamber identified you by your . . . photograph.

"We set the resurrector so that the next time your body was to be recreated, an alarm would notify us, and we would bring you here to this place."

But Burton had not died again. Somehow, they had located him while he was alive. Though he had run away again, he had been caught. Or had he? Perhaps, as he ran through the night, he had been killed by lightning. And they were waiting for him in the PR bubble. That vast chamber which he supposed was somewhere deep under the surface of this planet or in the tower of the polar sea.

Loga said, "We've made a thorough search of your body. We have also screened every component of your . . . psychomorph. Or aura, whichever word you prefer."

He pointed at the flashing, whirling globe above the Burton who sat in the chair facing him.

Then the Ethical did a strange thing.

He turned and looked out into the mists and pointed at Burton, the watcher.

"We found no clues whatsoever."

The dark figure in the wings chuckled.

The Burton in the pit called out, "You think there are only twelve of you! There are thirteen! An unlucky number!"

"It's quality, not quantity, that matters," the thing off-stage said.

"You won't remember a thing that occurs down here after we send you back to the Rivervalley," Loga said.

The Burton in the chair said something that he had not said in the original inquisition.

"How can you make me forget?"

"We have run off your memory as if it were a tape recording," Thanabur said. He talked as if he were lecturing. Or was he warning Burton because he was X?

"Of course, it took a long time to run your memory track for the seven years since you've been here. And it required an enormous amount of energy and materials. But the computer Loga monitored was set to run your memory at high-speed and stop only when you were visited by that filthy renegade. So, we know what happened then exactly as you knew what happened. We saw what you saw, heard what you heard, felt what you touched, what you smelled. We even experienced your emotions.

"Unfortunately, you were visited at night, and the traitor was effectively disguised. Even his voice was filtered through a distorter which prevented the computer from analyzing his—or her—voice-prints. I say his or her because all you saw was a pale thing without identifiable features, sexual or otherwise. The voice seemed to be masculine, but a female could have used a transmitter to make it seem a man's.

"The body odor was also false. The computer analyzed it, and it's obvious that a chemical complex altered that.

"In short, Burton, we have no idea which of us is the renegade, nor do we have any idea why he or she would be working against us. It is almost inconceivable that anyone who knew the truth would try to betray us. The only explanation is that the person is insane. And that, too, is inconceivable."

The Burton in the pit knew, somehow, that Thanabur had not spoken those words during the first performance, the real drama. He also knew that he was dreaming, that he was sometimes putting words in Thanabur's mouth. The man's speech was made up of Burton's own thoughts, speculations, and fantasies which were afterthoughts.

The Burton in the chair now voiced some of these.

"If you can read a person's mind—tape it, as it were—why don't you read your own minds? Surely you have done that? And just as surely, you would have found your traitor."

Loga, looking uncomfortable, said, "We submitted to a reading, of course. But . . ."

He raised his shoulders and spread out his palms upward.

Thanabur said, "So, the person you call X must have been lying to you. He is not one of us but one of the second-order, an agent. We are calling them in for memory scanning. That takes time, however. We have plenty of that. The renegade will be caught."

The Burton in the chair said, "And what if *none* of the agents is guilty?"

"Don't be ridiculous," Loga said. "In any event your memory of awakening in the preressurection bubble will be erased. Also, your memory of the renegade's visit and all events from that time on will be a blank space. We are truly sorry to have to do this violent act. But it is necessary, and the time will come, we hope, when we can make amends."

The Burton in the chair said, "But . . . I will have many recollections of the preressurection place. You forget that I often thought of that between the time I awoke on the banks and X's visit. Also, I told many people about it.''

Thanabur said, ''Ah, but do they really believe you? And if they do, what can they do about it? No, we do not want to remove your entire memory of your life here. It would cause you great distress; it would remove you from your friends. And''—here Thanabur paused—''it might slow down your progress.''

''Progress?''

''There is time for you to find out what that means. The insane person who claims to be aiding you was using you for his own purposes. He did not tell you that you were throwing away your opportunity for eternal life by carrying out his designs. He or she, whoever the traitor is, is evil. Evil, evil!''

''Now, now,'' Loga said. ''We all feel strongly about this but we must not forget. The . . . unknown is sick.''

The jewel-eyed man said, ''To be sick is, in a sense, to be evil.''

The Burton in the chair threw back his head and laughed loudly and long.

''So you bastards don't know everything?''

He stood up, the gray fog supporting him as if it were solid, and he shouted, ''You don't want me to get to the headwaters of The River! Why? Why?''

Loga said, ''*Au revoir*. Forgive us for this violence.''

A woman pointed a short, slim blue cylinder at the Burton on the stage, and he crumpled. Two men, wearing only white kilts, emerged from the fog. They picked up the senseless body and carried it into the mists.

Burton tried again to get at the people on the stage. Failing, he shook his fist at them, and he cried, ''You'll never get me, you monsters!''

The dark figure in the wings applauded, but his hands made no noise.

Burton had expected to be placed in the area where he had been picked up by the Ethicals. Instead, he awoke in Theleme, the little state which he had founded.

Even more unexpected was that he had not been deprived of his memory. He remembered everything, even the inquisition with the twelve Ethicals.

Somehow, X had managed to fool the others.

Later, he got to wondering if they had lied to him and had not intended to tamper with his memory. That made no sense, but then he did not know what their intentions were.

At one time, Burton had been able to play two games of chess at the same time while blindfolded. That, however, only required skill, a knowledge of the rules, and familiarity with the board and the pieces. He did not know the rules of this game, nor did he know the powers of all the chessmen.

The dark design had no pattern.

3

GROANING, BURTON HALF-AWOKE.

For a moment, he didn't know where he was. Darkness surrounded him, darkness as thick as that which he felt filled him.

Familiar sounds reassured him. The ship was rubbing up against the dock, and water lapped against the hull. Alice was breathing softly by him. He touched her soft, warm back. Light footsteps came from above, Peter Frigate on night watch. Perhaps he was getting ready to wake up his captain. Burton had no idea what time it was.

There were other well-known sounds. Through the wooden partition the snores of Kazz and his woman, Besst, gurgled. And then, from the compartment behind theirs, the voice of Monat issued. He spoke in his native language, but Burton could not distinguish the words.

Doubtless, Monat was dreaming of far-off Athaklu. Of that planet with its "wild, weird clime" which circled the giant orange star, Arcturus.

He lay for a while, rigid as a corpse, thinking, *Here I am, a one-hundred-and-one-year-old man in the body of a twenty-five-year-old.*

The Ethicals had softened the hardened arteries of the candidates. But they had not been able to do anything about atherosclerosis of the soul. That repair was apparently left up to the candidate.

The dreams were going backward in time. The inquisition by the Ethicals had come last. But now he was dreaming that he was experiencing again the dream he'd had just before he awoke to the Last Trump. However, he was watching himself in the dream; he was both participant and spectator.

God was standing over him as he lay on the grass, as weak as a newly born baby. This time, He lacked the long, black, forked beard, and He was not dressed like an English gentleman of the fifty-third year of Queen Victoria's reign. His only garment was a blue towel wrapped around his waist. His body was not tall, as in the original dream, but was short and broad and heavily muscled. The hairs on His chest were thick and curly and red.

The first time, Burton had looked into God's face and seen his own. God had had the same black straight hair, the same Arabic face with the deep, dark eyes like spearpoints thrusting from a cave, the high cheekbones, the heavy lips, and the thrust-out, deeply cleft chin. However, His face no longer bore the scars of the Somali spear that had sliced through Burton's cheek, knocking out teeth, its edge jammed into his palate, its point sticking out the other cheek.

The face looked familiar, but he couldn't name its owner. It certainly was not that of Richard Francis Burton.

God still had the iron cane. Now He was poking Burton in the ribs.

"You're late. Long past due for the payment of your debt, you know."

"What debt?" the man on the grass said.

The Burton who was watching suddenly realized that fog was swirling around him, casting veils between the two before him. And a grey wall, expanding and contracting as if it were the chest of a breathing animal, was behind them.

"You owe for the flesh," God said. He poked the ribs of the man on the grass. Somehow, the standing Burton felt the pain.

"You owe for the flesh and the spirit, which are one and the same thing."

The man on the grass struggled to get onto his feet. He said, gasping, "Nobody can strike me and get away without a fight."

Somebody snickered, and the standing Burton became aware of a dim, tall figure in the fog beyond.

God said, "Pay up, sir. Otherwise, I'll be forced to foreclose."

"Damned money lender!" the man on the grass said. "I ran into your kind in Damascus."

"This is the *road to* Damascus. Or it should be."

The dark figure snickered again. The fog enclosed all. Burton awoke, sweating, hearing the last of his whimperings.

Alice turned and said sleepily, "Are you having a nightmare, Dick?"

"I'm all right. Go back to sleep."

"You've been having many nightmares lately."

"No more than on Earth."

"Would you like to talk?"

"When I dream, I *am* talking."

"But to yourself."

"Who knows me better?" He laughed softly.

"And who can deceive you better," she said a little tartly.

He did not reply. After a few seconds, she was breathing with the gentle rhythm of the untroubled. But she would not forget what had been said. He hoped that morning would not bring another quarrel.

He liked arguing; it enabled him to explode. Lately, however, their fights had left him unsatisfied, ready at once for another.

It was so difficult to blaze away at her without being overheard on this small vessel. Alice had changed much during their years together, but she still retained a ladylike abhorrence of, as she put it, washing their dirty linen in public. Knowing this, he pressed her too hard, shouted, roared, getting pleasure out of seeing her shrink. Afterward, he felt ashamed because he had taken advantage of her, because he had caused her shame.

All of which made him even more angry.

Frigate's footsteps sounded on the deck. Burton thought of relieving Frigate early. He would not be able to get back to sleep; he'd suffered from insomnia most of his adult life on Earth and much here, too. Frigate would be grateful to get to bed. He had trouble staying awake when on watch.

He closed his eyes. Darkness was replaced by greyness. Now he saw himself in that colossal chamber without walls, floor, or ceiling. Naked, he was floating in a horizontal position in the abyss. As if suspended on an invisible, unfelt spit, he was turning slowly. Rotating, he saw that there were naked bodies above, to the sides, and below. Like him, their heads and pubic regions were shaven. Some were incomplete. A man nearby had a right arm which was skinless from the elbow down. Turning, he saw another body that had no skin at all and no muscles in the face.

At a distance was a skeleton with a mess of organs floating inside it.

Everywhere, the bodies were bounded at head and foot by red metallic-looking rods. They rose from the unseen floor and ascended to the unseen ceiling. They stood in rows as far as he could see, and in a vertical line between each pair hovered the wheeling bodies, rank on rank of sleepers, bodies as far down, bodies as far up, as the eye could encompass.

They formed vertical and horizontal lines stretching into grey infinity.

This time, watching, he felt some of the bewilderment and the terror of the first moment of awakening.

He, Captain Sir Richard Francis Burton, Her Majesty's consul at the city of Trieste in the Austro-Hungarian Empire, had died on Sunday, October 19, 1890.

Now he was alive in a place that was like no heaven or hell he had ever heard of.

Of all the millions of bodies he could see, he was the only one alive. Or awake.

The rotating Burton would be wondering why he was singled out for this unsought honor.

The watching Burton now knew why.

It was that Ethical whom Burton called X, the unknown quality, who had roused him. The renegade.

Now the suspended man had touched one of the rods. And that had broken some kind of circuit, and all the bodies between the rods had started to fall, Burton among them.

The watcher felt almost as much terror as when it had first occurred. This was a primal dream, the universal human dream of falling. Doubtless, it originated from the first man, the half-ape half-sentient, for whom the fall was a dread reality, not just a nightmare. The half-ape had leaped from one branch to another, thinking in his pride that he could span the gulf. And he had fallen because of his pride, which distorted his judgment.

Just as Lucifer's fall had been caused by his pride.

Now that other Burton had grabbed a rod and was hanging on while the bodies, still turning slowly, hurtled past him, a cataract of flesh.

Now he looked up and saw an aerial machine, a green canoe shape, sinking down through the space between nearby rods. It was wingless, propellerless, apparently buoyed up by some kind of device unknown to the science of his day.

On its bow was a symbol: a white spiral which ended pointing to the right and from which point white threads flared.

In the reality, two men had looked over the side of the flying machine. And then, suddenly, the falling bodies slowed in their fall, and an invisible force seized him and brought his legs up and tore him loose from the rod. He floated upward, revolving, went past and above the canoe, and stopped. One of the men pointed a pencil-sized metal object at him.

Screaming with rage and hate and frustration, that Burton shouted, "I'll kill! I'll kill!"

The threat was an empty one, as empty as the darkness that stilled his fury.

Now, only one face looked over the edge of the machine. Though he could not see the man's face, Burton thought it looked familiar. Whatever the features, they belonged to X.

The Ethical chuckled.

4

BURTON SAT UPRIGHT AND GRABBED FOR THE THROAT OF X.

"For God's sake, Dick! It's me, Pete!"

Burton opened his hands from around Frigate's throat. Starlight as bright as Earth's full moon beamed in through the open doorway and silhouetted Frigate.

"It's your watch, Dick."

"Please be less noisy," Alice murmured.

Burton rolled off the bed and felt the suit hanging from a peg. Though he was sweating, he shivered. The little cabin, hot from the night-long radiation of two bodies, was cooling now. The cold fog was pressing in.

Alice said, "Brrr!" and sounds indicated she was pulling the thick towels over her. Burton caught a glimpse of her white body before it was covered. He glanced at Frigate, but the American had turned and was heading up the ladder. Whatever his faults, he was not a Peeping Tom. Not that he could really blame the fellow if he had taken a look. He was more than half in love with Alice. He had never said so, but it was obvious to Burton, to Alice, and to Loghu, Frigate's bunkmate.

If anybody was to blame, it was Alice. She had long ago lost her Victorian modesty. Though she would deny it, she may have, subconsciously, of course, teased Frigate with a quick flash of herself.

Burton decided not to bring that subject up. Though he was angry at both Frigate and Alice, he'd look like a fool if he said anything about this. Alice, like most people, bathed in The River in the nude, seemingly indifferent to the passersby. Frigate had seen her hundreds of times without clothing.

The night suit was composed of a number of thick towels held together by magnetic tabs underneath the cloth. Burton opened it and fitted the cloths to make a hooded garment around legs and body. He buckled on a belt of hornfish skin holding scabbards containing a flint knife, a chert axe, and a wooden sword. The edges of the latter were lined with tiny flint chips and its end held a sharp hornfish's horn. He removed from a rack a heavy ash spear tipped with horn and went up the ladder.

Gaining the deck, he found that his head was above the fog. Frigate was his same height, and his head seemed to float bodiless above the swirling wool of the mists. The sky was bright, though The Riverworld had no moon. It blazed with stars and with vast, shining gas clouds. Frigate believed that this planet was near the center of Earth's galaxy. But it could be inside some other galaxy, for all anybody knew.

Burton and his friends had built a vessel and had sailed from Theleme. The *Hadji II*, unlike its predecessor, was a cutter, a fore-and-aft rigged single-master. Aboard it were Burton, Hargreaves, Frigate, Loghu, Kazz, Besst, Monat Grrautut, and Owenone. The latter was a woman of ancient pre-Hellenic Pelasgia who did not mind at all sharing the Arcturan's bunk. With his peculiar crew (Burton had a not always fortunate talent for collecting an un-homogeneous band of followers), he had voyaged up-River for twenty-five years. One of the men with whom he had shared many adventures, Lev Ruach, had decided to stay in Theleme.

The *Hadji II* had not gotten as far as Burton had hoped. Since the crew had little elbow room, its members were in too close and constant contact with each other. It had been necessary to take long shore leaves so they could cool off their cabin fever.

Burton had decided that it was about time for another long liberty when the boat had sailed into this area. This was one of the rare widenings of The River, a lake about 20 miles or 32 kilometers long and 6 miles or 9.6 kilometers wide. At its western end the lake narrowed into a strait about a quarter-mile or 321 meters wide. The current boiled through this, but fortunately the prevailing wind here was behind a vessel going upstream. If the *Hadji II* had had to sail against the wind, it would have had little space to tack.

After looking at the strait, Burton thought that the passage could be made, though it would be close. However, now was the time to take a long rest. Instead of putting into one of the banks, he had stopped the boat alongside one of the scores of rocks that jutted up from the middle of the lake. These were tall spires with some level land at their bases. Some of them had grailstones, and around these were gathered a few huts.

The island-spire nearest the strait had a few floating docks. They would have been more convenient if they had been on the down-current side, but they were not, so the boat was taken alongside one. It was secured by lines to the posts and against the bumpers, bags of tough skins of alligator-fish filled with grass. The island's inhabitants approached them cautiously. Burton quickly assured them of his peaceful intentions, and he politely asked if his crew could use the grailstone.

There were only twenty islanders—short, dark people whose native language was unknown to Burton. They spoke a degraded form of Esperanto, however, so there was little language barrier.

The grailstone was a massive mushroom-shaped structure of grey red-flecked granite. The surface of its top was as high as Burton's chest and bore seven hundred round indentations in concentric circles.

Shortly before sunset, each person put in one of the shallow holes a tall cylinder of grey metal. English-speakers called it a grail, a pandora (or its shortened form, dora), a tucker box, lunch pail, glory bucket, and so on. The most popular name was that given it by the missionaries of the Church of the Second Chance. This was the Esperanto *pandoro*. Though the grey metal was as thin as a sheet of newspaper except for the base, it was unbendable, unbreakable, and indestructible.

The owners of the grails retreated about fifty paces and waited. Presently, intense blue flames roared upward from the top of the stone to 20 feet or a little over 6 meters. Simultaneously, every one of the stones lining the banks of the lake spat fire and shouted thunder.

A minute later, several of the little dark people climbed onto the stone and handed down the grails. The party sat down under a bamboo roof by a fire of bamboo and driftwood and opened the lids of the cylinders. Inside were racks holding cups and deep dishes, all filled with liquor, food, crystals of instant coffee or tea, cigarettes and cigars.

Burton's grail contained both Slovene and Italian food. He had been first resurrected in an area consisting mainly of people who had died in the Trieste area, and the grails of these usually gave the type of food they had been accustomed to eat on Earth. About every ten days, however, the grails served something entirely different. Sometimes it was English, French, Chinese, Russian, Persian, or any of a hundred national foods. Occasionally it offered dishes which were disgusting, such as kangaroo meat, burned on the surface and raw underneath, or living grubworms. Burton had gotten this Australian aborigine meal twice.

Tonight the liquor cup contained beer. He hated beer, so he traded it for Frigate's wine.

The islanders' grails contained food much of which reminded Burton of Mexican cuisine. However, the tacos and tortillas were packed with venison, not beef.

While they ate and talked, Burton questioned the locals. From their descriptions, he surmised that they were pre-Columbian Indians who had lived in a wide valley in the Southwest desert. They had been composed of two different tribes speaking related but mutually unintelligible languages. Despite this, the two groups had lived peacefully side by side and had formed a single culture, each of the groups differing only in a few traits.

He decided that they were the people whom the Pima Indians of his time had called the Hohokam, The Ancient Ones. These had flourished in the area which the white settlers would call the Valley of the Sun. It was there that the village of Phoenix of the Arizona Territory had been founded, a village which, according to what he had been told, had become a city of over a million population in the late twentieth century.

These people called themselves the Ganopo. In their Terrestrial time they had dug long irrigation ditches with flint and wooden tools and turned the desert into a garden. But they had suddenly disappeared, leaving the American archaeologists to explain why. Various theories had been advanced to account for this. The most widely accepted was that belligerent invaders from the north had wiped them out, though there was no evidence for that.

Burton's hopes that he could solve this mystery were quickly dissipated. These people had lived and died before their society came to an end.

They all sat up late that night, smoking and drinking the alcohol made from the lichen which coated their rock spire. They told stories, mostly obscene and absurd, and rolled on the ground with laughter. Burton, when he told Arabic tales, found it necessary not to use unfamiliar references or to explain them if they were simple enough to be understood. But they had no trouble grasping the stories of Aladdin and his magic lamp or of how Abu Hasan broke wind.

The latter had been a great favorite with the Bedouins. Burton had often sat around a fire of dried camel dung and sent his listeners into shrieks of laughter though they had heard it a thousand times.

Abu Hasan was a Bedouin who had left his nomadic life to become a merchant of the city of Kaukaban in Yemen. He became very rich, and after his wife died he was urged by his friends to marry again. After some resistance, he gave in and arranged a marriage to a beautiful young woman. There was much feasting of rices of several colors and sherbets of as many more, kids stuffed with walnuts and almonds and a camel colt roasted whole.

Finally, the bridegroom was summoned to the chamber where his bride, clad in many rich robes, waited. He rose slowly and with dignity from his divan but, alas! He was full of meat and drink, and as he walked toward the bridal chamber, lo and behold! he let fly a fart, great and terrible.

On hearing this, the guests turned to each other and talked loudly, pretending not to have noticed this social sin. But Abu Hasan was greatly humiliated, and so, pretending a call of nature, he went down to the horsecourt, saddled a horse, and rode away, abandoning his fortune, his house, his friends, and his bride.

He then took ship to India, where he became the captain of a king's bodyguard. After ten years he was seized with a homesickness so terrible that he was about to die of it, and so he set out for home disguised as a poor fakir. After a long and dangerous journey, he drew near to his city, and he looked from the hills upon its walls and towers with eyes flowing with tears. However, he did not dare venture into the city until he knew that he and his disgrace had been forgotten. So he wandered around the outskirts for seven days and seven nights, eavesdropping upon the conversations in street and marketplace.

At the end of that time he chanced to be sitting at the door of a hut, thinking that perhaps he could now venture into the city as himself. And then he heard a young girl say, "O my mother, tell me the day I was born, for one of my companions needs to know that so she can read my future."

And the mother replied, "You were born, O daughter, on the very night when Abu Hasan farted."

The listener no sooner heard these words than he rose from the bench and fled, saying to himself, "Truly your fart has become a date, which shall last forever."

And he did not quit traveling and voyaging until he returned to India and there lived in self-exile until he died, and the mercy of God be upon him.

This story was a great success, but before he told it Burton had to preface his story with the explanation that the Bedouins of that time considered farting in company a disgrace. In fact, it was necessary that everyone within earshot pretend that it had not happened, since the disgraced one would kill anyone who called attention to it.

Burton, sitting cross-legged before the fire, noted that even Alice seemed to enjoy the story. She was a middle-Victorian, raised in a deeply religious Anglican family, her father a bishop and the brother of a baron, descended from John of Gaunt, King John's son, her mother the granddaughter of an earl. But the impact of Riverworld life and a long intimate association with Burton had dissolved many of her inhibitions.

He had then gone on to the tale of Sinbad the Sailor, though it was necessary to adapt this to the experiences of the Ganopo. They had never seen a sea, so the sea became a river, and the roc which carried off Sinbad became a giant golden eagle.

The Ganopo, in their turn, told stories from their creation myths and the ribald adventures of a folk hero, the trickster Old Man Coyote.

Burton questioned them about the adaptation of their religion to the reality of this world.

"O Burton," their chief said, "this is not quite the world after death which we had envisioned. It is no land where maize grows higher than a man's head in one day and deer and jackrabbit give us a good hunt but never escape our spears. Nor have we been reunited with our women and children, our parents and grandparents. Nor do the great ones, the spirits of the mountains and the river, of the rocks and the bush, walk among us and talk to us.

"We do not complain. In fact, we are far happier than in the world we left. We have more food, better food, than we had there, and we do not have to work to get it, though we had to fight to keep it in the early days here. We have far more than enough water, we can fish to our heart's content, and we do not know the fevers that killed or crippled us nor do we know the aches and pains of old age and its enfeeblements."

5

HERE THE CHIEF FROWNED, AND WITH HIS NEXT WORDS A SHADOW fell upon them and the smiles faded.

"Tell me, you strangers, have you heard anything about the return of death? Of death forever, I mean? We live upon this little island and so do not get many visitors. But from the few we do meet and from those we talk to when we visit the banks, we have heard some strange and troubling stories.

"They say that for some time now no one who has died has been raised again. A person is killed, and he or she does not wake up the next day, his wounds healed, his grail beside him, upon a bank far from the scene of his death. Tell me, is this true or is it just one of those tales that people like to make up to worry others?"

"I do not know," Burton said. "It is true that we have traveled for thousands of kilometers . . . I mean, we have passed by an uncountable number of grailstones on our voyage. And for the past year, we have noticed this thing of which you speak."

He paused for a moment, thinking. From the very second day after the great resurrection, the lesser resurrections, or translations, as they were generally called, had occurred. People were killed or killed themselves or had fatal accidents, but, at dawn the next day, they found themselves alive. However, they were never raised at the scene of their deaths. Always, they found themselves far away, often in a different climatic zone.

Many attributed this to a supernatural agency. Many more, among whom was Burton, did not think that there was any agency except an advanced science which accounted for this. There was no need to call in the supernatural. "No ghosts need apply,"—to quote the immortal Sherlock Holmes. Physical explanations sufficed.

Burton knew from his own experience, apparently a unique one, that a dead person's body could be duplicated. He had seen that in the vast space where he had awakened briefly. Bodies were somehow made from some kind of recording, their wounds healed, diseased flesh regenerated, limbs restored, the ravages of old age repaired, youth restored.

Somewhere under the crust of this planet was an immense thermionic energy-matter converter. Probably, it was fueled by heat from the nickel-iron core. Its machinery operated through the complex of grailstones, the roots of which reached deep under the earth, forming a circuit so complex that it staggered the mind to think of it.

Was the recording of the dead person's cells made by something in the stones themselves? Or was it made as Frigate had suggested, by unseen orbital satellites which kept an eye upon every living being, much as God was supposed to note even the fall of a sparrow?

Nobody knew, or, if they did, they were keeping the secret to themselves.

Energy-matter conversion through the grailstone system also accounted for the free meals every citizen of The Riverworld found in his grail three times a day. The base of each of the metal cylinders must conceal a tiny converter and an electronic menu. The energy was transmitted through the grailstone complex into the grails. And there electricity became complex matter: beef, bread, lettuce, etcetera, and even luxuries, tobacco, marijuana, booze, scissors, combs, cigarette lighters, lipstick, dreamgum.

The towel-like cloths were also provided via the stone system, but not through the grails. They appeared in a neat pile next to the resurrected body and the grail.

There had to be some sort of mechanism inside the underground roots of the stone complex. This somehow could project through many meters of earth the vastly complicated configuration of molecules of human bodies, grails, and cloths at precisely a centimeter above ground level.

Literally, people and things formed from the air.

Burton had sometimes wondered what would happen if the translatee should happen to be formed in an area occupied by another object. Frigate said that there would be a terrible explosion. This had never happened, at least not to Burton's knowledge. Thus, the mechanism "knew" how to avoid this intermingling of molecules.

There was, however, as Frigate had pointed out, the volume of atmosphere which the newly formed body had to displace. How were the molecules of air kept from a fatal mingling with the molecules of the body?

No one knew. But the mechanism must somehow remove the air, make vacuums into which the body, grail, and cloths appeared. It would have to be a perfect vacuum, too, something which the science of the late 10th century had not succeeded in making.

And it did it silently, without the explosion of a mass of suddenly displaced air.

The question of how bodies were recorded still did not have a satisfactory answer. Many years ago, a captured agent of the Ethicals, a man calling himself Spruce, had said that a sort of chronoscope, an instrument which could look back in time, recorded the

cells of human beings. Of every person who had ever lived from
about two million B.C. to 2008 A.D.

Burton did not believe this. It did not seem possible that anything
could go backward in time, bodily or visually. Frigate had expressed his disbelief, too, saying that Spruce probably had used
"chronoscope" in a figurative sense. Or perhaps he had lied.

Whatever the whole truth, the resurrection and the grail food
could be explained in purely physical terms.

"What is it, Burton?" the chief said politely. "You have been
seized by a spirit?"

Burton smiled and said, "No, I was just thinking. We too have
talked to many who said that no one has been translated for a year in
their areas. Of course, this may just mean that the places through
which we voyaged may not have had any translatees. It is possible
that there have been translatees elsewhere. After all, The River may
be . . ."

He paused. How could he put across the concept of a River which
was possibly 10,000,000 or more kilometers long to people who did
not understand any number above twenty?

"It may be so long that a man who sailed from one end of The
River to the other would take as many years to do it as the combined
lifetimes of your grandfather, father, and yourself on Earth.

"Thus, even though there may be as many deaths as there are
blades of grass between two grailstones, that still would not be
much compared to the numbers who live along The River. Even
though we have voyaged very far, we still have not gone far
compared to the length of The River. So, there may be many areas
where the dead have risen.

"Also, not as many people die now as in the first twenty years
here. The many, many little states have been permanently established. Few slave states now exist. People have made states which
keep order among their own citizens and protect them from other
states. The evil people who lusted for power and the food and goods
of others were killed off. It is true they popped up elsewhere, but in
other areas they found themselves without their supporters. Things
are fairly well settled now, though, of course, there are still accidents, mainly from fishing, and individuals do kill, though chiefly
from passion.

"There are not so many dying nowadays. It is possible that the
areas through which we went just were not the areas in which
translatees appeared."

"Do you really believe that?" the chief said. "Or are you saying
that merely to make us feel happy?"

Burton smiled again. "I do not know."

"Perhaps," the chief said, "it is as the shamans of the Church of
the Second Chance tell us. That this world is only a stepping stone, a

way station, to another. A world even better than this one. The shamans say that when a person becomes a very good man here, much better than he was on Earth, he goes on to a world where the great spirits truly dwell. Though the shamans do insist that there is only one great spirit. I cannot believe that, since everybody knows that there are many spirits, both high and low.''

"That is what they say," Burton replied. "But how should they know any more than you or I know?''

"They say that one of the spirits that made this world appeared to the man who founded their church. This spirit told the man that this was so.''

"Perhaps the man who claims this is mad or a liar," Burton said. "In any event, I would have to talk to this spirit myself. And he would have to prove that he was indeed a spirit.''

"I do not trouble myself about such matters," the chief said. "It is better to leave the spirits alone, to enjoy life as it is and to be one whom the tribe finds good.''

"Perhaps that is the wisest course," Burton said.

He did not believe this. If he did, why was he so determined to get to the headwaters of The River and to the sea behind the mountains ringing the north pole, the sea that was said to have at its center a mighty tower in which the secret makers and rulers of this world lived?

The chief said, "I mean no offense, Burton, but I am one who can see into a person. You smile and you tell funny stories, but you are troubled. You are angry. Why do you not quit voyaging on that small vessel and settle down? You have a good woman, all, in fact, that any man needs. This is a good place. There is peace, and thieves are unknown, except for an occasional passerthrough. There are not many fights except between men who want to prove that one is stronger than the other or between a man and his woman because they cannot get along with each other. Any sensible person would enjoy this area.''

"I am not offended," Burton said. "However, for you to understand me, you would have to listen to the story of my life, here and on Earth. And even then you might not understand. How could you when I don't understand it myself?''

Burton fell silent then, thinking of another chief of a primitive tribe who had told him much the same thing. This was in 1863 when Burton, as Her Majesty's consul for the west African island of Fernando Po and the Bight of Biafra, visited Gélélé, king of Dahomey. Burton's mission was to talk the king into stopping the bloody annual human sacrifices and the slave trade. His mission had failed, but he had collected enough data to write two volumes.

The drunken, bloody-minded, lecherous king had acted high-handedly with him, whereas when Burton had visited Benin its king

had crucified a man in his honor. Still, they had gotten along rather
well, considering the circumstances. In fact, on a previous visit,
Burton had been made an honorary captain of the king's Amazon
guard.

Gélélé had said that Burton was a good man but too angry.

Primitive people were good at reading character. They had had to
be to survive.

Monat, the Arcturan, sensing that Burton's withdrawal was low-
ering the high spirits of the occasion, began to tell stories of his
native planet. Monat had somewhat awed the islanders at first
because of his obviously nonhuman origin. However, he had no
trouble in warming them, since he knew exactly how to make a
human being feel at ease. He should have; he had had to do this
every day of his life on The Riverworld.

After a while, Burton arose and said that his crew should be
getting to bed. He thanked the Ganopo for their hospitality but said
that he had changed his mind about staying there for several days.
His original intention to rest there while he studied them was gone.

"We would like very much for you to stay here," the chief said.
"For a few days or for many years. Whichever you prefer."

"I thank you for that," Burton said. He quoted the words of a
character from *The Thousand and One Nights*. "Allah afflicted me
with a love of travel."

He then quoted himself, "Travelers like poets are mostly an
angry race."

That at least made him laugh, and he went to the boat feeling less
gloomy. Before going to bed, he set the watches. Frigate protested
that a guard wasn't needed in this isolated place where the few
inhabitants seemed to be honest. He was overruled, which was no
surprise to him. He knew that Burton thought that acquisitiveness
was the mainspring of human action.

6

BURTON WAS THINKING OF THIS AND OTHER EVENTS OF LAST NIGHT, including the dreams. He stood for a while, smoking a cigar, while Frigate stood by him. The assemblage of closely packed stars and wide-spreading gas sheets paled as they silently watched. Dawn would be coming within a half-hour. Its light would wash out most of the celestial objects, would spread out for some time before the sun finally cleared the northern mountain wall.

They could see the fog, like a woolly blanket, covering The River and the plains on both banks. It lapped against the tree-covered hills, on the sides of which were a few lights. Beyond the hills of the valley were the mountains, inclined at an angle of forty-five degrees for the first thousand feet or 305 meters or so, then ascending straight up, smooth as a mirror, for 10,000 feet or about 3048 meters.

During his first years here, Burton had estimated the mountains to be about 20,000 feet or 6096 meters high. He was not the only one to make that error when only the eye was available for calculation. After he had been able to construct rather crude surveying instruments, however, he had determined that the mountain walls were, generally, twice as low as he had thought. Their blue-grey or black rock created an illusion. Perhaps this was because the valley was so narrow, and the walls made the dwellers feel even more pygmyish.

This was a world of illusions, physical, metaphysical, and psychological. As on Earth, so here.

Frigate had lit a cigarette. He had quit smoking for a year, but now, as he put it, he had "fallen from grace." He was almost as tall as Burton. His eyes were hazel. His hair was almost as black as his companion's, though it reflected a reddish undercoating in sunlight. His features were irregular: bulging supraorbital ridges, a straight nose of average size but with large nostrils, full lips, the upper very long, a clefted chin. The latter seemed to recede because of his unusually short jaw.

On Earth he had been, among many other things, one of that rare but vigorous breed which collected all literature by, about, and relevant to Burton. He had also written a biography of him but had eventually novelized it as *A Rough Knight for the Queen*.

On first meeting him, Burton had been puzzled when Frigate had identified himself as a science fiction writer.

"What in Gehenna is that?"

"Don't ask me to define science fiction," Frigate had said. "No one was ever able to give it a completely satisfactory definition. However, what it is . . . was . . . was a genre of literature in which most of the stories took place in a fictional future. It was called science fiction because science was supposed to play a large part in it. The development of science in the future, that is. This science wasn't confined to physics and chemistry but also included extrapolations of the sociological and psychological science of the author's time.

"In fact, any story that took place in the future was science fiction. However, a story written in 1960, for instance, which projected a future of 1984, was still classified as science fiction in 1984.

"Moreover, a science fiction story could take place in the present or the past. But the assumption was that the story was possible because it was based on the science of the author's time, and he merely extrapolated, more or less rigorously, what a science could develop into.

"Unfortunately, this definition included stories in which there was no science or else science poorly understood by the author.

"However (there are a lot of howevers in science fiction), there were many stories about things which could not possibly happen, for which there was no scientific evidence whatsoever. Like time travel, parallel worlds, and faster-than-light drives. Living stars, God visiting the Earth in the flesh, insects tall as buildings, world deluges, enslavement through telepathy, and more in an endless list."

"How did it come to be named science fiction?"

"Well, actually, it was around a long time before a man named Hugo Gernsback originated the label. You've read the Jules Verne novels and Mary Shelley's *Frankenstein*, haven't you? Those were considered to be science fiction."

"It sounds as if it were just fantasy," Burton had said.

"Yes, but all fiction is fantasy. The difference between mundane fantasy, what we called mainstream literature, and science fiction was that mainstream stories were about things which could have happened. They also always took place in the past or the present.

"Science fiction stories were about things that could not happen or were highly improbable. Some people wanted to name it speculative literature, but the term never caught on."

Burton never thoroughly understood what science fiction was, but he did not feel bad about it. Frigate couldn't explain it clearly either, though he could give numerous examples.

"Actually," Frigate had said, "science fiction was one of those many things that don't exist but nevertheless have a name. Let's talk about something else."

Burton had refused to drop the subject. "Then you were in a profession which didn't exist?"

"No, the profession of writing science fiction existed. It was just that science fiction *per se* was nonexistent. This is beginning to sound like a dialog in *Alice in Wonderland*."

"Was the money you made from your writings also nonexistent?"

"Almost. Well, that's an exaggeration. I didn't starve in a garret, but I also wasn't driving a gold-plated Cadillac."

"What's a Cadillac?"

Thinking of that now, Burton found it strange that the woman who slept with him was the Alice who had been the inspiration for Lewis Carroll's two masterpieces.

Suddenly, Frigate said, "What's that?"

Burton looked eastward toward the strait. Unlike the areas above and below it, the strait had no banks. High hills rose abruptly along its length, hills which were smooth walls. Below the strait something—no, two objects—were moving toward him, seemingly suspended above the fog.

He climbed a rope ladder to get a better look. The two objects were not suspended in the air. Their lower parts were just hidden by the mists. The nearest was a wooden structure with what seemed to be a human figure on its top. The second, much farther back, was a large, round, black object.

He called down. "Pete! I think it's a raft! A very large one! It's moving with the current, and it's headed directly toward us! There's a tower with a pilot on it. He isn't moving, though, just standing there. Surely . . ."

No, not surely. The man on the tower had not moved. If he were awake, he would have seen that the raft was on a collision course.

Burton hooked an arm around a rope, cupped his hands, and bellowed warnings. The figure leaning against the guardrail did not move. Burton stopped shouting at him.

"Wake up everybody!" he thundered at Frigate. "On the double! We must get the boat out of the way!"

He climbed swiftly down and went over the side onto the dock. Here, where his head was below the surface of the fog, he could see nothing. By running one hand along the hull, however, he could feel his way to the mooring posts. By the time he had untied two lines, he heard the others on the deck above. He shouted that Monat and Kazz should get onto the dock on the other side and untie the lines there.

In his haste, he rammed into a post and for several seconds hopped around holding his knee. Then he resumed his work.

Having completed his part of unloosing, he groped back along the hull. Someone had by then let down the gangway. He went up it, his hands sliding along the railing, and came aboard. Now he could see the tops of the women's heads and the American's face.

Alice said, "What's going on?"

"Have you gotten the poles out?" he said to Frigate.

"Yeah."

He swung up onto the rope ladder again. The two objects were still on a course that must end at the docks. The man on the watch tower had not moved.

By now there were voices coming from the island. The Ganopo were awake and calling out questions.

Monat's head and shoulders rose from the greyness. He looked like a monster sliding up out of the fog of a Gothic novel. The skull was similar to that of a human being's, but the fleshy features made him seem only semihuman. Thick black eyebrows curved down alongside the face to knobbed cheekbones and flared out to cover them. Thin membranes that swung with the movement of his head hung from the lower part of his nostrils. At the end of his nose was a deeply cleft boss of cartilage. His lips were like a dog's, thin, black, and leathery. The lobeless ears were convoluted like seashells.

Kazz bellowed somewhere near Monat. Burton could not see him since he was the second shortest of the crew, only about 5 feet or 1.5 meter tall. Then he came very close, and Burton could make out the squat figure.

"Get the poles and push the boat from the docks!" Burton yelled.

"Where in hell are they?" Besst called.

Frigate said, "I pulled them from the rack. They're on the deck below it."

Burton said, "Follow me," and then he cursed as he stumbled over something and fell flat on his face. He was up again at once, only to bump into somebody. From the bulky shape, he thought it must be Besst.

After some confusion, the poles were gotten and their wielders were stationed along the sides. At Burton's orders, they thrust the ends against the top of the dock, there being no room between the hull and the side of the dock for the poles to shove against the stone bottom of the underwater shelf. Since they had to fight against the current, which was strongest in the middle of the lake, they could only move the vessel very slowly. Once past the dock, they lowered the ends of the poles into the water and pushed against the rocky bottom. Even so, the poles slipped on the bare, smooth rock.

Burton ordered that they should let the prow of the boat swing around. This was done, and then the polers on the port side moved to the starboard to help the others keep the vessel from drifting sidewise against the spire. At this point, both the beach and the underwater shelf abruptly ceased. Now they had to hold the poles horizontally and shove against the wall of the spire.

Burton, hearing an unknown voice, looked back. The dark figure on the tower was moving now and screaming down into the fog. Other voices, fainter than the pilot's, came through the mists.

The large, round, dark object had become even larger. In the starlight it looked like the head of a giant. He estimated that the distance between the tower and the other object was about 100 meters. That meant that the raft which carried them was huge. He had no idea how wide it was, and he hoped he did not find out until after the boat was on the other side of the island.

Just before he turned back to his task, he saw another man appear on the tower. He was waving his hands, and his shrill voice dominated the other man's.

"Here it comes!" Frigate called out.

Burton didn't blame him for sounding panicked. He was in a frenzy himself. All that weight and momentum, hundreds, perhaps thousands of logs, were moving toward the *Hadji II*.

"Push your guts out!" he yelled. "We'll be crushed if you don't!"

By then the bowsprit, the large spar projecting forward of the ship, had cleared the spire. About ten more pushes should clear the corner, and the *Hadji II* would be taken by the current past the spire, away from the danger.

The yelling from the raft was loud and close. Burton spared a glance at the tower. It was only a little over 400 feet or 122 meters away. Furthermore, the side of the tower had turned a little. He cursed. That meant that the raft had turned, or been turned, off its course to avoid striking the island in its center part. Unfortunately, it was going to the left instead of to the right.

"Heave!" Burton shouted.

He wondered where the tower was located. Was it on the very prow of the raft or was it set back? If the latter was the situation, then there would be a large part of the raft forward of the tower. That meant that somewhere under the fog the forward part of the raft was very near the boat.

In any case, the raft was not going to miss the island. He did not care about that if it did not strike the boat.

A man on the tower was screaming orders in an unknown language down into the mists.

The prow of the *Hadji II* was now past the spire. But here the strong current at the corner had pressed the boat against the rocky wall, and their poles were slipping on the rock, which was smoother than that just passed.

"Push, you sons of bitches, push!" Burton thundered.

There was a roar, an abrupt lifting of the deck, a tilting inward toward the rock. Burton was dashed against a bright hardness that made him go soft and black inside. Dimly, he was aware that he had fallen back onto the deck, was lying on his back, was trying to get up in the dark greyness. Screams arose from around him. These and the snapping of smashed timbers and a final explosion, the impact of the forward part of the raft against the rock, were the last things he heard.

7

Fog blinded Jill Gulbirra.

By keeping close to the right bank of The River, she could barely discern the grailstones. They looked ominous, like giant toadstools in a dismal wasteland.

The next one should be the end of her odyssey. She had been counting them as she passed them, counting all night.

Now, a phantom in a ghost canoe, she paddled on. The wind was dead, but she revived it a little, or made it a pseudowind, by her own motion, driving against the current. The heavy wet air rubbed against her face like ectoplasmic curtains.

Now she saw a fire by the stone which had to be her destination. It had been a small spark. Now it was bigger, glowing palely, a ghost of a fire. From near it the voices of men. Disembodied voices.

She herself, she thought, must look like the spirit of a nun. White cloths held together by concealed magnetic tabs swathed her body. One cloth formed a hood so that anyone near enough in the fog would see her face as a darker blank in the dark greyness.

Her few belongings crouched on the floor of the canoe. In this wet, dim woolliness, they were two small beasts, white and grey. Near her was a tall grey metal cylinder, her "tucker box." Beyond it was a bundle, cloths containing various items. A bamboo flute. A ring of oak set with polished jadeite stone, her lover's gift, a lover departed but dead in only one sense—as far as she knew. A bag of dragonfish leather, crammed with artifacts and memories. Tied to the bundle, but invisible in this darkness, was a leather case holding a yew bow and a quiver of arrows.

Under her seat lay a spear, a bamboo shaft tipped with a hornfish horn. By it lay two heavy oak war-boomerangs and a bag containing two leather slings and forty stones.

As the fire brightened, the voices became louder. Who were they? Guards? Drunken revelers? Slavers hoping to catch just such as she? Early worms out to catch a bird?

She smiled grimly. If they wanted violence, they would get it.

However, they sounded more like drunks. If what she had been told down-River was true, she was in peaceful territory. Neither Parolando nor its neighboring states practiced grail slavery. She could have sailed the canoe boldly in daylight, according to her information. She would be welcomed and free, free to come or to go. Moreover, it was true that they, *Parolandoj*, were building a giant airship.

But distrust was her native element, though she could not be blamed for that. Consider her terrible experiences. So, she would scout around in the dark. It would require more work and inconvenience; it would be inefficient. You had to make your choice between survival and efficiency, though in the long run survival was optimum efficiency, no matter how much time and effort it took.

Death was no longer a temporary event in the Rivervalley. Resurrection seemed to have stopped, and with its cessation the ancient terror had returned.

Now the fire was bright enough for her to see the huge toadstool shape. The blaze was just beyond it. Four figures, black outlines, moved by the flames. She could smell the smoke of bamboo and pine, and she thought she whiffed cigars. Why had the disgusting cigars been provided by the Mysterious Donors?

They were talking in somewhat slurred English. Either they had been drinking or English was not their native tongue. No. The voice now booming through the fog belonged to an American.

"No!" the man bellowed. "By the holy flaming rings of buggered Saturn, no! It's not sheer ego, downright stinking hubris! I want to build the biggest ever built, a fabulous ship, a true queen of the skies, a colossus, a leviathan! Bigger than Earth or The Riverworld has ever seen or will ever see again! A ship to make everybody's eyes bug out, make them proud they're human! A beauty! A wondrous behemoth of the air! Unique! Like nothing that ever existed before! What? Don't interrupt, Dave! I'm flying high, and I'm going to keep on flying until we get there! And then some!"

"But, Milt!"

"But me no buts! We need a big one, the biggest, the grandest, for purely logical scientific reasons. My God, man, we have to go higher, further, than any dirigible ever has! We have to range 16,900 kilometers maybe, depending upon where the boat is! And God only knows what winds we'll run into! And it's all one vast one-shot! Do you hear me, Dave, Zeke, Cyrano? A one-shot!"

Her heart would not quit racing. "Dave" had spoken with a German accent. They must be the very men she was looking for. What luck! No, not luck. She had known how many kilometers distant, counted by the grailstones spaced along the bank, her destination was. And she had been told exactly where the headquarters of Milton Firebrass was. And she knew that David Schwartz, the Austrian engineer, was one of Firebrass' lieutenants.

"It'll take too much time, too much material," a man said loudly. His speech was that of a native of Maine. There was something, or was it just her overactive imagination, of the shriek of the wind in rigging, the creaking of rope and wood in a rolling ship, the thunder of surf, the flapping of sails, in his voice? Imagination, of course.

"Stop that, Jill," she told herself. If Firebrass had not called him Zeke, she would not now be imposing open-sea-sailing-ship images on the voice. He would be Ezekiel Hardy, captain of a New Bedford whaler, killed by a sperm whale off the coast of Japan—1833?—and he had convinced Firebrass that he would make an excellent helmsman or navigator for the airship. After suitable training, of course. Firebrass must really be hard up for a crew if he signed on an early-nineteenth-century whaling ship skipper. The man had probably never even seen a balloon, maybe not even a steam-driven riverboat.

The grapevine had it that Firebrass had had little success so far in finding experienced airshipmen. *Men*, of course. Always men. So, he had accepted candidates who seemed most likely to benefit from training. Airplane pilots. Balloonists. Sailors. Meanwhile, the word had spread up and down The River for 60,000 kilometers, perhaps 100,000, that Firebrass wanted lighter-than-air men. Always men.

What did Firebrass know about building and flying a gasbag? He may have journeyed to Mars and Ganymede, orbited Jupiter and Saturn, but what did that have to do with dirigibles? David Schwartz, it was true, had designed and built the first truly rigid dirigible. It had also been the first to have a structure and skin made completely from aluminum. This was in 1893, sixty years before she had been born. He'd then started to build a better airship—in Berlin, 1895?—but work had stopped on it when Schwartz had died—January, 1897?

She was not sure now. Thirty-one years on The River had dimmed much of memories on Earth.

She wondered if Schwartz knew what had happened after he had died. Probably not unless he'd met some gasbag freak, a layman Zepfan. Schwartz's widow had carried on his work, and yet no book Jill had read had bothered to note her first name or her maiden name. She was *only Frau* Schwartz. She had gotten the second ship built, despite being *only* a woman. And some male jackass had flown the aluminum ship (which looked more like a thermos bottle than anything else), had panicked, and had wrecked it.

All that was left of Schwartz's dream and his wife's devotion to it was a crumpled mass of silvery-looking metal. So much for dreams in a high wind when a big phallus, lilliputian brains, and mouse courage were at the controls. Now, if the jackass had been a woman, her name would have been recorded. See what happens when a woman leaves the kitchen? If God had intended . . .

Jill Gulbirra trembled, a hot ache in her chest. Get hold of yourself, she murmured. Cool does it or you blow it.

She started from her reverie. While she had been dreaming of Frau Schwartz's dream, she had allowed the canoe to be carried down-River. The fire had become smaller, and the voices fainter, and yet she had not noticed. Better bloody watch out, she told herself. She had to be ever alert, or she would never convince the powers-that-be that she was qualified to be one of the airship crew. To be captain?

"There's plenty of time!" Firebrass thundered. "This isn't any government-contract, low-fund, high-pressure project! It'll be thirty-seven years or more before Sam gets to the end of The River. It'll only take two—maybe three—years to complete the beast. Meanwhile, we'll use the blimp for training. And then we're off, heigh ho for the wild blue yonder, the misty sea of the north pole, where no Santa Claus, but somebody who's given us gifts that make Saint Nick look like the world's worst tightwad, lives! Off to the Misty Tower, the Really Big Grail!"

The fourth man spoke up now. He had a pleasant baritone, but it was evident that English was not his natal speech. What was it? It sounded like a French accent in some ways but : . . Yes, of course. That could be Savinien de Cyrano de Bergerac, if she could believe what she had heard at about hundredth hand. It just did not seem possible that she would soon be talking to him. Perhaps she wouldn't be, since there were so many phonies on The River.

There was silence for a moment, the silence that only the River-valley knew—when people kept their mouths shut. No birds, no animals (especially no barking dogs), no mechanical monsters roaring, bellowing, buzzing, screeching, no tooting horns, no whooping or screaming sirens, no shrieking brakes, no loud radios, no blaring loudspeakers. Only water lapping against shore and then a splash as a fish leaped out and fell back. And the crackle of wood in the fire.

"Ah!" Firebrass said. "Smooth! Better'n anything I ever had on Earth! And free, free! But when, when will the airmen show up? I need more men with experience, real gasbaggers!"

Schwartz made a smacking sound—Jill could see the bottle tilted above his lips now—and he said, "So! You are not so unworried!"

The canoe touched shore, and she got out of it without tipping it. The water was up to her waist, but the magnetically sealed cloths kept the cold liquid out. She waded closer and lifted the long, heavy canoe, moving forward until she was on shore. She let the craft down and dragged it until its entire length was out of the stream. The bank was only about 30 centimeters above the water level. She stood for a moment, planning her entrance, then decided not to go armed.

"Oh, I'll get them eventually," Firebrass was saying.

She stepped closer, sliding her feet over the short grass.

"I'm the one you're looking for," she said loudly.

The four whirled, one almost falling and grabbing another. They stared, their mouths and eyes dark holes in paleness. Like her, they were covered with cloths but theirs were brightly colored. If she had been an enemy, she could have put an arrow into each one before they could grab their weapons—if they had such. Then she saw that they did have guns, placed on the edge of the mushroom top of the grailstone.

Pistols! Made of iron! So, it was true!

Now she suddenly saw a rapier, a long, steel sharp-pointed blade, in the hand of the tallest man there. His other hand brushed his hood back and revealed a long, dark face with a big nose. He had to be the fabled Cyrano de Bergerac.

Cyrano reverted to seventeenth-century French, of which she could understand only a few words.

Firebrass pushed his hood back, too.

"I almost crapped in my britches! Why didn't you warn us you were coming?"

She lowered her hood.

Firebrass stepped closer and looked keenly at her. "It's a woman!"

"Nevertheless, I'm your man," Jill said.

"What'd you say?"

"Don't you understand English!" she said angrily.

Her displeasure was more at herself. She had been so excited, though pretending to be composed, that she'd reverted to her Toowoomba dialect. She might as well have spoken in Shakespearean English for all they understood. She repeated, in the standard Midwestern American she'd learned so painstakingly, "Nevertheless, I'm your man. My name, by the way, is Jill Gulbirra."

Firebrass introduced himself and the others, then said, "I need another drink."

"I could use one myself," Jill said. "It's a fallacy that alcohol warms you up, but it does make you think you're warmed up."

Firebrass stopped and picked up a bottle—the first glass Jill had seen for years. He handed it to her and she drank the scotch without wiping the mouth of the bottle. After all, there were no disease germs on The River. And she had no prejudices about drinking from a bottle that had been in the mouth of a half-black. Wasn't her grandmother an aborigine? Of course, abos were not Negroes. They were black-skinned archaic Caucasians.

Why was she thinking such thoughts?

Cyrano, his head stuck forward, his back bent, walked up to her. He looked her over, shook his head, and said, "*Mordioux*, the hair is shorter than mine! And there is no makeup! Are you sure she is a woman?"

Jill moved the scotch around in her mouth and swallowed it. It was delicious, and it warmed all the way down.

"We shall see," the Frenchman said. He put his hand on her left breast and squeezed gently.

Jill sank a fist into his hard belly. He bent over, and Jill brought her knee up against his chin. He fell heavily.

Firebrass said, "What the hell?" and stared at her.

"How would you react if he felt your crotch to see if you were a man?"

"Simply thrilled, honey," Firebrass said. He whooped with laughter and danced around while the other two men looked at him as if they thought he was crazy.

Cyrano got onto his hands and knees and then onto his feet. His face was red, and he was snarling. Jill wanted to back away, especially after he picked up the rapier. But she did not move, and she said, her voice steady, "Do you always take such familiarities with strange women?"

A shudder went over him. The redness faded away, and the snarl became a smile. He bowed. "No, madame, and my apologies for such inexcusable manners. I do not usually drink, since I do not like to cloud my mind, to become bestial. But tonight we were celebrating the anniversary of the departure of the Riverboat."

"No sweat," Jill said. "Just don't let it happen again."

Though she smiled, she was cursing herself for having begun in such a bad way with a man for whom she had a great admiration. It was not her fault, but she could not expect him to forgive her for having felled him so easily before witnesses. No male ego could survive that.

8

THE MIST THINNED. NOW THEY DID NOT NEED THE FIRELIGHT TO see each other's faces. Below their waists the grey-white coils were still dense, however. The sky was brightening, though it would be some hours before the sun cleared the eastern peaks. The great white gas sheets that covered one-sixth of the sky had faded away with the lesser stars. Thousands of the giants still flamed red, green, white, blue, but their intensity, like gas jets slowly being turned off, was diminishing.

Westward, a dozen structures towered up from the mists. Her eyes widened, though she had heard about these through the grapevine and the drum-telegraph. Some were four-and-five-story-high buildings of sheet-iron and aluminum. Factories. But the colossus was an aluminum building, a hangar.

"It's the biggest I ever saw," she murmured.

"You ain't seen nothing yet," Firebrass said. He paused, then said, wonderingly, "So you have come to sign up?"

"I said that once."

He was The Man. He could hire and fire her. But she'd never been able to conceal irritation at stupidity. Repetition was wasteful and hence stupid. Here was a man who had a Ph.D. in astrophysics and a master's in electronic engineering. And the United States had not sent any dummies into space, though they may not have been brilliant. Maybe it was the liquor that made him seem stupid. As it did every man. And every woman, she hastened to remind herself. Be fair.

He was close, breathing the whiskey fumes up into her face. He was a head shorter than she, his broad shoulders, muscular arms, and deep chest making a curious contrast with long, skinny legs. His large eyes were brown, the balls bloodshot. His head was large, his forehead bulged, his bronze hair was so curly that it was almost kinky, his skin was bronze-red. He was supposed to be a mulatto, but the Caucasian and Onondaga Indian genes seemed to be dominant. He could pass for a Provençal or Catalonian. Or just about anything South European.

He looked her up and down. Was his bold stare supposed to challenge her to knock him down as she had Cyrano?

Jill said, "What are you thinking of? My qualifications for airship officer? Or what kind of body is under these baggy towels?"

Firebrass burst out laughing. When he had recovered, he said, "Both."

Schwartz looked embarrassed. He was short and slight, blue eyed and brown haired. Jill glared at him, and he turned away. Ezekiel Hardy was, like Cyrano, almost as tall as she. He was narrow faced, high cheekboned, black haired. He stared at her with hard pale-blue eyes.

"I'll repeat this because it needs to be stressed," she said. "I'm as good as any man and ready to prove it. And I'm a godsend. I have an engineering degree and I can design an airship from A to Z. I have 8342 hours flight-time in four different types of blimp. I can handle any post, including captain."

"What proof do we have?" Hardy said. "You could be lying."

"Where are *your* papers?" Jill said. "And even if you were skipper of a whaling ship, so what? What qualification is that for a dirigible man?"

"Now, now," Firebrass said. "Don't let us get our bowels in an uproar. I believe you, Gulbirra. I don't think you're one of the many phonies I've had to put up with.

"But let's get one thing straight. You are a hell of a lot more qualified than I am—as of this moment, anyway—to command the ship. But nevertheless, I am the captain, the boss, the head cheese! I'm running this whole show from start to finish. On the ground and up there. I didn't give up being chief engineer on Clemens' boat so I could take a minor position in this project.

"It's *Captain* Firebrass, and don't ever forget that. If that's okay, signed and sealed in blood, then I'll be jumping with joy to welcome you aboard. You might even be first mate—no sexual implications involved—though I can't promise that. The roster is a long way from being filled."

He paused, cocked his head, and narrowed his eyes.

"First thing off. You have to swear by your personal honor—and by God, if you believe in one—that you'll obey the laws of Parolando. No ifs, ands, buts."

Gulbirra hesitated. She licked her lips, feeling their dryness. She desired—no, lusted for—the airship. She could visualize it even now. It hovered over them, casting a shadow over her and Firebrass, shining silvery where the imaginary sun struck it.

"I'm not going to sacrifice any of my principles!" she said. She spoke so loudly that she startled the men. "Are men and women equal here? Is there any discrimination in sex, race, nationality, and so forth? Especially in sex?"

"No," Firebrass said. "Theoretically and legally, that is. Actually, that is, personally, there is, of course. And there is, as there has always been everywhere and everytime, discrimination based on competency. We have high standards here. If you're one of those who think that a person should be given a job just because he—or she—belongs to a group that has been discriminated against, forget it. Or move your ass on out of here.''

She was silent for a moment. The men looked at her, obviously aware of the struggle inside her.

Firebrass grinned again. ''You're not the only one in agony,'' he said. ''I want you in the worst way, just as you want in the worst way, that is, the best way, to be one of the crew. But I've got my principles, just as you have yours.''

He jerked a thumb at Schwartz and Hardy. ''Look at them. Both nineteenth-century. One's an Austrian; one, a New Englander. But they've not only accepted me as the captain, they're good friends. Maybe they still believe, way deep down, that I'm an uppity nigger, but they'd take a poke at anyone who called me that. Right, men?''

They nodded.

''Thirty-one years on The Riverworld changes a person. If he's capable of being changed. So, what do you say? Want to hear the constitution of Parolando?''

''Of course. I wouldn't make a decision until I knew what I was getting into.''

''It was formulated by the great Sam Clemens, who left on his boat, the *Mark Twain*, almost a year ago.''

''The *Mark Twain?* That's pretty egostistical, isn't it?''

''The name was chosen by popular vote. Sam protested, though not very strongly. Anyway, you interrupted me. There's an unwritten rule that nobody interrupts the captain. So here goes. *We, the people of Parolando, do hereby declare . . .*''

There was no hesitation nor, as far as she knew, any mistakes in the long recital. The almost total lack of the written word had forced the literate population to rely on memory. A skill that once had flourished only among preliterates—and actors—was now general property.

While the words rose to the sky, the sky became brighter. The mists shrank to their knees. The valley floor was still covered with what looked at a distance like snow. The foothills beyond the plains were no longer distorted. The long hillgrass, the bushes, the iron-trees, oaks, pines, yews, and bamboo no longer looked like a Japanese painting, misty, unreal, and far off. The huge flowers that grew from the thick vines intertwined on the irontree branches were beginning to collect color. When the sun would hit them, they would glow with vivid reds, greens, blues, blacks, whites, yellows, stripes and diamonds of mixed colors.

The western precipices were blue-black stone on which were

enormous splotches of bluish-green lichen. Here and there, narrow cataracts fell dull-silvery down the mountain sides.

All of this was familiar to Jill Gulbirra. But each morning awoke in her the same sense of awe and wonder. Who had formed this many-million-kilometers-long Rivervalley? And why? And how and why had she, along with an estimated thirty-four to thirty-seven billion people, been resurrected on this planet? Everybody who had ever lived from about 2,000,000 B.C. to 2008 A.D. seemed to have been raised from the dead. The exceptions were children who'd died at or under the age of five and the mentally retarded. And also, possibly, the hopelessly insane, though there was doubt about the definition of *hopelessly*.

Who were the people who had done this? Why?

There were rumors and tales, strange, disturbing, and maddening, of people who had appeared among the lazari. Briefly. Mysteriously. They were named, among other things, the Ethicals.

"Are you listening?" Firebrass said. She became aware that they were staring at her. "I can give you back, almost verbatim, what you've said so far," she answered.

This wasn't true. But she was sensitized—keeping one ear open, as it were, like an antenna receiving on a single frequency—for what she considered important.

Now the people were coming out of the huts, stretching, coughing, lighting up cigarettes, heading for the bamboo-walled latrines, or walking toward The River, grails in hand. The hardy wore only a towel; most were clad from head to foot. Bedouins of the Rivervalley. Phantoms in a mirage.

Firebrass said, "Okay. You ready to be sworn in? Or do you have mental reservations?"

"I never have those," she said. "What about you? In regard to me, I mean?"

"It wouldn't matter, anyway." He grinned again. "This oath is only a preliminary one. You'll be on probation for three months, then the people vote on you. But I can veto the vote. Then you take the final oath, if you pass. Okay?"

"Okay."

She didn't like it, but what could she do? She certainly wasn't going to walk out. Besides, though they didn't know it, they'd be on probation with her.

The air became warmer. The eastern sky continued to brighten, quenching all but a few giant stars. Bugles blew. The nearest was on top of a six-story bamboo tower, in the middle of the plain, and the bugler was a tall, skinny black wearing a scarlet towel around his waist.

"Real brass," Firebrass said. "There are some deposits of copper and zinc a little ways upstream. We could have taken them away from the people who owned it, but we traded instead. Sam wouldn't let us use force unless it was necessary.

"South of here, where Soul City used to be, were big deposits of cryolite and bauxite. The Soul Citizens wouldn't keep their side of the bargain—we were trading steel weapons for the ores—so, we went down and took it. In fact," he waved his hand, "Parolando now extends for 64 kilometers on both sides of The River."

The men removed all cloths except for those around the waist. Jill kept on a green-and-white-striped kilt and a thin, nearly transparent cloth around her breasts. They had looked like desert Arabs; now they were Polynesians.

The dwellers of the plains and the bases of the foothills were gathering by the Riverside. A number shucked all their cloths and jumped into the water, whooping at the cold and splashing each other.

Jill hesitated for a minute. She had sweat all day and all night paddling her canoe. She needed a bath, and sooner or later she'd have to disrobe entirely. She dropped her towels and ran to the bank and dived flatly out. After swimming back, she borrowed a bar of soap from a woman and lathered the upper part of her body. She came out of the water shivering and rubbed herself vigorously.

The men stared frankly, seeing a very tall woman, slim, long legged, small breasted, wide hipped, deeply tanned. She had short, straight, russet hair and large russet eyes. Her face, as she well knew, was nothing to write home about. It was passable except for large buck teeth and a nose a little too long and too hawkish. The teeth were an inheritance from her blackfeller grandmother. There was nothing she could do about them. Nor was there anything she wanted to do about them.

Hardy's gaze was fastened on her pubic hair, which was extraordinarily long, thick, and ginger colored. Well, he'd get over that, and he was as close to it as he was ever going to get.

Firebrass went around the side of the grailstone and returned with a spear. Just below the steel head, attached to the shaft, was a large vertebral bone from a hornfish. He drove the spear straight into the ground beside her canoe.

"The bone means it's my spear, the captain's," he said. "I stuck it in the ground by the canoe to tell everybody that it's not to be borrowed without permission. There are a lot of things like that for you to learn. Meanwhile, Schwartz can show you your quarters and then give you a guided tour. Report to me at high noon under that irontree there."

He indicated a tree about 90 meters to the west. Towering over 300 meters, it had a thick, gnarly grey bark, scores of great branches extending 90 meters outward, huge elephant's-ear leaves with green and red stripes. Its roots surely drove down at least 120 meters, and its unburnable wood was so hard it would resist a steel saw.

"We call it The Chief. Meet me there."

The bugles rang out again. The crowds organized themselves into a military formation under the directions of officers. Firebrass pulled himself onto the top of the grailstone. He stood there, watching while the roll call was made. The corporals reported to the sergeants and the sergeants to the lieutenants, and they to the adjutant. Then Hardy to Firebrass. A moment later, the mob was dismissed. However, they did not leave. Firebrass got off the mushroom-shaped stone, and the corporals took his place. These put the grails in the depressions on the surface of the stone.

Schwartz was beside her. He cleared his throat. "Gulbirra? I'll take care of your grail."

She took it from the canoe and handed it to him. This was a grey metal cylinder, 45.72 centimeters across, 76.20 centimeters high, weighing empty about 0.55 kilogram. It had a lid which, once shut, could be lifted only by the owner. There was a curved handle on the lid. Tied to it by a bamboo fiber rope was her I.D., a tiny baked-clay dirigible. It bore her initials on both sides.

Schwartz ordered a man to place her grail on the stone. The man did so quickly, glancing often at the eastern peaks. But he was safe by two minutes. At the end of that time, the sun ballooned over the top. A few seconds later, the mushroom-shape spouted blue flames over 9 meters high. The roar of its discharged electricity mingled with the thunder of every stone on both sides of The River for as far as could be seen. All these years had not inured Jill to the sight nor sound. Though expecting it, she jumped a little. The report rolled back from the reflector of the mountains, echoed again, and died out with a mutter.

Everybody had breakfast.

9

THEY WERE ON A FOOTHILL. THE TALL ESPARTO-LIKE GRASS HAD been recently mown to about a centimeter and a half-length. "We have some machines that do that, though much cutting is done with sickles," David Schwartz said. "The grass is made into ropes."

"We didn't have any machines where I come from," Jill said. "We used flint sickles. But we made rope from it, of course."

It was shady and cool here. The branches of an irontree spread out to cover a small village, a scattering of square or round huts of bamboo. Many of them were thatched with the scarlet and green leaves of the irontree. A rope ladder dangled from the lowest branch of the colossus, 33 meters up. Near it, a hut sat on a platform supported on two branches. There were other rope ladders, other platforms and huts here and there.

"Perhaps you will be assigned one of them after your probation," Schwartz said. "Meanwhile, here's your home."

Jill entered the indicated doorway. At least, she did not have to stoop in this. So many people were short and had therefore built low entrances.

She set her grail and bundles down on the floor. Schwartz followed her in. "This belonged to a couple killed by a dragonfish. It came up out of the water as if it had been fired from a cannon. It bit off one end of the fishing craft. Unfortunately, the couple were standing on the end and were swallowed along with the logs.

"It was also unfortunate that this happened after the resurrections ceased. So, they won't be appearing elsewhere, I suppose. You haven't heard anything about new lazari, have you? Recently?"

"No, I haven't," she said. "Nothing reliable, anyway."

"Why do you suppose it stopped? After all these years?"

"I don't know," she said sharply. Talking about this made her uneasy. Why had the gift of immortality been so suddenly withdrawn?

"Bloody hell with it," she said loudly. She looked around. The floor was hidden under grass that reached almost to her crotch. The blades rasped against her legs. She would have to cut the grass close to the ground and then bring in earth to cover it. Even then the blades might not die. The roots went so deep and were so interconnected that the grass could flourish without benefit of sunshine. Apparently they could draw their sustenance from the roots of those exposed to light.

A steel sickle hung from a peg on the wall. Steel was so common here that this tool, priceless elsewhere, had not been stolen.

She moved around, slowly, so that the sharp edges of the grass would not cut her legs. She found two clay pots—thundermugs—in the tall green. A jar for drinking water was on a bamboo table which had not as yet been overturned by the pressure of the growing grass. A necklace of fishbones hung on another peg. Two bamboo cots and pillows and mattresses, made from magnetically locked cloths stuffed with leaves, were partially hidden by the grass. Near them lay a harp made from turtlefish shell and fish intestines.

"Well, it's not much," she said. "But then it never is, is it?"

"It's big enough, though," Schwartz said. "Plenty of room for you and your mate—when you find one."

Jill took the sickle from the peg and swiped at the grass. The blades fell like so many heads. "Hah!"

Schwartz looked at her as if he wondered if she would go from the grass to him.

"Why do you assume that I want a lover?"

"Why, why, why, everybody, that is, everybody does."

"Everybody doesn't," she said. She hung the sickle back onto the peg. "What's next on this Cook's tour?"

She had expected that, when they were alone in the hut, he would ask her to go to bed with him. So many men did. It was evident now that he would like to ask her, but he didn't have the guts. She felt relief mixed with contempt. Then she told herself that it was a strange feeling, self-contradictory. Why should she look down on him because he behaved as she wanted him to behave?

Perhaps some disappointment was also present. When a man got too aggressive, despite her warnings, then she chopped his neck with the edge of her hand, squeezed his testicles, kicked him in the stomach while he writhed on the ground. No matter how big and strong a man, he was taken by surprise. They were all helpless, at least while the agony in the testicles lasted. Afterward . . . well, most of them left her alone. Some had tried to kill her, but she was ready for that. They didn't know how handy she was with a knife—or with any weapon.

David Schwartz was unaware of how narrowly he had escaped crippling and a permanent dent in his ego.

"It's quite safe to leave your belongings here. We've never had a case of theft yet."

"I'll take the grail. I'd feel nervous if I couldn't keep my eye on it."

He shrugged and took a cigar from the leather bag hanging from his shoulder. One of this morning's offerings from his grail.

"Not in here," she said quietly. "This is my home, and I don't want it stunk up."

He looked surprised, but he shrugged again. As soon as they had stepped out, however, he lit it. And he moved from her left side to upwind, puffing vigorously, blowing in her direction.

Jill repressed the remark she wanted so much to make. It would be indiscreet to offend him too much, to give him a chance to blackmark her. After all, she was on probation; she was a woman; she wouldn't needlessly antagonize a man with such a high position, a good friend of Firebrass'. But she would bend her principles, her neck, only so far.

Or would she? She had taken a lot of crap on Earth because she had wanted to be an airship officer. And smiled and gone home and smashed dishes and pottery and written dirty words on the wall. Childish, but satisfactory. And here she was, in a similar situation, undreamed of until several years ago. She couldn't go someplace else, because there wasn't any other place. Here was where the only airship in the world would be built. And that was to be a one-shot, a single-voyage phenomenon.

Schwartz stopped on top of the hill. He pointed at an avenue formed by ridgepole pines. At its end, halfway down the hill opposite, was a long shed.

"The latrine for your neighborhood," he said. "You'll dump your nightpots in it first thing every morning. The urine in one hole and the excrement in the one next to it."

He paused, smiled, and said, "Probationers are usually given the task of removing the stuff every other day. They take it up the mountain to the gunpowder factory. The excrement is fed to the powderworms. The end product of their digestion is potassium nitrate, and . . ."

"I know," she said, speaking between clamped teeth. "I'm not a dummy. Anyway, that process is used wherever sulfur is available."

Schwartz teetered on his heels, happily puffing his cigar, tilted upward. If he had had suspenders, he would have snapped them.

"Most probationers put in at least a month working in the factory. It's unpleasant, but it's good discipline. It also weeds out those who aren't dedicated."

"Non carborundum illegitimatus," she said.

"What?" he said out of the side of his mouth.

"A Yank saying. Jack-Latin. Translation: *Don't let the bastards grind you down*. I can take any crap handed me—if it's worth doing it. Then it's my turn."

"You're a tough one."

"Too right. You have to be if you survive in a man's world. I thought perhaps things would be different here. They weren't, and aren't, but they will be."

"We've all changed," he said slowly and somewhat sadly. "Not always for the better. If you'd told me in 1893 that I'd be listening to a woman, an upper-class woman, not a whore or a millhand, mind you, spewing filth and subversive . . ."

"Instead of subservient, you mean," she said harshly.

"Allow me to finish. Subversive suffragette rot. And if you'd told me that it wouldn't particularly bother me, I'd have said you were a liar. But live and learn. Or, in our case, die and learn."

He paused and looked at her. The right side of her mouth jerked; her eyes narrowed.

"I could tell you to stick it," she said. "But I must get along with you. I will take only so much, however."

"You didn't understand all I said," he replied. "I said it doesn't bother me now. And I said, live and learn. I am not the David Schwartz of 1893. I hope you are not the Jill Gulbirra of . . . when did you die?"

"In 1983."

They walked down the hill in silence, Jill carrying her grail on the end of her spear, which was on her shoulder. Schwartz stopped once to point out a stream that ran down from the hills. Its source was a cataract in the mountains. They came to a small lake between two hills. A man sat in a rowboat in the middle of the lake, a bamboo fishing pole in his hand, the float drifting toward a bush overhanging the bank. Jill thought he looked Japanese.

Schwartz said, "Your neighbor. His real name is Ohara, but he prefers to be called Piscator. He's crazy about Izaak Walton, whom he can quote verbatim. He says a man needs only one name in this world, and he's chosen Piscator. Latin for fisher. He's a fish freak, as you can see. Which is why he's in charge of the Parolando Riverdragon fishing. But today's his day off."

"That's interesting," she said. He was, she believed, leading up to something unpleasant for her. The slight smile looked sadistic.

"He'll probably be the first mate of the airship," he said. "He was a Japanese naval officer and during the first part of World War I he was attached to the British Navy as an observer and trainee on dirigibles. Later, he was a trainee-observer on an Italian Navy airship which made bombing raids on Austrian bases. So, you see, he's had enough experience to rank him very high on the list."

"And he is a man." She smiled, though seething inside. "And though my experience is much much more than his, still, he's a man."

Schwartz backed away from her. "I'm sure Firebrass will appoint officers according to their merits only."

She did not reply.

Schwartz waved at the man in the boat. He rose from his seat and, smiling, bowed. Then he sat down, but not before giving her a look that seemed to sweep over her like a metaphysical radar beam, locating her place in the world, identifying her psychic construction.

Imagination, of course. But she thought that Schwartz was right when he said, "An extraordinary man, that Piscator."

The Japanese's black eyes seemed to burn holes in her back as she walked away.

10

BLACKNESS OUTSIDE. INSIDE, A NIGHT WRITHING WITH SNAKES OF pale lightning, twisty and fuzzy. Some time later, in a place where there was no time, a bright beam ahead shone as if from the lens of a movie projector. The light was a whisper in the air; in her mind, it was bellowing. The film was being shown on a cathode-ray oscilloscope; it was a series of letters, broken words, signs, and symbols, all part of an undeciphered code. Perhaps: undecipherable.

Worse, it seemed to run backward, spun back into the reel(ity?). It was a documentary made for television, for the boobish (boobed?) viewer of the boob tube. Yet, backward was an excellent technique. Images flashed to suggest, to reverberate, to echo, to evoke, to flap intimation upon intimation with electronic quickness. Like flipping the pages of an illustrated book from back to beginning. But the text, where was the text? And what was she thinking of when she thought of images? There were no images. No plot. Yes, there was a plot, but it had to be put together from many pieces. Ah, many pieces. She almost had it, but it had slipped away.

Moaning, she awoke. She opened her eyes and listened to the rain beating upon the thatched roof.

Now she remembered the first part of the dream. It was a dream of a dream, or what she thought was a dream but was not sure. It was raining, and she had half-awakened or had seemed to do so. The hut was 20,000 kilometers from this one, but it was almost identical, and the world outside the hut, as seen by occasional flashes of lightning, would not have differed much. She had turned, and her hand had not felt the expected flesh.

She had sat up and looked around. A lightning streak, close enough to make her jump, showed that Jack was not in the hut.

She had got up and lit a fish-oil lamp. Not only was he not there, his cloths, weapons, and grail were gone.

She had run out into the stormy night to look for him.

She never found him. He was gone, and no one knew where or why.

The only one who might have been able to tell her had also sneaked out that same night. He, too, had left his hutmate without saying a word about his intentions. It was apparent to Jill that the two had run off together. Yet, as far as she knew, they had been only casual acquaintances.

Why had Jack left her, so silently and heartlessly?

What had she done?

Was it just that Jack had decided that he did not want to put up with a woman who wouldn't play second fiddle in their relationship? Also, the wanderlust had gotten him again? With both motives pushing him, he had just up and went, to use one of his corny Americanisms?

Whatever was the truth, she was living with no man anymore, ever again. Jack was the best, and the last was the best, as it should be, but he had not been good enough.

She was on the rebound when she met Fatima, the little sloe-eyed Turk. Fatima, one of the hundreds of concubines of Mohammed IV (ruled Turkey from 1648-1687), had never gone to bed with him. She had, however, not suffered overmuch from lack of sexual satisfaction. There were plenty of fellow prisoners of the Seraglio who preferred their own sex as lovers, either through natural inclinations or conditioning. She became a favorite of Kosem, Mohammed's grandmother, though there was nothing overtly homosexual in their relationship.

But Turhan, Mohammed's mother, sought to get control of the government from Kosem, and eventually Kosem was caught by a party of Turhan's assassins and strangled to death with the cords from her own bed curtain. It was Fatima's bad fortune to be attending Kosem when this happened and so she had to share her fate.

Jill took the sexy little Turk in as hutmate after Fatima had quarreled with her lover, a French ballet danseuse (died 1873). Jill was not in love with her, but she was sexually exciting and, after a while, she became fond of her. Fatima, however, was ignorant and, worse, unteachable. She was selfish and would remain so, was infantile and would remain so. Jill got tired of her after a year. Even so, she was grief-stricken when Fatima was raped and then beaten to death by three drunken Sikeli (born 1000 B.C.?). Her grief was intensified by the knowledge (or belief, since there was no proof) that Fatima was truly dead. Resurrection had apparently stopped. No more would a dead person rise the next day at dawn far, far from the scene of his or her demise.

Before succumbing to her sorrow, however, Jill had put an arrow into each of Fatima's murderers. They were not going to rise elsewhere either.

Years later, she had heard rumors of the great dirigible that was being built up-River. She did not know if they were true or not, but there was only one way to find out.

So here she was, though it had taken a long time to get here.

11

FROM *The Daily Leak*, A FIVE-PAGE NEWSPAPER. OWNER AND owner and publisher: the state of Parolando. Editor: S.C. Bagg. In the upper left-hand corner above the headline is the standard notice:

CAVEAT LECTOR

By law, the reader must place this journal in a public recycling barrel the day after receipt. In case of emergency, it may be used for toilet paper. We recommend the *Letters to the Editor* page as most appropriate for this purpose. First offense: a public reprimand. Second: confiscation of all booze, tobacco, and dreamgum for a week. Third: permanent exile.

Prominent in the *Newcomers* section:

JILL GULBIRRA

We welcome, in spite of the advice of many, our latest female candidate for citizenship. On Sunday last, this tall drink of water appeared out of the predawn fog and accosted four of our leading public figures. Despite their certain state of inebriation and possibly lecherous thoughts, two conditions leading to mental fogginess, the quartet finally comprehended that their unexpected guest had traveled approximately 32,180 kilometers (or 20,000 miles, for you dummies and dodos). She had done this alone and in a canoe (and not been raped or dunked once) and all this odyssey was performed just to make sure that our airship project proceeds on proper lines. While not exactly demanding that she be appointed commander of the dirigible when it is commissioned, she did intimate that it would be to everybody's good if she did obtain this post.

After a few snorts of the divine product of Caledonia, the

quartet partially recovered from this onslaught. (One witness thus describes her appearance: "Amazonly, with a demeanor of sheer brass nerves and ironclad guts, unseemly in any woman worthy of the name.")

The famous four inquired as to her credentials. She furnished these, which, if valid, are impressive indeed. A prominent citizen interviewed on the subject by our intrepid reporter, Roger "Nellie" Bligh, affirms that she is indeed what she claims to be. Though never having met her in his Terrestrial existence, he did read about her in various periodicals and once viewed her on television (a mid-twentieth-century invention which your editor did not live long enough to see and from all accounts was fortunate to have missed).

It seems that, unless this woman bears a remarkable physical resemblance to the genuine Jill Gulbirra, she is not one of the numerous phonies that have plagued this Rivervalley for far too long a time.

The Office of Vital (some say Deadly) Statistics has furnished us with the following information. Gulbirra, Jill (no middle name). Female. Natal name: Johnetta Georgette Redd. Born February 12, 1953, Toowoomba, Queensland, Australia. Father: John George Redd. Mother: Marie Bronze Redd. Heredity: Scotch-Irish, French (Jewish), Australian aborigine. Unmarried on Earth. Attended schools in Canberra and Melbourne. Graduated 1973 from Massachusetts Institute of Technology, master's degree in aeronautical engineering. Commercial aviator's license, four-motor. Free balloonist's license. Engineer-navigator on West German freighter blimp serving Nigerian government, 1977-78. Blimp pilot for Goodyear, United States, 1979. Blimp pilot for the Sheik of Kuwait, 1980-81. Blimp instructor for British Airways Systems, 1982. Became in 1983 the only qualified woman airship captain in the Western world. Logged 8342 hours airship flight time.

Died April 1, 1983 A.D., automobile accident near Howden, England, just before assuming command of the newly commissioned rigid airship *Willows-Goodens*.

Profession: obvious from above.

Skills: flute, archery, fencing, kendo, quarterstaff, martial arts, badmouthing.

She is pretty good with her dukes, too, having slammed a distinguished citizen, Cyrano "Schnozzola" de Bergerac in the breadbasket, following with a knee to the jaw, rendering him *hors de combat* and speechless. This phenomenon occurred as a result of his having laid hands (without permission) upon her teat. Normally, the fiery Frenchman would have challenged anyone who handled him so savagely to a duel to the death (across the Parolando boundary, of course, since dueling is illegal in our fair state). But he is so old-fashioned that he would feel, as he put it *"comme un imbécile,"* if he were to fight a woman. Moreover, he feels that he was in the wrong for having made advances without invitation "verbal" or "ocular."

An hour after suppertime yesterday, your enterprising intrepid appeared at the door of Gulbirra's hut and knocked. There were some grunts and then a querulous voice called. "What in hell do you want?" Apparently, the would-be interviewee didn't give a hoot about the identity of her caller.

"Miss Gulbirra, I'm Roger Bligh, reporter for *The Daily Leak*. I'd like to interview you."

"Well, you'll have to wait. I'm on the pot."

Your journalist lit up a cigar to pass the time. He also planned to use its burning tip later to clear out the fumes in the hut. After some time, during which he heard splashing of water in a basin, he heard, "Come on in. But leave the door open."

"Gladly," said your dauntless.

He found the subject seated at a chair by the table and smoking a joint. What with the cigar and maryjane and residue of the subject's recent occupation and the smoke from several fishwax candles, neither visibility nor olfactoriness were at an optimum.

"Miss Gulbirra?"

"No. Miz."

"What does the title mean?"

"Are you asking just to get my views or don't you really know? There are plenty of people of my time around. Surely, you've encountered *Miz* before?"

Your reporter confessed his ignorance.

Instead of enlightening Mr. Bligh, the subject said, "What is the position of women in Parolando?"

"In the daytime or at night?" Mr. Bligh said.

"Don't get smart with me," Miz Gulbirra said. "Let me put it simply so your mind can grasp exactly what I'm talking about. Legally, that is, theoretically, women have equal rights here. But in practice, in reality, what is the male attitude toward females?"

"Mainly lecherous, I'm afraid," the intrepid replied.

"I'll give you one more chance," the subject said. "Then it'll be a question of chance and gravity which strikes the ground first outside the door, your ass or your stinking cigar.''

''My apologies,'' the intrepid said. ''But, after all, I am here to interview you, not vice versa. Why don't you ask our female citizens what they think of the male attitude toward them? Anyway, are you here to conduct a suffragette crusade or to build and to man (if I may use the word) the proposed dirigible?''

''Are you making fun of me?''

''The farthest thing from my mind,'' the dauntless said hastily. ''We are quite modern here, even though the late-twentieth-centurians constitute only a small percentage of the population. The state is dedicated to the construction of the airship. To that goal, strict discipline during working hours is maintained. But a citizen may do what he damn well pleases on his hours off, as long as he doesn't hurt anybody else. So, let's get down to business. What is a Miz, not to be confused with amiss?''

''You aren't putting me on?''

''I'd swear by a stack of Bibles, if any existed.''

''Briefly, it's a title which the members of the women's liberation movement in the sixties adopted. *Miss* and *Mrs.* were too indicative of male sexual attitudes. To be a *Miss* was to be unmarried, which automatically evoked contempt, consciously or unconsciously, on the part of the male, *if* the Miss were past marriageable age. It implied that something was lacking in the woman, and also that the Miss must be dying to be referred to as Mrs. That is, without an identity of her own, regarded as an appendage to her husband, a second-class citizen. Why should a Miss, for that matter, be known by her father's name? Why not her mother's?''

''In the latter case,'' our intrepid replied, ''the name would still be a man's, the woman's father's name.''

''Exactly. That is why I changed my name from Johnetta Georgette Redd—you'll notice that both my so-called Christian names are feminizations of masculine names—I changed it to Jill Gulbirra. My father raised hell about that, even my mother protested strongly. But she was a typical Aunt Dora—brainwashed.''

''Interesting,'' Mr. Bligh said. ''Gulbirra? What kind of a name is that? Slavic? And why did you choose it?''

''No, it's Australian aborigine, you dummy. A *gulbirra* is a kangaroo that catches dogs and eats them.''

''A carnivorous kangaroo? I thought they were all vegetarians?''

"Well, actually, it may not have existed. But the abos claimed that it did exist in the outlands. It may have been mythical, but what's the difference? It's the symbolism that counts."

"So you identify with the gulbirra? I can imagine what the dogs symbolize."

At this point, Miz Gulbirra smiled so terrifyingly that your correspondent felt compelled to down a snort of the Dutch courage he always carries in his shoulderbag.

"Not that I chose that name because I identify with, or sympathize with, blackfellow culture," the Miz said. "I am one-quarter abo, but so what? It was a male chauvinist culture through and through, women were mere objects, subject to slavery, they did all the hard work and they were often beaten by their fathers and husbands. A lot of Caucasian males have sentimentalized about the destruction of abo society, but I personally thought it was a good thing. Of course, I deplore the suffering that went along with its disintegration."

"Deploration, unlike defloration, is usually managed without pain," Mr. Bligh said.

"Virginity! That's another male myth, invented solely to aggrandize the male ego and enforce his opinions about his property rights," Miz Gulbirra said bitterly. "Fortunately, that attitude changed considerably during my lifetime. But there are still plenty of pigs around, fossil boars, I called them, who . . ."

"That's all very interesting," the dauntless dared to interrupt. "But you can reserve your opinions for the *Letters to the Editor* page. Mr. Bagg will print anything you say, no matter how scurrilous. Our readers just now would like to know what your professional plans are. Just how do you see yourself as contributing to Project Airship, as it's officially called? Just where do you think you'll fit into the hierarchy?"

By now, the heavy acrid fumes of marijuana overrode all others. A wild, fierce light glittered in her drug-expanded pupils. Your correspondent felt it necessary to expand his rapidly shrinking dauntless state with another pull on the divine bottle.

"By all logic and by right of superior knowledge, experience, and capability," she said slowly but loudly, "I should be in charge of the project. And I should be captain of the airship! I've checked out everybody's qualifications, and there's no doubt at all that I am by far the best qualified.

"So why am I not put in charge of the construction? Why

am I not even considered as a candidate for the captaincy? Why?''

"Don't tell me," your intrepid answered. Possibly he was overly emboldened by the liquid lava coursing through his veins and dulling his otherwise fine sensibilities. "Don't tell me. Let me hazard a guess. Could it be, I'm just groping for an explanation, mind you, could it be that you are relegated to an inferior position because you are only a woman?"

The subject stared at your correspondent, took another puff, drew it deep into her lungs, causing a slight lifting of slight breasts, and finally, face bluish with lack of oxygen, discharged the tag-ends of fumes through her nostrils. Your intrepid was reminded of pictures of dragons he had seen during his Terrestrial existence. He, however, thought of the better part of valor and did not remark upon the similarity.

"You've got it," she said. "Maybe you're not so dense after all."

Then, gripping the edge of the table as if she'd squeeze the wood, she sat up straight. "But just what do you mean by *only* a woman?"

"Oh, that's only my verbalization of your thoughts," the intrepid said hastily. "I was being ironic. Or whatever . . ."

"If I were a man," she said, "which, thank God I am not, I'd have been made at least first mate on the spot. And you wouldn't be sitting there sneering at me."

"Oh, you're mistaken about that," our dauntless said. "I am not sneering at you. However, there is a point that you may have overlooked. It wouldn't make any difference what your sex is; you could have the biggest balls for 40,000 kilometers around, and you still wouldn't be put in charge.

"Long before the Riverboat was built—the second one, I mean, not the one King John stole—it was agreed that Firebrass would be in charge of the airship project. It's even in the Parolando constitution, which you must know, since he himself recited it chapter and verse to you. You were aware of that and by taking the oath you accepted that. So, tell me, why all the bitching?"

"You don't understand after all, do you, you clown?" she said. "The point is that that rule, that arrogantly imperious law, should never have been made."

Your correspondent swallowed some more of the stuff that encourages-and-stupefies—and said, "The point is that it *was* made. And if a man came along twice as qualified as you, he'd still have to accept the fact that he could never be higher than second. He could be Captain Firebrass' chief construction assistant and first mate on the ship. But that's all."

"There isn't any such creature as twice as qualified as me," she said, "unless an officer from the *Graf Zeppelin* should show up. Listen, I'm getting tired of this."

"It is rather hot and smoky in here," your correspondent said, wiping the sweat off his brow. "However, I would like to get more of your background, details of your earthly life, you know, human interest stuff. And also the story of what happened to you right after Resurrection Day. And . . ."

"Are you hoping I'll get turned on by this joint and by your overwhelming male charm and virility?" she said. "Are you getting ready to make a pass at me?"

"God forbid," I said. "This is a strictly professional visit. Besides . . ."

"Besides," she said, and she was the one sneering now, "you're scared of me, aren't you? You're all alike. You have to be dominant, the superior. If you meet a woman with more brains, one who is able to handle you in a fight, who is clearly the superior, then the hot air whistles out of you like a pricked balloon. A balloon with a prick."

"Now, really, Miz Gulbirra," your dauntless said, feeling his face heat up.

"Bug off, little man," the subject said.

Your correspondent thought it was wise to obey this imperative. The interview, though not complete from our viewpoint, was terminated.

12

JILL PICKED UP NEXT EVENING'S *Leak* FROM THE DISTRIBUTION shack outside the press building. Some people who obviously had already read the news snickered or grinned at her. She opened the paper to the *Newcomers* page, suspecting what she would find there, angry before reading it.

The pages rattled in her shaking hands. The interview was bad enough, though she should have known that a late-nineteenth-century man like Bagg would print such rot. What had he been, editor of some crummy yellow rag of some frontier town in the Arizona Territory? Yes, that was it. Tombstone. Firebrass had told her something about him.

What really enraged her was the photograph. She hadn't been aware of it, but someone in the crowd her first morning here had snapped her picture. There she was, caught in a silly-looking, almost obscene, posture. Naked, bending over, her breasts hanging straight down like a cow's udders, the towel in one hand behind her and one before as she sawed it, drying her crotch. She was looking up, her mouth open, and she seemed all nose and buckteeth.

Surely, the cameraman had taken other shots. But Bagg had chosen this one just to make her a laughingstock.

She was so furious she almost forgot to pick up her grail. Swinging it from one hand, thinking how she was going to brain Bagg with it, the newspaper clutched in the other—it was also going to be jammed all the way up—she stormed toward the building. But when she got to the door, she stopped.

"Come on, Jill!" she told herself. "You're reacting just as he hoped you would, just as they all hope you will. Play it cool; don't be a knee-jerk. Sure, it'd make you feel great to slam him around his office a little. But it might ruin everything. You've endured worse, and you've come out on top."

She walked slowly homeward, the handle of the grail looped over one arm. In the fading light, she read the rest of the paper. She wasn't the only one Bagg had libeled, slandered, and mocked. Firebrass himself, though treated gently in the write-up on her, was severely criticized elsewhere and not only by Bagg. The *vox pop* page contained a number of signed letters from citizens outraged by Firebrass' policies.

As she left the plain and started her winding way through the hills, she was softly hailed. Turning, she saw Piscator. He smiled as he walked toward her and said in an Oxford accent, "Good evening, citizen. May I accompany you? We will be happier in each other's company than alone? Or perhaps not?"

Jill had to smile. He spoke so gravely, almost in a seventeenth-century style. This impression was strengthened by his hat, a tall cylinder sloping inward to the top and with a wide circular brim. It reminded her of the hats of the New England Pilgrims. It was made of dark-red leather from the scaleless redfish. Several aluminum alloy flies were snagged in its brim. A black cloth was over his shoulders, held together at the throat. A dark-green cloth served as a kilt, and his sandals were of redfish leather.

Over his shoulder was a bamboo rod. In the other hand was the handle of his grail. A newspaper was clamped by an arm to his body. A wicker basket hung by a strap from the other shoulder.

He was tall for a Japanese, the top of his head coming to her nose. And his features were attractive, not too Mongolian.

"I suppose you've read the paper?" she said.

"Unhappily, most of it," he said. "But don't be grieved. As Solomon says of scoffers, Proverbs xxiv. 9. *They are an abomination to mankind.*"

"I prefer *humankind*," she said.

He looked puzzled. "But what . . .? Ah, I see, you obviously object to *man* in mankind. But *man* means man, woman, and child in this usage."

"I know it does," she said as if she were repeating this for the thousandth time, which she was. "I know it does. But the use of *man* conditions the speaker and the hearer to think of *man* as the human male only. The use of *humankind*, or *personkind*, conditions people to think of *Homo sapiens* as consisting of both sexes."

Piscator drew breath in through his teeth. She expected him to say, "Ah, so!" but he did not. Instead, he said, "I have in this basket three of the savory tench, if I may call them that. They are remarkably similar in appearance and taste to Terrestrial fish of that name. They are not quite as delicious as the grayling, if I may call them that, which are caught in the mountain streams. But they are much sport, a cunning and lusty fish."

She decided that he must have learned his English from *The Compleat Angler*.

"Would you care to share some of the fish with me tonight? I'll have them baked piping hot at 16:00 by the waterclock. I will also have a plentiful supply of skull-bloom."

This was the local name for alcohol made from the lichen scraped off the mountain face. It was watered down, three parts to one, and then blossoms from the irontree vines were dried, crushed, and mixed with alcohol. After the blossoms had given a purplish color and a roselike fragrance to the liquid, it was ready to be served.

Jill hesitated for several seconds. She did not mind being alone—most of the time. Unlike most of her contemporaries, she did not get desperate, panicked, if she were thrown on her own resources. But she had been her only company for too long. The voyage up The River had taken four hundred and twenty days, and during most of that time she had been utterly alone by day. At night, she had eaten and talked with strangers. She had passed an estimated 501,020,000 people and had not seen one face she had known on Earth or Riverworld. Not one.

But then she had seldom gotten close enough to the banks during the day to have recognized facial features. Her socializing at night was limited to a few people. What was mental agony, or would have been if she permitted herself such an emotion, was that she might have passed by some people she had loved on Earth, or, at least, liked. There were some she wanted very much to see again.

Perhaps the one she most longed to talk to was Marie. What had Marie felt when she learned that her senseless jealousy had been responsible for the death of her lover, Jill Gulbirra? Would she have been grief-stricken, perhaps have taken her own life because of guilt? After all, Marie was suicide-prone. Or, rather, to be exact, prone to taking just enough pills to endanger her but not enough so that she could not get medical assistance in time to save her. Marie had come close to death at least three times that Jill knew about. But not very close.

No, Marie would have been plunged into gloom and self-reproach for about three days. Then she would have swallowed about twenty phenobarbitols and called her closest friend, probably another lover, Jill thought, her breast hurting—the bitch!—and the lover would have called the hospital, and then there would be the stomach pump and the antidotes and the long, anxious waiting in the lobby and then the attendance by the bed while Marie rambled on half-mindlessly, still fogged by the drug but not so fogged that she would not be deliberately working on her lover's emotions. It would not just be sympathy that she would be evoking. The sadistic little bitch would also make a few wounding remarks to her lover, getting across some criticisms which she would claim later that she did not remember making.

Then Marie would be taken to her apartment by her lover, and tenderly taken care of for a while, and *then* . . . Jill could not bear fantasizing that *then*.

At these times she had to laugh, though grimly, at herself. It was thirty-one years after she had stormed out of the house and driven off, tires screaming, rubber burning, and raced recklessly through three stoplights and then . . . then the blinding lights and the blaring horn of the huge lorry and the savage wrenching at the wheel to turn the Mercedes-Benz, the frozen sickness inside her, the looming of the juggernaut, and . . .

And she had awakened with countless others, naked, her thirty-year-old body restored to a twenty-five-year-old state—minus certain blemishes and imperfections—on the banks of the Rivervalley. Nightmare in paradise. Or what could have been paradise if so many human beings did not insist on making a hell of it.

Thirty-one years ago. Time had not mended all hurts, not, at least, this one. By now she should have gotten over the mingled fury and grief. It should have receded beyond the horizon of things that mattered now. She should have no slightest emotion about Marie now. But she did.

She was suddenly aware that the Japanese was looking at her. He evidently expected her to reply to something he had just said.

"I'm sorry," she said. "Sometimes, I get lost in the past."

"I am sorry, too," he said. "Sometimes . . . if one is using dreamgum as a means to rid oneself of painful or crippling memories or undesirable psychic states, one instead . . . gets lost."

"No," she said, trying to keep the anger out of her voice. "It's just that I have been alone so long, I have fallen into the habit of reverie. Why, when I was sailing the canoe up The River, I would do so automatically. Sometimes, I would realize that I had put ten kilometers behind me and not even been aware, consciously anyway, of what had happened during that time.

"But now that I'm here, where I have a job that requires constant mental alertness, you will see that I can be as much on my toes as anyone."

She added that because she knew that Piscator might report her to Firebrass. Absentmindedness was not to be tolerated in an airship officer.

"I am sure you will," Piscator said. He paused, smiled, and said, "By the way, do not be worried about competition from me. I am not ambitious. I will be satisfied with whatever rank or position I am given, because I know that that will fit my abilities and experience. Firebrass is fair.

"I am curious about our goal, the so-called Misty Tower or Big Grail or the dozen other titles it bears. In fact, I am eager to journey there, to inquire into what may hold the secret of this world. Eager but not anxious, if you understand what I mean. I readily admit that I do not have your qualifications, and so I anticipate being ranked under you."

Jill Gulbirra was silent for a moment. This man belonged to a nation which practically enslaved its women. At least, in his own time (1886-1965), it had. It was true that after World War I there had been a certain amount of liberation. He would, theoretically, still have the attitude of the old-fashioned Japanese man toward women. Which was a terrible attitude. On the other hand, The Riverworld did change people. *Some* people.

"You really wouldn't mind?" she said. "Not really, deep down!"

"I seldom lie," he said. "And that only to spare the feelings of someone or to keep from wasting time with fools. I think I know what you are thinking. Would it help you to know that one of my masters in Afghanistan was a woman? I spent ten years as her disciple before she decided that I was not as stupid as when I had come to her and that I could go on to my next sheik."

"What were you doing there?"

"I would be happy to discuss that some other time. As of the moment, let me assure you that I am not prejudiced against women or against non-Japanese. I was, but that foolishness was emptied out of me a long time ago. For instance, at one time, for some years after World War I, I was a Zen monk. First, though, do you know anything about Zen?"

"There were many books written about it after 1960 or thereabouts," Jill said. "I read a few."

"Yes. Did you know any more after reading these than you did before?" he said, smiling.

"A little."

"You are truthful. As I was saying, I retired from the world after I resigned from the Navy and I resided at a monastery in Ryukyu. The third year, a white man, a Hungarian, came to the monastery as a humble novitiate. When I saw how he was treated, I suddenly acknowledged what I had known unconsciously but had resisted bringing to light. That was that many years in the discipline of Zen had not rid either the disciples or masters, no one in the monastery, except myself, of their racial prejudices. Their national prejudices, I should say, since they showed hostility and even contempt for Chinese and Indo-Chinese, fellow Mongolians.

"After being honest for the first time with myself, I acknowledged to myself that the practice of Zen had not resulted in anything deeply worthwhile in myself or the others. Of course, you must realize that Zen does not have goals. To have goals is to frustrate the attaining of goals. Is that contradictory? It is.

"It is also nonsense, as is that business of *emptying* oneself. Perhaps the state of being empty is not nonsense, but the methods used to achieve it were, as far as I was concerned. And so, one morning, I walked out of the monastery and took ship to China. And I began my long wanderings, called by some inaudible voice toward Central Asia. And from thence . . . well, that is enough for the time being. I can continue this later if you wish.

"I see that we are getting close to our homes. I bid you adieu then until tonight. I will set out two torches, which you may see from your window, to announce when our little gathering begins.''

''I did not say that I was coming.''

''But you had nevertheless accepted,'' he said. ''Is that not true?''

''Yes, but how did you know?''

''It's not telepathy,'' he said, smiling again. ''A certain posture, a certain relaxation of muscles, the dilation of your pupils, an undertone to your voice, undetectable except to the highly trained, told me that you were looking forward to the party.''

Jill said nothing. She had not known herself that she was pleased with the invitation. Nor was she sure now. Was Piscator conning her?

13

AN IRONTREE GREW FROM THE TOP OF A HILL 200 METERS FROM Jill's hut. Piscator's hut was near the top, nestled between the upper parts of two roots. Its back rested upon a shelf of earth; its front was held up by bamboo pylons to keep it from slipping down the steep slope.

Jill went up the hill without Jack, though there would be Jack-asses at its top, she thought. She went under the house and up a bamboo staircase which entered the structure through the floor halfway along its length.

The building was larger than most of those in this area, three rooms on the ground floor and two on the first story. According to a neighbor, it had once housed a commune. Like all such nonreligious organizations composed of Occidentals, it had dissolved after a while. Piscator had moved in then, though Jill did not know why one man wanted such a large house. Was it because it was a prestige symbol? He did not seem to be the sort of man who would care for such things.

Along the railing were bright acetylene lamps behind white, green, or scarlet shades made from fish intestines. Piscator, at the top of the steps, smiled and nodded at Jill. He was wearing a kimonolike arrangement of varicolored towels. In his hand he held a bouquet of huge blooms plucked from the vines entwining the upper reaches of the irontree.

"Welcome, Jill Gulbirra."

She thanked him, breathing deeply the strong odor of the flowers, reminiscent of honeysuckle with a very slight scent of old leather. A peculiar but pleasing combination.

Gaining the top of the steps, she found herself in the largest room of the house. Its ceiling was about three times her height; from it hung a score of Japanese lamps. The bamboo floor was covered here and there with throwrugs made from bamboo fiber. The furniture was of bamboo, light, simple forms the seats of which were sof-tened with cushions. Some of the chair arms and table legs and the posts supporting the ceiling were, however, of oak or yew. Heads of animals, demons, Riverfish, and human beings had been carved from these. They did not look as if they had been done by a

Japanese. Probably, a previous occupant had sculptured them.

Tall, wasp-waisted bell-mouthed vases stood on the floor. Shorter versions stood on top of spindly legged round-topped tables. These were formed on a potter's wheel, baked, and glazed or painted. Geometrical designs were on some vases; others bore marine scenes from Earthlife. The boats were lateens; the sailors, Arabs. Blue dolphins leaped from a blue-greenish sea; a monster opened its mouth to swallow a ship. However, since there were large fish called dolphins in The River, and the colossal Riverdragon did bear a faint resemblance to the monster, it was possible that the artist had represented Riverlife.

The doorways to the neighboring rooms were filled with dangling strings of white and red hornfish vertebrae; these emitted a tinkling when disturbed. Mats of woven fibers from irontree vines hung on the walls, and transparent intestines of Riverdragons, stretched on bamboo frames, were above each window.

All in all, though there were some things, such as the acetylene lamps, not found elsewhere, the room was a variation of what many called Riparian Culture; others, Riverine Polynesian.

The lamp lights strove to pierce the heavy clouds of tobacco and marijuana. A band played softly on a small podium in a corner. It was providing its services in return for booze and a chance to please itself with useful work. The musicians were beating or brushing drums, blowing on a bamboo flute, a clay ocarina; stroking a harp made of a turtlefish shell and fish guts; sawing on a fiddle of fish intestines and English-yewlike wood with a yew bow fitted with the horsehairlike mouth cilia of the blue dolphin; hammering a xylophone; blowing a saxophone, a trumpet.

The music was unrecognizable, at least for Jill. But she thought that it was derived from a Central or South American Indian piece.

"If this were tête-à-tête, instead of a large party, I would be able to give you tea, my dear," Piscator said. "But it is not possible. My grail does not provide me with tea daily, but only one small bagful once a week."

He had not changed so much that he did not miss the ceremony of tea, so beloved by all Japanese. Jill regretted the scarcity of the herb, too. Like most of her nation, she felt that something vital was missing if she didn't get her tea at the proper time.

Piscator dipped a glass in a huge glass bowl full of skull-bloom and handed it to her. She sipped on it while he told her how happy he was to see her here. He sounded as if he really meant it. She found herself warming to him, though she did remind herself that he came from a culture which conditioned males to regard females as pleasure and work objects. Then she warned herself—for the ten thousandth time?—that she must not be as guilty of prejudice as others. Find the facts first and study them before judgment.

Her host led her around, introducing her briefly. Firebrass waved at her from a corner. Cyrano smiled thinly and bowed. They had encountered each other a number of times since that morning, but each had been aloof though polite. She did not want it that way. After all, he had apologized, and she was very curious about this flamboyant seventeenth-centurian.

She said hello to Ezekiel Hardy and David Schwartz, whom she saw every day in the office inside the hangar and in the factories nearby. Hardy and Schwartz were friendly enough; they had learned by now that she was thoroughly knowledgeable in her field. In many, in fact. She had bridled her impatience and anger at their ignorance and their assumed superiority. It had paid off, though she did not know how long she could repress herself.

"Don't bottle up," she told herself. "Empty yourself."

How many times had she done that, or tried to do that? And it had seemed to work so many times, though not always by any means. Yet, here was this Japanese, Ohara, calling himself by the goofy name of Piscator—how weird—telling her than Zen was nonsense. Well, not exactly nonsense. But he had certainly indicated that it was overrated. She had not liked to hear that. It struck her below the belt of her self-image; it injured her. Which it should not have done. She should have laughed at him, even if only inwardly. But he had seemed so sure.

14

ONE OF THE WOMEN SHE WAS INTRODUCED TO WAS JEANNE JUGAN. Piscator mentioned that she had once been a servant in her native France but then had become one of the founders of the Roman Catholic religious order of the Little Sisters of the Poor, established in 1839 in Brittany.

"I am his disciple," Jugan said, nodding at Piscator.

Jill's eyebrows rose. "Oh!" She had no chance to continue the conversation. Piscator steered her away with a light touch on the elbow.

"You may talk to her later."

Jill wondered what particular religion, sect, or mental discipline Piscator belonged to. He wasn't a member of the Church of the Second Chance. A Chancer always wore a hornfish spiral vertebra or its wooden facsimile on a string from his neck.

However, the next person she met did wear that emblem, three, in fact, indicating that he was a bishop. Samuelo, short, very dark, and hawk faced, had been born sometime around the middle of the second century A.D. He had been a rabbi of the Jewish community at Nehardea in Babylonia. According to Piscator, he was somewhat famous in his time for his knowledge of traditional law and for some attainments in science. One of his feats was the compilation of a calendar of the Hebrew year. His chief claim to fame, however, lay in his efforts to adjust the Jewish law to the law of the land in which the Jews of the Diaspora lived.

"His principle was *The law of the state is the binding law*," Piscator said.

Samuelo introduced his wife, Rahelo. She was even shorter, though not as dark, and she had very broad hips and heavy legs, but a face of startling sensuality. Replying to Jill's questions, she said that she had been born in the Krakow ghetto in the fourteenth century A.D. Piscator would tell Jill later that Rahelo had been abducted by a Polish nobleman and imprisoned for a year in his castle. Tiring of her, he had then kicked her out, though not without a fat purse of gold coins. Her husband had murdered her because she had not had the grace to kill herself because of her dishonor.

Samuelo sent Rahelo running several times to get him a drink from a bowl filled with nonalcoholic bloom juice. He also gestured for her to light his cigar. She obeyed quickly and then resumed her position behind him.

Jill felt like kicking Rahelo for putting up with her ancient degradation and Samuelo for his ancient complacency. She could visualize him at prayers, thanking God that he was not born a woman.

Later, Piscator said to her, "You were furious with the bishop and his wife."

She did not ask him how he knew. She said, "It must have been a hell of a shock for him to wake up here and find out that he was not one of God's chosen people. That everybody, idol worshipper, cannibal, swine eater, uncircumcised dog of an infidel, all God's children, were here, all were chosen."

"We were all shocked," Piscator said. "And terrified. Weren't you?"

She stared at him for a moment, then laughed, and said, "Of course. I was an atheist, and I still am. I was sure that I was just so much flesh that would become so much dust. And that was that. I was horribly frightened when I awoke here. But at the same time, well, not at first but a little later, I was relieved. So, I thought, there *is* eternal life. Then, even later, I saw such strange things, and we were in such a strange place, nothing like heaven or hell, you know . . ."

"I know," he said. He smiled. "I wonder what Samuelo thought when he saw that the uncircumcised *goyim* of Earth had been resurrected without their foreskins? That must have been as puzzling as the fact that men could no longer grow beards. On the one hand, God had performed a *briss* upon all the Gentiles who needed it and so He must be a Jewish god. On the other hand, a man could no longer sport the full beard demanded by God, so He surely could not be a Jewish god.

"It was, and is, such things that should have and should be changing our patterns of thinking," Piscator said.

He came close, looking up at her with dark brown eyes set in fleshy slits. "The Second Chancers have some excellent ideas about why we have been raised from the dead and who has done it. They are not too far wrong about the way, or ways, one must take to attain the goal. A goal which mankind should desire and the gate to which our unknown benefactors have opened for us. But exactness is rightness. The inexact Church has wandered off the main road, or, I should say, the only road. Which is not to say that there is not more than one road."

"What are you talking about?" she said. "You sound as weird as those Chancers."

"We shall see—if you care to see," he said. He excused himself and walked to the big table, where he started talking to a man who had just entered.

Jill sauntered toward Jeanne Jugan, intending to ask her what she meant by calling herself Piscator's *disciple*. De Bergerac, however, placed himself in front of her. He was smiling broadly now.

"Ah, Ms. Gulbirra! I must beg your pardon for that unfortunate incident again! It was the liquor which caused me to behave so unforgivably, well not unforgivably I hope, but so barbarically! It is seldom that I drink more than an ounce or two, since I abominate the dulling of my senses. Alcohol makes one a swine, and I do not care for the beast on the hoof, though I adore him sliced and fried in a pan or roasted on a spit. But that night we were fishing . . ."

"I didn't see any fishing equipment," she said.

"It was on the other side of the grailstone. And the fog was thick, remember, mademoiselle?"

"Ms."

"And we got to talking of things on Earth, places, people we had known, friends who had come to a bad end, children who had died, how our parents had misunderstood us, enemies, why we were here, and so on, understand? I became depressed, thinking of what might have been on Earth, especially what my cousin Madeleine and I might have done if I had been more mature or had not been so naive at that time. And so . . ."

"And so you got drunk," she said, her face grave.

"And offended you, Ms., though I swear that I did not believe that you were a woman. The fog, the baggy clothing, my own addled wits . . ."

"Forget it," she said. "Only . . . I believed you would never forgive me, since you would have lost face after a woman punched you out. Your ego . . ."

"You must not stereotype!" Cyrano cried.

"And you are right," she said. "That is a failing I loathe, and yet I find myself doing it all the time. However, so often . . . well, most people are living stereotypes, aren't they?"

They stood there, talking for a long time. Jill sipped on the purple passion, feeling her belly slowly warm up. The marijuana fumes became thicker, and she added to their intensity by drawing on the burning joint between her fingers. The voices were becoming louder, and there was much more laughter. Some couples were dancing now, their arms around each other's necks, shuffling languorously.

Piscator and Jugan seemed to be the only ones who were not drinking. Piscator was smoking a cigarette now, the first, she believed, that he had lit up since she had entered.

The combination of liquor and pot had given her a pleasant halo now. She felt as if her flesh must be leaking a red-colored light. The smoke clouds were forming into almost-shapes. Sometimes, out of the corners of her eyes, she would glimpse a definite figure, a dragon, a smokefish, once, a dirigible. But when she turned her head toward them, she could see only amorphous masses.

When she saw a metal tub float by to one side, she knew that she had had it. No more booze and grass the rest of the night. The reason for the appearance of the tub was apparent, since Cyrano had been telling her about crime and its punishments in the France of his day. A counterfeiter, for instance, was stretched out upon a large wheel. The executioner then broke his arms and legs with an iron bar, sometimes pounding them to a pulp. Executed criminals were hung in chains in marketplaces and left to rot until the bodies fell through the chains. The guts of others were left in big open tubs so that they could remind the citizens of what happened to transgressors.

"And the streets ran with sewage, Ms. Gulbirra. No wonder that those who had the money drenched themselves with perfume."

"I thought it was because you seldom bathed then."

"True," the Frenchman said. "I mean, true that we did not bathe often. It was thought to be unhealthy, un-Christian. But one can get used to the stench of unwashed bodies. I was not often aware of it since I was, as you might say, immersed in it, as unconscious of it as a fish is of water. But here, *helas!* Where so few clothes are worn and where running water is so at hand, and where one encounters so many who cannot endure the odor of long-dirty humans, then one learns new habits. I, myself, now, I must confess that I saw no reason to be so fastidious, but then after some years I met a woman with whom I fell into love almost as passionately as I had with my cousin. She was Olivia Langdon . . ."

"You can't mean Sam Clemens' wife?"

"But yes. Though of course that meant nothing to me when I first met her and still does not. I understood that he was the great writer of the New World—she told me much about what happened since I had died on Earth—but I do not think much about it. And then Olivia and I wandered down The River and suddenly we were confronted with that classical situation which so many people dread. We met the former, the Terrestrial, spouse, of one's hutmate.

"By then, though I was still fond of her, my passion had cooled off. Each of us did so many things to annoy, even enrage the other, and why not? Is that not something commonplace here, where man and woman may be not only from different nations but from different times? How can the seventeenth-century person mesh with the nineteenth? Well, sometimes such a mismatch can be reshaped to match. But add the temporal differences to those that naturally exist between individuals, and what do you have? Quite often, a hopeless case.

"Livy and I were far up The River when I heard about the boat that was being built. I had heard of the meteorite that fell here, but I did not know that it was Sam Clemens who had seized the meteorite. I wanted to be one of the crew, and especially I wanted to feel a steel rapier in my hand again.

"And so, my dear Ms. Gulbirra, we came to this place. The shock was powerful indeed for Sam. I felt sorry for him, for a while, and regretted having forced this reunion that was not a reunion. Olivia showed no inclination to leave me for Clemens even though our passion was not quite what it had been. She did feel guilt about not feeling love for him. This was all the stranger when it is considered that they were deeply in love on Earth.

"But there had been many frictions, deeply hidden hostilities. She said that when she was in her terminal illness she did not want to see him. This hurt him very much, but she could not help it. And why, I asked her, had she not cared to admit him into her sickroom? She replied that she did not know. Perhaps it was because their only son had died because of Sam's negligence. Criminal negligence, she called it, though she had never used, or even thought of, that word on Earth.

"I said that that was a long time ago and on another planet. Why did she still hold that fierce grievance within her breast? Did it matter now? Was not little . . . I forget his name . . ."

"Langdon," Jill said.

". . . risen from the dead now? And she said, yes, but she would never see Langdon. He had died when he was two, and no one under five years of age at death had been resurrected. At least not here. Maybe on another world. In any event, even if he had been raised here, what chance would she have of running across him? And what if she did? He would be full grown now, he would not even remember her. She would be a stranger to him. And God only knew what kind of a boy he would be. He might have been resurrected among cannibals or Digger Indians and not even know English or table manners."

Jill grinned and said, "That sounds like something Mark Twain would say, not his wife."

Cyrano grinned back and said, "She didn't say that. I made that up, paraphrasing her. There was, of course, much more to her feeling than the accidental death of her baby. Actually, I can't blame Clemens. Being a writer, he was very absentminded when he was pondering upon a story. I am that way myself. He did not notice that the coverings of the baby had slipped aside and that the icy air was blowing full upon the unprotected infant. He was automatically driving the horse which was drawing the sledge through the snows while his mind was intent upon that other world—his fiction.

"However, Olivia was certain that he was not as absentminded as he believed. She insisted that he could not have been, that some part of his mind must have observed the baby's situation. He did not really want a son. Unlike most men, he preferred daughters. Besides, the baby was sickly from birth, a nuisance. To Sam, I mean.''

"That's one thing in his favor," Jill said. "I mean, that he preferred girls. Though I suppose, to be fair, that it is as neurotic to prefer a female infant as to prefer a male. Still, he did not have that male chauvinism . . .''

Cyrano said, "You must comprehend that Olivia did not consciously acknowledge all this during her Terrestrial existence. At least, she claimed not to have done so, though I suspect that she had such thoughts, was ashamed of them, and so put them away in the deep, dark files of her soul. But it was here, in this Valley, when she became addicted to chewing the *soi-disant*, the so-called dreamgum, that she perceived her true feelings.

"And so, though she still loved Clemens, in a manner of speaking, she hated him even more.''

"Did she quit using the gum?''

"Yes. It upset her too much. Though she now and then had some ecstatic or fantastic visions, she had too many horrible experiences.''

"She should have stuck with it," Jill said. "But under proper guidance. However . . .''

"Yes?''

Jill compressed her lips, than said, "Perhaps I shouldn't be too bloody critical. I had a guru, a beautiful woman, the best and wisest woman I ever knew, but she couldn't keep me from running headlong into . . . well, no need to go into it here . . . it was too . . . dismaying? No, horrifying. I chickened out. So I shan't be criticizing anyone else, shouldn't anyway. I have been considering taking it up again, but I don't trust the Second Chancers' use of it, even though they claim to have excellent, quite safe, techniques. I couldn't put full confidence in people who have *their* religious beliefs.''

"I was a free thinker, a *libertin*, as we styled ourselves," Cyrano said. "But now . . . I do not know. Perhaps there is after all a God. Otherwise, how does one account for *this* world?''

"There are a score of theories," Jill said. "And no doubt you've heard them all.''

"Many, at any rate," Cyrano said. "I was hoping to hear a new one from you.''

15

AT THAT MOMENT, SEVERAL PEOPLE INVADED THE CONVERSATION. Jill broke off from the clump and drifted around, looking for another clump, a temporary colony, to attach herself to. In The Riverworld, as on Earth, all cocktail or after-dinner parties were alike. You spoke briefly, trying to make yourself heard above all the chatter and music, and then changed partners or groups until you had made a complete circuit. If you were intrigued or even interested in someone, you could make arrangements to see him or her some other time, when you could have a chance for an uninterrupted and quiet conversation.

In the old days, long ago, when she was young in mind, she had often met men or women at such gatherings who enthralled her. But then she had been full of booze or pot or both and so wide open. It was easy to fall in love with a mind or body—or both at the same time. Sobering up usually meant wising up. A disappointment. Not always. Just most of the time.

Here was a gathering all of whom had the bodies of twenty-five-year-olds. Chronologically, she was sixty-one. Some here might actually be one hundred and thirty-two or even more. The youngest could not be under thirty-six.

The index of wisdom should be high, if it was true that age brought wisdom. She had not found that to be true about most people on Earth. Experience was something it was difficult to avoid, though many people had managed to keep it to a minimum. Experience did not by any means give wisdom, that understanding of the basic mechanics of humanity. Most oldsters she had known had been as governed by conditioned reflexes as when they had been nineteen.

So it was expected that people would not have benefited much from their experiences here. However, the hammer blows of death and resurrection had broken open the seals of the minds of many.

For one thing, absolutely no one had expected this type of afterlife, if you could call this an afterlife. No religion had described such a place, such events. Though, to tell the truth, those religions which did promise paradises and hells were remarkably lacking in descriptive detail. Perhaps not so remarkably, since very few persons had actually claimed to have seen the postmortem world.

And there certainly was nothing supernatural about this place and the raising of the dead in it. Everything—well, not everything but almost everything—could be explained in physical, not metaphysical, terms. This did not keep people from originating religious theories or reshaping old ones.

Those religions which had no eschatology of resurrection or immortality in the Western sense, Buddhism, Hinduism, Confucianism, Taoism were discredited. Those which did have such, Judaism, Islamism, Christianity, were equally discredited. But here, as on Earth, the death of a major religion was the birth pang of a new one. And there were, of course, minorities who refused stubbornly, despite all evidence, to admit that their faith was invalid.

Jill, standing near Samuelo, ex-rabbi, present bishop of the Church of the Second Chance, wondered what his reaction had been that first year on this world. There was no Messiah come to save the Chosen People, nor, indeed, any Chosen People assembled together at Jerusalem on Earth. No Jerusalem, no Earth.

Apparently the shattering of his faith had not shattered him. Somehow he had been able to accept that he had been wrong. Although a superorthodox rabbi of ancient times, he had a flexible mind.

At that moment Jeanne Jugan, who was hostess, offered Samuelo and Rañelo a dish of bamboo tips and fileted fish. Samuelo looked at the fish and said, "What is that?"

"Toadfish," Jeanne said.

Samuelo tightened his lips and shook his head. Jeanne looked puzzled, since the bishop was obviously hungry and his fingers were only a few centimeters from seizing the tips. These, as far as Jill knew, were not tabu according to the Mosaic laws. But they were on the same plate as the forbidden scaleless fish and so contaminated.

She smiled. It was much easier to change a person's religion than his/her food habits. A devout Jew or Moslem could give up his creed but would still feel nauseated if offered pork. A Hindu whom Jill had known had become an atheist on The Riverworld, but he still could not abide meat. Jill, though of partial blackfellow descent, could not force herself to eat worms, though she had tried. Genetic descent had nothing to do with dietary matters, of course; it was social descent that determined food choices. Though not always. Some people could adapt easily enough. And there was always the individual taste. Jill had ceased eating mutton the moment she had quit her parents' house. She hated it. And she preferred hamburger to beef roast.

The whole point to this reverie, she thought as she emerged from it, shedding thoughts as a surfacing diver sheds water, the whole point was that we are what we eat. And we eat what we do because of what we are. And what we are is determined partly by our environment and partly by our genetic makeup. All my family except myself loved mutton. A sister shared my indifference to beef roast and my love for hamburgers.

All my brothers and sisters, as far as I know, are heterosexual. I am the only bisexual. And I don't want that. I want to be one way or the other, a gate that is latched, not swinging either way depending upon which way the wind is blowing. My internal wind which shifts from east to west or vice versa, twirling the windcock this way or that way.

Actually, she did not want it one way or the other. If she had her choice—and why shouldn't she?—she would be a woman lover.

Woman lover. Why didn't she say to herself: lesbian? The English language was the greatest in the world, but it had its faults. It was often too ambiguous. Woman lover could mean a man who loved women, a man or woman who loved women, or a woman who was a lover.

There, she'd said it. Lesbian. And she didn't feel any shame. What about Jack? She had loved him. What about . . . ?

She had come up from the reverie only to dive down again.

Across the room, Firebrass, though talking to others, was looking at her. Had he noticed her tendency to become a statue, slumped, her head slightly cocked to the left, her eyelids lowered, and the eyes slightly rolled up? And if he had, then had he decided she was too moody and hence untrustworthy?

At that, she felt a slight panic. Oh, God, if he rejected her as a candidate just because she was pensive now and then! She was not that way when on duty! Never. But how could she convince Firebrass of that?

She would have to be alert, always act as if she were on her toes, extroverted, prepared, trustworthy. As if she were a Girl Scout.

She walked up to a circle in the center of which was Bishop Samuelo. The dark little man was telling some stories about La Viro. Jill had heard a number of them, since she had attended many Second Chancer meetings and talked with its missionaries. In Esperanto, the official language of the Church, La Viro meant The Man. He was also called La Fondinto, The Founder. Apparently, no one knew his Terrestrial name or else it was not considered important by the Second Chancers.

Samuelo's tale concerned the stranger who had approached La Viro one stormy night in a cave high in the mountains. The stranger had revealed that he was one of the people who had reshaped this planet into one long Rivervalley and who had then resurrected the people of Earth.

The stranger had instructed La Viro to found the Church of the Second Chance. He was given certain tenets to preach, and he was told that after he had spread these up and down the Valley, he would then be given more revelations. As far as she knew, these new "truths" had not yet been forthcoming.

But the Church had spread everywhere. Its missionaries had traveled on foot or boat. Some, it was said, had journeyed in balloons. The fastest means of transportation had been death and resurrection.

Actually, those who had killed the Chancer preachers were doing the Church a service. It ensured that the faith spread around The Riverworld in a much faster time.

Martyrdom was a convenient means of travel, Jill thought. But it took great courage to die for your religion now when *once dead always dead*. She had heard that there had been a great falling away from the Church recently. Whether that was caused by the permanency of death now, or it was just that the movement had lost its steam, she did not know.

One of the group was a man to whom she had not been introduced. Piscator had, however, pointed to him across the room and said, "John de Greystock. He lived during Edward I of England's reign. Thirteenth century? I have forgotten much of British history, though I studied it intensively when I was a naval cadet."

"Edward ruled from about 1270 to very early 1300, I think," Jill said. "I do remember that he ruled thirty-five years and died when he was sixty-eight. I remember it because that was a long life in those days, especially for an Englishman. Those chilly, drafty castles, you know."

"Greystock was made a baron by Edward and accompanied him on his Gascon and Scottish expeditions," Piscator said. "I don't really know much about him. Except that he was governor of *La Civito de La Animoj*—Soul City in English—a little state some forty-one kilometers down-River. He came here before I did, not too long after King John stole Clemens' boat. He enlisted in Parolando's army, rose rapidly in rank, and distinguished himself during the invasion of Soul City . . ."

"Why would Parolando invade Soul City?" Jill said.

"Soul City had made a sneak attack on Parolando. It wanted to get control of the meteorite iron supply here and the *Not For Hire* too. It almost succeeded. But Clemens and several others blew up a big dam. This had been built to store water from a mountain stream so it could be used to generate electrical power. The blowing up of the dam released many millions of liters of water. The invaders were wiped out, along with thousands of Parolandans. It also swept the aluminum and steel mills and the factories into The River. The Riverboat, too, but that was recovered almost undamaged.

"Clemens had to rebuild almost from scratch. During our vulnerable situation, the Soul Citizens allied with some other states and attacked again. They were repulsed but with heavy losses. The Parolanders badly needed Soul City's bauxite, cryolite, cinnabar, and platinum. It had the only supply in the Valley. The bauxite and cryolite were needed to make more aluminum. Cinnabar is the ore of mercury, and platinum is used as electrical contacts for various scientific apparatuses, and as absolutely required catalysts in various chemical reactions."

"I know that," Jill said with some asperity.

"Forgive me," Piscator said, smiling slightly. "After the unsuccessful attack by the Soul Citizens, Greystock was made a colonel. And after Parolando's successful invasion of Soul City, he was made its governor. Clemens wanted a tough, ruthless man, and like most feudal lords, Greystock was that.

"However, several weeks ago Soul City voluntarily became one of the states in the United States of Parolando, fully equal with the mother state.

"Of course"—here Piscator smiled lopsidedly—"by now the supply of minerals in Soul City is almost exhausted. Project Airship doesn't need Soul City anymore. Also, through the process which Greystock calls *attrition*, a very euphemistic term, I fear, the original makeup of the population there has changed considerably. It was once a majority of mid-twentieth-century American blacks, with a minority of medieval Arabs—fanatical Wahhabis—and Dravidian speakers of ancient India. Because of the wars and Greystock's harsh governorship, its population became about half-white."

"He sounds so savage," she said. "With due apologies to the savages."

"He had several rebellions to put down. No one was forced to stay at Soul City, you know. Clemens would not permit slavery. Everybody was given a chance to leave, to go peacefully and with all his possessions elsewhere. Many citizens stayed there, swore loyalty to Parolando, but then became saboteurs."

"Guerrilla warfare?"

"Hardly," Piscator said. "You know that the topography just isn't fitted for guerrilla activity. No. It seems that a number of Soul Citizens thought that sabotage would be a method of recreation."

"Recreation?"

"It gave them something to do. It was better than drifting on down The River. Besides, many of them wanted revenge.

"To give Greystock his due, he usually just kicked any saboteurs he caught out of the state. Actually, he threw them into The River. Well, that is history, and it happened before I came here. Anyway,

Greystock has come here because he wants to be a member of the airship crew."

"But he has no qualifications!"

"True—in one sense. He does not come from a highly technological culture, relatively speaking. But he is intelligent and curious, and he can learn. And though he was once a baron of England and governor of Soul City, he is willing to be a lowly crewman. The idea of flying fascinates him. It's akin to magic—for him. Firebrass has promised him that he can go—if there are not enough qualified airshipmen. Of course, if by chance the crew of the *Graf Zeppelin* or the *Shenandoah* should just happen to come along . . ."

Piscator had smiled.

Greystock was about 1.8 meters, a very tall height during the medieval period. His hair was black, long, and straight; his eyes, large and grey; his eyebrows, thick; his nose, slightly aquiline. His features harmonized into a ruggedly good-looking face. His shoulders were broad; his waist, narrow; his legs, thickly packed with muscle but long.

At the moment, he was speaking to Samuelo, his grin and his tone both sarcastic. Piscator had said that Greystock hated priests, though he had been very devout during his Terrestrial existence. Apparently, he had never forgiven the clergy for falsely claiming to know the truth about the afterlife.

Using Esperanto, Greystock said, "But surely you must have some idea of who and what La Viro was on Earth? What race was he? What nationality? When was he born, when died? Was he prehistoric, ancient, medieval, or what the later peoples called modern? What had he been on Earth, a religionist, agnostic, or atheist? What was his trade or profession? His education? Was he married? Did he have children? Was he a homosexual?

"Was he unknown during his time? Or was he, perhaps, *Christ*? And is that why He is remaining anonymous, knowing that no one is going to believe His lies a second time?"

Samuelo scowled, but he said, "I know little of this Christ; only what has been told me and that is not much. All I know of La Viro is what I have heard through word of mouth. They say that he is very tall, white skinned though very dark, and some say that they think he might have been Persian.

"But all this is irrelevant. It is not his background or his physical appearance that matters. What does matter is his message."

"Which I have heard from many preachers of your Church many times!" Greystock said. "And which I believe no more than I do the stinking falsehoods the stinking priests offered me as God's own truths in my own time!"

"That is your privilege, though not your right," Samuelo said.

Greystock looked puzzled. Jill did not understand what he meant either.

Greystock said loudly, "All you priests talk mumbo-jumbo!" and he walked away scowling.

Piscator, watching him, smiled. "A dangerous man. But interesting. You should get him to tell the story of his journey with an Arcturan."

Jill's eyebrows went up.

"Yes, he knew a being who came to Earth from a planet of the star Arcturus. Apparently, this being came with some others in a spaceship in 2002 A.D. But he was forced to kill almost all human beings. He died, too, though. It's a horrible story, but true.

"Firebrass can give you the details. He was on Earth when it happened."

16

EAGER TO TALK TO GREYSTOCK, JILL MADE HER WAY THROUGH THE crowd toward him. But she was stopped by Firebrass before she could reach the Englishman.

"A messenger just told me that radio contact's been made with the *Mark Twain*. Want to come along and get in on the pow-wow? You might get to talk to the great Sam Clemens himself."

"Too right I would!" she said. "And thanks for the invitation."

Jill followed Firebrass to the jeep, which was near the foot of the staircase. It was made of steel and aluminum and had pneumatic nylon tires. Its six-cylinder motor was fueled by wood alcohol.

There were five passengers: Firebrass, Gulbirra, de Bergerac, Schwartz, and Hardy. The jeep took off swiftly, following the narrow valleys among the hills. Its bright beams showed the grass, closely cut by machines, huts here and there, stands of the incredibly quick-growing bamboo, some 31 meters or over 100 feet high. Leaving the hills, it sped over the plain gently sloping to The River.

Jill could see the lights of the aluminum-processing factory, the steel mill, the distillery, the welding shop, the armory, the arms factory, the cement mill, and the government building. The latter housed the newspaper and radio station offices, and the top government officials had residences there.

The colossal hangar was down-River and hence downwind of the other buildings. Up in the mountains to the west were strings of lights. These were on the dam constructed to replace the one that Clemens had blown up.

The jeep passed the hangar. A steam locomotive, burning alcohol, chuffchuffed by, hauling three flatbed cars piled with aluminum girders. It entered the blazing interior of the hangar, stopped, and a crane hook swung down to the rear car. Workers gathered around it to connect hooks to the steel cables around the girders.

"City Hall" was the northernmost building. The jeep stopped before its porch. The riders got out and went between two massive Doric columns. Jill thought that the building was an abomination, architecturally speaking. Nor did it fit in with the surroundings. Seen from a distance, this area looked as if both the Parthenon and a section of the Ruhr had been teleported to a remote section of Tahiti.

Firebrass' suite of offices was to the left of the entrance to the immense lobby. Six men stood guard before its entrance, each armed with a single-shot rifle firing .80-caliber plastic bullets. They also carried cutlasses and daggers. The radio "shack" was a large room next to the conference hall and Firebrass' sanctum sanctorum. They entered the former to find several men standing around the operator. He was adjusting dials on the big panel before him. On hearing the door slam open under his commander's overvigorous shove, he looked up.

"I've been talking to Sam," he said. "But I lost him about thirty seconds ago. Hold on. I think I got him."

A series of squeals and crackles issued from the loudspeaker. Suddenly, the interference eased off, and a voice could be heard above the noise. The operator made a final adjustment and gave up his chair to Firebrass.

"Firebrass speaking. Is that you, Sam?"

"No. Just a moment."

"Sam here," a pleasant drawling voice said. "Is that you, Milt?"

"Sure is. How are you, Sam? And what's doing?"

"As of today, Milt, the electronic log says we've traveled 792,014 miles. You can convert that into kilometers if you wish. I prefer the old system, and that's what we're . . . well, you know that. Not bad for three years' travel, heh? But downright aggravating. A snail could go to the North Pole faster than we can, if it could go on a straight line. Or, pardon me, a great curve. It would have time to build a hotel for us and make an enormous fortune renting rooms to the walruses until we arrived. Even if the snail was traveling only a mile every twenty-four hours and we're averaging about eight hundred miles a day.

"As of . . ." sputter, crackle ". . . little trouble."

Firebrass waited until reception was clear before speaking again. "Is everything all-go, Sam?"

"Copacetic," Sam said. "Nothing unusual has happened. Which means that there are always emergencies, always trouble, but not mutinies, among the crew. I've had to boot a few out now and then. If this keeps up, by the time we get to our million-mile mark, I'll be the only person who was on the boat when it left Parolando."

More crackles. Then Jill heard a voice that was so deep, so bottom-of-the-well, that cold ran over her neck.

Sam said, "Yeah? Oh, all right, I forgot you, though that's not easy with you breathing booze down my neck. Joe says he'll still be here, too. He wants to say hellow to you. Joe, say hello."

"Hello, Milt."

Thunder in a barrel.

"How're thingth going? Thwell, I hope. Tham here, he'th kinda thad becauthe hith girl friend left him. Thye'll be back, though, I think. He'th been havingk bad dreamth about that Erik Bloodakthe again. I told him if he'd lay off the boothe, he'd be okay. He hathn't got any ekthcyuthe to drink, thinthe he hath me ath a thyining ekthample of thobriety."

Jill looked at Hardy, saying, "What the . . ."

Hardy grinned and said, "Yeth, he lithpth. Joe Miller is as big as two Goliaths put together but he lisps. Joe belongs to a species of subhuman which Sam named *Titanthropus clemensi*, though actually I think Joe's kind is really just a giant variant of *Homo sapiens*. Anyway, it became extinct an estimated fifty thousand to one hundred thousand years ago. He and Sam met many years ago, and they've been real pals since. Damon and Pythias. Roland and Oliver."

"More like Mutt and Jeff or Laurel and Hardy," someone muttered.

Hardy said, "Hardy?"

Firebrass said, "Mute it. Okay, Sam. Everything's in orbit. We got a great new candidate, real first-class officer material. Australian, named Jill Gulbirra. She's got over eight hundred hours dirigible experience and she has an engineering degree. How do you like that?"

Crackle. Then, "A woman?"

"Yeah, Sam, I know they didn't have female riverboat pilots or railroad engineers in your day. But in my day we had women airplane pilots and horse jockeys and even astronauts!"

Jill unfroze and started forward. "Let me talk to him," she said. "I'll tell that son of a bitch . . ."

"He isn't objecting. He's just surprised," Firebrass said, looking up at her. "Take it easy. What do you care? He's all right. Even if he wasn't, he couldn't do anything. I'm *Numero Uno* here.

"Sam, she said she's pleased to meet you."

"I heard her," Sam said, and he chuckled. "Listen . . ." Crackle, hiss, sputter. ". . . when?"

"Static shot that all to hell," Firebrass said. "And you're drifting off. I don't think we can keep contact much longer. So here goes, fast. I'm a long way from having a full crew, but it'll be a year before the big ship's finished. By then I might have enough. If not, what the hell? Airplane pilots and mechanics are a dime a dozen and they can be trained for dirigible operation.

"Listen."

He paused, looked around—though why Jill did not know—and said, "Heard from X? Have . . ."

Static rolled over his voice, chewed it up, and wouldn't let go of the pieces. After trying for several minutes to get hold of Clemens again, Firebrass gave up.

Jill said to Hardy, "What is this about hearing from X?"

"I don't know," the New Englander said. "Firebrass says it's a private joke between Sam and him."

Firebrass turned off the radio and got up from his chair. "It's getting late, and we have a lot to do tomorrow. Do you want Willy to drive you home, Jill?"

"I don't need anyone to protect me," she said. "And I don't mind walking. No thanks."

Covered with the magnetically attached towels, she walked across the plain. Before she had reached the first hill, she saw clouds racing across the blazing sky. She took a stick of dreamgum from her shoulderbag, tore off half of it, and thrust it into her mouth. It had been years since she had chewed it.

Now, as she moved the coffee-tasting chicloid around in her mouth, she wondered why she had suddenly, almost involuntarily, decided to try it again. What secret motive did she have? It had been almost an unconscious act. If she had not gotten into the habit of closely observing herself, she might not even have been aware of what she was doing.

Lightning flashed to the north. Then the rain fell as if dumped from a ballast bag. She put her head down under her hood and hunched her shoulders. Her bare feet were wet, but the cloth over her body repelled the drops.

She unlatched the door of her hut. Inside, she put down the bag, opened it, and removed the heavy metal lighter provided twice a year by her grail. She groped toward the table which held an alcohol lamp, a gift from Firebrass. The lightning came nearer, and by its increasing brightness, she could see the lamp.

Something touched her shoulder.

She screamed and whirled, dropping the lighter. Her right fist struck out. A hand gripped her right wrist. Her knee came up, aiming at the groin she hoped was in its path. It slid by a hip, and another hand caught her other wrist. She sagged, and the attacker was deceived. He chuckled and pulled her close. She could see him vaguely now as flashes of light dimly illumined the interior of the hut. His nose was in front of her and close, though below her, since he was short.

She bent her head swiftly, bit down on the end of the nose, and jerked her head savagely. The man screamed and released her. He staggered backward holding his nose. She followed him, and this time her foot shot up between his legs. Though she had no shoes, her hard-driven toes sent him writhing to the ground, clutching his genitals.

Jill came up and leaped up and down, landing on his side. His ribs snapped loudly. Stepping off him, she bent down and grabbed both ears. He tried to reach up then, but she yanked outward. The ears came loose with a ripping sound.

The man, ignoring his injured genitals and broken ribs, came up off the floor. Jill caught the side of his neck with the edge of her palm. He fell, and she went to the table and lit the lamp with a lighter in a shaking hand. The wick took hold, and then the flame brightened as she turned the knob on the side of the lamp. After trimming it, she turned, and she yelled again.

He had risen and had seized a spear from its wall brackets and was thrusting it at her.

The lamp flew from her hand in unthinking but deadly reaction. It struck him in the face, shattered, and the alcohol spilled out.

Flames exploded. He screamed and ran blindly—his eyes were on fire—toward her. She screamed. Only now did she recognize him.

She shrieked, "Jack!" and then he was on her, had wrapped his burning arms around her, knocked her upon her back, the breath coming out of her in a whoof. Unable to breathe for a moment, but in a frenzy to escape his fiery arms, she tore herself loose and rolled away. Her fireproof clothing had kept her from being burned.

Before she could get up, however, he had grabbed her garment hem and yanked on it. The magnetic tabs separated. Naked, she leaped to her feet and ran for the spear, lying where he had dropped it. She bent down to get it, and Jack was on her from behind, blazing hands grabbing her breasts, his blazing erection driving into her. Their screams bounced around the walls of the hut, seeming to mount in intensity with each echo. She was being fried, seared, inside her, on her buttocks, on her breasts, and in her ears—as if the echoes were flames, too. She could only roll over and over until brought up short against the wall.

Jack was on his hands and knees now, his hair burned off, his scalp black, crinkled, and ridged, his skin broken open to reveal reddish-black blood and grey-black bone. The only illumination was the fire still consuming his face and chest and belly and the penis—which was swollen as if with the passion of hate—and the lightning cracking into the earth outside.

She was up and running toward the door to get to the outside, where the blessed rain would put out the fire and soothe her external burns. Somehow, he grabbed hold of her ankle. She fell heavily, knocking her breath out again. Jack was on top of her again, muttering strange croaking sounds—his tongue was burned, too?—and both were enfolded in fire.

She slid down a scream of pure agony toward a hole far below, a hole which expanded swiftly and received her as she fell toward the center of this world and toward the heart of all things.

17

JACK'S FACE WAS HANGING ABOVE HER. IT WAS UNCONNECTED TO a body, floating freely like a balloon. The curly reddish hair, the broad handsome face, the bright blue eyes, the strong chin, the full lips, smiling . . .

"Jack!" she murmured, and then the face dissolved and became another, attached to a body.

The face was broad and handsome, the cheekbones high, the eyes black, slanted by epicanthic folds, the hair straight and black.

"Piscator!"

"I heard you screaming." He leaned down and took her hands. "Can you get up?"

"I think so," she said shakily. She came up easily enough with his help. She became aware that the thunder and lightning had ceased. Nor was it raining, though water was still dripping from the eaves. The door was open, showing only darkness. The clouds had not yet disappeared. No, there was the silhouette of a hill suddenly rising. Beyond was a break in the skycover and the white flare of a great gas sheet in which thousands of giant stars were embedded.

She also became aware that she was naked. She looked down and saw her breasts were reddened, as if they had been too near a fire. The red slowly faded away as she watched.

Piscator said, "I thought you had been slightly burned. Your breasts and your pubic area were inflamed, swollen, reddened. But there was no evidence of a fire."

"The fire was from within, *inside* me," she said. "Dreamgum."

His eyebrows arose. He said, "Ah, so!"

She laughed.

He helped her to the cot, and she lay down on it with a sigh. The slight warmth inside her vagina had subsided now. Piscator busied himself, placing towels over her, getting her a drink of rainwater from the bamboo barrel placed outside the door. She drank the water, holding the cup with one hand, leaning on the elbow of the other arm.

"Thanks," she said. "I should have known better than to chew the gum. I was depressed, and when I'm in that kind of a mood, I get strange effects from it. It all seemed so real, so horrible. I never questioned its reality, though it was clearly impossible."

He said, "The Second Chancers use dreamgum in their therapy, but it's done under supervision. It seems to have some beneficial results. But we do not use it except in the initial stages of education with some people."

"We?"

"*Al Ahl al-Hagg*, the followers of the Real. What you Occidentals call Sufis."

"I thought so."

"You should, since we have had this conversation once before."

She gasped and said, "When was that?"

"This morning."

"It must be the gum," she said. "I'm through with it. No more of this bloody stuff."

She sat up and said, "You won't tell Firebrass about this, will you?"

He was no longer smiling. "You are experiencing some very strong psychic disturbances. To cause burns, stigmata, on your body through mental means . . . well . . ."

"I won't be using the gum anymore. I'm not just making an empty promise you know. I'm not addicted. I am mentally stable."

"You're deeply troubled," he said. "Be honest with me, Jill. I may call you Jill, may I not? Have you had attacks similar to this? If so, how many and how serious were they? That is, how long did they last? How long did it take you to recover from them?"

"Not one recent attack, as you call it," she said.

"Very well. I will say nothing to anyone. That is, if there is no recurrence. You will be honest with me and inform me if you do suffer from any, won't you? You would not endanger your ship just because you want so desperately to be a member of the crew?"

"No, I would not," she said. But the words came hard.

"Then we'll let it stand at that, for the time being."

She rose on one elbow again, ignoring the slipping aside of the towel and the baring of her breast.

"Look, Piscator. Be honest. If you are given a rank inferior to mine, and it's likely, if Firebrass awards ranks according to experience, would you resent serving under me?"

"Not in the slightest," he said, smiling.

She lay back and pulled the towel up. "You come from a culture which held women in a very inferior position. Your women were practically on a level with the beasts of burden. They . . ."

"That is in the past, the long dead and faraway past," he said. "Nor was nor am I a typical male, Nipponese or not. You must avoid stereotyping. After all, that is what you hate, what you have fought all your life, have you not? Stereotyping?"

"You're right," she said. "But it's a conditioned reflex."

"I believe I said this once before to you. However, repetition has its uses in education. You should learn to think in a different pattern."

"And how do I do that?"

He hesitated, then said, "You will know when to attempt that. And whom to see about it."

Jill knew that he was waiting for her to ask him to accept her as his disciple. She was having none of that. She just did not believe in organized religion. Though Sufism was not a religion, its members were religious. There was no such thing as an atheist Sufi.

She was an atheist. Despite having been resurrected, she did not believe in a Creator. At least, she did not believe in a Creator who was personally interested in her or in any creature whatsoever. People who did believe in a deity who considered human beings as His children—and why was a spirit always *he?*—why not be logical since God had no sex, an *it?*— people who believed in Him were deluded. The believers in God might be intelligent, but they were mentally benighted. The gears in that part of the brain which dealt with religion had been put into neutral, and they were spinning. Or the circuit of religion had been disconnected from the main circuit of the intellect.

That was a bad analogy. People used their intellect to justify the nonintellective, emotionally based phenomenon called religion. Often brilliantly. But, as far as she was concerned, uselessly.

Piscator said, "You are going to sleep. Good. If you need me, though, feel free to call on me."

"You're no physician," she said. "Why should you . . ."

"You have potential. And though you sometimes act foolishly, you are no fool. Though you have fooled yourself from time to time and still are. Good night."

"Good night."

He bowed quickly and walked out, closing the door behind him. She started to call out, but she stopped. She had wanted to ask him what he was doing near the hut when he had heard her. It was too late. Nor was it important. Still . . . what had he been doing here? Had he intended to seduce her? Rape was out of the question, of course. She was bigger than he, and though he probably was a master of the martial arts, so was she. Moreover, his position as an airship officer would be seriously jeopardized if she were to accuse him.

No, he would not have been here either to seduce or to rape. He did not give the impression that he was that type of man. On the other hand, no matter how nice they acted, weren't they all? No, there was something about him—she hated to use the imprecise and unscientifically founded term *vibrations*—but there it was. He did not radiate that length of frequency classified as "bad vibes."

It was then she realized that he had not asked her to describe her experience. If he had been curious, he had managed not to show it. Perhaps he had felt that she would have volunteered if she had wanted to share the details with him. He was a very sensitive man, very perceptive.

What did that horrifying attack by Jack mean? That she was afraid of him, of men in general? Of the male sex? Of sex itself when in male form? She could not believe that. But the illusion? delusion? visitation? had revealed certain feelings of hate and destruction. Not just for men in general and for Jack in particular. She had set him afire but she had also burned and raped herself—in a sense. Which made no sense. She certainly did not subconsciously wish to be raped. Only a mentally sick woman would desire that.

Did she hate herself? The answer was, yes, at times. But who didn't?

Some time later, she sank into an uneasy sleep. Once, she dreamed of Cyrano de Bergerac. They were fencing with épées. The circling point of his blade dazzled her, and then her weapon was knocked up and his leaped in and its point sank deep into her navel. She looked down in surprise at the blade as it withdrew, but the navel did not spout blood. Instead, it swelled and thickened and then a tiny dagger issued from the tumor.

18

THE SHOCK OF COLD WATER FULLY AWOKE BURTON. FOR A MINUTE,
he was completely beneath the surface, and he did not know which
way was up in the darkness.

There was only one way to find out. After five strokes, he felt the
pressure on his eardrums increasing. Reversing position, he swam
in what he hoped was the opposite direction. For all he knew, he was
moving horizontally. But the pressure eased, and just as he feared
he could not possibly hold his breath anymore, he broke the surface.

At the same time, something rammed into the back of his head,
knocking him half-senseless again. His flailing hand hit an object
and he grabbed it. Though he could see nothing in the mists, he
could feel the thing that was holding him up. A massive log.

Bedlam was around him, screams, shouts, someone nearby calling for help. He released his hold as soon as he had regained all his
senses and swam toward the woman crying for aid. As he neared
her, he realized that it was Loghu's voice. A few strokes brought
him to her, close enough to see her face dimly.

"Take it easy," he said. "It's me, Dick!"

Loghu seized him by the shoulders, and they both went down. He
fought her, pushed her away, then grabbed her from behind.

Loghu said something in her native Tokharian. He answered her
in the same tongue.

"Don't panic. We'll be all right."

Longhu, gasping, said, "I've got hold of something. I won't
sink."

He released her and reached around her. Another log. The collision must have torn some of the forward logs loose. But where was
the boat and where was the raft? And where were Loghu and he?

It seemed probable that they had fallen into the gap made when
the lashings of the logs of the raft had been torn loose. But the
current would by now surely have carried the intact part against the
rock, crushing everything between it and the rock. Had they been
carried around the corner of the spire and were now drifting with the
current?

If so, they were in a tangle of logs and pieces from the boat. They
kept bumping against him and Loghu.

She moaned and said, "I think my leg's broken, Dick. It hurts so."

The log to which they were clinging was very thick and long, its ends so distant they could not be seen through the fog. They had to dig into the rough bark with their fingers. It would not be long before they would lose their grip.

Suddenly Monat's voice tore through the greyness.

"Dick! Loghu! Are you out there?"

Burton shouted, and a moment later something rapped along the log. It struck his fingers, causing him to yell with pain and to slip back into the water. He struggled back up, and then the end of a pole shot like a striking snake in ambush from the fog. It grazed his left cheek. A little to the right and it would have stunned him, perhaps broken his skull.

He seized it and called out that he was to be pulled in.

"Loghu's here, too," he said. "Be careful with that pole!"

He was dragged in by Monat to the edge of the raft where Kazz pulled him out with a single heave. Monat then stuck the pole into the darkness. A minute later, Loghu was drawn in. She was half-unconscious.

"Get some cloths and wrap her up in them. Keep her warm," he told Kazz.

"Will do, Burton-naq," the Neanderthal said. He turned and was enfolded in the mist.

Burton sat down on the wet, smooth surface of the raft. "Where are the others? Is Alice all right?"

"They're all here except Owenone," Monat said. "Alice seems to have some broken ribs. Frigate hurt his knee. As for the boat, it's gone."

Before he could recover from this shock, he saw torches flaring. They drew nearer, casting light enough for him to see their bearers. There were a dozen of them, short, dark-faced Caucasians with large, hooked noses, clad from head to foot in cloths of many stripes and colors. Their only arms were flint knives, all sheathed.

One of them spoke in a language which Burton thought was Semitic. If so, it was an ancient form of that family. He could understand a few words here and there, though. He replied in Esperanto, and the speaker switched to that.

There followed a swift dialog. Apparently, the man on the tower had fallen asleep because he had been drinking. He had survived the fall from the tower when the raft had crashed into the island and toppled him and the man whom Burton had seen climb up to him.

The second man had not been so lucky. He had died of a broken neck. As for the luck of the pilot, it had run out on him. He had been thrown overboard by his enraged fellows.

The great grinding noises Burton had heard before the boat struck came from the collision of the tip of the V-shaped prow with the docks and then the hard rock of the beach. This had crumpled the front half of the V and torn loose many of the fish-leather lashings. The V had also absorbed much of the shock, preventing more of the raft from being ripped apart.

A section of the northwest side had been ripped off, but it was forced on by the main body. It was this jumble of massive logs which had rammed into the *Hadji II*, crushing the lower half of the back part. After the torn-off front half of the boat had fallen into the water, the back half, knocked apart by the great blow, had fallen down from—and through—the log jam.

Burton had been thrown forward by the impact against the rock, had fallen back onto the deck, and then had been tilted off it as it slid into the water.

The crew was indeed lucky that no one had been killed or seriously hurt. No, Owenone was yet to be accounted for.

There were more things to find out. Just now, the wounded had to be attended to. He made his way to where the others lay beneath the blaze of three torches. Alice put out her arms to him and cried when he embraced her.

"Don't squeeze me," she said. "My side hurts."

A man came to him and said that he had been appointed to take care of them. The two women were carried by some raftsmen, while Frigate, groaning, hobbled along supported by Kazz. By then the daylight had increased somewhat so they could see further. After progressing for perhaps 61 meters or over 200 feet, they stopped before a large bamboo hut thatched with the great irontree leaves. This was secured to the raft by leather ropes tied at one end to pegs fitted into drilled holes in the logs.

Inside the hut was a stone platform on which a small fire burned. The injured were laid near this on bamboo beds. By then the fog was getting thinner. The light increased and presently they were startled by a noise like a thousand cannon shells exploding at once. No matter how often they heard it, they jumped.

The grailstones had spouted their energy.

"No breakfast for us," Burton said.

He raised his head abruptly.

"The grails? Did anyone get the grails?"

Monat said, "No, they were lost with the boat." His face twisted with grief, and he wept. "Owenone must have drowned!"

They looked at each other in the firelight. Their faces were still pale from their ordeal; even so, they lost a shade of color.

Some of them groaned. Burton cursed. He too felt grief for Owenone, but he and his crew were beggars, dependent upon the charity of others. It was better to be dead than without a grail, and in the old days those who had lost theirs could, and often did, commit suicide. The next day they would wake up, far from their friends and mates, but at least with their own source of food and luxuries.

"Well," Frigate said, "we can eat fish and acorn bread."

"For the rest of our lives?" Burton said, sneering. "Which may be forever for all we know."

"Just trying to look on the bright side of things," the American said. "Though even that is pretty dim."

"Why don't we deal with things as they come up?" Alice said. "For the moment, I'd like my ribs seen to, and I'm sure poor Loghu would like her broken bone set and splinted."

The man who had conducted them there arranged for treatment of the injured. After this was done and the pains of his patients had been eased with pieces of dreamgum, he went outside. Burton, Kazz, and Monat followed him inside. By then the sun was burning away the fog. Within a few minutes it would all be gone.

The scene was appalling. The entire V-shaped prow of the raft had broken up when its point had ridden up onto the beach and its port side had smashed into a corner of the spire. The docks and the boats of the Ganopo were smashed, buried somewhere in the pile of logs on the beach. The main part of the raft had also slid for at least 13 meters onto the shore. Several hundreds of the raftspeople were standing at the edge of the wreck, talking animatedly but doing nothing constructive.

To the left, logs were jammed against the sheer wall of the spire by the current. There was no sign of the *Hadji II*, or of Owenone. Burton's hope that he might be able to retrieve at least a few grails was not going to be realized.

He looked around the raft. Even though it had lost its forepart, it was still immense. It had to be at least 660 feet or 201 meters long with a breadth at its widest of 122 meters. Its stern was also V shaped.

In the center was the large, round, black object he had seen floating above the mists. It was the head of an idol 30 feet or over 9 meters tall. Black, squat, and ugly, it dominated the raft. It was sitting cross-legged, and its spine bore lizardlike crests. The head was a demon's, its blue eyes glaring, its wide, snarling mouth displaying many great white sharkfish teeth.

These, Burton assumed, had been removed from a dragonfish and set within the scarlet gums.

In the middle of its huge paunch was a round hole. Inside this was a stone hearth on which a small pile of wood blazed. Its smoke rose within the body and curled out of the batlike ears of the idol.

Forward, near the edge of the raft, the watch tower lay on its side, its supports broken off at the base by the force of the collision. A body still lay near it.

There were some large buildings here and there with many

smaller ones among them. A few of the smaller ones had collapsed, and one of the big constructions leaned crazily.

He counted ten tall masts with square-rigged sails and twenty shorter ones with fore-and-aft rigs. All of the sails were furled.

Alongside the edges were a number of racks holding boats of various sizes.

Behind the idol was the largest building of all. He supposed that this was the house of the chief or perhaps a temple. Or both.

Presently wooden trumpets blew and drums beat. Seeing the people streaming toward the great building, Burton decided to join them. They congregated between the idol and the building. Burton stood behind the mob where he could hear the proceedings but at the same time examine the statue. A little discreet scratching with a flint knife revealed that it was adobe covered with a black paint. He wondered where the paint for the body, eyes, and gums had been obtained. Pigments were rare, much to the sorrow of artists.

The chief, or the head priest, was taller than the others though still half a head shorter than Burton. He wore a cape and kilt with blue, black, and red stripes and an oaken crown with six points. His right hand held a long shepherd's staff of oak. He spoke from a platform at the building's entrance, gesturing often with the staff, his black eyes fiery, his mouth spewing a torrent of which Burton understood not one word. After about half an hour he got down from the platform, and the crowd broke up into various work parties.

Some of these went to the island to clear away the logs which had broken from the prow and piled onto the main body. Others went to the starboard rearside, where the V-shaped stern joined the main part. These lifted huge oars and fitted them to locks. Then, like a gang of galley slaves, working to a rhythm beat out on a drum, they began rowing.

Apparently, they were trying to bring the stern around so that the current would catch it on one side and then swing the entire raft. As soon as the vessel presented enough of its starboard side to the current, it would be turned around enough to be free of the island.

That was the theory, but the practice failed. It became apparent that the log jam would have to be cleared first and then leverage applied to push the front part from the beach.

Burton wished to talk to the headman, but he had gone around to the front of the idol and was bowing rapidly and chanting to it. Whatever Burton had learned or not learned, he knew that it was dangerous to interrupt a religious ritual.

He strolled around, stopping to look at the dugouts, canoes, and small sailboats in racks or on slides along the edge of the raft. Then he poked around the larger buildings. Most of these had doors which were barred on the outside. Making sure that no one was noticing him, he entered several.

Two were storehouses of dried fish and acorn bread. One was crammed with weapons. Another was a boatshed containing two half-finished dugouts and the pine framework of a canoe. In time the latter would be covered with fish-skin. The fifth building held a variety of artifacts: boxes of oak rings for trading, spiral bones and the unicornlike horns of the hornfish, piles of fish- and human-leather, drums, bamboo flutes, harps with hornfish guts for strings, skulls fashioned into drinking cups, ropes of fiber and fish-skin, piles of dried dragonfish intestines, suitable for sails, stone lamps for burning fish-oil, boxes of lipstick, face-paint, marijuana, cigarettes, cigars, lighters (all doubtless saved up for trading or tribute), about fifty ritual masks, and many more items.

When he went into the sixth building, he smiled. This was where the grails were kept. The tall grey cylinders were stacked in wooden racks, waiting for their owners. He counted three hundred and fifty. One grail for each of the approximately three hundred and ten raftspeople meant that there were thirty extra grails.

A few minutes' inspection showed him that all but thirty were tagged. The others had cords tied around the handles of the tops, the other ends of which cords were connected to baked clay tablets bearing cuneiform writing. These were the names of their owners. He examined some of the incised marks, which looked like those he had seen in photographs of Babylonian and Assyrian documents.

He tried to raise the lids of a number of the tagged cylinders but failed, of course. There was some sort of mechanism preventing anyone but its owner from opening it. There were several theories about the operation, one being that a sensitive device inside the grail detected the electrical field of the owner's skin and then activated an opening mechanism.

However, the untagged grails were of a different kind, called "freebies" by some English-speakers.

When over thirty-six billion of Earth's dead had awakened whole and young along the immense stretch of The River, they had found a personal grail at their side. At the same time, each of the grailstones bore in its central depression one grail. This apparently had been provided by the resurrectors to show the new citizens just how their grails worked.

Each stone had vomited noise and light, and when the thunder and lightning had ceased, curious people had climbed onto the stones to look into the grails left there. The lids were raised, and the contents were revealed. Wonder of wonders, joy of joys! The hollow interior held snap-down racks on which were dishes and cups full of food and various goodies.

The next time the stones discharged, the private grails were on the stones, and these, too, supplied everything they needed and more, though human nature was such that many people complained because there wasn't more variety.

The freebies had become very valuable; people bullied and thieved and killed to get them. If a person had a private grail and a freebie, he or she had twice as much food and luxuries as he or she was supposed to get.

Burton himself had never owned one, but here were thirty on racks before him.

The problem of the lost grails was solved—if he could get the headman to part with them. After all, his raft was responsible for the loss of the boat and the grails. He owed the crew of the *Hadji II*.

So far, he and his crew had been treated decently. He could think of other groups he had met that would have done nothing for them except throw them overboard—after mass-raping the women and perhaps sodomizing the men.

However, there might be a limit to the raftspeople's hospitality. The free grails were anything but free. This group might even have stolen these. However they got them, they would be saving them for emergencies, such as replacements for those they lost or as tribute if they ran into a particularly hostile and powerful group.

Burton left the building, barred the door after him, and walked around pondering. If he asked the chief to give him seven grails, he could be refused. That would make the man suspicious, and he would set up guards over this building. Not to mention the fact that he might get nervous having potential thieves around and would ask them, politely or otherwise, to leave.

Passing by the idol, he saw that the chief had stopped praying and was walking toward the island. Apparently, he intended to supervise the activities there.

Burton decided to ask him now about the grails. No use putting off the issue.

The man who sits on his arse sits on his fortune.

19

MUTU-SHA-ILI WAS HIS NATIVE NAME, MEANING "MAN OF GOD," but to Esperanto speakers he was Metuŝael. In English, Methusaleh.

For a delirious moment, Burton wondered if he had met the model for the long-lived patriarch of the Old Testament. No. Metuŝael was a Babylonian, and he had never heard of Hebrews until he had come to The Riverworld. He had been an inspector of granaries on Earth, but here he was the founder and head of a new religion and commander of the great raft.

"One night many years ago, while a storm raged outside, I was sleeping. And a god came to me in my dream, a god named Rushhub. I had never heard of this god, but he told me that he had once been a mighty god of my ancestors. Their descendants, however, had abandoned him, and in my lifetime on Earth only a small village at the edge of the kingdom had still worshipped him.

"But gods do not die, though they may take other forms and new names, or even become nameless, and he had lived in the dreams of many people through many generations. Now he had decided that the time was come to leave the dreamworld. Thus, he told me that I must arise and go forth and preach the worship of Rushhub. I must gather together a group of the faithful and build a giant raft and take my people down The River upon it.

"After many years, perhaps several generations as we knew generations on Earth, we would come to the end of The River, where it empties into a hole in the base of the mountains that ring the top of this world.

"There, we would go through the underworld, a great dark cavern, and then we would come out into a bright sea surrounding a land where we would live forever in peace and happiness with the gods and goddesses themselves.

"But before the raft was launched we must make a statue of the god Rushhub and set it upon the raft and worship it as the symbol of Rushhub. So do not say, as so many have said, that we are idolaters who mistake the physical symbol for the body of the god itself."

Burton thought the man was crazy, though he was discreet enough not to say so. He and his crew had fallen into the hands of fanatics. Fortunately, the god had told Metušael that his worshippers must harm no one unless it was in self-defense. However, he knew from experience that "self-defense" could mean whatever a person or group wanted it to mean.

"Rushhub himself told me that just before we enter the underworld, we must break the idol into little bits and cast them into The River. He did not say why we should do so. He merely said that by the time we reach the cavern, we will understand."

"That is all very well for you," Burton said. "But you are responsible for destroying our boat. Also, we have lost our grails."

"I am indeed sorry, but there is little I can do for you. What happened to you is the will of Rushhub."

Burton felt like striking the man in his face. Mastering himself, he said, "Three of my people are too injured at the moment to move them very far. Could you at least give us a boat so we could get to shore?"

Metušael glared with fierce black eyes, and he pointed at the island.

"There is the shore, and there is a foodstone. I will see that your injured are placed there, and we will give you some dried fish and acorn bread. In the meantime, please do not trouble me with any more requests. I have work to do. We must get our raft back into The River. Rushhub told me that we should not delay our journey for any reason whatsoever.

"If we take too long, we may find the gates to the land of the gods forever shut. Then we will be left to howl at the gates and repent in vain for our lack of faith and determination."

At that moment Burton decided that anything he did would be justified. These people owed him much, and he owed them nothing.

Metušael had walked away. Now he stopped suddenly, pointing at Monat, who had just come out of the building.

"What is that?"

Burton walked up to him and said, "That is a man from another world. He and some of his kind traveled from a distant star to Earth. This was over a hundred years after I died, perhaps four thousand years after you died. He came in peace, but the people of Earth discovered that he had a . . . drug which could keep people from aging. They demanded that he tell them its secret, but he refused. He said that Earth people had enough problems as it was with overpopulation. Besides, a person should not be given the chance to live forever unless that person was worthy of it."

"He was wrong then," Metušael said. "The gods *have* given us a chance to live forever."

"Yes, in a way. Though, according to your religion, only a very small group, just those on this raft, will become truly immortal. Am I right?"

"It seems hard," Metuŝael said. "But that is the way it is, and who are we to question the motives and methods of the gods?"

"It is, however, a fact that we only know what the gods desire through human beings who speak for them. I have never met a person yet whose motives and methods I would not question."

"The more fool you."

"Aside from that," Burton said, smiling to hide his anger, "the Arcturans, Monat and his people, were attacked by the Earth people. They were all killed, but before he died Monat caused almost all of the Earth people to die."

He paused. How could he explain to this ignoramus that the Arcturans had left their mother ship in orbit around Earth? And that Monat had transmitted a radio wave signal to the orbiting vessel and that it had projected an energy beam of such a frequency that only human beings had died?

He did not really understand it himself, since in his time such things as radio and spaceships had not existed.

Metuŝael was wide-eyed now. Looking at Monat, he said, "He is a great magician? He killed all those people through his powers?"

For a moment, Burton considered using Monat's supposed magic as a lever. Perhaps he could pry a boat and free-grails out of this man if he threatened him. But, though Metuŝael might be ignorant, and crazed, he was not unintelligent. He would ask why Monat, if he was such a sorcerer, had not protected the *Hadji II* from destruction and his companions from hurt. He also might ask why Burton needed a boat, since surely Monat could give them the power to fly through the air.

"Yes, he did slay them," Burton said. "And he also woke up on these banks, not knowing how or why. His magical tools were left on Earth, of course. However, he says that he will find the materials to make more tools some day, and he will regain his powers and be as mighty and as deadly as ever. Then those who have scorned and mocked him will have good reason to fear him."

Let Metuŝael chew on that.

Metuŝael smiled, and said, "By that time . . ."

Burton understood. By then the raft would be long gone.

"Besides, Rushhub will protect his people. A god is mightier than a man, even a demon from the stars."

"Why didn't Rushhub avert this accident then?" Burton said.

"I do not know, but I am sure that he will come to me in a dream, and he will tell me why. Nothing happens to the people of Rushhub without a purpose."

Metuŝael walked off. Burton returned to the building to check on his crew. Kazz stepped outside just as Burton was about to enter. He had removed all his cloths except for his kilt, revealing a very hairy, squat, big-boned, powerfully muscled body. His head was thrust forward on a bowed and bull-like neck. His forehead was low and slanting; his skull long and narrow; his face, broad. His supraorbital ridges were thick, bony shelves above shrewd dark-brown eyes. The nose was puggish but had flaring nostrils. The bulging jaws pushed out thin lips. The massive hands looked as if they could squeeze stone to powder.

Despite his fearsome appearance, he would not have gotten more than a passing glance in the East End of London in Burton's time if he had been clothed.

His full name was *Kazzintuitruaabemss*. In his native language, Man-Who-Slew-The-White-Tooth.

"What's up, Burton-*naq*?"

"You and Monat come in with me."

When he was in the hut, he asked the others how they felt. Alice and Frigate said they could walk but not run. Loghu's case was evident. She was in no pain because of the dreamgum given her, but she would not be restored to full health for four or five days. It took that long for a broken bone to knit completely. The fantastic speed in healing was due to causes unknown, perhaps something in their food.

Whatever the reason, bones healed, teeth and eyes regrew, torn muscles and burned flesh were renewed, all with a quickness that had once astonished the Valley-dwellers. Now it was taken for granted.

Burton had no sooner explained the situation to them than twelve armed men appeared. Their captain said he had orders to escort them to the island. Two men put Loghu on a stretcher and carried her out. Frigate, supported by Monat and Kazz, limped after them. They made their way, with some difficulty, over the wilderness of logs and onto the shore. Here they were met by the Ganopo, all angry but helpless.

Loghu was taken into a hut, and the guards left. Not, however, before their captain cautioned Burton that he and his crew must stay away from the raft.

"And if we don't?" Burton said loudly.

"Then you will be thrown into The River. Perhaps with a stone tied to your legs. Almighty Rushhub has told us not to spill blood except in self-defense. But he said nothing about drowning our enemies."

Shortly before the midday grailstone discharge, a store of dried fish and acorn bread was delivered to Burton.

"Metušael says that this will keep you from starving until you can catch more fish and make more bread."

"I'll save my thanks to deliver in person to him," Burton said to the captain. "He may not like its form, though."

Monat said, "Was that empty bluster or do you plan on some sort of revenge?"

"Revenge isn't my dish," Burton said. "I do intend, however, to see that we do not go grailless."

Two days passed. The front part of the raft was still beached. The log jam had been cleared away, and the raft had been pushed back toward the water several meters. This was a tedious, back-breaking job. The entire population of the raft, their leader excepted, pried away at the front end with small thin logs as levers. From sunup until sunset, the Babylonian words for "Heave! One, two three, heave!" bellowed from hundreds of mouths.

Every mass effort only succeeded in pushing back the immensely heavy raft a millimeter or so. Often, the stones wedged between the rock of the beach and the front edge of the raft would slip a little, and the raft, urged by the current, would move back onto the beach. Several times, the wedges were knocked out, and all gains were lost.

Since the wind blew from down-River, the sails on the masts were unfurled. Metušael hoped that the upstream wind would give the heavers an advantage. The theory would have worked if it had not been that the rock spire blocked off most of the breeze.

By the morning of the third day, the raft had been pushed back about a meter. At this rate, it would take seven more days to free it.

The Ganopo were busy meanwhile. Unable to borrow a boat from Metušael, they sent four strong swimmers out. These got to the right bank, where they explained the situation and were loaned a small sailboat. They returned with a fleet of twenty boats manned by the chiefs of the local state and the best fighting men. The head chief, a tall Shawnee, looked around and then conferred with the Ganopo. Burton and Monat sat in on the meeting.

There was a lot of talking, complaints from the Ganopo, various counsels offered, and a speech by Burton. He told them of the large store of goods on the raft, omitting mention of the free-grails, and suggested that perhaps the Babylonians would part with some of their stores if the locals loaned enough men to help free the raft.

The Shawnee thought this was a good idea. He talked to Metušael, who was polite but said he did not need any help.

Disgruntled, the Shawnee returned to the island.

"Those eagle-noses do not have much sense," he said. "Don't they know that we can take everything they have without giving anything in return? They have wrecked the boats and the docks of the Ganopo and offered nothing in restitution. They have wrecked the strangers' vessel, which took a year to build and cost them much tobacco and booze in trade for the wood with which to build it. They have caused a crewman to die. They have also caused the loss of the strangers' grails. A person might as well be dead as not have a grail.

"And what do they offer as payment? Nothing! They mock the Ganopo and the strangers. These are evil people, and they should be punished as such."

"Not to mention the valuable goods the chief and his chums will obtain," Burton murmured in English to Monat.

"What did you say?" the chief said.

"I was telling my friend, the man from the stars, that you have great wisdom and know what is right and wrong. That what you do to the eagle-noses will be right and just, and the great spirit will smile upon you."

"Your language says much in a few words."

"The tongue of my people is not forked."

And God forgive me for that remark, Burton thought.

Though the Shawnee did not say what he meant to do, it was evident to Burton that he would be planning a raid in force. Perhaps for that very night.

Burton called the others into his hut.

"Don't look so gloomy. I think we'll have grails after all, lose our beggar status. However, we must act tonight. How about it, Loghu, Pete, Alice? Do you feel up to some action? Some perhaps vigorous action?"

The three replied that they could walk. Running was as yet out of the question.

"Very well. Here is what we'll do, if you have no objections. If you do, we'll do it anyway."

20

THEY ATE THEIR EVENING MEAL, FISH AND BREAD WHICH DISGUSTED them before they put it in their mouths. The Ganopo, however, were kind enough to give them a few cigarettes and as much of the lichen-alcohol as they wanted. Before going into his hut, presumably to retire for the night, Burton walked around the beach. The Babylonians were either in their huts or talking in small groups before them. They were tired after three days of hard and frustrating labor and would soon be asleep. All, that is, except for the guards stationed along the edge of the raft. They would light pine torches soaked in fish-oil and pace back and forth under their illumination, waiting for their reliefs.

The largest groups were at the forward end. Metuŝael had placed them there to make sure that Burton's people did not try to sneak aboard to steal their goods. The little dark-skinned men watched him closely as he sauntered along. He grinned and waved at them. They did not return his greeting.

Having checked the situation, Burton walked back to his hut. On the way he passed the Ganopo chief, who was sitting before his hut and smoking one of the little briar pipes the grails offered once a year.

Burton squatted down by him.

"I am thinking, O chief, that tonight the raftspeople may be in for a big surprise."

The chief removed his pipe and said, "What do you mean?"

"It is possible that the chief of the people on the north bank may be leading a raid upon the raftspeople. Have you heard anything about that?"

"Not a word. The great chief of the Shaawanwaaki does not confide in me. However, I would not be surprised if he and his warriors did not resent the injuries and the insults which we Ganopo, who are under his protection, have suffered from the eagle-noses."

"If they did make this raid you suggest, when would they be likely to do it?"

"In the old days, when the Shaawanwaaki warred against the people on the south bank, they would cross The River just before dawn. The clouds are still thick then, and they could not be seen approaching. But soon after they had landed, the sun would come up and the clouds would burn away under its heat. Then the Shaawanwaaki could see to strike.''

"That is what I thought," Burton said. "However, one thing troubles me. It is an easy matter to cross a river or even a small lake in the fog and find the other side. This is a small island which would be difficult to find in the clouds. It is true the rock tower is very high, but the raiders would be in the fog and could not see it.''

The chief tamped down the coals in his pipe, and he said, ''That is no worry of mine.''

Burton said, "There is a ledge on the spire. It faces the north bank, but an outcropping of rock would prevent the raftspeople from seeing it. It would also prevent them from seeing a bonfire. A bonfire which anyone on The River north of the island might see even through the fog. Is that why some of the Ganopo have been busy all day carrying bamboo and pine up to this ledge?''

The chief grinned. "You have the curiosity of a wildcat and the eyes of a hawk. However, I promised the Shaawanwaaki chief not to say a word about this business.''

Burton stood up. "I understand. Many thanks for your hospitality, chief, whether or not I ever see you again.''

"If not in this world, perhaps in the next.''

It was difficult to get to sleep. After hours of tossing and turning, he was surprised to find himself being shaken awake by Monat. Burton freed himself of the Arcturan's three fingers and thumb and got up. Monat, who also came from a planet with a twenty-four hours' rotation, had a biological chronometer in his head. Burton had depended upon him to wake the others at the right time.

They moved around, talking softly while they drank instant coffee. The crystals, a gift from the islanders, provided a boiling heat as they dissolved.

After going over their plan once more, they moved outside and relieved themselves. The hut was just high enough to be above the mists, enabling them to see a faint glow high up on the spire. The Shaawanwaaki, even though in fog, would be able to discern it as a dim glow. That would be all they needed.

Frigate and Burton were the only ones who had been wearing a full suit of cloths when the *Hadji II* had gone down. The others, however, had cloths given them by the Ganopo. Clad from head to foot in these, they walked down into the fog. Burton led, one hand in Alice's, hers in Frigate's, and so on down the line. Depending upon an unusual sense of direction, Burton led them to the water's edge. Now they could see the glow of the torches in the fuzziness.

Burton took out his flint knife. Kazz had a club he'd fashioned from a stick of pine with a knife he'd borrowed from a Ganopo. Frigate's knife had been given to the Neanderthal woman, Besst. The rest were unarmed.

Burton moved cautiously forward until he was at the edge of the raft. There was enough space between the torches ranged along the edge for him to crawl through unseen. He proceeded to do this until he was well out of range of the guards' vision and hearing. He waited while, one by one, the others caught up.

"This is the easy part," he said. "From now on we'll be blind until we come across a torchlight. I have the location of the buildings and the boats in my head, but in this fog . . . well, follow me."

Despite his assurances, he blundered around for a while. Then, abruptly, the huge black figure of the idol, a fire in its hollow belly, was in front of him. He stood for a minute, estimating the probable number of paces from the statue to the building which held the grails.

Kazz said, "I can just see some lights to the right."

Keeping to the right of the torches, Burton led the others until he saw the square walls and conical roof of the storehouse. From the front of the building came the voices of the guards, speaking in low tones, stamping their feet now and then. After going behind the building, touching it with a finger to keep contact, Burton stopped on the other side.

Here he removed from under his cloths a coil of leather rope borrowed from the Ganopo chief, who had not asked him about its intended use. Monat and Frigate also carried coils. Burton tied their ends together to make a single rope. While Alice held one end, he moved out into the darkness with Frigate, Monat, Loghu, and Kazz. He knew that there was a boat-rack on the edge of the raft just opposite the storehouse. This time, he went straight to his target.

Cautioning them to move slowly and silently, he and the others eased a large canoe off the rack. It could hold ten people and so, though made of light pine and thin fish-skin, was heavy.

After the canoe was in the water and paddles placed in it, all returned except Loghu. It was her job to keep the canoe from drifting away.

Following the rope, they went swiftly back to the storehouse.

Just as they returned, Kazz grunted, and said, "Others coming!"

The flames of four torches became visible.

"It's a change of guards!" Burton said.

They had to move around to the other side of the building since the four armed men were headed toward them.

Burton looked upward. Was it his imagination or was the fog becoming less dark above?

They waited, some of them sweating despite the damp, cold air. The guards exchanged some words, somebody must have cracked a joke, judging by their laughter, then the relieved men said good night. The torches showed that two were going to homes in the forward part. The other two went in the opposite direction, causing a swift retreat by the invaders.

Burton, watching from the corner said, "Those two are separating. Kazz, do you think you could get one of them?"

"No sweat, Burton-*naq*," Kazz said, and he was gone.

Both the torches were almost out of sight when Burton saw one of them drop. A minute later it lifted, becoming more bright as it approached them.

By then, Burton had moved the group from the side to the back of the building. He did not want a guard to walk past the front and see the torch.

Kazz had thrown his hood back. His big, blocklike teeth gleamed in the light of the flames. In one hand he held the heavy oak spear tipped with a long hornfish horn which he had taken from the guard. His belt held a chert knife set in a heavy wooden handle and a flint-headed axe. These he passed out to Frigate and Alice. His club went to the Arcturan.

"I hope you didn't kill him," Monat whispered.

"That depends on how thick his skull is," Kazz said.

Monat grimaced. He had an almost pathological abhorrence of violence, though he could be an effective fighter in self-defense.

"Will your leg handicap you?" Burton said. "Think you can throw that axe as effectively as usual?"

"I think so," Frigate said. He was shaking now, though he would be steady when the fighting started. Like the Arcturan, he dreaded physical conflict.

Burton told them what to do, then he led Kazz and Alice around one side toward the front. The others went around the opposite corner.

Burton peered around the corner. The four guards were standing close together, facing each other, and talking. A moment later, a torchlight appeared around the corner. The guards did not see it until it was close. As soon as Burton saw them turn toward it, calling a challenge, he moved out.

Kazz, his features shrouded by his hood, got near to them before he was required to stop. Probably, the guards thought that he was one of the relieved men, returned for some reason.

By the time the mistake was discovered, it was too late for them. Kazz grasped his spear just behind its head, and, using it as a quarterstaff, struck its butt against the side of a guard's neck.

Burton, holding his knife in his left hand, chopped the edge of his right against the back of the neck of another man. He had no wish to kill, and he had ordered the bloodthirsty Kazz to avoid using the spearhead if he could do so.

Frigate's axe whirled out of the greyness and caught a third in the chest. It was thrown not quite accurately enough, or perhaps Frigate was trying not to kill. In which case, his axe-throwing was superb. The blunt forefront, not the cutting edge, struck, and the man fell back, the wind knocked out of him. Before he could recover it, he was knocked out by Burton's savage kick to the side of his head.

At the same time as the others, Monat struck, and the fourth crumpled from a blow on the head.

There was silence for a moment as they waited to find out if anyone had heard the fight. Then they picked up the torches from the deck, and Burton unbarred the door. The fallen were dragged inside, where Monat examined them.

"Very good. They're all alive."

"Some of them'll be coming to soon," Burton said. "Watch them, Kazz."

He held a torch above the free-grail rack. "We're beggars no longer."

He hesitated. Should just seven grails be taken? Why not all thirty? The extras could be used to trade for wood and sails for the new boat to be built.

Honour Not Honours was his motto, but this was a matter of recompense, not thievery.

He gave the order, and each took five grails. They put the wide handle of one grail over their head, letting it hang behind them by the neck and thrust each arm through the handles of two grails. Then they left the building, barred the door, and followed the leather cord to the canoe. The torches were left upon the deck outside the storehouse.

Loghu said, "Isn't it about time the Indians attacked?"

"Past time, I would say," Monat replied.

The canoe loaded, they paddled away. Their destination was the south bank, which they intended to follow up-River until just before dawn. Burton was worried about the extra grails. If the local authorities saw them, they might seize them. Even if they didn't, greedy individuals would try to steal them.

There was only one way to hide them. The extras were filled with water. Sections of leather line were cut, and one end of each was tied to a handle. The other end was tied to the upper part of the canoe framework through a hole punched in the skin.

The drag on the canoe was heavy, but fortunately they were very close to the bank. They stopped at a dock complex near a grailstone and tied the canoe to a piling under a dock.

They sat down under the stone and waited. Dawn and hundreds of citizens came. Burton's group introduced itself and requested permission to use the stone. This was given gladly, since the south-bank locals were peaceful. In fact, they welcomed strangers, a source of news and gossip.

The fog burned away. Burton got on top of the stone and looked toward the spire. Its base was about 2.5 nautical miles distant, which, from his altitude, put the horizon 4 miles away. He could see the larger buildings and the idol but the flames he had expected to be rising from them were nonexistent. Perhaps the Shaawanwaaki had not set them afire. After all, they might have wanted to keep the raft intact until it could be taken to the shore and dismantled. Its logs were valuable.

Instead of pushing on that day, he decided that they would rest. That afternoon a Ganopo party landed, the chief among them. Burton questioned him.

The chief laughed. "Those Shaawanwaaki turtleheads completely missed the raft. They couldn't see the fire, though how they could not, I don't understand. Anyway, they paddled around for hours, and when the fog lifted they found that the current had taken them five stones below the island. What a bunch of bums!"

"Did the Babylonians say anything to you about their missing canoe? Not to mention the guards we had to rough up?"

Burton thought it best not to say anything about the grails.

The chief laughed again. "Yes, they came storming ashore before the stone flamed. They were very angry, though they did not say why. They knocked us around a little, but the bruises and the insults did not bother us because we were happy that you had made fools of them. They searched the island thoroughly, but they did not find you, of course. They did find the ashes of the fire and asked us about it. I told them that it was a ceremonial fire.

"They didn't believe me. I think they must have guessed the truth. You won't have to worry about them sending out search parties for you. Every one of them, including Metusael, is straining to get the raft off today. They must expect another attack tonight."

Burton asked the chief why the Shaawanwaaki didn't attack in the daylight. They could easily overwhelm the Babylonians.

"That is because there is an agreement among the states in this area to protect strangers. So far, it has been honored and with good reason. The other states would be compelled to go to war against the aggressor. However, the Shaawanwaaki were hoping to keep it a secret. If they were to be found out, they would say that the raftspeople had refused to pay compensation for the damage done to us.

"I don't know. Perhaps the Shaawanwaaki will give up the idea.

Still, there are many among them who would like to make a raid just for the sake of excitement.''

Burton never found out what happened to the Babylonians. He decided that they should leave that day. After the canoe was on its way, the grails were pulled up, emptied, and placed in the bottom of the canoe.

21

AFTER TRAVELING 200 KILOMETERS, BURTON FOUND AN AREA suitable for boat construction. It was not determined by the wood available, since all places had plenty of pine, oak, yew, and bamboo. What was now difficult to find was flint and chert for cutting timber. Even in the beginning, these stones were restricted to certain sites, some being rich in them, others comparatively poor, and many lacking them entirely. Wars for flint had been common in the old days.

The minerals were even rarer now. Hard as they were, flint and chert wore out, and new supplies were almost unheard of. As a result, the end of 32 A.R.D. (After Resurrection Day) was also the near end of large-vessel construction. At least, it was in the countries through which Burton had passed, and he presumed that it was the same everywhere.

The area at which he stopped was one of the very few that still had a plentiful store. The locals, a majority of pre-Columbian Algonquins and a minority of pre-Roman Picts, were well aware of the value of their stones. Their chief, a Menomini named Oskas, haggled fiercely with Burton. Finally, he stated that his rock-bottom price was seven thousand cigarettes of tobacco, five hundred of marijuana, twenty-five hundred cigars, forty packages of pipe tobacco, and eight thousand cupfuls of liquor. He also suggested that he would like to sleep with the blonde, Loghu, every five days or so. Actually, he would prefer that it be every night, but he did not think his three women would like that.

Burton took some time to recover from his shock. He said, "That's up to her. I don't think either she or her man would agree to it. Anyway, you're asking far too much. None of my party would have booze or tobacco for a year."

Oskas shrugged and said, "Well, if it isn't worth it to you . . . ?"

Burton called a conference and told his crew what Oskas demanded. Kazz objected the most.

"Burton-*naq*, I lived all my life on Earth, forty-five summers, without whiskey or nicotine. But here I got hooked and if I go a day without either, I am ready, as you put it, to climb the wall. You know that I tried to quit both at different times, and before a week was gone I was ready to bite my tongue off. I was as mean as a cave bear with a thorn in his paw."

Besst said, "I haven't forgotten."

"If there was no alternative, we'd have to do it," Burton said. "It'd be cold turkey or no boat. But we do have the extra grails."

He returned to Oskas and, after they had smoked a pipe, he got down to business.

"The woman with the yellow hair and blue eyes says the only part of her you'll get is her foot, and you might have a hard time pulling it out of your ass."

Oskas laughed loudly and slapped his thigh.

When he had dried his tears, he said, "Too bad. I like a woman with spirit, though not with too much."

"It so happens that some time ago I got hold of a free-grail. Now, I am willing to trade that for a place in which to build our boat and the materials to build it."

Oskas did not ask him how he got it, though it was evident that he thought Burton had stolen it.

"If that is so," he said, smiling, "then we have a deal."

He stood up. "I will see that things are arranged at once. Are you sure that the blonde is not just playing hard to get?"

The chief took the grail to the council's stronghouse, adding it to the twenty-one free-grails there. These had been collected through the years for the benefit of himself and his subchiefs.

Here, as everywhere, special people made sure that they got special privileges.

It took a year to build another cutter. When it was half-finished, Burton decided not to name it after its predecessors, *Hadji I* and *Hadji II*. Both had come to bad ends, and, though he denied it, he was superstitious. After some talk with his crew, it was agreed that *Snark* was suitable. Alice liked the name because of her association with Lewis Carroll, and she agreed with Frigate that it was most appropriate.

Smiling, she recited part of the Bellman's speech from *The Hunting of the Snark*.

> "He had bought a large map representing the sea,
>   Without the least vestige of land:
> And the crew were much pleased when they
>   found it to be
> A map they could all understand.

> " 'What's the good of Mercator's North Poles and
>   Equators,
> Tropics, Zones, and Meridian Lines?'

> *So the Bellman would cry: and the crew would*
> *   reply*
> *'They are merely conventional signs!*
>
> *" 'Other maps are such shapes, with their islands*
> *   and capes!*
> *But we've got our brave Captain to thank'*
> *(So the crew would protest) 'that he's bought us*
> *A perfect and absolute blank!' "*

Burton laughed, but he was not sure that Alice was not obliquely insulting his abilities as a captain. Lately, they had not been getting along so well.

"Let's hope the voyage in the new boat won't be another agony in eight fits!" Alice cried.

"Well," Burton said, grinning savagely at her, "this Bellman knows enough not to get the browsprit mixed up with the rudder sometimes!"

"Nor," he added, "is there a Rule 42 of the boat's code. *No one shall speak to the Man at the Helm.*"

"Which," Alice said, her smile gone, "was decreed by the Bellman himself. *And the Man at the Helm shall speak to no one.*"

There was a short silence. All felt the tension between the two, and they looked uneasy, dreading another violent explosion of their captain's temper.

Monat, eager to avoid this, laughed. He said, "I remember that poem. I was especially struck by 'Fit the Sixth, The Barrister's Dream.' Let me see, ah, yes, the pig was on trial for having deserted its sty, and the Snark, dressed in gown, bands, and wig, was defending it.

> *"The indictment had never been clearly expressed,*
> *   And it seemed that the Snark had begun,*
> *And had spoken three hours, before any one*
> *   guessed*
> *What the pig was supposed to have done."*

He paused, rolled his eyes, and said, "I have it. That one quatrain which so impressed me.

> *"But their wild exultation was suddenly checked*
> *   When the jailor informed them with tears,*
> *Such a sentence would not have the slightest effect,*
> *   As the pig had been dead for some years."*

They all laughed, and Monat said, "Somehow, that verse squeezes out the essence of Terrestrial justice, its letter if not its spirit."

"I am amazed," Burton said, "that in your short time on Earth you managed not only to read so much but to remember it so well."

"*The Hunting of the Snark* was a poem. I believe that you can understand human beings better through poetry and fiction than through so-called fact-literature. That is why I took the trouble to memorize it.

"Anyway, an Earth friend gave it to me. He said that it was one of the greatest works of metaphysics that humanity could boast of. He asked me if Arcturans had anything to equal it."

Alice said, "Surely he was pulling your leg?"

"I don't think so."

Burton shook his head. He had been a voracious reader, and he had an almost photographic memory. But he had been on Earth sixty-nine years, whereas Monat had lived there only from 2002 to 2008 A.D. Yet, during the years they had voyaged together, Monat had betrayed a knowledge that no human could have accumulated in a century.

The conversation ended since it was time to go back to work on the boat. Burton had not forgotten Alice's seeming barb, however. He brought it up as they got ready to go to bed.

She looked at him with large, dark eyes, eyes that were already retreating into another world. She almost always withdrew when he attacked, and it was this that heated his anger from red to white-hot.

"No, Dick, I wasn't insulting you. At least, I wasn't doing so consciously."

"But you were doing it unconsciously, is that it? That's no excuse. You can't plead that you have no control of that part of you. What your unconscious thinks is just as much *you* as the conscious is. It's even worse. You can dismiss your conscious thoughts, but what you really believe is what that shadowy thing believes."

He began pacing back and forth, his face looking like a demon's in the faint light cast by the small fire on the stone hearth.

"Isabel worshipped me, yet she was not afraid to argue violently with me, to tell me when she thought I was doing something wrong. But you . . . you harbor resentment until it makes an absolute bitch of you, yet you won't come out with it. And that makes things even worse.

"There's nothing evil about a hammer-and-tongs, screaming, throwing argument. It's like a thunderstorm, frightening when it happens; but it clears the air after it's over.

"The trouble with you is that you were raised to be a lady. You must never lift your voice in anger, you must always be calm and cool and collected. But that shadowy entity, that hindbrain, that inheritance from your ape ancestors, is tearing at the bars of its cage. And, incidentally, tearing at you. But you, you won't admit it.''

Alice lost her dreamy look, and she shouted at him.

"You're a liar! And don't throw up your wife to me! We agreed never to compare each other's spouse, but you do it every time you wish to get me angry! It isn't true that I lack passion. You of all people should know that, and I don't just mean in bed.

"But I won't go into a rage over every petty word and incident. When I get mad it's because the situation demands it. It's worth getting angry about. You . . . you're in a perpetual state of rage.''

"That's a lie!"

"I don't lie!"

"Let us get back to the point," he said. "What is there about my capacity as commander that you don't like?"

She bit her lip, then said, "It's not how you run the boat or how you treat your crew. That's such an obvious matter, and you do fine at it. No, what troubles me is the command, or lack of it, over yourself.''

Burton sat down, saying, "Let's have it. Just what are you talking about?"

She hitched forward on the chair and leaned over so that her face was close to his.

"For one thing, you can't stand to stay in one place more than a week. Before three days are up, you get uneasy. By the seventh day you're like a tiger pacing back and forth in his cage, a lion throwing himself against the bars.''

"Spare me the zoological analogies," he said. "Besides, you know that I have stayed in one place for as much as a year.''

"Yes, when you were building a boat. When you had a project going, one which would enable you to travel even more swiftly. Even then, you took short trips, leaving the rest of us to work on the boat. You had to go see this and that, investigate rumors, study strange customs, track down a language you didn't know. Never mind what the excuse was. You had to get away.

"You have a blight of the soul, Dick. That's the only way I can describe it. You can't endure to stay long in one place. But it's not because of the place. Never! It's you yourself that you can't tolerate. You must run so you can get away from yourself!''

He stood up and began pacing again.

"You say then that I can't endure myself! What a pitiable fellow! He doesn't love himself, which means that no one else can love him!''

"Nonsense!"

"Yes, all you're saying is pure rot!''

"The rot is in you, not in what I say."

"If you can't stand me, why don't you leave?"

Tears slid down her cheeks, and she said, "I love you, Dick!"

"But not enough to put up with my trifling eccentricities, is that it?"

She threw up her hands. "*Trifling?*"

"I have an itch to travel. So what? Would you taunt me if I had a physical itch, say athlete's foot?"

She smiled slightly. "No, I'd tell you to get rid of it. But this isn't just an itch, Dick. It's a compulsion."

She got up and lit a cigarette. Waving it under his nose, she said, "Look at this. In my time on Earth I would never have dared smoke, wouldn't even have considered it. A lady did not do such things. Especially a lady whose husband was of the landed gentry, whose father was a bishop of the Anglican church. Nor did she ever drink strong liquor to excess or curse. And she would never have considered bathing nude in public!

"But here I am, Alice Pleasance Liddell Hargreaves of the estate of Cuffnells, a most proper Victorian female aristocrat, doing all that and much more. By much more, well, I'm doing things in bed that even the French novels my husband was so fond of reading would not even have hinted at.

"I've changed. So why can't you?

"To tell the truth, Dick, I'm sick of traveling, always moving on, cooped up inside a small vessel, never knowing what tomorrow will bring. I'm no coward, you know that. But I would like to find a place where they speak English, where the people are of my own kind, where there is peace, where I can settle down, put down roots. I'm so *tired* of this eternal voyaging!"

Burton was moved by her tears. He put his hand on her shoulder and said, "What can we do about it? I must keep going on. Now, my . . ."

"Isabel? I'm not she. I'm Alice. I do love you, Dick, but I'm not your shadow, trailing you wherever you go, present when there's light, gone when there's darkness, a mere appendage."

She got up to put out the half-smoked cigarette in a baked-clay ashtray. Turning to him, she said, "But there's more! There's something else that bothers me very much. It hurts me that you don't fully confide in me. You have a secret, Dick, a very deep, very dark secret."

"Perhaps you can tell me what it is. I certainly don't know."

"Don't lie! I've heard you talking in your sleep. It has something to do with those Ethicals, doesn't it? Something happened to you you didn't tell anyone about when you were gone all those years.

"I've heard you muttering about bubbles, about killing yourself seven hundred and seventy-seven times. And I've heard names you never mention when you're awake. Loga. Thanabur. And you speak of Ecks and the mysterious stranger. Who are these people?''

"Only the man who sleeps alone can keep a secret," Burton said.

"Why can't you tell me? Don't you trust me—after all these years?"

"I would if I could. But it would be too dangerous for you. Believe me, Alice, I have said nothing because I must say nothing. It is for your own good. No arguments now. I won't give in, and I'll get very angry if you persist in questioning me."

"Very well then. But keep your hands to yourself tonight."

It was a long time before he fell asleep. Some time in the night he awoke, aware that he had been talking. Alice was sitting up, staring at him.

22

OSKAS, HALF-DRUNK AS USUAL, VISITED BURTON DURING LUNCH hour. Burton did not mind, especially since the chief gave him a skin containing at least two liters of bourbon.

"Have you heard the rumors of this great white boat which is said to be coming from down-River?" the Indian said.

"Only a deaf man would not have heard," Burton said, and he took a long pull of the whiskey. It had a winey odor and went down smoothly, needing no dilution with water. But then the grails never delivered anything but the best.

He said, "Aah!" and then, "I find it hard to believe the stories. From the description, the vessel is propelled by paddlewheels. That would mean that its engines are of iron. I doubt that anyone could gather enough ore to make engines of any size. Also, I have heard that the hull of the boat is made of metal. There's not enough iron in the whole planet to make a vessel that big. If it is as big as the rumors say."

"You are full of doubts," Oskas said. "That is bad for the liver. However, if the stories are true, then the great boat will be coming along some day. I would like to have such a boat."

"You and millions more. But if such a boat can be made, then its maker could have iron weapons, perhaps firearms. You have never seen these though you do have some gunpowder bombs. Firearms, however, are metal tubes which can shoot metal projectiles to a great distance. Some of these can fire so fast that a man could not shoot one arrow before he was hit ten times. And then there are cannons. These are giant tubes which shoot large bombs farther than the mountains.

"So, you can assume that others have tried to take this boat away from its owners and have died before they could get within arrow range. Besides, what would you do with it if you did get it? It takes highly trained people to operate such a boat."

"Those could be gotten," Oskas said. "You, for instance. Could you operate it?"

"Probably."

"Would you be interested in helping me take it? I would be grateful. You would be first among my subchiefs."

"I am not a warlike man," Burton said. "Nor am I greedy. However, just for the sake of conversation, let us say that I was interested. Here is what I would do."

Oskas was fascinated by the intricate but fantastic plan that Burton proposed. When he left he said that he would send Burton more whiskey. They must talk about this some more. Smiling broadly, Oskas staggered away.

Burton thought the chief was very gullible. He did not mind stringing him along, however. It would keep him happy.

The truth was that Burton had some plans of his own.

If the stories were true, then the boat was a means for traveling much faster than by sail. Somehow, he was going to get on it. Not by force but by cunning. The main trouble was that he had no idea as yet how he could accomplish that.

For one thing, the boat might not, probably would not, stop at this area. For another, it might not have room for more people. Also, why should its captain want to take him and his crew on?

The rest of the day, he was silent, absorbed in his thoughts. After he had gone to bed, he lay a long time considering every possibility. One of the things he considered was that of going along with Oskas' plan. Then, at the last moment, he could betray him. That might get him into the good graces of the boat's captain.

He rejected that almost instantly. In the first place, even if Oskas was rapacious and treacherous, he, Burton, would feel dishonored if he deceived him. Secondly, it was inevitable that many of Oskas' people would be killed and wounded. He did not wish to be responsible for that.

No, there had to be another way.

Finally, he found it. Its success depended upon stopping the boat or at least getting the attention of those aboard it. How he would do it if it passed during the night, he did not know. Somehow, he would.

Smiling, he fell asleep.

Two months passed. In another week, the *Snark* would be launched. In the meantime, details about the approaching paddle-wheeler had come in piecemeal. These had arrived by drum, smoke, fire, and mica-mirror signals. Putting the items together, Burton had built a picture of the vessel. It was probably larger than any Mississippi riverboat of his time. It was undoubtedly of metal, and it traveled at least 15 miles an hour or a little over 24 kilometers per hour. Sometimes, it had been seen going twice as fast. The calculations were crude, of course, since none of the observers had a stopwatch. But seconds could be counted as it passed from one grailstone to the next.

Burton had presumed from the first reports that the boat was a steamer. However, later messages said that the vessel seldom took in wood. This was for a boiler which heated water for showers and made steam for machine guns. Burton could not understand how steam propelled bullets. Monat suggested that the weapon used a synchronizing system to drop projectiles into the barrel, through which steam at considerable pressure was shot at regular intervals.

The motors of the boat used electricity, drawn from a grailstone when it discharged.

"Then they not only have steel, they have copper for the windings of the electrical motors," Burton said. "Where did they get all that metal?"

Frigate said, "The boat could be mainly aluminum. And aluminum could be used for the windings, though it's not as efficient as copper."

More data came in. The vessel bore its name on its sides in big black Roman letters. *Rex Grandissimus*. Latin for "The Greatest King," that is, greatest in manner or style of life. Its commander, according to informants, was none other than the son of Henry II of England and Eleanor, divorced wife of Louis VII of France, daughter of the Duke of Aquitaine. King John, surnamed Lackland, was the captain. After his famous brother, Richard the Lion-Hearted, had died, John had become *Joannes Rex Angliae et Dominus Hiberniae*, etc. He had also gained such a bad reputation that there was an unwritten law in the British royalty that no heir to the throne should ever be named John.

On first learning the captain's name, Burton had gone to Alice. "One of your ancestors commands the paddlewheeler. Perhaps we could appeal to his family affections to get him to take us aboard. Though, from what history said, he did not seem to have much family loyalty. He led a rebellion against his father, and he is said to have murdered his nephew, Arthur, whom Richard had made heir to the crown."

"He was no worse than any other king of that time," Alice said. "And he did do some good things, despite what people think. He reformed the coinage, he supported development of the Navy, he did all he could to develop trade, he urged the completion of London Bridge. He was also unusual among the monarchs of his time in that he was an intellectual. He read Latin books and French histories in the vernacular, and wherever he went he took his library with him.

"As for his opposition to the Magna Carta, that has been misrepresented. The barons' revolt was not in the interests of the common people; it was no democratic movement. The barons wanted special privileges for themselves. The freedom for which they fought was the freedom to exploit their subjects without opposition from the king.

"He fought hard against the barons, and he battled to keep the French provinces under the English crown. But there was no way he could get out of that; he had inherited old conflicts from his father and brother.''

"Well!'' Burton said. "You make him sound like a saint.''

"He was far from that. He was also far more interested in England itself, the welfare of its people, than any previous Anglo-Norman king.''

"You must have done much reading and thinking about him. Your opinions go against the grain of everything I've read.''

"I had much time to read when I lived in Cuffnells. And I form my own opinions.''

"Bully for you. Nevertheless, the fact remains that somehow this medieval monarch has gotten control of the greatest artifact, the most superb machine, on this world. I can deal with him when I get to him. The problem is, how do I do it?''

"You mean, how do *we* do it?''

"Right. My apologies. Well, we shall see.''

The *Snark* was let down the ways into The River amid much cheering and drinking. Burton was not as happy as he should have been. He had lost interest in it.

During the festivities, Oskas took him aside.

"You don't intend to leave soon, I hope? I am counting on you to help me take the great boat.''

Burton felt like telling him to go to hell. That would, however, not be diplomatic, since the chief might decide to confiscate the *Snark* for himself. Worse, he might quit resisting the temptation to take Loghu to his bed. During the year he had given her some trouble, though he had made no violent moves. Whenever he got very drunk, which was often, he had openly asked her to move in with him.

There had been many uneasy moments when it looked as if he was going to take her by force. Frigate, whose nature was anything but belligerent, had intended to challenge him to a duel, though he thought that it was a stupid way to solve a problem. But honor demanded it, manhood demanded it, there was no other way out unless he and Loghu sneaked away some night. He would not leave the people with whom he had been so intimate so many years.

Loghu had told him, "No, you will not get killed or kill that savage and so arouse his people to kill you. Leave it to me.''

Loghu had then astonished everybody, Oskas most of all, by challenging him to a fight to the death.

After recovering from the shock, Oskas had roared with laughter. "What? I should fight a *woman?* I beat my wives when they anger me, but I would not fight one. If I were to do this, it would not matter that I would kill you easily. I would be laughed at; I would no longer be Oskas, The Bear Claw, I would be The Man Who Fought a Woman.''

"What will it be?" Loghu had said. "Tomahawk? Spear? Knife? Or bare hands? You have seen me in the contests. You know how good I am with all weapons. It is true that you are bigger and stronger, but I know many tricks you don't. I've had some of the best instructors in the world."

What she did not mention was that he was very intoxicated, very fat, and very much out of condition.

Had it been a man who talked to him like that, Oskas would have leaped upon him. Drunk as he was, he knew that he was in a quandary. If he killed this woman, he would be a public jest. If he didn't accept the challenge, he would be said to be afraid of her.

Monat, smiling, stepped forward. "Chief, Loghu is my very good friend. I am also a friend of yours. Why don't we drop this matter? After all, it is the drink that is speaking in you, not you yourself, Oskas, the chief, a mighty warrior on Earth and along The River. No one can blame you for refusing to fight a woman.

"However, it is not right that you should bother another man's woman. You would not do it if you were not full of whiskey. So, I say that from now on you must not treat this woman with anything but the respect you demand from other men toward your women.

"Now, as Burton has told you, I was once a great magician. I still have some powers left, and I will not hesitate to use them if you harm Loghu. I would do so reluctantly, since I have great respect for you. But I will if I have to."

Oskas turned pale beneath the dark skin and the flush of whiskey-heated blood. He said, "Yes, it must be the drink. No one can blame me for what I do when I am drunk."

No more was said that night, and the next day Oskas claimed to have been so intoxicated he did not remember anything about the party.

For several months, he had been cool though polite to Loghu. Lately, he had resumed making remarks to her, though he had not touched her. This may have been because Loghu had told him, in private so that he would not lose face, that she would slice open his belly if he so much as laid a hand on her. Following which, she would crush his testicles.

She reported that he had only laughed at her. Despite which, he was aware that, given a chance, he could do just what she said. Nevertheless, Oskas had a compulsive passion for her. Now that the time was drawing close for her to leave, he was again after her.

Burton, talking to him now, kept this in mind. It wouldn't do to have him think that he had little time left to get Loghu into his bed.

"No, we are not leaving. We will follow the plan that I have worked out for you, and I and my people will be among the vanguard when we seize the boat.

"However, as you know, it is essential that we get to the boat when it has stopped to draw lightning from a stone. If it's moving we have no chance. Now, I have calculated the area where the boat will stop nearest to this place. I can't pinpoint it. But I can say within four or five grailstones where it will stop in the evening.

"Our boat needs a shakedown cruise. I propose to take it on one tomorrow. I'll sail down to the place where the great boat will stop, and I'll look over the situation. We need to know the lay of the land if we are to attack the mighty vessel with any chance of success.

"Would you like to come along?"

Oskas had been looking at him narrow-eyed. Now his face cleared, and he smiled.

"Of course I will go along. I do not blunder blind into a battle."

That took care of Oskas' unvoiced suspicion that the *Snark* would not return from the cruise. Even so, he stationed four men in a hut nearby to keep an eye on the boat, though he said nothing of it to Burton. That night, the entire crew sneaked out through the fog to the hills. There they retrieved the free-grails from a hole in the base of the mountain and brought them back to the boat. These were put in a hiding place behind what looked like a solidly secured bulkhead.

The next day, after breakfast, Oskas came aboard with seven of his best warriors. They crowded the vessel, but Burton did not complain. He began passing out lichen-alcohol flavored with ground irontree leaves. His crew had orders to be very abstemious. By midafternoon, the chief and his men were loud-mouthed, laughing drunks. Even their lunch had not been enough to sober them to any extent. Burton kept pressing his guests with drinks. About an hour before they were to stop for dinner, the Indians were staggering around or lying on deck asleep.

It was easy to push the still conscious ones into the water and then throw the unconscious after them. Fortunately, the shock of the water woke up the latter. Otherwise, Burton would have felt compelled to pick them up and take them ashore.

Oskas, treading water, shook his fist at them and raved in Menomini and Esperanto. Laughing, Burton bent his thumb and all except the middle finger and jerked his hand upward. Then he held out his hand with the first and fourth fingers extended, the ancient sign of the "evil eye," a sign that in modern times had come to mean "bullshit."

Oskas became even more violent and colorful in his description of the many ways he would get revenge.

Kazz, grinning, threw the chief's grail to him so accurately that it struck him on the head. The warriors had to dive down after him. When they brought him up, two were forced to support him until he could regain consciousness.

Kazz thought that putting a lump on Oskas' head was very funny.

He would have considered it to be even a better joke if the chief had drowned. Yet, among his crewmates, he was as sociable, tender, and compassionate a man as anyone could ask for. He was a primitive, and all primitives, civilized or preliterate, were tribal people. Only the tribe consisted of human beings and were treated as such. All outside the tribe, though some might be considered friends, were not quite human. Therefore, they did not have to be treated as if they were completely human.

Though the Neanderthal had lost his tribe on Earth, he had regained it in the crew of the *Snark*. This was his family, his tribe.

23

THE *Snark* DID NOT STOP WHERE BURTON HAD TOLD OSKAS IT would wait for the paddlewheeler. It would have been foolish to do so. Oskas could have made his way back quickly to his territory by renting or stealing a boat. He would then return with many warriors before the arrival of the *Rex Grandissimus*.

The cutter sailed on past the designated stop and continued down-River for two days. Meanwhile, its crew saw and heard messages sent by Oskas via heliograph, fire and smoke signals, and drum. The chief claimed that Burton's party had stolen cigarettes and booze from him and then had kidnapped him. Oskas offered a reward to anyone who would seize and hold the "criminals" until he could arrive to take them into custody.

Burton had to act quickly to counteract this, though it was doubtful that any authorities of the small states would arrest the crew of the *Snark*. Oskas was not popular because of the troubles he had given them over the years. However, individuals might organize privateering groups.

Burton went ashore with a box of tobacco and liquor and some oak rings. With these he paid the head of the local branch of the signal company to send out a message for him. This was that Oskas lied, and the truth was that the chief had wanted to take a female crew member by force and so she and her companions had been compelled to flee. Oskas had pursued them but his warcanoe had been sunk when he had tried to board the *Snark*.

Burton then added that he knew that the chief and his councillors had a great treasure, a hoard of free-grails numbering at least a hundred.

This was a lie, since Oskas, when drunk, had told Burton that the headmen only had twenty. Burton did not mind stretching the truth. Attention would now be diverted from him to the chief. His people would hear this, and they would be raising hell about it. Undoubtedly, they would demand that the proceeds of the free-grails be added to the communal stockpile. Also, Oskas would now have to worry about thieves. Not only would these be of his own people, but many from other states would be planning how they could steal the grails.

Oskas was going to be too busy to worry about revenge.

Burton chuckled as he thought about this.

The *Snark* came to an area where the current of The River slowed down considerably. The boat had encountered many of these, places where a river should no longer be able to flow downward. On Earth this would have meant that The River would have spread out into a lake, deluging the Valley.

However, after passing through the almost dead current, the cutter came to an area where the water picked up speed. Once again, it was running toward the faraway mouth, that legendary great cavern leading to the north polar sea. There were a number of explanations for this phenomenon, none of which had so far been proved valid.

One was that there were enough variations in local gravity to permit the impetus of The River to overcome the lack of downward gradient. Those who favored this theory said that the unknown makers of this world might have installed underground devices which caused a weaker gravity field in appropriate areas.

Others suggested that water was pumped under great pressure from pipes deep beneath The River.

A third school speculated that the ceaseless current-flow was caused by a combination of pressure pumps and "light-gravity" generators.

A fourth maintained that God had decreed that the water go uphill and so there was no use wondering about the phenomenon.

The majority of people never thought about it.

Whatever the cause, The River never stopped rolling along its many-million-meter course.

At the end of the second day, the *Snark* docked in the locality where the great metal boat should stop. The news here was that the *Rex* had stopped traveling for several days. Its crew was taking a short shore leave.

"Excellent!" Burton said. "We can get to it by tomorrow and have a whole day to talk Captain John into enlisting us."

Though he sounded cheerful, he did not feel so. If his plan did not work, he'd have to take the *Snark* through Oskas' area in daylight since there was little wind at night. Warned by the signal system that it was coming, the chief would be waiting for it with his full force. Burton felt that he should have turned back up-River after getting rid of the Indians and sailed far past their land. However, the paddle-wheeler might then have passed by the *Snark*, and Burton would have had no chance to talk to its commander.

Sufficient unto the day is the evil thereof, and the best-laid plans of mice and men gang aft agley. He'd enjoy tonight and take care of tomorrow tomorrow. Despite which reassurance, he worried.

The locals here were a majority of sixteenth-century Dutch, a minority of ancient Thracians, and the usual small percentage of people from many places and many times. Burton met a Fleming who had known Ben Jonson and Shakespeare, among other famous persons. He was talking to him when a newcomer joined the crowd sitting around a bonfire. He was a Caucasian of medium stature, thin bodied, black haired, and blue eyed. He stood for a minute, looking intently at Frigate. Then he smiled broadly and ran up to him.

He cried out in English, "Pete! For God's sake, Pete! It's me, Bill Owain! Pete Frigate, by the Lord! It is you, isn't it, Pete?"

Frigate looked startled. He said, "Yes? But you, you're . . . what did you say your name was?"

"Bill Owain! For Christ's sake, you haven't forgotten me, Bill Owain, your old buddy! You look a little different, Pete. For a moment, I wasn't sure! You don't quite look like I remember you! Bill Owain! I didn't recognize you at first, it's been so long!"

They embraced then and both talked swiftly, laughing now and then. When they let loose of each other, Frigate introduced Owain.

"He's my old schoolmate. We've known each other since fourth grade in grammar school. We went to Peoria Central High together and buddied around for some years afterward. When I finally settled down in Peoria after working around the country, we used to see each other now and then. Not very often, since we had our own lives to live and belonged to different circles."

"Even so," Owain said, "I don't see how you could have failed to recognize me right off. But then I wasn't quite sure about you either. I remembered you differently. Your nose is a little longer and your eyes are greener and your mouth isn't quite as broad and your chin seems bigger. And your voice—you remember how everybody kidded you because it was a dead ringer for Gary Cooper's? It doesn't sound like it used to, like I thought it did. So much for memory, eh?"

"Yeah, so much for memory. You know, Bill, mine was never very good. Besides, we remember each other as middle-aged and old men, and now we look like we did when we were twenty-five. Also, we're not wearing the clothes we did then, and it's a shock, a real shock, to run across somebody I knew then. I was stunned!"

"I was, too! I wasn't quite sure! Listen, do you know you're the first person I've met that I knew on Earth?"

Frigate said, "You're the second for me. And that was thirty-two years ago, and the guy I met wasn't one I cared to associate with!"

That, Burton thought, would be a man called Sharkko. A publisher of hardcover science fiction books in Chicago, he had cheated Frigate in a rather complicated deal. The business had taken several years, at the end of which Frigate's writing career had been almost wrecked. But one of the first persons Frigate had encountered after being resurrected was Sharkko. Burton had not witnessed the meeting, but Frigate had recounted how he had avenged himself by punching the fellow in the nose.

Burton himself had met only one person he had known on Earth, though his acquaintances had been numerous and worldwide. That was also a meeting he could have passed up. The man had been one of the porters on his expedition to find the source of the Nile. On the way to Lake Tanganyika (Burton and his companion Speke were the first Europeans to see it), the porter had purchased a slave, a girl about thirteen years old. She had become too sick to continue with them, so the porter had cut off her head rather than allow someone else to own her.

Burton had not been present to prevent the murder, nor would it have been discreet to punish the man. He had the legal right to do with his slave as he wished. However, Burton would punish him for other things, such as laziness, thievery, and breakage of goods, and he laid the whip on him whenever the opportunity arose.

Now Owain and Frigate sat down to drink lichen-alcohol and to talk of old times. Burton noticed that Owain seemed to remember incidents and friends much better than Frigate did. This was surprising, since Frigate had very good recall.

"Remember how we used to see the shows at the Princess, Columbia, and Apollo theaters?" Owain said. "Do you remember the Saturday we decided to find out how many movies we could see in one day? We went to a doublefeature at the Princess, then a double-feature at the Columbia, a triple-feature at the Apollo, and a midnight show at the Madison."

Frigate smiled and nodded. But his expression showed that his recollection was faulty.

"Then there was that time we took a trip to St. Louis with Al Everhard and Jack Dirkman and Dan Doobin. Al's cousin got some dates for us; they were nurses, remember? We drove out to the cemetery—what was it called?"

"Damned if I remember," Pete said.

"Yes, but I'll bet you haven't forgotten how you and that nurse stripped and you were chasing her around the cemetery and you jumped over a tombstone and fell smack into a wreath and got all torn up from the thorns and roses! Bet you haven't forgotten that!"

Frigate grinned embarrassedly. "How could I?"

"It sure took the wind out of your sails! And everything else! Haw, haw!"

There was more reminiscence. After a while, the talk turned to their reactions on awakening along the banks of The River. The others joined in then, since this was a favorite topic. That day had been so frightening, so awe-inspiring, so alien that no one would ever forget that. The horror, the panic, and confusion were still with them. Burton sometimes wondered if people were still talking so much about that experience because the recapitulation was a form of therapy. They hoped to rid themselves of the trauma by a verbal discharge.

There was a general agreement that everybody had acted somewhat silly that day.

"I remember how absurdly formal and dignified I was," Alice said. "Not that I was the only one. However, most people were hysterical. We were all in great shock. The wonder is that nobody died of a heart attack. You'd think that waking up in this strange place after you'd died would be enough to kill you again—at once."

Monat said, "Perhaps, just before resurrection, our anonymous benefactors injected some sort of drug into us that eased the impact of the shock. Also, the dreamgum we found in our grails may have acted as a sort of postoperative anesthesia. Though I must say that its effect caused some terribly savage behavior."

Alice looked at Burton then. Even after all these years, she still blushed at the memory. All their social inhibitions had been stripped off for a few hours, and they had acted as if they were minks whose sole diet was Spanish fly. Or as if their secret fantasies had taken control.

The conversation then centered on the Arcturan. Previously, despite his warm manner, he had encountered the standoffishness he met everywhere at first from strangers. His obvious nonhuman origin made them shy or caused repulsion.

Now they questioned him about his life on his native planet and his experience on Earth. A few had heard tales of how the Arcturans had been forced to slay almost all the people on Earth. No one present, however, except Frigate, had been living when the Arcturans' ship had arrived on Earth.

Burton said, "You know, that is peculiar, though I suppose it's to be expected. There were, according to Pete, eight billion people living in 2008 A.D. Yet, aside from Monat and Frigate here, and one other person, I've never met anyone who lived then. Did any of you?"

Nobody had. In fact, the only locals who had lived past the seventies of the twentieth century were Owain and a woman. She had died in 1982; he, in 1981.

Burton shook his head. "There must be at least thirty-six billion along The River. The biggest majority should be those who lived between 1983—I choose that date because I've met only three who lived past it—those who lived between 1983 and 2008. Yet, where are they?''

''Maybe there are some at the next grailstone,'' Frigate said. ''After all, Dick, nobody's taken a census. What's more, nobody is able to do that. You pass hundreds of thousands every day, but how many do you get to talk to? A few dozen a day. Sooner or later you're bound to run into one.''

They speculated for a while about why and how they had been resurrected and who could have done it. They also talked about why the growth of facial hair in men was inhibited, why all males had awakened circumcised, and why women had their hymens restored before resurrection. As for not needing to shave, half the men thought it a good thing while the other half resented not being able to grow moustaches and beards.

There was also some wonder about why the grails of both men and women occasionally yielded lipstick and other cosmetics.

Frigate said that he thought that their benefactors probably did not like to shave and that both their sexes painted their faces. That was, to him, the only reasonable explanation.

Then Alice brought up Burton's experience in the preresurrection bubble. This got everybody's attention, but he told them that he had no memory of that. He'd suffered a blow on his head which had wiped out all recollection of it.

As always, when he told this lie, he caught Monat smiling slightly at him. He suspected that the Arcturan guessed that he was prevaricating. However, the fellow had never said so. He respected Burton's reasons for concealment even if he did not know what they were.

Frigate and Alice recounted Burton's tale as they remembered it. They made several mistakes, which he, of course, could not correct.

''If that is so,'' a man said, ''then the resurrection isn't a supernatural thing. It was done through scientific means. Amazing!''

''Yes, it is,'' Alice said. ''But why are we no longer resurrected? Why has death, permanent death, returned?''

A gloomy pensiveness fell upon them for a minute.

Kazz broke it by saying, ''There is one thing which Burton-*naq* has not forgotten. That's the business with Spruce. The agent of the Ethicals.''

That brought forth more questions.

''What are Ethicals?''

Burton took a long drink of scotch and launched into the story. At one time, he said, he and his party had been captured by grail-slavers. There was no need to explain this word. Everybody had had some experience with grail-slavers.

Burton told them how his boat had been attacked and how they had been put into a stockade. Thereafter, they had left it only to work under a heavy guard. All of their tobacco, marijuana, dream-gum, and liquor were taken by their captors. Moreover, these kept half of the food for themselves, leaving their prisoners on a bare-minimum diet.

After a few months, Burton and a man named Targoff had led a successful revolt against the slavers.

24

"A FEW DAYS AFTER WE'D WON OUR FREEDOM, FRIGATE, MONAT, and Kazz came to me. They greeted me, and then Kazz spoke excitedly.

" 'A long time ago, before I could speak English good, I see something. I try to tell you then, but you don't understand me. I see a man who don't have this on his forehead.'

"My friend here, my *naq*, as he calls it in his speech, indicated the center of his forehead and that of all of us.

"Kazz then said, 'I know you can't see it. Pete and Monat can't either. Nobody else can. But I see it on everybody's forehead. Except on that man I try to catch long time ago. Then, one day, I see a woman who don't have it, but I don't say nothing to you. Now, I see a third who don't have it.'

"I still did not understand. Monat, however, explained.

" 'He means that he is able to perceive certain symbols of characters on the forehead of each and every one of us. He can see these only in bright sunlight and at a certain angle. But everyone he's ever seen has had those symbols—except for the three he's mentioned.'

"Frigate added that Kazz somehow could see a little further into the color spectrum than non-Neanderthals could. Into the ultraviolet, as a matter of fact, since the symbols were bluish. At least that is the way Kazz described them. All of us, except certain individuals, seem to bear this mark. As if we're branded cattle. Since that time, Kazz, and his woman Besst, have observed these on people's foreheads, when the lighting conditions were right, of course."

This news, as always, resulted in astonishment, indignation, and even shock. Burton waited until the furor died down before speaking.

"Some of you late-twentieth-centurians may know that the so-called Neanderthal man was reclassified. The anthropoligists decided that he was not a separate species but a variant of *Homo sapiens*. Nevertheless, just as he differed somewhat in physical build and teeth from us, he also has the ability to see into the ultraviolet."

Besst said, "I am not a Neanderthal man but a woman, and I, too, have this ability."

Burton grinned and said, "Women's lib has penetrated into the Old Stone Age. However, let me point out that events will show that Whoever made this world and stamped us with, in a manner of speaking, the mark of the beast, did not know that *Homo neanderthalis* had a special visual ability. This means that Whoever is not omniscient.

"To resume my narrative. I asked for the identity of the person who lacked the symbol. Frigate replied, 'Robert Spruce!'

"Spruce had also been a grail slave. He claimed to be an Englishman born in 1945. That was about all I knew of him.

"I said that we would get him and question him. Frigate told me that we'd have to catch him because he was probably long gone. It seems that Kazz told Spruce he'd noticed Spruce lacked the mark on his forehead. Spruce had turned pale, and a few minutes later he left hurriedly. Frigate and Monat sent search parties out, but at the time they reported to me he hadn't been found.

"It seemed to me that his flight was an admission of guilt, though I didn't know what he was guilty of. A few hours later, he was discovered hiding in the hills. He was brought before the newly formed council of our newly formed state. Spruce was pale and trembling, though he looked us straight in the eye defiantly enough.

"I informed him that we suspected that he was an agent for the Ethicals if not an Ethical himself. I also told him that we would go to any lengths, including torture, to get the truth from him. This was a lie, since we would have been no better than the men who'd enslaved us if we had resorted to torture. Spruce, however, did not know that.

"Spruce said, 'You may be denying yourself eternal life if you torture me. It will at least set you far back on your journey, delay your final goal.'

"I asked him what that final goal was, but he ignored that question. Instead, he said, 'We can't stand pain. We're too sensitive.'

"There was some more exchange, but he would not answer our questions. Then one of the councillors suggested that he be suspended above a fire. Monat spoke up then. He told Spruce that he was from a culture somewhat more advanced than that of Earth's. He felt he was more qualified to make guesses about the truth than the rest of us, and no one argued with him about this. Monat said that he would like to spare him the pain of the fire and also the pain of betraying his trust. Perhaps Monat could make some speculations about the Ethicals and their agents, and Spruce could merely affirm or deny the speculations. In this way, Spruce would not be making a positive betrayal of his trust, whatever that was."

Bill Owain said, "That was a peculiar arrangement."

"True. But Monat hoped to get him to talking. You see, we were not going to use any brutal methods of inquisition. If we couldn't scare him, then we were going to try hypnosis. Both Monat and I are skilled mesmerists. However, as it turned out, we didn't have to resort to that.

"Monat said, 'It's my theory that you are a Terrestrial. You come from an age chronologically far past 2008 A.D. In fact, you are a descendant of the few people who survived the death beam projected from our orbital ship.' Monat guessed that the technology and energy required to reconstruct this planet into one vast Rivervalley was very advanced. He suggested that Spruce was born in the fiftieth century A.D.

"Spruce replied that he should add two thousand years.

"Monat then said that not everyone had been resurrected. There wasn't enough room on this world. It was known that no children who had died before the age of five were here. And though it couldn't be proved, it seemed likely that no imbeciles and idiots had been resurrected here. Nor was anyone who lived after 2008 A.D., with the exception of Spruce here.

"Where were these people?

"Spruce answered that they were elsewhere, and that was all he would say on the subject.

"Monat then asked him how the people of the Earth had been recorded. That is, what device had the Ethicals used to make recordings of our bodies? Since it was obvious that scientific, not supernatural, means were used to resurrect us, that meant that everyone from the Old Stone Age to 2008 A.D. had somehow been observed, the structure of every cell of a person's body recorded, and this recording was stored somewhere to be used later in the re-creation of the body.

"Monat said that the recordings must be placed in an energy-matter converter, whereupon the body was duplicated. The effects of injuries, wounds, and diseases that had caused death were cancelled. Amputated limbs and organs were restored. I myself saw some of this regeneration process when I awoke in the preresurrection space. Also, those aged past twenty-five were rejuvenated.

"Monat further speculated that the bodies in the PR bubble were destroyed after the regeneration process was completed. But recordings of the new bodies had been made, and these recordings were used in the final stage, the great resurrection, when all of us appeared together on that never-to-be-forgotten day.

"Monat supposed that the resurrection was accomplished through the metal of the grailstone system. That is, all the stones are connected deep underground to form a circuit of some sort, and the energy is supplied from the hot nickle-iron core of this planet.

"Monat then said, "The big question is why?'

"Spruce said, 'If you had it in your power to do all this, would you not think it your *ethical* duty?'

"Monat said that he would think so. But he would bring back to life only those who deserve a second life.

"Spruce became angry then. He replied that Monat was setting himself up as an equal of God. Everybody, no matter how stupid, selfish, petty, brutal, etcetera, must be given another chance to redeem themselves, to make themselves worthy. It would not be done *for* them; they must, somehow, lift themselves by their own moral bootstraps.

"Monat asked Spruce how long this process would take. A thousand years? Two? A million?

"Spruce became angry, and he shouted, 'You will stay here as long as it takes you to be rehabilitated! Then . . .'

"He paused, glaring at us as if he hated us, and he said, 'Continued contact with you makes even the toughest of us take on your characteristics. We then have to go through a rehabilitation process ourselves. Already, I feel unclean . . .'

"One of the councillors, wishing to press him, urged that he be put over the fire until he would talk freely.

"Spruce cried, 'No, you won't! I should have done this long ago! Who knows what . . .' "

Burton paused dramatically.

"Then Spruce fell dead!"

There were gasps, and someone said, *"Mein Gott!"*

"Yes, but that isn't the end of the story. Spruce's body was taken away for dissection. It seemed too coincidental that he should have had a heart attack. Not only was it too convenient for him, it was unheard-of.

"While he was being dissected, we discussed what happened. Some thought that he was lying to us. Or, at least, only giving us half-truths. We did agree on one thing. That was that there were people in this Valley who were agents of the Ethicals or perhaps the Ethicals themselves. These did not bear the mark on their foreheads.

"But it seemed likely that we would not be able to distinguish them anymore by using Kazz's peculiar visual powers. Spruce would be resurrected wherever their headquarters was. He would report to the others that we now knew about the symbols. And of course they would put the mark on their agents.

"This would take time, and in the meantime Kazz might detect others. But this has not happened. Neither he nor Besst has seen anybody unmarked. Again, of course, this does not mean too much. They have to get a close look under certain conditions to see the mark.

"Three hours later, the surgeon reported to us. There was nothing remarkable about Spruce. Nothing to distinguish him from other members of *Homo sapiens*."

Once more, Burton paused.

"Except for one small item! This was a very tiny black sphere! The doctor had found it on the surface of Spruce's forebrain. It was attached to the cerebral nerves by extremely thin wires. This led us to conclude that Spruce had literally thought, or wished, himself to die.

"Somehow, the sphere interacted with his mental processes in such a manner that he could think himself dead. Perhaps he thought of a certain code sequence, and this released a poison into his system. The doctor could find no evidence of this, but then he lacked the necessary chemical means to make an accurate analysis.

"In any event, Spruce's body showed no damage. Something had stopped his heart, but the doctor did not know what that was."

A woman said, "Then there could be such people among us? Now, here, in this group?"

Burton nodded, and everybody started talking at once. After fifteen minutes of this babel, he stood up and indicated to his crew that it was time to go to bed. On the way to the cutter, Kazz drew him aside.

"Burton-*naq*, when you mentioned you and Monat were hypnotists . . . well, that made me think about something. I've never thought about it before . . . maybe there's nothing funny about it . . . only . . ."

"Well?"

"It's nothing, I'm sure. Only it was funny. You see, I told Spruce I could see he didn't have no sign on his head. He left a few minutes later, but I could smell the fear in his sweat. There were others there, all eating breakfast, Targoff, Doctor Steinborg, Monat, Pete, and a number of others. Targoff said we should convene the council, though this was some time after Spruce had taken off. Monat and Pete agreed. But they said they wanted to question me a little more. You know, what the marks looked like. Were they all alike or did they differ?"

"I said they differed. A lot of them were . . . what you say? . . . similar, yes, that's it. But each one . . . what the hell, you know what they look like, I've drawn pictures of them for you."

Burton said, "Aside from some looking something like Chinese ideograms, they resemble nothing I've ever seen. My guess is that they're symbols of a numbering system."

"Yeah, I know what you said. The thing is, Monat and Frigate took me aside before we went to your place to tell you what'd happened. In fact, we went to Monat's hut."

Kazz paused. Impatiently Burton said, "Well?"

"I'm trying to remember. But I can't. I went into the hut, and that's all!"

"What do you mean, that's all?"

"Burton-*naq*, I mean that's all. I don't remember a thing about going into that hut. I remember starting through the door. The next I remember is walking with Monat, Pete, and the other councillors to your hut!"

Burton felt a slight shock, yet he had no idea what had caused it.

"You mean that you don't remember anything from the time you entered until the time you walked out?"

"I mean that I don't remember walking out. All of a sudden, there I was, a hundred paces from Monat's house and walking along, talking to Monat."

Burton frowned. Alice and Besst were standing on the dock, looking back as if wondering why they had dropped behind.

"This is most peculiar, Kazz. Why haven't you told me about this before? After all, it's been many years since it happened. Didn't you think about this before?"

"No, I didn't. Ain't that funny? Not one frigging thought. I still wouldn't remember even entering the hut if Loghu hadn't said something about it the other day. She saw me go in, but she wasn't with the group that day and so didn't know what was going on until later.

"What happened was that she was standing in the doorway of her and Frigate's hut. Frigate, Monat, and me was going to go into Frigate's hut. When they found she was there, they went to Monat's. It was just by chance that she mentioned this yesterday. We was talking about when we was grail slaves, and this brought up Spruce. That's when she asked me what Monat, Pete, and me was talking about. She said she wondered sometimes why they wanted to talk to me in private.

"She just never brought it up before because it didn't seem important. It still wasn't, but she was curious, and since the subject was brought up, she remembered to ask me. You know how curious women are."

"Women have the curiosity of cats," Burton said, and he chuckled. "Whereas men are as curious as monkeys."

"What? What does that mean?"

"I don't know, but it sounds deep. I'll think up an explanation later. So, it was Loghu's remarks that made you remember the events preceding and following your entry into Monat's place?"

"Not right away, Burton-*naq*. I got to puzzling about what she said. I really strained my brain. I could hear the tissues ripping. Finally, I could remember, in a dim way, how we meant to go into Pete's hut. Then I could remember Loghu being there and Monat saying they'd use his hut. And after a while . . . I could faintly recollect going into there.

"While you was talking didn't you notice me sitting there by the fire, frowning away like there was a thunderstorm on my brow?"

"I just thought you'd taken too much to eat and drink, as usual."

"That, too. But it wasn't no farts storming around inside me. It was gas on the brain."

"Since you've recalled this, you haven't said anything to Monat or Frigate about it?"

"No."

"Don't, then."

Kazz had a low forehead, but he was not unintelligent.

"You think there's something phony about those two?"

Burton said, "I don't know. I'd hate to think so. After all these years . . . and they are good friends. At least . . ."

"It don't seem possible," Kazz said. He sounded as if his heart were about to break.

"What doesn't?"

"I don't know what. But it has to be something *bad*."

"I don't know that," Burton said. "There may be a very good explanation other than the one I'm thinking of. Anyway, don't mention this to anyone."

"I won't. Only . . . listen, those two do have symbols on their heads. They always had them. So, if them agents didn't have them at one time, Pete and Monat couldn't be agents!"

Burton smiled. Kazz's thoughts were his. Nevertheless, he had to look into this. How could he do it without putting the two on guard? Of course, they might have nothing to hide.

"Yes, I know. Don't forget that Besst has also seen their symbols. So we have double confirmation, not that we need it.

"In any course, mum's the word until I say otherwise."

They started to walk toward the *Snark*. Kazz said, "I don't know. I sure have a bad feeling about this. Wish I'd kept my mouth shut. Loghu *would* say something about it."

BURTON PACED BACK AND FORTH ON THE DECK IN THE FOG. THOUGH his body was warm in the cloths, his face was chilled. An unusually cold body of air had moved into the area, and as a result the mists were piled halfway up the mast. He could not see beyond his outstretched arms.

As far as he knew, everybody aboard except himself was asleep. His only company were his thoughts. These tended to stray as if they were sheep on a hillside. Burton had to work hard to bring them back, arrange them in an orderly band, keep them moving toward pasture. And what was pasture? Bitter eating.

There were thirty-three years to cover in his memory. It was a selective process, one which concentrated on Monat and Frigate. What actions, what words of theirs were suspicious? What could be fitted into a dark jigsaw puzzle?

There were very few people available. There might be more, but he could be looking at them and not even realize that they were pieces.

That terrible, joyous day, the day that he had awakened from the dead, he had met the Arcturan first of all. Of all those he had encountered that day, Monat had acted most calmly and rationally. He had taken stock of the situation amazingly fast, checked out the environment, and immediately understood the purpose of the grails.

The second person Burton had especially noticed was the Neanderthal, Kazz. He, however, had not tried to talk to Burton at first. He had merely followed him for a while. Peter Frigate had been the second person to talk to Burton. And, now that Burton considered it, Frigate had been rather easy and casual in manner. This was strange in view of Frigate's claim that he suffered from anxiety and hysteria.

Later events had seemed to confirm this. However, from time to time, and consistently in the past twenty years, Frigate had overcome his faults. Had he really attained self-mastery or had he just abandoned a role, ceased to play-act?

Certainly, it had been quite a coincidence that the second person Burton met had written a biography of him. How many biographers of his existed? Ten or twelve? What were the probabilities that one of them would be resurrected only a few meters from him? Twelve in thirty-six billion.

Still, it was within the realm of chance; it was not impossible.

Then Kazz had joined those who'd collected around Burton. Then Alice. Then Lev Ruach.

Today, while Kazz had been helmsman, Burton had stood by him and questioned him. Had Kazz talked to Monat and Frigate during Resurrection Day when Burton had not been around? Did he remember anything that was suspicious about them?

Kazz had shaken his thickly boned head. "I was with them several times when you were not in sight. But I don't remember nothing strange about them. That is, Burton-*naq*, there was nothing stranger than strange. Everything was strange that day."

"Did you notice the marks on people's foreheads that day?"

"Yes, a few. That was when the sun was highest."

"What about Monat and Frigate?"

"I don't remember seeing any on theirs that day. But then I don't remember seeing one on you, either. The light had to reflect at a certain angle."

Burton had taken out of his shoulderbag a pad of bamboo paper, a sharply pointed fish bone, and wooden bottle of ink. He took over the wheel while Kazz drew the marks he saw on the foreheads of the Arcturan and the American. Both were three parallel horizontal lines crossed by three parallel vertical lines juxtaposed to a cross enclosed in a circle. The lines were of even thickness and length except at the ends. Monat's lines broadened at the right; Frigate's, at the left.

"What about the sign on my forehead?" Burton had said.

Kazz showed him four wavy parallel horizontal lines next to a symbol like an ampersand (&). Below it was a short, thin, straight horizontal line.

"Monat's and Pete's are remarkably alike," Burton said.

At Burton's request, Kazz then drew the symbols on the foreheads of everyone of the crew. Not one resembled any other.

"Do you remember Lev Ruach's?"

Kazz nodded, and a moment later he handed Burton the drawing. He felt disappointed, though he had no conscious reason to be so. Ruach's symbol was not at all like his prime suspects'.

Now, walking on the deck, Burton wondered why he had expected it to be similar to the other two. Something tickled the back of his brain, some suspicion he could not scratch. There was a linkage among the three, but it slipped away just as he was about to grasp it.

He had done enough thinking. Now for action.

A white bundle lying against the cabin was the Neanderthal, wrapped in cloths. Guiding himself by the fellow's snoring, Burton went to him and shook him. Kazz, snorting, woke up at once.

"Time?"

"Time."

First, though, Kazz had to piss over the railing. Burton lit a fish-oil lantern, and they walked down the gangplank onto the dock. From there they moved slowly onto the plain, their destination an empty hut about two hundred paces away. They missed it, but after circling around, they found it. After they had entered, Burton shut the door. A bundle of logs and shavings had been placed in the stone hearth that evening by Kazz. In a minute, a small fire was blazing. Kazz sat down on a bamboo wickerwork chair near the fire. He coughed as he breathed smoke which had escaped the feeble draught of the chimney.

It was easy to place Kazz into a hypnotic trance. He had been one of Burton's subjects for years when Burton entertained locals by displaying his powers as a mesmerist.

Now that Burton thought about it, Monat and Frigate had always been present at these times. Had they been nervous then? If they had, they had successfully concealed it.

Burton took Kazz straight back to the time when he had mentioned to the breakfasting group that Spruce had no mark. Working forward, he took him then to the point where the Neanderthal had gone into Monat's hut. Here he encountered first resistance.

"Are you now in the hut?"

Kazz, staring straight ahead, his eyes seemingly turned inward upon the past, said, "I am in the doorway."

"Go on in, Kazz."

The fellow shook with effort.

"I can't, Burton-*naq*."

"Why not?"

"I do not know."

"Is there something you fear in the hut?"

"I don't know."

"Has anyone told you that there is something bad in the hut?"

"No."

"Then you have nothing to fear. Kazz, you are a brave man, aren't you?"

"You know I am, Burton-*naq*."

"Why can't you go on in then?"

Kazz shook his head. "I don't know. Something . . ."

"Something what?"

"Something . . . tells me . . . tells me . . . can't remember."

Burton bit his lower lip. The flaming wood cracked and hissed.

"Who tells you? Monat? Frigate?"

"Don't know."

"Think!"

Kazz's forehead wrinkled. Sweat poured down it.

The firewood crackled again. Hearing it, Burton smiled.

"Kazz!"

"Yes."

"Kazz! Besst is in the hut, and she's screaming! Can you hear her screaming?"

Kazz straightened up and looked from side to side, his eyes wide open, his nostrils distended, his lips drawn back.

"I hear her! What is the matter?"

"Kazz! There's a bear in the hut, and it's going to attack Besst! Take your spear and go in there and kill the bear, Kazz! Save Besst!"

Kazz stood up, and, his hand grasping the imaginary spear, sprang forward. Burton had to move swiftly to get out of his way. Kazz stumbled over the chair and fell upon his face.

Burton grimaced. Would the shock bring Kazz out of his trance? No, Kazz was up on his feet and about to run forward again.

"Kazz! You're in the hut! There's the bear! Kill it, Kazz! Kill it!"

Snarling, Kazz grabbed the phantom spear with both hands and thrust it.

"Ayee! Ayee!" And a gabble of harsh sounds followed. Burton, having learned his native language, understood them.

"I am the Man-Who-Slew-The-White-Tooth! Die, Hairy-One-Who-Sleeps-All-Winter! Die, but forgive me! I must, I must! Die! Die!"

Burton spoke loudly. "Kazz! It's run away! The bear has run out of the hut! Besst is safe now!"

Kazz stopped thrusting the spear. He stood upright now, looking from side to side.

"Kazz! It's a few minutes later. Kazz! Besst has left. You're *in* the hut now! *Inside* it. You've nothing to fear! You've entered the hut, and there is nothing to be afraid of! But who else is in there with you?

"Kazz! You're in the hut a few minutes after you saw that Spruce had no mark on his forehead. Who else is in the hut with you?"

The Neanderthal had lost his fierce expression. Now he looked dully at Burton.

"Who? Why, Monat and Pete."

"Very good, Kazz. Now . . . who first spoke to you there?"

"Monat did."

"Tell me what he said to you. Tell me what Frigate said, too."

"Frigate never said anything. Just Monat."

"Tell me what he said . . . what he is saying."

"Monat says, 'Now, Kazz, you will remember nothing that took place in this hut. We will talk a minute and then we will leave. After you leave you will not remember going into the hut or leaving it.

Everything between that time will be a blank. If anyone should ask you about this time, you will say that you don't remember. And you will not be lying because you will have forgotten everything. Isn't that right, Kazz?' "

The Neanderthal nodded.

" 'Also, Kazz, just to make sure, you will not remember the first time I told you to forget that you had mentioned to me and Frigate that we had no marks. Do you remember that time, Kazz?' "

Kazz shook his head. " 'No, Monat.' "

He gave a drawnout sigh.

"Who sighed?" Burton said.

"Frigate."

It was evidently an expiration of relief.

"What else is Monat saying? Tell me what you are saying, too."

" 'Kazz, when I talked to you that first time, the time just after you had told Frigate and me that we had no signs, I also told you to tell me whatever Burton said about meeting a mysterious person. By that I mean someone who might call himself an Ethical.' "

Burton said, "Aah!"

" 'Do you remember that, Kazz?'

" 'No.'

" 'Of course not. I told you not to remember that. But I now tell you to remember it. Do you remember it, Kazz?' "

A silence of about twenty seconds followed. Then the Neanderthal said, " 'Yes, I remember now.'

" 'Very good, Kazz. Now, forget it again, though what I told you then still is a command. Isn't that right?'

" 'Yes, that's right.'

" 'Now, Kazz. Has Burton ever said anything to you about this Ethical? Or about anyone, man or woman, who claimed to be one of those who brought us back from the dead?'

" 'No, Burton-*naq* never told me anything like that.'

" 'But if, in the future, he does tell you, you will come to me at once and tell me. You will only do this, however, when no one else is around. Where no one can overhear us. Do you understand that?'

" 'Yes, I understand.'

" 'If for some reason I am not available, if you cannot get hold of me because I am dead or gone on a journey, you will tell Peter Frigate or Lev Ruach, instead of me. Do you understand?' "

Burton said, in a low voice, "Ruach, too!"

" 'Yes, I understand. I will tell Peter Frigate or Lev Ruach instead of you.'

" 'And you will tell them only when no one is around, where no one else can overhear you two. Understand?'

" 'Yes, I understand.'

" 'And you will not tell anyone else about this, you will only tell Frigate, Ruach, or myself. Understand?'

" 'Yes, I understand.'

" 'Very good, Kazz. That's fine. We will go now, and when I snap my fingers twice, you will not remember this or the first time. Understand?'

" 'Yes, I understand.'

" 'Kazz, you will also . . . oh, oh! Someone's calling for us! No time for an excuse now. Let's go!' "

Burton had to guess what this last remark meant. Monat must have been about to tell Kazz what he should say if anyone asked him what the conversation had been about. That was a lucky break for Burton. If Kazz had had a reasonable story, then Burton would never have become suspicious.

26

BURTON SAID, "SIT DOWN, KAZZ. MAKE YOURSELF COMFORTABLE. You sit there for a minute. I'm leaving. Monat will be coming in, and he will talk to you."

"I understand."

Burton walked out of the hut and stood for a minute. He should have posed as Monat when he first started the session. That might have overcome Kazz's resistance more quickly, and Burton would not have had to resort to the trickery of the bear and Besst.

He re-entered, and said, "Hello, Kazz. How are you?"

"I'm fine, Monat. How are you?"

"Great! Very well, Kazz. I'll take over from where your friend, Burton, left off. We'll go back to that first time I talked to you, just after you had noticed that Frigate and I had no marks on our foreheads. You now remember that time, Kazz, because I, Monat, tell you to do so.

"You will go back to the second after you had told Monat. Are you there?"

"Yes, I am there."

"Where are you, Monat, and Frigate?"

"We are near a grailstone."

"What day, or night, is that?"

"I do not understand."

"I mean, how many days was it after Resurrection Day?"

"Three days."

"Tell me what happened after you spoke to them about the lack of the mark."

Kazz, speaking in a monotone, described the events immediately after. Monat had said that he and Frigate wanted to speak to him privately. They had walked across the plain and gone into the hills. There, behind a giant irontree, Monat had fixed his eyes upon Kazz's. Without the use of any mechanical devices, without even informing Kazz what he was doing, Monat had hypnotized him.

"It was as if something dark flowed from him to me, something dark and overpowering."

Burton nodded. He had seen Monat demonstrate this power, this "animal magnetism" as it was known in Burton's time. He was a stronger mesmerist than Burton, which was one reason why Burton had never permitted the Arcturan to attempt hypnotizing him. In fact, Burton had taken precautions against getting caught unawares by Monat. In an elaborate self-hypnosis, he had told himself that he must never allow himself to be mesmerized by Monat. However, Monat could be powerful enough to break down that command, so Burton had been extremely cautious about being alone with him.

That forearming had been based on the fear that Monat might stumble across the time when he had been visited by the Ethical. That was Burton's secret, one he wanted no one to know. He had had no idea then, of course, that Monat was one of Them.

He wondered if Frigate was also an expert hypnotizer. The fellow had never given any indication that he was. However, he had refused to let Burton try mesmerism on him. His plea had been that he could not endure the thought of losing his self-control.

Kazz remembered that, during the course of the session, Monat had remarked to Frigate about the Neanderthal's ability to see the symbols.

" 'We never knew about that. We'll have to tell HQ as soon as we get a chance.' "

So, Burton thought, Monat and Frigate were in communication from time to time with the Ethicals. How did they manage that? Were prearranged landings of the flying machines, which Burton had once glimpsed, one method of communicating? Those machines which flickered into and out of visibility as they flew along?

Those two must have been watching him closely. That was one of the reasons the Mysterious Stranger had visited him at night during a storm. The Ethical must have known that Monat and Frigate were in Burton's party. But he had never mentioned them, had not put him on his guard.

Perhaps he had meant to do so, but he *had* been hurried. He'd said that the Ethicals were coming soon in their flying machines. And he had left abruptly. Even so, he surely would have mentioned so grave a matter. A few words would have warned him. Why had he not done so? Was it possible that he did not know that Monat and Frigate were with him? And Ruach, too. He must not forget Ruach.

Why had three agents been assigned to him? Wouldn't one have been enough? Also, why was one so conspicuous as the Arcturan given the job?

Whatever the reasons for this, the matter of the lack of signs on the heads of the three agents was more pressing. Evidently, Ethicals, first-order or second-order, did not have such marks. Now that they were aware that Neanderthals could observe this, they had made sure that Kazz would not say anything about it.

Moreover, Monat had then told Kazz that from that moment on he would see the marks on the foreheads of himself and his two colleagues.

Why had he not then installed a command that Kazz would see these signs on everybody who did not have them?

Perhaps he thought that it would not be necessary. The chances of running across other Neanderthals, never a numerous people, were slight. Still, it would have eliminated any exposures of agents from then on.

The explanation might be simple. Monat would have had to describe the marks of every agent in the valley. Inasmuch as there might be hundreds, or thousands, for all Burton knew, that would have been impossible.

Monat had not been too wrong in thinking that encounters with Neanderthals would be rare. In fact, Burton had never seen more than a hundred. All of these except Kazz and Besst had been passed by swiftly and at a distance during the day.

Yet, they had come across Besst.

He tried to recollect the exact circumstances under which she had been met. It was three years ago that they had come ashore at evening. This was an area populated largely by fourteenth-century A.D. Chinese and ancient Slavs. Besst was living with a Chinese, but she had made it evident from the first that she wished to go on the boat with Kazz. It was dark, so she would not have noticed anything unusual about Frigate and Monat—aside from the latter's being nonhuman, of course.

The two had gotten together and talked until late that night. When her hutmate had ordered her to come with him, she had refused. There was a tense moment when it looked as if the Chinese were going to attack Kazz. Discretion won. He realized that, though he was bigger than the Neanderthal, he was also much weaker. Though very short, Kazz's massive bones and muscles made him stronger than any but the most powerful of modern men. In addition, his brutal face was enough to scare anybody.

The two had gone aboard to spend the night together. Yet they must have gone to sleep before dawn. Could Monat have gotten to her then? Probably. Burton did not know how he had done it. But Besst had never said anything about Frigate's and Monat's marks.

Kazz finished his account of the session. It was short and what Burton had expected.

He sent Kazz after Besst, telling him to be very quiet. In a few minutes he was back with her. Burton told her he would satisfy her curiosity later. For the time being, would she let him hypnotize her? Sleepily, she agreed, and she sat down on the chair Kazz had occupied.

After telling her he was Monat, he took her back to the mesmerizing by Monat. As he had thought, it had been done after she and

Kazz had gone to sleep. Monat had simply described to her the marks which he had hypnotized her mate into seeing on the three agents' foreheads. Then he had ordered her to see the same marks. The whole process would have been done very quietly and quickly.

Monat and his colleague had been lucky. Before Kazz had encountered Spruce, he had seen two other people without the marks. However, the first time had been on Resurrection Day. He had called out to the man, asking him why he had no mark. The man had fled, probably not because he understood what Kazz was saying but because he had misunderstood the Neanderthal's intentions.

Later, after meeting Burton, Kazz had tried to tell him what he had seen, but neither could speak the other's language yet. And Kazz had simply forgotten about it in the days following, when they were all busy trying to survive.

The second person he'd seen lacking a mark was a woman, a Mongolian. This had happened at high noon, and the woman had just come out of The River, where she was bathing. Kazz had tried to talk to her, but her hutmate, who did have a mark on his head, had taken the woman away. Evidently, he was jealous. Once more, Kazz's intentions were misunderstood.

At that time, Burton and the others had been talking to the local headman in the council house. Kazz had stayed behind to watch their boat. After the woman had gone, Kazz was offered some drinks of lichen-alcohol by several people who wanted to talk to him. These had never seen a Neanderthal before, and the liquor was an inducement to get him to talk. Kazz, easily induced and seduced by free booze, was half-drunk by the time his crewmates returned. Burton had reproached him so harshly that Kazz had never again drunk while on guard duty.

He also forgot about the woman.

After bringing Besst out of the trance, Burton sat for a while in thought. Besst and Kazz shifted uneasily and gave each other wondering looks. Finally, he made a decision. There was no longer any use keeping them in the dark. Nor would he exclude Alice from now on. He owed the Stranger nothing, and the fact that he had not reappeared again could mean that he, Burton, had no reason to keep silent. Besides, though he was naturally secretive, he longed now to share his experiences.

Though he gave only a bare outline, he took over an hour. Both Besst and Kazz were amazed, and they had many questions. He held up his hand for silence.

"Later! Later! As of now, we must question them. The Arcturan's a much tougher customer, so we'll tackle Frigate first."

He told them what they must do. Kazz said, "But wouldn't it be best to knock out Monat and tie him up? What if he wakes up while we're getting Frigate?"

"I don't want to make any more noise than we have to. If Loghu and Alice hear us, we'll have a brouhaha."

"A what?"

"An uproar. Let's go."

The three of them made their way through the fog. Burton thought of some more questions he would ask Frigate. For instance, Monat, Frigate, and Ruach must have known that Spruce was an agent. There had been plenty of opportunity for them to talk to him while they had been grail slaves. And Monat had had opportunities after the revolt to hypnotize Kazz so he would see a mark on Spruce. Why had he not done that?

If Monat had not been able to get to Kazz after the revolt, he should then have told Spruce to leave the area at once. Or, at least, to wear a cloth around his head when conditions were favorable for seeing the mark.

Could Spruce not have known that they were his fellow agents? They might be so numerous that each was familiar only with a few others. But surely all would know of Monat.

He stopped, and drew in his breath.

The Mysterious Stranger had never said anything about having his own agents. Yet, he was a renegade, and he might have enlisted a few highly trusted people. Could Spruce have been one? And could Monat somehow have found this out? And so gotten rid of him by not telling him about Kazz's visual abilities?

That did not seem probable. If Monat had found out that Spruce was on the Stranger's side—and how would he ever be able to do that?—would he not then have hypnotized Spruce? That would enable him to identify the Stranger, supposing, of course, that Spruce knew who he was.

There was another possibility. Monat knew of Spruce's ability to kill himself by means of the sphere on his forebrain. Thus, he was not worried that Spruce would be forced to divulge any information at all.

Also, he may have used Spruce as a messenger. He would have given him some information to pass on when Spruce was resurrected at HQ—if HQ meant *headquarters*.

Monat had taken part in Spruce's inquisition. How amused he must have been at that. Also, it was Monat who had given Spruce some leading questions.

Had Spruce been prepared by Monat to give the answers he had made? Were they all lies?

If so, why should he lie? Why were all resurrectees kept in the dark?

It was quite possible that Spruce, acting on Monat's orders, had deliberately ensured that Kazz would notice him.

By then, the three had boarded the *Snark*. The Neanderthals stayed above. Burton felt his way to the cabin, down the companionway, and, counting the compartment doors, stopped outside Frigate's and Loghu's. He opened the door slowly and stepped inside. It was a very small space, just large enough to hold two bunks against the bulkhead and room to climb down from them. The bunk-chambers were the only places where any privacy was available. Even defecation was done in them, in the bamboo chamber pots which were stored in a rack to one side.

Frigate usually slept in the top bunk. Burton moved forward, his hand outstretched. He would wake him gently, whisper that it was his watch, and then he would follow him to the deck. There Kazz would knock him out, and he would be carried to the hut.

Since it would be impossible to keep him from killing himself once he was fully conscious, Burton had decided to try to mesmerize him as he was regaining his wits. It would be a chancy procedure, but he would have to try it. Frigate, unlike Spruce, might not be so willing to commit suicide now that there were no more resurrections.

However, Burton was not sure that the Ethicals' agents were not resurrected.

His fingertips felt the smooth sideboard of the bunk. They moved up onto the cloths that served as a mattress. They stopped.

Frigate was not in his bunk.

Burton felt along the cloths though he knew that nobody was on the bunk. They were warm. Then he stood for a minute. Had Frigate gone above to relieve himself because he did not want to awake Loghu? Or had he awakened early and decided to talk to his captain a few minutes before going on guard duty?

Or had he . . . ? Burton felt furious. Had he sneaked out of bed and now was with Alice?

Feeling ashamed of himself, he rejected that idea. Alice was honest. She would never betray him. If she wanted another lover, she would have said so. She would have told him and then left him. Nor did he believe that Frigate would ever do anything like that to him, though he may have contemplated it in his mind.

He bent down and reached out until he touched cloth. His fingers moved along, traced a curve—Loghu's breast under the cloth—and he backed out and closed the door.

Silently, his heart thudding so fast he could almost believe that it could be heard throughout the cabin, he moved to Monat's partition. His ear against the door, he listened. Silence. He straightened, opened the door, and felt into the upper bunk. Monat was not there, but he could be sleeping in the lower bunk. If so, his breathing was not audible.

His hand slid over unoccupied cloths.

Cursing softly, he groped back to the deck.

Kazz stepped out of the fog with his fist raised.

"*Wallah!* What's the matter?"

"They're both gone," Burton said.

"But . . . how could that be?"

"I don't know. Maybe Monat knew that something was wrong. He's the most sensitive person I've ever met; he can read your slightest expression, detect the feeblest nuance in your voice. Or perhaps he heard you wake up Besst, investigated, and guessed the truth. For all I know, he may have been listening to us outside the door of the hut."

"Neither Besst or me made any noise. We was as silent as a weasel sneaking up on a rabbit."

"I know. Look around. See if our launch is missing."

He met Kazz coming around the other way.

"The boats're all here."

27

BURTON ROUSED LOGHU AND ALICE. WHILE THEY DRANK HOT coffee, he outlined everything that had happened to him in connection with the Ethicals. They were stunned, but they kept silent until he had finished. Questions hailstormed him then, but he said that he would answer them later. It would be dawn shortly, which meant that they had to put their grails on the stone for breakfast.

Alice was the only one who had not said anything. It was evident from her narrowed eyes and tight lips that she was furious.

"I am sorry that I had to keep all this from you," Burton said. "But surely you can see how necessary it was? What if I told you everything and then the Ethicals grabbed you, as they did me? They could have read your mind and discovered that they had erred in thinking they had erased relevant portions of my memory."

"They didn't do so," she said. "Why should they have even thought of that?"

"How do you know they didn't?" he said. "You wouldn't remember it if they had done it."

That gave her another shock. Nevertheless, she did not speak again until after breakfast.

This took place in unusual weather. Normally, the sun quickly burned off the fog. The sky was clear the rest of the day in the tropical zone or until midafternoon in the temperate zones. In the latter, clouds quickly gathered, rain fell for fifteen minutes or so, and then the clouds disappeared.

This morning, however, black masses rolled between sun and earth. Lightning flickered as if chips of the bright sky above the clouds were falling through. Thunder was the muttering of a giant behind the mountains. A pale light spread over the land, staining it brownish-yellow. The faces around the grailstone looked as if a blight had settled upon them.

Kazz and Besst hunched down uneasily over their food and looked around as if they expected an unwelcome visitor. He muttered in his native tongue, "The-Bear-Who-Collects-The-Bad is walking."

Besst almost whined. "We must find a hut to hide in. It is not good to be near the water when he walks."

The others looked as if they were going to seek shelter, too. Burton stood up and said loudly, "One moment, please! I'm interested in finding out if any of you are missing a boat!"

A man said, "Why?"

"Two of my crew deserted last night, and it's possible that they stole a boat to get away."

Forgetting about the coming storm, the party scattered to look along the bank. Within a minute, a man reported that his dugout was gone.

"They're far away by now," Kazz said. "But did they go up or down The River?"

"If there was a signal system in this area, we could find out quickly enough," Burton said. "Unless, of course, they beached their boat and went into the hills to hide."

Alice said, "What do we do now, Dick? If we stay here to look for them, we'll not be able to get on the *Rex*."

Burton stifled the impulse to tell her not to point out the obvious to him. She was still simmering; no sense in making her boil again.

"Monat and Frigate can hole up today and sneak out tonight and steal another boat. It would be futile to try to catch them. No, we'll try to get aboard the paddlewheeler. But those two will come along some day, and when they do . . ."

"We'll tear them apart?" Kazz said.

Burton shrugged and spread his palms upward.

"I don't know. They've got the advantage. They can either drop dead on us or lie to us. Until we get to the tower . . ."

Alice spoke then, her eyes dark with accustomed reverie:

> *"If at his counsel I should turn aside*
> *Into that ominous tract which, all agree,*
> *Hides the Dark Tower. Yet acquiescingly*
> *I did turn as he pointed; neither pride*
> *Nor hope rekindling at the end descried,*
> *So much as gladness that some end might be.*
>
> *"For, what with my world-wide wandering,*
> *What with my search drawn out thro' years, my hope*
> *Dwindled into a ghost not fit to cope*
> *With that obstreperous joy success would bring—*
> *I hardly tried now to rebuke the spring*
> *My heart made, finding failure in its scope.*
>
> *"There they stood, ranged along the hillsides, met*
> *To view the last of me, a living frame*
> *For one more picture! in a sheet of flame*
> *I saw them and I knew them all. And yet*

Dauntless the slug-horn to my lips I set
And blew, 'Childe Roland to the Dark Tower came.' "

Burton grinned savagely. "Browning would have thought
. . . must think . . . that this world is even stranger than the setting of
his outré poem. I appreciate your sentiment, even if he said it first,
Alice. Very well, we will go to the Dark Tower."

"I don't know what Alice was talking about," Kazz said. "Anyway, just how're we going to get on that boat?"

"If King John has room for us, I'll offer him our treasure trove,
our free-grails. That should appeal even to the ungreediest heart."

"And if he doesn't have room?"

He was silent for a moment. That tickle in the back of his brain,
that feeling that he had overlooked some linkage between agents,
had returned while Alice was speaking. And now he saw, or thought
he saw, the means for scratching the itch, the kind of chain binding
the agents together.

How did they recognize each other? Monat was no problem; he
did not need identification. But what kind of secret signal would the
human agents use to identify each other?

If they possessed a Neanderthal's ability, they could see the
negative signal, lack of a sign, in their colleagues' foreheads.
Suppose, though, they did not have this ability? Spruce had been
surprised when he found out about Kazz's optical talent. Though he
had not said so, his manner had indicated that he had never heard of
such a thing. Evidently, machines were used to detect and translate
the symbols into whatever meaning they had. That would probably
be done in the PR bubble or whatever HQ was.

If, then, they could not see the symbols with the naked eye, they
would have another means of identification.

Suppose, just suppose, that there was a cutoff date. A period of
time at which no more people from Earth were resurrected, not, at
least, on this planet. According to Monat, Frigate, Ruach, and
Spruce, that cutoff date had been 2008 A.D.

What if that was not the true date? What if it were earlier than
2008 A.D.?

He had no idea what the true date would be, though he had never
met anyone, except the agents, who claimed to have lived past 1983
A.D. From now on, he would question every late-twentieth-centu-
rian he met. And if 1983 was the latest at which anybody had died,
then he would be fairly certain that that was the cutoff point.

So . . . perhaps the Ethicals had contrived a fiction which would
enable them to identify each other instantly. That was that they had
lived during 2008 A.D. And, of course, there would be a fixed story
about events from 1983, or whatever date it was, to 2008.

Which meant that perhaps it was untrue that the Arcturans had killed most of humanity in that year. The terrible slaughter might never have happened. In fact, anything he had heard about the years 1983-2008 might be a lie. Yet, there was Monat. He was not a Terrestrial. There was no reason to believe that he had not come from a planet of the Bear Watcher.

For the present, there was no way to explain his presence on The Riverworld.

Meanwhile, Burton had two means for catching an Ethical. Kazz was one; the 2008 story was another.

However—humanity lived not only in an *as-if* world, it was a *but-if* world, too—however, just possibly the agents had been recruited from a time past 1983. So, their stories could be true.

There were so many possibilities. For instance, how did he know that Monat, Frigate, and Ruach had told him the truth about what had happened to them when they were away from him? There was that incident when Frigate had claimed he had met the publisher who had cheated him on Earth. Frigate said he had gotten a long-delayed revenge by punching him on the nose.

There were bruises on Frigate, supposedly gotten during the fight with Sharkko and his gang. Those could have come from conflict with others, though. Frigate's nature was such that he dreaded violence, physical or verbal. He might fantasize revenge, but he would never carry it out.

Suppose, just suppose, that the agents adopted disguises based on real life Terrestrials. What if there was an actual Peter Jairus Frigate somewhere on this planet? The pseudo-Frigate could be pretending to be the man who had had such an intense interest in Burton's life. That would be one means of getting close to Burton, of making sure that Burton would let him attach himself to Burton. After all, it would be hard for any man to be indifferent to his biographer, to a person who seemed to worship him.

Yet, why would it be necessary for an agent to adopt such a disguise? Why not make up one from whole cloth?

Perhaps it was not necessary, it was just easier, more convenient. As for an agent encountering the person he was pretending to be, that was highly unlikely.

There were so many potentialities, so many questions to be answered.

Alice said, "Dick! What's the matter?"

He came out of his reverie with a start. Everybody except his crew and the man whose boat had been stolen had fled. The man looked as if he would like to ask for reparations but was hesitating because he had no one to back him up.

A wind was whipping the waves of The River and ruffling the thatches of the huts. The *Snark* thumped against the bumpers of its dock. The light had gone from brownish-yellow to pale grey, making the faces around him even more ghastly. Across the water lightning flashed its fiery tooth, and thunder bellowed like a bear in a cave. Kazz and Besst were obviously longing for him to give the word to look for shelter. The others were only somewhat less nervous.

"I was thinking," he said. "You asked what we'd do if King John doesn't have room for us? Well, monarchs have means for making room if they wish to do so. And if he refuses, I'll find some way to get aboard. I'm not going to be stopped by anything or anybody!"

Lightning struck nearby, cracking as if the back of the world had broken. Kazz and Besst led the headlong flight for the nearest building.

Burton, standing in the heavy rain that had immediately followed the bolt, laughed at them.

He shouted, "On to the Dark Tower!"

28

IN THE DREAM, PETER JAIRUS FRIGATE WAS GROPING THROUGH A fog. He was naked; somebody had stolen his clothes. He had to get home before the sun rose and burned the fog off and exposed him to the derision of the world.

The grass was wet and scratchy. After a while he got tired of walking on the shoulder of the road, and he stepped onto the asphalt pavement. Now and then, as he trudged along, the fog would thin a little, and he could see the trees to his right.

Somehow, he knew that he was far out in the country. Home was a long way off. But if he walked fast enough, he could make it before dawn. Then he'd have to get into the house without waking his parents. The doors and windows would be locked, which meant that he'd have to throw pebbles against the second-story window in the back. The rattle might wake his brother, Roosevelt.

But his brother, though only eighteen, was already a heavy drinker, a skirt chaser, roaring around on his motorcycle with his sideburned, leather-jacketed dese-and-dem pals from the Hiram Walker Distillery. This was Sunday morning, and so he'd be snoring away, filling the small attic bedroom he shared with Peter with stinking whiskey fumes.

Roosevelt was named after Theodore, not Franklin Delano, whom his father hated. James Frigate abominated "the man in the White House" and loved *The Chicago Tribune*, which was delivered on the doorstep every Sunday. His oldest son loathed the editorials, the whole tone of the paper, except for the comics. Ever since he had learned to read, he'd eagerly awaited every Sunday morning, right after the cocoa, pancakes, bacon, and eggs, for the adventures of Chester Gump and his pals in quest of the city of gold; Moon Mullins; Little Orphan Annie and her big Daddy Warbucks and his pals, the colossal magician Punjab and the sinister The Asp, and Mr. Am, who looked like Santa Claus, was as old as the Earth, and could travel in time. And then there was Barney Google and Smilin' Jack and Terry and the Pirates. Delightful!

And what was he doing thinking about those great comic-strip characters while walking naked along a country road in dark, wet-with-evil clouds? It wasn't difficult to figure out why. They brought a sense of warmth and security, happiness even, his belly filled with his mother's good cooking, the radio turned on low, his father sitting in the best chair reading the opinions of "Colonel Blimp." Peter would be sprawling on the living room floor with the comics page spread out before him, his mother bustling around in the kitchen feeding his two younger brothers and his infant sister. Little Jeannette, whom he loved so much and who would grow up and go through three husbands and innumerable lovers and a thousand fifths of whiskey, the curse of the Frigates.

All that was ahead, fading now from his mind, absorbed by the fog. Now he was dwelling in the front room, happy . . . no, it too faded away . . . he was outside the house, in the backyard, naked and shivering with the cold and the terror of being caught without his clothes and no way of explaining why it happened. He was throwing pebbles against the window, hoping their rattle wouldn't wake up his little brothers and sister sleeping in the tiny bedroom below and to one side of the attic bedroom.

The house had once been a one-room country schoolhouse outside the mid-Illinois town of Peoria. But the town had grown, houses sprang up all around it, and now the city limits were a half a mile to the north. A second story and indoor plumbing had been added sometime during the growth of this area. This was the first house he had lived in in which there had been an indoor toilet. Somehow, this once-country house became the farmhouse near Mexico, Missouri. Here he, at the age of four, had lived with his mother, father, and younger brother and the family of the farmer who'd rented out two rooms to the Frigates.

His father, a civil and electrical engineer (one year in Rose Polytechnic Institute in Terre Haute, Indiana, and a diploma from the International Correspondence School) had worked for a year at the generating plant in Mexico. It was in the farmyard behind the farmhouse that Peter had been horrified on realizing that chickens ate animals and he ate chickens that ate animals. That had been the first revelation that this world was founded on cannibalism.

That was not right, he thought. A cannibal was a creature that ate its own kind. He turned over and passed back into sleep, vaguely aware that he had been half-waking between segments of this dream and mulling over each before passing on to the next. Or he had been redreaming the entire dream each time. In one night he would have the same dream several times. Or a dream would recur a number of times over several years.

The series was his specialty in dreams or in fiction. At one time, during his writing career, he had twenty-one series going. He'd completed ten of them. The others were still waiting, cliff-hangers all, when that great editor in the skies arbitrarily canceled all of them.

As in life, so in death. He could never—never? Well, hardly ever—finish anything. The great uncompleted. He'd first become aware of that when, a troubled youth, he had poured out his torments and anxieties onto his college freshman advisor, who also happened to be his psychology teacher.

The professor, what was his name? O'Brien? He was a short, slim youth with a fiery manner and even fierier red hair. And he always wore a bow tie.

And now Peter Jairus Frigate was walking along in the fog and there was no sound except for the hooting of a distant owl. Suddenly, a motor was roaring, two lights shone faintly ahead of him, then brightly, and the motor screamed as he screamed. He dived to one side, floating, slowly floating, while the black bulk of the automobile sped slowly toward him. As he inched through the air, his arms flailing, he turned his head toward it. Now he could see, beyond the glare of its lights, that it was a Duesenberg, the long low, classy roadster driven by Cary Grant in the movie he's seen last week, *Topper*. A shapeless mass sat behind the wheel, its only visible features its eyes. They were the pale-blue eyes of his German grandmother, his mother's mother, Wilhelmina Kaiser.

Then he was screaming because the car had swerved and headed directly toward him and there was no way he could escape being hit.

He woke up moaning. Eve said sleepily, "Did you have a bad . . . ?" and she subsided into mumbles and a gentle snoring.

Peter got out of bed, a short-legged structure with a bamboo frame and rope supports for a mattress made of cloths magnetically attached around treated leaves. The earthen floor was covered with attached cloths. The windows were paned with the ising-glasslike intestinal membrane of the hornfish. Their squares shone faintly with the reflected light from the night sky.

He stumbled to the door, opened it, walked outside, and urinated. Rain still dripped from the thatched roof. Through a pass in the hills, he could see a fire blazing under the roof of a sentinel tower. It outlined the form of a guard leaning on the railing and looking down The River. The flames also shone on the masts and rigging of a boat he had never seen before. The other guard wasn't on the tower, which meant that he would be down by the boat. He'd be questioning the boat's skipper. It must be all right, since there were no alarm drums beating.

Back in bed, he considered the dream. Its chronology was mixed up, which was par for dreams. For one thing, in 1937, brother Roosevelt had been only sixteen. The motorcycle, the distillery job, and the peroxided blondes were still two years away. The family wasn't even living in that house anymore. It had moved to a newer, larger house a few blocks away.

There was that amorphous, sinister dark mass in the car, the thing with his grandmother's eyes. What did that mean? It wasn't the first time he had been horrified by a black hooded thing with Grandma Kaiser's almost colorless blue eyes. Nor the first time he'd tried to figure out why she appeared in such horrendous guise.

He knew that she had come from Galena, Kansas to Terre Haute to help his mother take care of him just after he'd been born. His mother had told him that his grandmother had also taken care of him when he was five. He didn't remember, however, ever seeing her before the age of twelve, when she had come to this house for a visit. But he was convinced that she had done something awful to him when he was an infant. Or it was something which had *seemed* awful. Yet she was a kindly old lady, though inclined to get hysterical. Nor did she have any control at all over her daughter's children when they were left in her care.

Where was she now? She'd died at about seventy-seven after a long and painful siege of stomach cancer. But he'd seen photographs of her when she was twenty. A petite blonde whose eyes looked a lively blue, not the washed-out red-veined things he remembered. The mouth was thin and tight, but all the adults in her family were grim lipped. Those brown-toned photogravures displayed faces that looked as if they'd had a very tough time but would never break under the strain.

The Victorians, judging by their photographs, were a hard-nosed, stiff-spined lot. His German grandma's family had been made of the same stern stuff. Persecuted by their Lutheran neighbors and the authorities because they had converted to the Baptist church, they left Oberellen, Thuringia for the land of promise. (Peter's family on both sides had always opted for the religion of the minority, usually a somewhat crank religion. Maybe they were trouble seekers.)

After years of moving from one place to another, never finding a single street paved with gold, after backbreaking labor, soul-searing poverty, and the deaths of many children and finally of parents and grandparents, the Kaisers had made it. They had become well-to-do farmers near, or owners of machine shops in, Kansas City.

Was it worth it? The survivors said that it was.

Wilhelmina had been a pretty, blue-eyed blonde of ten when she had come to America. At eighteen she had married a Kansan twenty years older than she, probably to escape poverty. It was said that old Bill Griffiths was part-Cherokee and that he had been one of Quantrill's guerrillas, but there was a lot of malarkey in Peter's family on both sides. They were always trying to make themselves look better, or worse, than they really were. Whatever old Bill's past, Peter's mother never wanted to talk about it. Maybe he was just a horse thief.

Where was Wilhelmina now? She'd no longer be the wrinkled,

bent old women he'd known. She'd be a good-looking, shapely wench, though still with the vacuous blue eyes and still speaking English with a heavy German accent. If he should run across her, would he recognize her? Not likely. And if he did, what could he find out from her about the traumas she'd inflicted on her infant grandson? Nothing. She wouldn't remember what would have been minor incidents to her. Or, if she did, she surely wasn't going to admit that she had ever mistreated him. If indeed the dark deed had ever been done.

During a brief stint of psychoanalysis, Peter had tried to break through the thick shadows of repressed memory to the primal drama in which his grandmother played such an important role. The effort had failed. More extended attempts in dianetics and scientology had resulted in zilch also. He had kept on sliding past the traumatic episodes, like a monkey on a greased pole, on past his birth and into previous lives.

After being a woman giving birth in a medieval castle, a dinosaur, a prevertebrate in the postprimal ocean, and an eighteenth-century passenger in a stage coach going through the Black Forest, Peter had abandoned scientology.

The fantasies were interesting, and they revealed something of his character. But his grandmother evaded him.

Here, on The Riverworld, he had tried dreamgum as a weapon to pierce the thick shadows. Under the guidance of a guru, he had chewed half a stick, a heavy load, and dived after the pearl hidden in the depths of his unconscious. When he woke from some horrible visions, he found his guru, battered and bloody, unconscious on the floor of the hut. There was no mystery about who had done this deed.

Peter had left the area after making sure that his guide would live without serious aftereffects. He could not stay in the area nor could he feel anything but guilt and shame whenever he saw his guru. The fellow had been very forgiving, had, in fact, been willing to continue the sessions—if Peter was tied up during them.

He could not face the violence that he felt dwelt deep within him. It was this fear of violence in himself that made him so afraid of violence in others.

The fault, dear Brutus, lies not in the stars but in our lousy genes. Or in failure of one's conquest of one's self.

The fault, dear Brutus, is in our fear of knowing our self.

The next, almost inevitable, scene in this drama of recollection was the seduction of Wilhelmina. How easy to think of this fantasy as potentially real, since it was possible that he would meet her. After some mutual questioning, they would discover that they were grandmother and grandson. Then the long talk with her telling what had happened to her daughter and her husband (Peter's father) and her grandchildren and great-grandchildren and great-great-grandchildren. Would she be horrified when she found that a great-granddaughter had married a Jew? Undoubtedly. Anyone of rural stock born in 1880 was bound to be deeply prejudiced. Or what if he told her that his sister had married a Japanese? Or that a brother and a first cousin had married Catholics? Or that a great-granddaughter had converted to Catholicism? Or that a great-grandson had become a Buddhist?

On the other hand, The Riverworld might have changed her attitudes, as it had done to so many. However, many more were as psychologically fossilized as when they had lived on Earth.

To get on to the fantasy.

After a few drinks and long talk, bed?

Rationally, one could not object to incest here. There would be no children.

But when did people ever think rationally in such situations?

No, the thing to do would be to say nothing about their relationship until after they'd been to bed.

The construction crumbled then. To reveal that would make her grievously ashamed. It would be cruel. And no matter how much he wanted revenge, he could not do that to her. To anyone. Besides, it would be revenge for some act that he only thought might have been committed. Even if it had occurred, it might have been something only a child would have thought terrible. Or something misinterpreted in his infant mind. Or something that she, being a product of her times, would have thought only natural.

It was exciting to think about laying your grandmother. But, in reality, it just wouldn't happen. He was sexually drawn only to intelligent women, and his grandmother had been an ignorant peasant. Vulgar, too, though not in an obscene or irreligious way. He remembered when she was eating with the family on a Thanksgiving holiday. She'd sneezed, the snot had landed on her blouse, and she had wiped it off with her hand and deposited it on her skirt. His father had laughed, his mother had looked stricken, and he had lost his appetite.

There went the whole fantasy, dissolved in disgust.

Still, she might have changed.

To hell with it, he told himself, and he turned on his side and went to sleep.

29

DRUMS BEAT, AND WOODEN TRUMPETS BLEW. PETER FRIGATE WOKE
up in the midst of another dream. It was three months after Pearl
Harbor, and he was an air cadet at Randolph Field being chewed out
by his flight instructor.

The lieutenant, a tall young man with a thin moustache and big
feet, was almost as hysterical as Grandma Kaiser.

"The next time you turn left when I tell you to turn right, Frigate,
I'm bringing us in right now, cutting the goddamn flight, and I'm
refusing to go up with you! You can get an instructor who doesn't
give a shit if his dumb student kills him or not! Jesus Christ, Frigate,
we coulda been killed! Didn't you see that plane on your left! Are
you suicidal! That's all right with me, but don't take me and two
others with you! And do it on your own time, off the field, and not
with government property! What the hell is the matter with you,
Frigate! Do you *hate* me!"

"I coudn't hear you, sir," Peter said. Though he was sweating in
the heavy flight clothes in the warm room, he was shivering and he
felt a painful urge to urinate. "I just can't seem to hear through those
tubes."

"There's nothing wrong with the tubes! I could hear you all right!
And there's nothing wrong with your ears! You had a medical
checkup only two weeks ago, didn't you? All you pissy-assed
cadets are examined when you transfer here! Aren't you?"

Peter nodded and said, "Yes sir, just like you were."

The lieutenant, his face red, eyes bugging, said, "What do you
mean by that? Are you saying I was a pissy-assed cadet?"

"No, sir," Peter said, feeling the sweat pour out from his
armpits. "I would never say 'pissy-assed' in reference to you, sir."

"What would you say?" the lieutenant said, almost screaming.

Peter looked from the corners of his eyes at the other cadets and
instructors. Most of them were paying no attention or pretending not
to. Some were grinning.

"I would never mention you," Peter said.

"What? Because I'm not worth mentioning, is that it? Frigate,
you *try* me! I don't like your attitude on the ground or in the air. But
to get back to the subject despite all your efforts to avoid it! Why in

hell can't you hear me when I can hear you? Is it because you don't want to hear me?

"Well, that's dangerous, Frigate! It's frightening, too. You scare the hell out of me! Do you know how many of those stubby-winged BT-12's spin in every week? Those sons of bitches have got a builtin spin, cadet. Even when an instructor tells his ape-brained student to spin it deliberately, and he's got his hand on the stick, ready to take over, the sons of bitches sometimes still keep on spinning!

"So I sure as hell don't want to tell you to turn right and have you think I'm telling you to spin her and catch me off guard. You could have us twenty feet deep in the ground before I could take to the chute! Okay, what is the matter with your ears?"

"I don't know," Peter said miserably. "Maybe it's wax. Wax builds up in my ears. It's a family trait, sir. I have to have the wax blown out every six months."

"I'll blow out more than wax out of another place than your ears, mister! Didn't the doctor check out your ears? Sure he did! So don't tell me it's wax! You just don't want to hear me! And why? God knows why! Or maybe you hate me so much you don't care if you die just so you take me with you? Is that it?"

Peter would not have been surprised to see the lieutenant foaming at the mouth.

"No, sir."

"No, sir, what?"

"No, sir, to any of that."

"You mean you're denying everything? You did turn left when I said turn right, didn't you? Don't tell me I'm a liar!"

"No, sir."

The lieutenant paused, then said, "Why are you smiling, Frigate?"

"I didn't know I was," Peter said. That was true. He was really in mental and physical distress. So why had he smiled?

"You're crazy, Frigate!" the lieutenant shouted. A captain, standing behind him, frowned. But he made no move to interfere.

"I don't want to see you again, Frigate, until you have a written testimonial from a doctor that your ears are okay. Do you hear that?"

Peter nodded.

"Yes, sir, I hear you."

"You're grounded until I get that report. But I want it at flight time, tomorrow, when I take you up again, God help me!"

"Yes, sir," Peter said and almost saluted. That would have been another excuse for the instructor to ream him out. Saluting was not done in the flight room.

He looked back as he checked in his parachute. The captain and

the lieutenant were talking earnestly. What were they saying about
him? That he ought to be washed out?

Maybe he should be. He really couldn't hear his instructor. Only
half of the lieutenant's frenzied gabble came through intelligibly on
the tubes. It wasn't because of wax. Or the high altitude. Or
anything physically wrong with his hearing.

It would be years later before he knew that he just did not want to
hear the lieutenant.

"He was right," Peter said.

"Who was right?" Eve said. She was sitting up in bed, leaning
on one arm, looking down at him. Her body was covered with thick
varicolored towels tabbed together, and the hood still shrouded her
face.

Peter sat up and stretched. The inside of the hut was dark; the
drums and bugles along the bank sounded faintly. Nearby, a neighbor was banging on his fish-skin-and-bamboo drum as if he were
trying to wake up the whole world.

"Nothing."

"You were groaning and mumbling."

"Earth is always with us," he said, and he left her to figure that
out for herself. With him he took the thunder mug to the neighborhood deposit hut which was about a hundred paces away. There he
greeted a score of men and women, all on the same task. They
dumped the contents of the pots into a large bamboo wagon. After
breakfast, this would be hauled out of the building by a team of men
into the foothills to the base of a mountain. There the excrement
would be treated to make potassium for black gunpowder. Frigate
worked two days a month there and four days on the sentinel towers.

A grailstone was just on the other side of the hill on which their
hut stood. Usually, he and Eve took their grails to it. This morning,
however, he wanted to talk to the crew of the boat that had arrived
during the night. Eve would not object if he went by himself, since
she had to finish stringing necklaces of hornfish vertebrae,
varicolored helical bones in demand as ornaments. She and Frigate
traded them for tobacco and liquor and flints. Frigate also made
boomerangs and, occasionally, dugouts and canoes.

Frigate carried his grail with his left hand and his yew-wood flint-
tipped spear in the other. A fish-skin belt around his waist held a
sheath containing a chert axe. A quiver of arrows, flint tipped and
fletched with thin, carved bones, was slung over one shoulder. A
bow of yew, wrapped in bamboo paper, was strapped to the quiver
to protect it from the early-morning moisture.

The little state of which he was a citizen, Ruritania, was not at
war or under threat of war. The law requiring that all have their
weapons handy was a hangover from the old days of turbulence.
Obsolete laws had almost as hard a time dying here as on Earth.

Social inertia was everywhere, though its resistance to change varied from state to state.

Frigate walked among the huts spread out over the plain. Hundreds, covered like him from foot to head against the chill, joined him. About a half-hour after the sun rose, they began to shed their cloths. While eating breakfast, Frigate looked for new faces. There were fifteen, all from the newly arrived schooner, the *Razzle Dazzle*. They sat in a group, eating and talking to those interested in the newcomers. Peter sat down by them to watch and listen.

The captain, Martin Farrington, also known as the Frisco Kid, was a muscular man of medium height. His handsome face looked Irish. His hair was reddish-bronze and curly; his eyes, large and deep blue; his chin, strong. He talked energetically, smiling often, cracking jokes. His Esperanto was fluent but not perfect, and it was evident that he preferred English.

The first mate, Tom Rider, also known as Tex, stood about 5.08 centimeters or 2 inches shorter than Frigate's 1.8 meter or 6 feet.

He was what the pulp magazine writers of Frigate's youth called "ruggedly handsome." Not as muscular as the captain, he moved quickly though gracefully with a confidence that Frigate envied. His dark hair was straight and if his tanned skin had been two shades browner, he could have passed for an Onondaga Indian. His Esperanto was perfect, but, like Farrington, he was pleased to find some English-speakers in the crowd. His voice was a pleasant baritone which combined a Southwestern drawl with a Midwestern pronunciation.

Frigate learned much about the crew just by listening to their uninhibited account of themselves. They were the usual motley collection met on the larger boats that wandered up and down The River. The captain's woman was a nineteenth-century South American Caucasian; the first mate's, a citizen of the Roman city of Aphrodita of the second century A.D. Frigate remembered that its ruins had been discovered by archaeologists in Turkey sometime around the 1970's.

Two of the crew were Arabs. One was Nur el-Musafir (The Traveler). The other had been the wife of a captain of a South Arabian ship which had traded with the southwest African empire of Monomotapa in the twelfth century A.D.

The Chinese crewman had ended his Earthly life by drowning when Kubla Khan's invasion fleet was destroyed by a storm enroute to Japan.

There were two eighteenth-centurians, Edmund Tresillian, a Cornishman who lost a leg in 1759 during the capture of Hood's *Vestal* of the French *Bellona* off Cape Finisterre. Pensionless, and with a wife and seven children, he was reduced to begging. Caught stealing a purse, he died in prison of a fever while waiting for his trial. The second man, "Red" Cozens, had been a midshipman on the *Wager*, a rebuilt Indiaman merchant accompanying Admiral Anson's flotilla on its voyage around the world. It had been wrecked off the coast of Patagonia. After innumerable sufferings and hardships, part of its crew had gotten to civilization, where the Spanish government of Chile imprisoned them for a while. However, poor Cozens had been shot and killed by a Captain Cheap a few days after the wreck in the mistaken belief that he was a mutineer.

John Byron, the poet's grandfather, also a midshipman then, had criticized Cheap for this in *The Narrative of the Honourable John Byron (Commodore in a Late EXPEDITION round the WORLD) Containing An Account of the Great Distresses Suffered by Himself and His Companions on the Coast of Patagonia, from the Year 1740, till their Arrival in England, 1746*, etc., London, 1768.

Frigate had owned a first edition of this book, in which he had found a description of an animal encountered by Byron which had to be a giant sloth.

He would have liked to have run across Byron. The little man had to have been incredibly tough to survive his experiences. Later, he had become an admiral, nicknamed "Foul Weather Jack" by his sailors. Just about every time he put out to sea, his fleet was hit by a bad storm.

Other interesting crew members were a late-twentieth-century Rhode Island millionaire and yachtsman; an eighteenth-century Turk, a bos'n's mate who had died of syphilis, a common sailor's disease then; and Abigail Rice, Earthly wife of an early-nineteenth-century second mate on a New Bedford whaler. Binns, the yachtsman, and Mustafa, the Turk, were obviously in love with each other.

As Peter would find out later, Cozens, Tresillian, and Chang shared Abigail Rice. This made Frigate wonder what she had been doing while her husband was spending two to three years chasing whales. Perhaps nothing she shouldn't have been doing. Perhaps she had been so sexually starved on Earth that she had exploded here.

And then there was Umslopogaas. Pogaas for short. He was a Swazi, son of a king of that South African nation which had been enemies of the great Zulu people. He had lived during the expansion of the British and the Boers and the conquests of the bloody military genius, Shaka. On Earth, he had killed twelve warriors in duels; here, at least fifty.

He would have been unnoticed by history, despite his fighting prowess, if he had not happened to be attached in his old age to the mission of Sir Theophilus Shepstone. With Shepstone was a young man, H. Rider Haggard, who had been much attracted by the stately figure and the tall stories of the old Swazi. Haggard was to immortalize Umslopogaas in three novels, *Nada the Lily*, *She and Allen*, and *Allan Quatermain*. However, he made the Swazi a Zulu, which must have disturbed his model.

Now Pogaas lounged near the ship, leaning on a long-handled war-axe of flint. He was tall and slim and his legs were extraordinarily long. His features were not Negroid but Hamitic, thin lipped, hawk nosed, and high cheekboned. He seemed friendly enough, but there was something about his bearing that told all but the most insensitive that he was not to be trifled with. He was also the only person on the crew who did not help handle the ship. His specialty was fighting.

Frigate was tinkled pink when he discovered the identity of this man. Imagine that! Umslopogaas!

After talking to various crew members, Frigate went back to a spot near the two officers. From what he heard, they were in no hurry to get to any particular place. The captain did, however, comment that he would like to get to the headwaters of The River some day. Which was, to say, in a hundred years or so.

Frigate finally spoke up, asking the captain and Rider about their Terrestrial origins. Farrington said he'd been born in California, but he gave no birthdate or place. Rider said he'd been born in Pennsylvania in 1880. Yes, he had spent a lot of time, most of his life, in fact, in the West.

Frigate swore softly. He had thought the two looked familiar. However, they wore their hair longer than on Earth and the lack of Terrestrial clothes gave them a different appearance. What Rider needed was a big white ten-gallon hat and a flashy pseudo-Western coat and breeches and a pair of ornamented cowboy's boots. And a horse to sit upon.

As a child, Frigate had seen him in just such garments and on a horse. That had been during a parade preceding a circus—Sells and Floto? Never mind. Frigate had stood with his father on Adams Street, just south of the courthouse, and waited eagerly for his favorite Western film hero to ride by. And so the hero had, but, being drunk, he had fallen off his horse. Unhurt, he had swung into the saddle again, riding off to the mingled laughter and cheers of the crowd. He must have sobered up after that, for he gave a great demonstration of riding and roping in the Wild West Show following the main events.

At that time, Frigate regarded drunkards as moral lepers and thus should have been completely disillusioned about Rider. But his worship of Rider was so intense that he was willing to forgive him. What a little prig he'd been!

Frigate was well acquainted with Farrington's portrait since he'd seen it so many times in biographies and on the back of dust jackets. Frigate had begun reading his works at the age of ten, and when he was fifty-seven he had contributed a foreword to a collection of Farrington's fantasies and science fiction.

For some reason, both his heroes were traveling under false names. He, Peter Frigate, was not going to expose them—not unless he had to. No, he wouldn't do it even then, but if he were forced to threaten them with exposure, he would do so. He'd do almost anything to get aboard the *Razzle Dazzle*.

After a while, the Frisco Kid announced that he and Tex would now interview anyone who'd like to sign on as a deckhand. Two folding chairs were set up on the end of the dock, and the "employment" line formed in front of the seated officers. Frigate immediately got into the line. Three men and a woman were ahead of him. This gave him a chance to listen to the questioning and to decide what he would tell his prospective employers.

30

THE FRISCO KID, SITTING ON A FOLDING BAMBOO CHAIR AND smoking a cigarette, ran his eyes up and down Frigate.

"Peter Jairus Frigate, heh? American. Midwest. Right? You look strong enough, but what's your nautical experience?"

"Not much on Earth," Peter said. "I used to sail a small boat on the Illinois River. But I've done a lot here. I sailed on a large single-masted catamaran for three years and I put in a year on a two-masted schooner like yours."

That was a lie. He'd only shipped on the two-master for three months. But that was enough for him to know, literally, the ropes.

"Hm. Did these ships make short local trips or were they on long voyages?"

"Long ones," Frigate said. He was glad he hadn't referred to the vessels as boats. Some sailors were very touchy about the distinction between "boats" and "ships." For Frigate, anything on a river was a boat. But Farrington was a seafaring man, even if there were no more seas.

"In those areas," he added, "the wind was usually from up-River. So we were sailing close-hauled most of the time."

"Yeah, anybody can sail with the wind," Martin Farrington said.

"*Why* do you want to sign up?" Rider asked suddenly.

"Why? I'm fed up with life here. Rather, I'm dissatisfied with doing the same old thing day after day. I . . ."

"You know how it is on a ship," Farrington said. "It's cramped, and you spend most of your time with just a few people. And it's pretty much the same old thing day after day."

"I know that, of course," Frigate said. "Well, I'd like to travel to the end of The River, for one thing. The catamaran I was on was going there, but it got burned during an attack by slavers. The schooner was sunk by a dragonfish while we were helping some locals fish for it. It was Moby Dick and the *Pequod* all over again."

"You were Ishmael?" Rider said.

Frigate looked at him. Rider was supposed to have been able to quote great chunks of Shakespeare, to be well read indeed. But that could have been Hollywood publicity crap.

165

''You mean, was I the lone survivor? No, six of us got to shore. It was scary, though.''

''Was . . . ?''

Farrington stopped, cleared his throat, and looked at Rider. Rider raised thick, dark eyebrows. Farrington was evidently considering how to rephrase the question.

''Who were the captains of these two crafts?''

''The catamaran captain was a Frenchman named DeGrasse. The schooner captain was a rough son-of-a-bitch named Larsen. A Norwegian of Danish birth. He'd been captain of a sealer, I believe.''

Nothing he said about Larsen was true. But Peter couldn't resist testing Farrington's reaction.

The captain's eyes narrowed, then he smiled. He said slowly, ''Was Larsen nicknamed *Wolf?*''

Peter kept his face blank. He wasn't falling for that trap. If Farrington thought that he was trying to tell him circuitously that he recognized him, Farrington would not take him on.

''No. If he had a nickname, it was 'Bastard.' He was about six and a half feet tall and very dark for a Scandinavian. His eyes were as black as an Arab's. Did you know him?''

Farrington relaxed. He dubbed out his cigarette on a baked-clay ashtray, and lit up another. Rider said, ''How good are you with that bow?''

''I've been practicing for thirty years. I'm no Robin Hood, but I can shoot six arrows in twenty seconds with reasonable accuracy. I've studied the martial arts for twenty years. I never look for a fight and I avoid one if it's possible. But I've been in about forty major actions and a lot of minor ones. I've been badly woulded four times.''

Rider said, ''When were you born?''

''In 1918.''

Martin Farrington looked at Rider, then said, ''I suppose you saw a lot of movies when you were a kid?''

''Didn't everybody?''

''And what about your education?''

''I got a B.A. in English literature with a minor in philosophy and I was a compulsive reader. Lord, how I miss reading!''

''Me, too,'' Farrington said.

There was a pause. Rider said, ''Well, our memories of Earth get dimmer every day.''

Which meant that if Frigate had seen Rider in the films and Farrington on the dust jackets of books, he did not remember them. The captain's question about his education might, however, have a double interest. He would want a crewman who could talk intelligently about many matters. On Earth, Farrington's forecastle companions had been brutal and illiterate, not exactly his soulmates. So, for that matter, had been most of the people he knew until he had gone to college.

"We seem to have about ten in all to interview," Farrington said. "We'll make our choice after we've talked to everybody. We'll let you know before noon."

Peter wanted desperately to be chosen, but he was afraid that too much eagerness might put them off. Since they were, for some reason, traveling under pseudonyms, they might be wary of someone who was trying too hard to sign on. Why, he did not know.

"One thing we forgot," Rider said. "We don't have room for more than one hand. You can't take your woman along. Is that okay?"

"No problem."

"You can take turns with Abigail," Rider said. "If you don't mind sharing with three others. And if she likes you, of course. But she hasn't shown many antipathies so far."

"She's a luscious woman," Peter said. "But that sort of thing doesn't appeal to me."

"Mustafa kind of likes you," Farrington said, grinning. "He's been eyeing you."

Frigate looked at the Turk, who winked, and he blushed.

"That appeals even less."

"Just make that plain, and you won't be bothered by him or Binns," Farrington said. "I'm no homo, but I saw a lot of buggery. Any man who sails under the mast has; every ship, naval or commercial, has been a viper's nest of sodomy since Noah. Those two are real he-men, aside from their lack of interest in the fair sex. And they're damn good sailors. So just tell them to back off. If, that is, we accept you. But I don't want any bitching about being hard up. You can catch up when we go ashore, and if we lose a man you can get a woman for your bunkmate. She has to be a good sailor, though. Everyone pulls his weight on this ship."

"Abigail's looking more appealing by the second," Frigate said.

Farrington and Rider laughed, and Frigate moved on.

For a while, he stood by the dock area. This was a shallow bay which had been hacked with much labor out of the bank. Stone cut from the base of the mountains had been carried down here and used to line the shore. Wooden docks had been extended from the bank, but these held mainly small catboats, lugboats, and catamarans. Two giant rafts with masts were tied up here, too. These were used for dragonfishing. A number of warcanoes, capable of holding forty men each, were beached near the rafts. Canoes and rowboats were putting out now for fishing. By noon, The River would be heavily salted with small and large boats.

The *Razzle Dazzle* was too large to fit within the piers. It was anchored near the mouth of the bay behind a breakwater of large black rocks. It was a beautiful ship, long and low, built of oak and pine. There wasn't a nail in it, and the pegs had been cut with flint. The sails were made of treated outer skin of the dragonfish, so thin they were translucent. The oaken figurehead was a full-busted mermaid holding a torch.

The ship was a wonder, and the wonder was how its crew had managed to avoid having it taken from them. Many had been murdered for much lesser craft.

Feeling anxious, he walked past Farrington and Rider. The interviews were by no means over. Word had gotten around, and now there were about twenty men and ten women waiting in line. If this continued, the questioning might take all day. There was nothing he could do about it, so he shrugged and went back home. Eve was gone, which was just as well. There was no need to tell her what he was doing until he found out if he was leaving. If he was turned down, he'd say nothing to her.

Part of his duty as a Ruritanian citizen was to assist in alcohol-making. He might as well work off a half-day today. The labor would help keep him from worrying. He walked through the passes between the hills until these gave out. There were four more hills to climb, each increasingly higher. The trees were thicker here; the huts, fewer. Presently he was on top of the highest hill, which was at the base of the mountain. Its smooth stone ran straight up for an estimated 1228 meters or about 6000 feet. A waterfall thundered about 91 meters or 100 yards away, spilling thousands of liters a minute into a pool. From this, the water ran in a broad channel which would thread a course through the hills to The River.

Frigate passed by the fires, the wooden, glass, and stone equipment, and the odor of alcohol. He climbed up a bamboo ladder until he was on a platform placed against an area of stone from which lichen had not yet been removed. He reported to a foreman, who gave him a chert scraper. The foreman took from a rack a pine stick with Frigate's initials cut into it. It bore alternating horizontal and vertical lines, the former indicating the days he'd worked, the latter the number of months.

"Next year you'll be using a stick to scrape off the stuff," the foremen said. "We'll be saving the chert and flint for weapons."

Peter nodded and went to work.

In time, the supply of flint would be exhausted. Technology on The Riverworld would go backward. Instead of progressing from a wooden to a stone age, humanity would reverse the procedure.

Frigate wondered how he was going to get his flint-tipped weapons out of the state. If he sailed on Farrington's craft he would, according to the law, have to leave his precious stones behind.

The time put in by Frigate on this work was estimated by the foreman. Except for the sun, there were few clocks of any type. The little glass available was used in the alcohol-making process, so there were not even hourglasses. For that matter, the sand used to make the glass had been imported from a state 800 kilometers down-River. That had cost Ruritania several boatloads of tobacco and booze and piles of dragonfish and hornfish skins and bones. The tobacco and alcohol had been contributed by the citizens from their grails. Frigate had given up smoking and drinking for two months during this time of sacrifice. When it was over, he continued his abstinence from smoking, trading his cigarettes and cigars for whiskey. But, as had happened on Earth and here, he had slipped back into the arms of Demon Nicotine.

He worked hard, scraping off the thick green-blue plant growth from the black rock and stuffing it into the bamboo buckets. Others lowered the buckets on ropes to the ground, where their contents were dumped into vats.

Shortly before noon, he knocked off for the lunch hour. Before going down the ladders, he looked out over the hills. Far below, the white hull of the *Razzle Dazzle* shone in the bright sun. Somehow, he was going to be on it when it up-anchored.

Peter walked back to the hut, noted that Eve wasn't there, and went on down to the plain. The line of interviewers did not look any shorter. He passed along the edge of the plain where its short grass abruptly stopped and the long grass of the hills began. What made for the line of demarcation? Were there chemicals in the hill soil that halted the encroachment of plain grass? Or was it vice versa? Or both? And why?

The archery range was about half a kilometer south of the dock area. He practiced shooting at a target of grass on a bamboo tripod for about thirty minutes. Then he went to the gymnasium area and ran sprints and made long jumps and engaged in judo, karate, and spear-fighting for two hours. At the end of the time, he was sweating and tired. But he was bursting with joy. It was wonderful to have a twenty-five-year-old body, the tiredness and feebleness of middle and old age gone, the aches and pains, the fat, the hernia, the ulcer, the headaches, the long-sightedness, all no more. Replacing it, the ability to run or swim swiftly and far, to feel sexual desire every night (and a good part of the day).

The worst thing he had done on Earth was to get a desk job as a technical writer at the age of thirty-eight and then at fifty-one, to become a fulltime fiction writer. He should have stayed in the steel mill. It was monotonous work, but while his body was handling the hot, heavy work, his mind was busy dreaming up stories. At night he would read or write.

It was when he had started to sit on his butt all day that he had begun drinking so heavily. And his reading had diminished, too. It was too easy after working on a typewriter eight hours a day to sit in front of the TV all evening and swill Bourbon or Scotch. TV, the worst thing that had happened to the twentieth century. After the atom bomb and overpopulation, of course.

No, he told himself, that wasn't fair. He didn't have to be a boob before the tube. He could have used the self-discipline which enabled him to write to turn the set off except at highly selected times. But the lotus-eater syndrome had gotten him. Besides, there were programs on TV which were really excellent, both entertaining and educational.

Still, this world was good in that there were no TV's or automobiles or atom bombs or gross national production or paychecks or mortgages or medical bills. Or air or water pollution and almost no dust. And nobody gave a damn about communism or socialism or capitalism, because they didn't exist. Well, that was not quite true. Most states did have a sort of primitive communism.

31

HE WALKED TO THE RIVER AND PLUNGED IN, CLEANING OFF THE sweat. Then he trotted along the bank (no huts allowed within 30 meters of it) to the dock area. He hung around until dinnertime, talking to friends. In between, he watched the two from the *Razzle Dazzle*. They were still interviewing, though lubricating their throats with frequent drinks. Wasn't that line ever going to end?

Just before it was suppertime, Farrington stood up and announced in a loud voice that he was taking no more applications. Those still in the line protested, but he said that he'd had enough.

By then the head of Ruritania, "Baron" Thomas Bullitt, had appeared with his councillors. Bullitt had had some small claim to fame in his day. In 1775 he had explored the Ohio River falls by the area which would become Louisville, Kentucky. Commissioned by the William and Mary College of Virginia, he surveyed the area. And thereafter disappeared from history. His aide-de-camp, Paulus Buys, a sixteenth-century Dutchman, was with him. Both invited the crew of the *Razzle Dazzle* to a party in their honor that night. The main reason for the invitation was to hear the adventures of the crew. River-dwellers loved gossip and exciting tales, since their fields of entertainment were limited.

Farrington accepted, but said that six of the crew would have to stay on the ship as guards. Frigate followed the crowd to a large roofed-over area, the Town Hall. Torches and bonfires drove back the darkness, and an orchestra played while the local variety of square-dancing began. Frisco and Tex stood around for a while, talking to the chief statesmen and their wives and close friends. Frigate, as one of the *hoi polloi*, was not admitted to the sacred circle. He knew, however, that the event would become much less formal later on. While he was standing in line to get the free liter of pure alcohol allowed per person at such functions, he was joined by his hutmate.

Eve Bellington waved at him and then got into line twelve persons behind him. She was tall, full figured, black haired, blue eyed, a Georgia peach. Born 1850, died two days before her one hundred first birthday. Her father was a wealthy cotton planter with a distinguished record as a major in the Confederate cavalry. The Bellington plantation was burned down during Sherman's march through Georgia, and the Bellingtons had become penniless. Her father had then gone to California and found enough gold to buy a partnership in a shipping firm.

Eve had loved being wealthy again, but she still had not forgiven him for leaving her mother and herself to struggle through the occupation and the early years of Reconstruction.

During her father's absence, Eve and her mother had lived with her father's brother, a handsome man only ten years older than Eve. He had raped her (without too much resistance, Eve admitted) when she was fifteen. When her mother had found that her daughter was pregnant, she had shot the uncle in the legs and the genitals. He survived a few years as a crippled eunuch in prison.

Mrs. Bellington then moved to Richmond, Virginia, where her husband joined them. Eve's son by the uncle grew up to be tall and handsome, dearly beloved by his mother. After a furious quarrel with his uncle-grandfather, he left to seek his fortune in the West. A letter from Silver City, Colorado, was the last Eve ever heard from him. He'd disappeared somewhere in the Rockies, according to a report sent by a detective.

Her mother had died in a fire, and her father had died of a heart attack while trying to rescue her mother. Eve's first husband died of cholera shortly thereafter, and before she was fifty she had lost two more husbands and six of her ten children.

Her life was that of a heroine of a novel on which Margaret Mitchell and Tennessee Williams might have collaborated. She didn't think it was very funny when Peter had told her that.

After thirty-plus years on The Riverworld, Eve had gotten over her prejudice against niggers and her hatred of bluebellies. She had even fallen in love with a Yankee. Peter had never told her that his great grandfather had been with an Indiana regiment on that "infamous" march with Sherman. He hadn't wanted to strain her affection.

Peter moved on up the line and received the alcohol in his soapstone mug. He mixed one part of alcohol with three parts of water in a bamboo bucket and walked back to talk to Eve, who was still in line. He asked her where she had been all day. She replied that she had been wandering around, thinking.

He didn't ask her what her thoughts had been. He knew. She was trying to think of a way to break off their relationship without pain. They'd been drifting apart for some months, their love suddenly and unaccountably cooled. Peter had done some thinking on this subject himself. But each was waiting for the other to take the initiative.

Peter said he would see her later, and he pushed through the noisy crowd toward Farrington. Rider was on the dance floor, whooping and whirling with Bullitt's woman.

Peter waited until the captain was through telling about his adventures in the 1899 Yukon gold rush. Farrington's tale, which involved losing some of his teeth from scurvy, somehow became a hilarious experience.

Peter said, "Mr. Farrington, have you made up your mind yet?"

Farrington paused, his mouth open to launch on another story. His reddened eyes blinked. He said, "Oh, yes! You're . . . ah . . . um . . . named Frigate, right? Peter Frigate. The one who's read a lot. Yes, Tom and I've made up our minds. We'll announce our choice some time during the party."

"I hope it's me," Peter said. "I really want to go with you."

"Enthusiasm counts for a great deal," Farrington said. "Experience counts for even more. Put the two together, and you have a fine jack-tar."

Peter breathed deeply and took the plunge.

"This uncertainty is getting me down. Could you at least tell me if I've been eliminated? If I have been, I can drown my sorrow."

Farrington smiled. "It really means that much to you? Why?"

"Well, I do want to get to the end of The River."

Farrington cocked his eyebrows. "Yeah? Do you expect to find the answers to all your questions there?"

"*I don't want millions, I want answers to my questions*," Peter said. "That's a quotation from a character in Dostoyevsky's *Brothers Karamazov*."

Farrington's face lit up.

"That's great! I'd heard of Dostoyevsky but I never had a chance to read him. I don't think there was an English translation of his books in my time. At least, I never ran across any."

"Nietzsche admitted that he'd learned a lot about psychology just from reading the Russian's novels," Peter said.

"Nietzsche, heh? You know him well?"

"I've read him in both English and German. He was a great poet, the only German philosopher who could write in anything but waterlogged prose. Well, that's not fair, Schopenhauer could write stuff that wouldn't put you to sleep or give you a nervous breakdown while you were waiting for the sentence to end. I don't go along with Nietzsche's conception of the Ubermensch, though. *Man is a rope across an abyss between animal and superman*. That may not be the exact quotation; it's been a hell of a long time since I read *Thus Spake Zarathustra*.

"Anyway, I do believe that man is a rope between animal and superman. But the superman I'm thinking of isn't Nietzsche's. The real superhuman, man or woman, is the person who's rid himself of all prejudices, neuroses, and psychoses, who realizes his full potential as a human being, who acts naturally on the basis of gentleness, compassion, and love, who thinks for himself and refuses to follow the herd. That's the genuine dyed-in-the-wool superman.

"Now, you take the Nietzschean concept of the superman as embodied in Jack London's novel *The Sea Wolf*."

Peter paused, then said, "Have you read it?"

Farrington grinned. "Many times. What about Wolf Larsen?"

"I think he was more London's superman then Nietzsche's. He was London's idea of what the superman ought to be. Nietzsche would have been appalled by Larsen's brutality. However, London did kill him off with a brain tumor. And I suppose that London meant to show by this that there was something inherently rotten about Larsen as superman. Maybe he meant to tell the reader that. If he did, it went over the heads of most of the literary critics. They never got the significance of Larsen's manner of death. Then, too, I think London was also showing that man, even superman, has his roots in his animal nature. He's part of Nature, and no matter what his mental attainments, no matter how much he defies Nature, he can't escape the physical facts. He is an animal, and so he's subject to disease, such as brain tumors. *How are the mighty fallen*.

"But I think that Wolf Larsen was also, in some respects, what Jack London would have liked to be. London lived in a brutal world, and he thought that he had to be a superbrute to survive. Yet, London had empathy; he knew what it was to be one of the people of the abyss. He thought that the masses could find relief from their sufferings, and realize their human potential, through socialism. He fought for it all his life. At the same time, he was a strong individualist. This conflicted with his socialism, and when it did, his socialist beliefs lost out. He wasn't any Emma Goldman.

"In fact, his daughter Joan criticized him for that in her study of his life."

"I didn't know that," Farrington said. "She must have written it after I died. Did you know much about her, what happened to her after London died, how she died?"

"I knew a London scholar who knew her well," Peter said.

Actually, the scholar had only corresponded with her a little and had met her briefly. Peter didn't mind exaggerating if it would get him a berth on the ship.

"She was a very active Socialist. She died in 1971, I think. Her book about her father was very objective, especially considering that he had divorced her mother for a younger woman.

"Anyway, I think that London wanted to be a Wolf Larsen because that would have made him insensitive to the world's woes. A man who doesn't feel for others can't be hurt himself. At least, he thinks he can't. Actually, he's hurting himself.

"London may have realized this and was, in fact, trying to put this idea across. At the same time, he wished to be a Larsen, even if this meant being frozen inside, that is, a superbrute. But writers have countercurrents in their psychic sea, as all humans do. That's why, when the critics have done with them, great writers are still enigmas. *When skies are hanged and oceans drowned, the single secret will still be man.*"

"I like that!" Farrington cried. "Who wrote that?"

"e.e. cummings. Another line of his that's a favorite of mine is: *Listen! There's a hell of a good universe next door . . . Let's go!*"

Peter thought that he might be pouring it on too thick. Farrington, however, seemed to be enjoying it.

Once Frigate was on the ship, he could bring up subjects which might anger and would certainly irritate Farrington. For instance, the man's knowledge of Nietzsche had been gotten mostly from dialogs with a friend, Strawn-Hamilton. He had apparently made some attempt to read the philosopher in English. But he had been so taken by the poetic phrases and the slogans that he had not taken in the full philosophy. He had picked what he liked from Nietzsche and ignored the rest—as Hitler had done. Not that Farrington was any Hitler.

What was it his daughter had said? " 'The glad perishers,' 'the Superman,' 'live dangerously!—these were more potent than wine.' "

As for Farrington's knowledge of socialism, he had not read anything of Marx's except *The Communist Manifesto*. But, as his daughter had said, ignoring Marx was a common practice among American Socialists then.

There were many other things to discuss—and contemn. London had wanted socialism only for the benefit of the Germanic peoples. He firmly believed that men were superior to women. Might made right. And he was not, in one sense of the word, a true artist. He wrote only for money, and if he had enough money would have quit writing. At least he had claimed he would. Frigate doubted this. Once a writer, always a writer.

"Well," Peter said, "whatever else can be said against London, Fred Lewis Patton probably had the final word. He said it was easy to criticize him, easy to deplore him, but impossible to avoid him."

Farrington liked that even more. But he said, "Enough of London, though I would like to meet him some day. Listen. Your idea of the superman sounds a lot like the ideal man of the Church of the Second Chance. It sounds even more like that of one of my crew, you know, the little Arab, though he isn't really an Arab. He's a Spanish Moor, born in the twelfth century A.D. He's not a Chancer, though."

He pointed to a man Frigate had seen among the crew of the *Razzle Dazzle*. He was standing in the center of a circle of Ruritanians, holding a drink and a cigarette. His speech seemed to be amusing; at least those around him were laughing. He was about 163 centimeters or a little less than 5 feet 5 inches tall, thin but with a suggestion of wiry strength, very dark, and big nosed. He looked like a young Jimmy Durante.

"Nur-ed-din el-Musafir," Farrington said. "Nur for short."

Frigate said, "In Arabic that means Light-of-the-Faith the-Traveler."

"You know Arabic?" Farrington said. "I never could get the hang of any foreign language except Esperanto."

"I picked up a lot of words from Burton's *Arabian Nights*."

He paused. "Well, what about it? Am I eliminated?"

Farrington said, "Yes and no." He laughed at Frigate's puzzled expression, and he clapped him on the shoulder.

"Can you keep your mouth shut?"

"Like a Trappist monk."

"Well, I'll tell you, Pete. Tom and I had picked out that big Kanaka there." He pointed at Mauï, a giant Marquesan, looking very Polynesian in a white cloth around his waist and a big dark-red bloom in his thick, black, curly hair.

"He was top's'l man in a whaler and then a harpooner for thirty years. He looks like he'd be a hellcat in a fight. Tom and I agreed that he was easily the best qualified. But he doesn't know anything about books, and I need educated people around me. That may sound snobbish, but so what?

"I'll tell you now. I just changed my mind. You're signed up—as far as I'm concerned. No, wait a minute! Don't look so happy. I have to talk to Tom about this. You wait. I'll be right back."

He plunged among the dancers, caught Rider by the hand, and dragged him off protesting to one side. Peter watched them talking. Rider looked at him several times but did not seem to be arguing.

Peter was glad that he had not had to play his trump card. If he hadn't been chosen, he would have told the two that he knew their true identities. What would have happened then, he couldn't guess. The two had some good reason to go under fake names. Perhaps they would have rushed off, leaving him behind if he had threatened to expose them. Or perhaps they would have taken him along, just to keep his mouth shut, and then thrown him overboard far up The River.

Possibly Farrington had caught on to what he was doing. He must have wondered why a man so familiar with London's works would not recognize him. In which case, Farrington would have decided that Frigate was playing some kind of game. He would go along with it until they were well up The River and then find out just what he was up to.

However, Peter did not think he was in any danger of being killed. Neither Farrington mor Rider were murderers. Still, if some changed for the better on this world, others changed for the worse. And he had no idea how deep and desperate this game was.

Rider came over, shook his hand, and told him he was welcome aboard. A few minutes later, Farrington stopped the music and announced his choice of the new deckhand. By then, Peter had taken Eve outside and given her the news.

Eve was quiet for a while. Then she said, "Yes, I knew you were trying to get on that ship. It's not easy to keep a secret here, Peter. I do feel bad, though mostly because you hadn't told me you were going to go away."

"I tried to get hold of you," he said. "But you had gone off without telling me where."

Eve began to cry. Peter's eyes were moist. But she wiped the tears, sniffled, and said, "I'm not grieved because you're leaving me, Pete. I'm full of sorrow because our love died. I once thought that it would last forever. I should have known better, though."

"I'm still fond of you."

"But not fond enough, is that it? Of course it is. I'm not blaming you, Peter. I feel the same way. It's just that . . . I wish we could have gone on feeling like we first did."

"You'll find someone else. At least, we didn't part with hatred."

"It would have been better that way. It's bad enough when you love each other but can't get along. But to have love just die out, cold! I can't stand indifference."

"You've stood a lot more than that," he said. "If we'd still been in love, I would've stayed here or I would've tried to get them to take us both."

"And then you would've resented me. No, this may not be the best way, but it's the only way."

He pulled her to him to kiss her, but she gave him her cheek.

"Goodbye, Peter."

"I won't forget you."

"A lot of good that'll do us," she said, and she walked away.

Peter went back under the roof. People crowded around to congratulate him. He didn't feel happy. Eve had upset him, and he felt uncomfortable when he was the focus of public attention. Then Bullitt was shaking his hand.

"We'll be sorry to see you go, Frigate," he said. "You've been a model citizen. However, there is one thing."

He turned to the sergeant-at-arms next to him and said, "Mr. Armstrong, please confiscate Mr. Frigate's weapons."

Peter did not protest, since he had sworn to give them up if he quit Ruritania. However, he had not given his word not to steal them back. Early that morning, while it was still dark, he did just that.

He told himself that he had put in too much labor making the weapons to give them up. Besides, he had been wounded once in the service of this state. Ruritania owed him those weapons.

He had not gotten more than a kilometer up The River when he felt like going back and surrendering the weapons. That fit of honesty lasted for a day, and then he was cured.

Or he thought that he was. The recurring dream came back again. This time it progressed past the point where he was standing naked outside the house. He threw pebbles against the window of the bedroom but repeated casts failed to wake Roosevelt. He went around trying the doors and windows, and when he got to the front door, he found it unlocked. He crept in through the front room, into the small kitchen, and he took the two steps needed to get to the door opposite the bathroom. This led up a steep stairway to the attic, a section of which had been made into a tiny bedroom. He would have to go slowly, walking on the ends of the steps. They squeaked abominably if he stepped in their middle.

It was then that he saw that the doors to his parents' bedroom and the younger children's were open. Moonlight came in. (Never mind that it had been dawn just as he opened the front door. This was a dream.) By its bright light he saw that his parents' big old-fashioned brass bed was empty. And so was his little sister's. He looked around the corner and saw that the bunkbeds of Mungo and James, Junior were also deserted.

Nor was Roosevelt in his bed.

In a panic, he looked out the back window. The doghouse in the backyard was empty.

Everybody, even the dog, had gone off without a word.

What nameless crime had he committed?

32

"THE TRAINING BLIMP WILL BE COMPLETED WITHIN A MONTH," Firebrass said. "Jill Gulbirra is the most experienced aeronaut by far, so she'll take charge of the training. In fact, I'm making her captain of the trainer. How about that, Jill? If you can't be commander of the big ship, you will be unchallenged chief honcho of the little one. Don't ever say I never did anything for you."

The other men offered her their congratulations, though some did so sourly. Cyrano seemed genuinely delighted, and if he had not been aware of her dislike for being touched, would doubtless have embraced her tightly and kissed her. On impulse, Jill pulled him to her and gave him a quick hug. After all, he was trying to make up for his offensive behavior on the Riverbank.

Twenty minutes later, she, Firebrass, Messnet, Piscator, and ten engineers began working on the blueprints for the big airship. The specifications had been determined during three weeks of hard work, usually twelve to fourteen hours a day. Instead of drawing lines on paper, however, they made blueprints on the cathode-ray tube of a computer. This was much faster, mistakes or alterations were erased quickly, and the computer itself double-checked the proportions. Of course, the computer had to be programmed first, and Jill participated in this. She loved this sort of work. It was creative and gave her a chance to play with mathematical relations.

Nevertheless, it did cause nervous tension. To relieve this and to stay in good physical shape, Jill fenced for two hours almost every day. Sword exercise here was not what it had been on Earth. The light, supple foil was discarded for the heavier, stiffer rapier. Moreover, every point of the body was a target, requiring that the fencers wear padded garments on their legs.

"We are not playing now," Cyrano told her. "You will be learning to fence for more than just points. The time may come when you will be striving in deadly earnest to keep your opponent from running you through while you try to pierce him from front to back."

She had been an excellent fencer. A great teacher, an Olympic champion, had told her that she could become a top contender in world competition if she would devote enough time to training. That had been impossible since her job required too much time away from the fencing courts. But when she had a chance to practice, she had taken it. She loved fencing; it was in some respects a very physical form of chess, which she also loved.

It was a joy to take a blade in hand again and to relearn all the long-unused, but not quite forgotten, skill. It was an even greater joy to find that she could beat most of her male opponents. Though she looked awkward, once she had gripped the handle of the rapier, she became all grace and liquid speed.

There were two men she could not master. One was Radaelli, the Italian master, author of *Istruzione per la scherma di spada a di sciabola*, published in 1885. The other, the indisputable champion, was Savinien Cyrano de Bergerac.

Jill was surprised at this. For one thing, fencing in his time had not yet developed into a fine art. It was not until near the end of the eighteenth century that the art neared its apex of technique. Cyrano had died in the middle of the seventeenth century before the foil had been invented, when men fought, often to the death, with techniques somewhat primitive, if spectacular. The Italians had put together the basic structure of modern swordplay by the early seventeenth century, but not until the beginning of the nineteenth century had the techniques reached the ultimate.

Thus Cyrano had established a reputation as the greatest swordsman of all times without having to compete with the more sophisticated fencers of a later age. Jill had believed that his reputation had been wildly exaggerated. After all, no one knew if the famous incident of the Porte de Nesle was true or not. No one except the Frenchman himself, and he would not talk about it.

However, he had learned all later refinements from Radaelli and Borsody. Within four months of starting his education, he was steadily outscoring his mentors. In five months, he was unbeatable. So far, at least.

Though rusty at first, Jill soon gained polish and began to give him a better battle. Never once, however, did she win more than one point of the total five within the six-minute limit of a match. And he always made four points before she got one. This led her to believe that he was giving her the one point to soften the defeat. Once, after a match in which she became furious because of her frustration, she accused him of patronizing her.

"Even if I were in love with you and desired very much to keep from hurting your feelings," he said, "I would not do *that!* It would be dishonest, and while it is said that all is fair in love and war, it is not so for me. No, you have gotten your points fairly because of your quickness and skill."

"But if we were playing for keeps," she said, "with unblunted points, you would have killed me every time. You always strike first.''

He raised his mask and wiped his forehead. "True. But surely you are not thinking about challenging me to a duel? You are still not angry with me are you?''

"About that incident on the bank? No. Not about that.''

"About what, then, if I may be so bold to ask?''

She would say nothing then, and he would raise his eyebrows and shrug his shoulders in a completely Gallic manner.

Cyrano *was* better than she. No matter how much she practiced, no matter how hard her determination to best him, because he was a man, because she did not like to lose to anybody, male or female, she always lost. Once, when she had jeered at his ignorance and superstitions and so had made him furious (she had done it on purpose), he had attacked her with such vigor that he had touched her five times in one and a half minutes. Instead of losing his head, he had become even more a being of cold fire, moving with certitude and swiftness, doing everything exactly right, one hundred percent anticipatory of her every movement.

It was she who was humiliated.

Rightfully so, she told herself, and she apologized, though it was a double humiliation to do so.

"I was terribly wrong to sneer at your lack of knowledge of science and at your mistaken beliefs,'' she said. "It is not your fault that you were born in 1619, and I should not have taunted you with that. I did so just to make you so mad I'd get an edge on you. It was a rotten thing to do. I promise not to do it again, and I most abjectly beg your pardon. I did not really mean it.''

"Then you said those nasty vicious things merely as a trick?'' he said. "A verbal device to gain points? There was nothing personal in those so-cutting remarks?''

She hesitated a moment, then said, "I have to be honest. My main purpose was to make you lose your head. But I was not so cool myself. At the moment, I did feel that you *were* an ignorant simpleton, a living fossil. But that was my own anger speaking out in me.

"Actually, you were far ahead of your time. You rejected the superstitions and the barbarisms of your time, as far as anybody is able to reject his culture. You were an exceptional man, and I honor you for being that. And you'll never hear such words from me again.''

She hesitated again, then said, "But is it true that you repented on your deathbed?''

The Frenchman's face became red. He grimaced and said, "But yes, Ms. Gulbirra, I did indeed say that I was sorry for my blasphemies and my unbelief and I asked the good God for His pardon. I, who had been a violent atheist since the age of thirteen! I, who hated the fat, smug, oily, stinking, ignorant, hypocritical, parasitical priests! And their unfeeling, merciless, cruel God!

"But you do not know, you who lived in a freer and more permissive age, you do not know the horrors of hellfire, of eternal damnation! You cannot know what it was to have the fear of hell soaking you, drowning you! It was taught us from earliest childhood, ground into our flesh, our bones, our deepest mind!

"And so, when I knew for sure that I was dying from a combination of that filthy disease with the lovely bucolic name of syphilis and a blow on the head from that beam, fallen accidentally or dropped by an enemy of mine, and I who only wanted to love all mankind, and womankind, too . . . where was I?

"Ah, yes, knowing for sure that I was to die, and with the terrors of the devils and of eternal tortures swarming around me, I gave in to my sister, the toothless bitch and withered nun, and my good, too good friend, Le Bret, and I said, yes, I repent, I will save my soul, and you may rejoice, dear sister, dear friend, I will probably go to purgatory, but you will pray me out of it, won't you?

"Why not? I was frightened as I had never been in all my life, and yet, and yet, I did not wholly believe that I was destined for damnation. I had some reservations, believe me. But then, it could not hurt to repent. If Christ was indeed available for salvation, not costing a centime, mind you, and there was a heaven and a hell, then I would be a fool not to save my worthless skin and invaluable soul.

"On the other hand, if all was emptiness, nothingness, once one had died, what had I to lose? I would make my sister and that superstitious but kind-hearted Le Bret happy."

"He wrote a glowing panegyric of you after you died," she said. "It was his preface to your *Voyage to the Moon,* which he edited two years after you died."

"Ah! I hope he did not make me out to be a saint!" Cyrano cried.

"No, but he did give you a fine character, a noble if not quite saintly one. However, other writers . . . well, you must have had many enemies."

"Who attempted to blacken my name and reputation after I was dead and couldn't defend myself, the cowards, the pigs!"

"I don't remember," she said. "And it doesn't actually matter now, does it? Besides, only scholars know the names of your detractors. Unfortunately, most people only know you as the romantic, bombastic, witty, pathetic, somewhat Don-Quixotish hero of a play by a Frenchman written in the late nineteenth century.

"There was a belief for a long time that you were insane by the time you had written *The Voyage to the Moon* and *The Voyage to the Sun.* That was because your books were so heavily censored. By the time the churchly Grundies had slashed your texts, much of it made no sense. But the text was eventually restored as much as possible, and by the time I was born, an unexpurgated text had been published in English.''

"I am happy to hear that! I knew from what Clemens and others said that I had become a literary Olympian, if not a Zeus at least a Ganymede, a cupbearer in the ranks of the exalted. But your sneering remark that I was superstitious hurt me very much, mademoiselle. It is true, as you observed, that I believed that the waning moon did suck up the marrow from the bones of animals. Now you say that that is sheer rot. Very well, I accept that. And I was wrong, along with millions of others of my time and God knows how many before my time.

"But this was a minuscule, a harmless error. What did it matter, what injury did it do to anyone, to have this misconception? The superstition, the grave error, that really harmed people, many millions of human beings, I assure you, was the stupid, barbarous belief in sorcery, in the ability of human beings to wreak evil through spells, chants, black cats, and the enlistment of devils as allies. I wrote a letter against that ignorant and vicious belief, that social system, rather. I contended that the grotesque legal sentences and the savagely cruel tortures and executions inflicted upon insane or innocent people in the name of God and the battle against Evil were themselves the essence of evil.

"Now, it is true that this letter I speak of, *Against Sorcerers,* was not published while I was alive. With good reason. I would have been tortured and burned alive. It was, however, circulated among my friends. It did show that I was not as you made me out to be. I was ahead of my time in many respects, though I was not, of course, the only person in that unhappy situation.''

"I know this," she said. "And I apologized once. Would you have me do it again?''

"It is not necessary," he said. His broad smile made him look handsome, or at least attractive, despite his large nose.

Jill picked up her grail by its handle and said, "Just about dinnertime.''

Jill knew something about the man called Odysseus, having heard occasional references. He had appeared without notice, seemingly from nowhere, when Clemens' and King John's forces were battling invaders who wanted to seize the meteorite ore. He had killed the enemy leader with a well-placed arrow, worked havoc among the other officers, and so had given the defenders the advantage they needed for victory.

Odysseus of Ithaca claimed to be the historical Odysseus on whom Homer's mythical character was based. He was one of the host who had fought before the walls of Troy, though he stated that the real Troy was not where the scholars said it was. Its location was elsewhere, much further south on the coast of Asia Minor.

Jill, first hearing about this, had not known whether to believe that the man was truly Odysseus or not. There were so many impostors on the Riverworld. But there was one thing that made her think that he might actually be the historical Ithacan. Why should he say that Troy VIIa, which even the archaeologists and Hellenists of her day had said was the true Ilion, was not the genuine site? Why would he claim that the historical Troy was some place else?

Whatever the reason, he was no longer around. He had disappeared as mysteriously as he had appeared. Agents sent to track him down had failed. Firebrass had continued to search for him after Clemens left on the *Mark Twain*. One of the searchers, Jim Sorley, had finally found some trace of the Greek, though it showed only that he had not been murdered by John's men.

Jill had wondered several times why Odysseus had volunteered to fight for Clemens' side. Why would a stranger who had seemingly blundered onto the battle pick out one force and risk his life for it? What had he to gain, especially since it seemed that he had known none of the participants on either force? She had once asked Firebrass about this, and he had said that he just did not know. Sam Clemens might be able to enlighten her, but he had never volunteered a word on the subject.

Firebrass had added, "However, Odysseus may have been here for the same reason that Cyrano and I were. We wanted to get on the paddlewheeler so we could get to the polar sea."

She thought it was strange that no one had thought of building a dirigible until shortly before the second riverboat was completed. Why take decades traveling to the arctic region on a surface vessel when an airship could get there in a few days?

Firebrass said, grinning, "Just one of those mysteries of life. Man, pardon me, humanity, sometimes can't see the nose on his own face. Then somebody comes along and holds up a mirror to him."

"If mankind had a nose like mine," Cyrano said, "he would never have that trouble."

In this case the person with the mirror had been August von Parseval. On Earth he had been a major in the German Army, and he had also designed airships for a German company. His type of dirigible was used by both the German and the British governments between 1906 and 1914.

Shortly before the *Mark Twain* was ready to leave Parolando, von Parseval had come along. He was amazed that no one had suggested that a *Luftschiff* would be a faster means of transportation than a boat.

After Firebrass had mentally kicked himself for this oversight, he had hastened to Clemens, taking the German with him.

Surprisingly, Clemens said that he had long ago considered building a dirigible. After all, had he not written *Tom Sawyer Abroad?* Had not Tom, Jim, and Huckleberry traveled from Missouri to the Sahara in a balloon?

Amazed, Firebrass asked him why he had not mentioned this.

"Because I knew some all-fired fool would want to drop all the work on the boat faster than a burglar drops his tools when he sees a policeman! He'd want to abandon the Riverboat and put all work and materials into a flying machine!

"No, siree! This boat takes precedence over everything else, as Noah said when his wife wanted to knock off work to go to a rain dance.

"By the blazing balls of the Bull of Bashan, there'll be no dirigible! It's a chancy thing, a dangerous device. Why, I wouldn't even be allowed to smoke a cigar on it, and if I can't do that, what's the use of living?"

Clemens gave additional objections, most of them more serious. Firebrass, however, perceived that Clemens was not going to voice his main reason. Getting to the tower was not genuinely important to Clemens. It was the voyage itself that mattered to him. To build the greatest Riverboat that had ever been built, to be its captain, its lord, to voyage for millions of kilometers in the splendid vessel, to be admired and adored and wondered at by billions, that was what Sam Clemens desired.

Moreover, he wanted revenge. He wanted to track and then to catch up with and destroy King John for having robbed him of his first boat, his first love, the *Not For Hire.*

It might take forty years to get from Parolando to the mountains that ringed the polar sea. Sam did not care. Not only would he be the revered owner and operator of the biggest and most beautiful Riverboat mankind had ever seen, he would be going on the longest voyage any vessel, bar none, had ever taken. Forty years! Put that in your pipe, Columbus, Magellan, and smoke it!

Also, he would be seeing and talking to hundreds of thousands. This delighted Sam, who was as curious about human beings as a housewife was about new neighbors.

If he went in an airship he would have no strangers to talk to.

Though Firebrass was as gregarious as a flock of ducks, he did not understand this attitude. He himself was too eager to solve the mystery of the tower. The key to all that puzzled humanity might be there.

He did not point out to Clemens what he believed to be his real reason for his objections to the airship. It would do no good. Sam would look him straight in the eye and deny everything.

However, Sam did know that he was in the wrong. And so, sixty days before the *Mark Twain* was to depart, he called Firebrass in.

"After I leave, you can build your highly inflammable folly, if you insist on it. Of course, that means you'll have to resign as chief engineer of the most magnificent creation of man. But you must use the dirigible for observation only, as a scout."

"Why?"

"Now how by the brass balls of burning Baal could it be used for anything else but that? It can't land on the tower or anyplace else, can it? According to Joe Miller, the mountains are sheer and there's no beach. And . . ."

"How would Joe know there's no beach? The sea was covered by fog. All he saw was the upper part of the tower."

Sam had puffed smoke that looked like angry dragons. "It stands to reason the people that made that sea wouldn't make a beach. Would they make a place from which invaders could launch a boat? Of course not.

"Anyway, what I want you to do is to find out the lay of the land. See if there's a passage through the mountains other than what Joe described. Find out if the tower can be entered otherwise than by the roof."

Firebrass had not argued. He would do what he wished to do when he got to the pole. Clemens would have no control of him then.

"I took off then, happy as a dog that's rid of his fleas. I told von Parseval about Sam's decision, and we had a big celebration. But two months later poor old August was swallowed by a dragonfish. I barely missed going down its gullet with him."

At this point in his story, Firebrass revealed a secret to Jill.

"You must swear by your honor not to tell anyone else. I wouldn't be telling you, except that the boat is long gone, and there's no way you could get the information to King John. Not that you would, of course."

"I promise to keep it to myself—whatever it is."

"Well . . . one of our engineers was a Californian scientist. He knew how to make a laser with a range of 404 meters. Within that distance, it could slice the *Rex* in two. And we had just enough materials to make one. So Sam had it done.

"It was a highly secret project, so secret that there are only six men on the *Mark Twain* who know of its existence. The laser is concealed in a compartment known only to these six, of whom Sam is one, of course. Even his buddy, Joe, doesn't know about it.

"When the *Mark Twain* catches up with the *Rex,* the laser will be brought out and mounted on a tripod. The battle ought to be short and sweet. Sweet for Sam, bitterly short for John. It'll also cut down the casualties tremendously for both sides.

"I was in on the secret because I was one of the engineers on the project. Before it was completed, I asked Sam if it could be left behind. I wanted to take it on the airship and use it to burn an entrance into the tower if we could not get in otherwise.

"But Sam flat out refused. He said that if anything happened to the airship, the laser would be lost. I wouldn't be able to return it to the *Mark Twain*. I argued like mad, but I lost. And Sam did have a strong point. There's no way of knowing what dangers we'll run into, meteorological or otherwise.

"However, it was very frustrating."

33

JILL WAS ABOUT TO ASK HIM IF HE HAD NOT SENT SCOUTS OUT TO LOOK for materials to make another laser. At that moment Firebrass' secretary knocked at the door. Would Mr. Firebrass see Piscator?

Firebrass said he would. The Japanese entered and, after inquiring about their health, said that he had good news. The engineers making the synthetic diesel-oil fuel would be able to deliver the first supply a week ahead of time.

"That's great!" Firebrass said. He grinned at Jill. "That means you can take the *Minerva* up tomorrow! Start the training seven days ahead of schedule! Fabulous!"

Jill felt even happier.

Firebrass proposed a drink to celebrate. The skull-bloom had no sooner been poured, however, than the secretary entered again.

Smiling broadly, she said, "I wouldn't interrupt if it weren't so important. I think we've got a new airshipman for you, one with much experience. He just got here a few minutes ago."

Jill's near-ecstasy whistled out of her, like gas from a ruptured cell. Her chest seemed to be caving in on her. So far, she had seemed to have the post of first mate secured. But here was a person who might have as much, or even more, experience than she. A male, of course. He might even be an officer of the *Graf Zeppelin* or the *Hindenburg*. A veteran of the large rigid dirigibles would have more clout, in Firebrass' estimation, than one with only blimp experience.

Her heart beating hard, she looked at the man who followed the secretary into the office. She did not recognize him, but that meant little. There were scores of airship personnel of her day and of the pre-*Hindenburg* era whose photographs she had not seen. Besides, those pictures had been of middle-aged men who wore civilian clothes or uniforms. And many of them had facial hair.

"Chief Firebrass," Agatha Rennick said. "Barry Thorn."

The newcomer wore fish-skin sandals, a bright red-, white-, and blue-striped kilt, and a long black cloth fastened at the throat. The handle of his grail was in one hand and the neck of a large fish-skin bag in the other.

He stood about 1.7 meter tall, and his shoulders seemed to be almost half that wide. His physique was massive, irresistibly evoking to Jill the image of a bull. Yet his legs, though thickly muscled, were long in proportion to his trunk. His chest and arms were gorillalike, but he had almost no pectoral hair.

Short, curly yellow hair framed on a broad face. The eyebrows were straw colored; the eyes, a dark blue. His nose was long and straight. The lips were full. Smiling, he revealed very white teeth. The jaw was thick, ending in a prominent rounded, deeply cleft chin. The ears were small and close to his head.

At Firebrass' invitation he put down the grail and bag. He flexed his fingers as if they had been carrying a load for a long time. Probably, though, he had been paddling a canoe for a long distance. Despite the broadness of his hands, the fingers were long and slim.

He seemed very much at ease despite being with strangers and facing an interview on his qualifications. In fact, he radiated a well-being and a magnetism that inevitably made Jill think of that much overused and often inappropriate word ''charisma.''

Later, she would find that he had a curious gift of being able to shut that off as if it were light from a lamp. Then, despite his obvious physical qualities, he seemed almost to become one with his background. A psychic chameleon.

Jill, glancing at Piscator, saw that he was intensely curious about the stranger. His black eyes were narrowed, and his head was cocked slightly to one side, as if he were listening to some soft, faraway sound.

Firebrass shook hands with Thorn.

''Wow! What a grip! Glad to have you aboard, sir, if you are what Agatha claims you are. Sit down, take a load off your feet. Have you traveled a long way? You have? Forty thousand stones? Would you care for food? Coffee? Tea? Booze or beer?''

Thorn declined everything except the chair. He spoke in a very pleasant baritone without the usual pauses, hesitations, and incomplete phrases that distinguished the speech of most people.

Finding that Thorn was a Canadian, Firebrass switched from Esperanto to English. In a few minutes of questioning, he got a capsule biography of the newcomer.

Barry Thorn was born in 1920 on his parents' farm outside Regina, Saskatchewan. After getting a degree in electromechanical engineering in 1938, he enlisted in the British Navy while in England. During the war, he was the commander of a naval blimp. He married an American girl and after the war went to the States to live because his wife, an Ohioan who wanted to be close to her parents, had insisted. Besides, the opportunities were better there for blimp pilots.

He picked up a commercial pilot's license also, intending to work for the American airlines. But after his divorce he quit Goodyear and became a bush pilot for several years in the Yukon. Then he had returned to Goodyear and married again. After his second wife died, he had gotten a job with a newly formed British-West German airship company. For some years he had captained a great blimp-tug which towed floating containers of natural gas from the Middle East to Europe.

Jill asked him a few questions in the hope that his answers would jog her memory. She had known a few airshipmen at Thorn's company, and some of these might have mentioned him. He replied that he remembered one of them—he thought. He wasn't sure because that had been so long ago.

He had died in 1983 while on leave in Friedrichshafen. He did not know the cause of his death. Heart failure, probably. He had gone to sleep one night and when he had awakened he was lying naked on a bank of The River—along with everybody else.

Since then he had been wandering up and down the Valley. One day, hearing a rumor that a giant dirigible was being built down-River, he had decided to find out for himself if the tale was true.

Firebrass, beaming, said, "This is luck! You're more than welcome, Barry. Agatha, will you make arrangements to house Mr. Thorn?"

Thorn shook hands with everybody and left. Firebrass almost danced with delight. "We're coming along famously."

Jill said, "Does this change my situation?"

Firebrass looked surprised. "No. I said you'd be the head instructor and captain of the *Minerva*. Firebrass always keeps his promises. Well, almost always.

"Now, I know what you're thinking. I made no promises about who'll be the first mate of the *Parseval*. You're a strong contender for the post, Jill. But it's too early to decide on that. All I can say is, 'May the best man win. Or the best woman.' "

Piscator patted her hand. At another time, she would have resented the gesture. Now, she felt warmed.

Later, after they had left the office, Piscator said, "I am not certain that Thorn is telling the truth. Not all of it, anyway. His story may be true as far as it goes. But there's something that rings falsely in his voice. He could be concealing something."

"Sometimes you frighten me," she said.

"I could be wrong about him."

Jill got the impression that he did not believe that.

34

EACH DAY, BEFORE DAWN, THE *Minerva* LIFTED FOR A TRAINING flight. Sometimes it stayed aloft until an hour after noon. Sometimes it cruised all day, landing at evening. For the first week, Jill was its only pilot. Then she let each of the trainee pilots and the control gondola officers handle the controls.

Barry Thorn did not enter the blimp until four weeks after aerial training started. Jill insisted that he attend ground school first. Though he was experienced, he had not been in an airship for thirty-two years and it could be presumed that he had forgotten much. Thorn did not object.

She watched him closely while he was in the pilot's seat. Whatever Piscator's suspicions of him, Thorn handled the ship as if he had been doing it steadily for years. Nor was he any less competent at navigation or at dealing with the simulated emergencies which were part of the training.

Jill felt disappointed. She had hoped that he was not all he claimed to be. Now she knew that he was the stuff from which captains could be made.

Thorn was, however, a strange man. He seemed at ease with everybody and he could appreciate a joke as much as anybody. Yet he never cracked one himself, and off duty he kept to himself. Though he was given a hut only 20 meters from Jill's, he never dropped in on her or invited her to visit him. In a way, this was a relief to Jill, since she did not have to worry about advances from him. Inasmuch as he made no effort to get a woman to move in with him, he could have been homosexual. But he also did not seem interested, sexually or otherwise, in either gender. He was a loner, though, when he wished, he could open up and be very charming. Then suddenly his personality would close like a fist, and he became pale neutral, almost a living statue.

The entire potential crew of the *Parseval* was under intense surveillance. Each had to undergo psychological tests for stability. Thorn passed both the observation and the tests as if he had made them up himself.

"Just because he's a little odd in his social life doesn't mean he isn't a first-class aeronaut," Firebrass said. "It's what a man does when he's aloft that counts."

Firebrass and de Bergerac proved to be natural dirigible pilots. This was not surprising in the American's case, since he had many thousands of hours in jetplanes, helicopters, and spacecraft. The Frenchman, however, came from a time when not even balloons had existed, though they had been envisioned. The most complicated mechanical device he had handled then were matchlock, wheel-lock, and flintlock pistols. He had been too poor to afford a watch, which, in any case, required the owner only to wind it.

Nevertheless, he quickly absorbed the instruction in ground school and aerial flight, nor did he have much trouble with the necessary mathematics.

Firebrass was very good, but de Bergerac was the best pilot of all. Jill reluctantly admitted that to herself. The Frenchman's reactions and judgment were almost computer-swift.

Another surprising candidate was John de Greystock. This medieval baron had volunteered to be part of the crew that would man the semirigid *Minerva* when it attacked the *Rex*. Jill had been skeptical about his ability to adapt to aerial flight. But, after three months of flight, he was considered by both Firebrass and Gulbirra to be the best qualified to command the ship. He was combatwise, ruthless, and utterly courageous. And he hated King John. Having been wounded and thrown overboard by John's men when the *Not For Hire* was highjacked, he lusted for revenge.

Jill had come to Parolando near the end of the month called Dektria (Thirteenth in English). Parolando had adopted a thirteen-month calendar since this planet had neither season nor moon. There was no reason except sentiment to keep the year at 365 days, but sentiment was good enough. Each month was made of four seven-day weeks, twenty-eight days in all. Since twelve months only made 336 days, an extra month had been added. This left one day extra, which was generally termed New Year's Eve Day, Last Day, or Blow-Your-Top Day. Jill had landed three days before this in 31 A.R.D.

Now it was January of 33 A.R.D., and though work on the big airship had started, it would be almost another year before it was ready for the polar flight. This was partly due to the inevitable unforseen difficulties and partly due to Firebrass' grandiose ideas. These had caused many revisions of the original plans.

As of now, the crew had been chosen, but the appointment of the officers had not been determined. As far as she was concerned, the list was fairly definite—except for the posts of first and second mate. One would go to Thorn and the other to herself. This had not caused her much anxiety—except in her dreams—since Thorn did not seem to care which position he got.

On this Wednesday of January or First-Month, she was happy. The work on the *Parseval* was going so well that she decided to quit early. She'd get her fishing pole and cast for some of the "chub" in the little lake near her hut. As she climbed the first of the hills, she saw Piscator. He was also carrying fishing tackle and a wickerwork basket.

She called to him, and he turned but did not give her his usual smile in greeting.

"You look as if you've got something on your mind," she said.

"I do, but it is not my problem, except that it concerns one whom I like to think is my friend."

"You don't have to tell me," she said.

"I think I do. It concerns you."

She stopped. "What's the matter?"

"I just learned from Firebrass that the psychological evaluation tests were not finished. There is one more to go, and every one of the flight crew will have to take it."

"Is that something I should worry about?"

He nodded. "The test involves deep hypnosis. It's designed to probe for any residue of instability which previous tests might have overlooked."

"Yes, but I . . ."

She paused again.

"I'm afraid that it might disclose these . . . ah . . . hallucinations that have disturbed you from time to time."

She felt faint. For a moment, the world around her seemed to dim. Piscator held her elbow and her arm to support her.

"I am sorry, but I thought it best that you be prepared."

She pulled away, saying, "I'm all right."

Then, "Godalmighty! I've had no trouble with those for eight months! I've had no dreamgum since that time you found me in the hut, and I'm sure that any residual effects are gone. Furthermore, I've never had those hallucinations except late at night when I was home. You don't really think that Firebrass would eliminate me, do you? He doesn't have enough reason to do so!"

"I don't know," Piscator said. "Perhaps the hypnosis might not uncover these attacks. In any event, if you will forgive me for trying to influence you, I think that you should go to Firebrass and tell him about your troubles. Do so before the tests are made."

"What good would that do?"

"If he finds out that you have been holding back on him, he probably would discharge you immediately. But if you are candid, confess before you get official word of the test, he might listen to your side of the case. I myself do not think that you are any danger to the welfare of the ship. But my opinion doesn't count."

"I won't beg!"

"That wouldn't influence him anyway—except negatively."

She breathed deeply and looked around, as if there might be an escape route to another world nearby. She had been so sure, so happy only a moment ago.

"Very well. There's no use putting it off."

"That's courageous," he said. "And commonsensical. I wish you luck."

"See you later," she said, and she strode off, her jaw set.

Nevertheless, by the time she had climbed the stairs to the second story, where Firebrass' apartment was, she was breathing hard, not from poor physical condition but from anxiety.

Firebrass' secretary had told her that he had gone to his suite. She was surprised at this but did not ask Agatha why he had quit work so early. Perhaps he, too, felt like relaxing.

The door to his apartment was halfway down the hall. Before it stood the bodyguard that usually accompanied him. Two assassination attempts in the last six months had made this necessary. The would-be killers had been slain themselves and thus could give no information. No one knew for certain, but it was believed that a ruler of a hostile state down-River had sent the men. He had made no bones about his desire to get hold of Parolando's mineral wealth and marvelous machines and weapons. It was possible that he had hoped that, if he removed Firebrass, he might be able to invade Parolando. But this was all speculation by Firebrass.

Jill walked up to the ensign in command of four heavily armed men.

"I'd like to talk to the chief."

The ensign, Smithers said, "Sorry. He gave orders he wasn't to be disturbed."

"Why not?"

Smithers looked curiously at her. "I wouldn't know, sir."

Anger caused by her fear overcame her.

"I suppose he has a woman in there!"

The ensign said, "No, not that that is any of your business, sir."

He grinned maliciously and said. "He's got a visitor. A newcomer named Fritz Stern. He just got here an hour ago. He's a German, and, from what I heard, a hotshot Zeppelin man. I heard him tell the captain he was a commander for NDELAG, whatever that means. But he's got more flight time than you."

Jill had to restrain herself from hitting him in his teeth. She knew that Smithers had never liked her, and no doubt he enjoyed needling her.

"NDELAG," she said, hating herself because her voice was trembling. "That could be *Neue Deutsche Luftschifffahrts-Aktien-Gesellschaft.*"

Now her voice seemed to be coming from far away, from someone else. "There was a Zeppelin line called DELAG in the days before Wórld War I. It carried passengers and freight in Germany. But I never heard of an NDELAG.''

"That would be because it was formed after you died,'' Smithers said. He grinned, enjoying her obvious distress. "I did hear him tell the captain that he graduated from the Friedrichshafen academy in 1984. He said he ended his career as commander of a super-Zeppelin named *Viktoria.*''

She felt sick. First Thorn and now Stern.

There was no use staying here. She squared her shoulders and said, in a firm voice, "I'll see him later.''

"Yes, sir. Sorry, sir,'' Smithers said, grinning.

Jill turned away to go back down the stairs.

She whirled around as a door banged and somebody shouted. A man had run out of Firebrass' apartment and slammed the door behind him.

He stood for several seconds, frozen, facing the guards. These were pulling their heavy pistols from their holsters. Smithers had his sword halfway from its sheath.

The man was as tall as she. He had a beautiful physique, broad shouldered, slim waisted, long legged. His face was handsome but rugged; his hair, wavy ash blond; his eyes, large and dark blue. But his skin was unhealthily pale and blood was flowing from a wound on the shoulder. He held a bloodied dagger in his left hand. Then the door opened, and Firebrass, a rapier in his hand, appeared. His face was twisted, and his forehead bled.

The ensign shouted, "Stern!''

Stern whirled and ran down the hall. There was no stairway at its end, only a tall window. Smithers cried, "Don't fire, men! He can't get away!''

"He can if he goes through the window!'' Jill screamed.

At the end of the hall, Stern leaped with a shout, whirling so that his back would strike the plastic and holding an arm over his face.

The window refused to give way. Stern hit it with a thud and bounced back, falling flat with another thud on his face. He lay there while Firebrass, the ensign, and the guards behind him, ran toward Stern.

Jill followed them a second later.

Before the group could reach him, Stern got to his feet. He stared at the men racing toward him, looked at the dagger, which he had dropped on the floor when he had hit the window. Then he closed his eyes and crumpled to the floor.

35

By THE TIME JILL GOT THERE, FIREBRASS WAS FEELING THE MAN'S pulse.

"He's dead!"

"What happened, sir?" the ensign said.

Firebrass stood up.

"I wish I could say *why* it happened. All I can tell you is *what* happened. We were getting along fine, drinking and smoking, joking, and he was giving me the details of his professional career. Everything was A-okay. And then all of a sudden he leaps up, pulls a dagger, and tries to stab me!

"He must have gone crazy, although he seemed quite rational until the moment he attacked. *Something* went wrong in him. Otherwise, why would he drop dead of a heart attack?"

Jill said, "A heart attack? I haven't ever heard of anyone having a heart attack here. Have you?"

Firebrass shrugged and said, "There's always a first time. After all, the resurrections have stopped, too."

"He looks bloody cyanotic for a heart attack," Jill said. "Could he have swallowed a poison? I didn't see him put anything in his mouth."

"Where would he get cyanide or prussic acid or any poison except here in Parolando?" Firebrass said. "He hasn't been here long enough to do that."

He looked at Smithers. "Wrap up the body and take it into one of my bedrooms. Take it out after midnight and drop it into The River. The dragonfish can have him."

"Yes, sir," Smithers said. "What about that cut on your forehead, sir? Should I get a doctor?"

"No, I'll patch it up myself. And not a word about this to anybody. Have you got that, all of you? You, too, Jill. Not a word. I don't want to upset the citizens."

They all nodded. Smithers said, "Do you suppose that that bastard Burr sent this man, too?"

"I don't know," Firebrass said. "Or care. I just want you to get rid of him, okay?"

He turned to Jill. "What're you doing here?"

"I had something important to talk about," she said. "But I'll do it later. You're in no condition to talk."

"Nonsense!" he said, grinning. "Sure I am. You don't think this is going to shake me up, do you? Come on in, Jill, and we'll talk after I fix up this scratch."

Jill sat down in an overstuffed chair in the living room of the luxurious suite. Firebrass disappeared into the bathroom, returning after a few minutes with a white tape slanting across his forehead.

Smiling cheerily as if this were a typical day, he said, "What about a drink? It might settle your nerves."

"*My* nerves?"

"Okay. Both our nerves. I'll admit I'm a little shaken up. I'm no superman, no matter what people say about me."

He poured purplish skull-bloom into two tall glasses half-filled with ice cubes. Neither the ice nor the glasses, like the band-aid, were available anywhere but in Parolando—as far as she knew.

For a minute they sipped on the cool, tangy drink, their eyes meeting but neither saying a word. Then Firebrass said, "Okay. Enough of the social amenities. What did you want to see me about?"

She could scarcely get the words out. They seemed to jam in her throat, then come tumbling out, broken by the pressure.

After pausing to take a long drink, she continued more slowly and smoothly. Firebrass did not interrupt but sat immobile, his brown eyes, flecked with green, intent on hers.

"So," she finished, "there you are. I had to tell you about this, but it's the hardest thing I ever did."

"Why did you finally decide to spill it? Was it because you heard about the hypnosis?"

For a second, she thought of lying. Piscator would not betray her, and she would look so much better if she had not been forced to admit the truth.

"Yes. I heard about it. But I'd been thinking for some time that I should tell you about it. It was just . . . it was just that I couldn't bear the thought of being left behind. And I really don't think I'm a danger to the ship."

"It would be bad if you had an attack during a crucial moment of flight. You know that, of course. Well, here's the way I look at it, Jill. Barring Thorn, you're the best airshipman—I mean, person— that we have. Unlike Thorn, who was a keen airman but doesn't make aeronauting his whole life, you're a fanatic. I honestly think you'd pass up a roll in the hay for an hour's flight. Myself, I'd try to combine both.

"I wouldn't want to lose you, and if I had to, I'd worry about your killing yourself. No, don't protest, I really think you would. Which makes you unbalanced in that respect. However, I have to consider the welfare of ship and crew first, so I'd discharge you if I had to, no matter how much it would grieve me.

"So I'm putting you on probation. If you don't have another attack or hallucination from now until the ship takes off for the big voyage, then you'll be in.

"The only trouble with this is that I'll have to depend on your word for it that you've not had an attack. Well, not really. I could put you under hypnosis to find out if you've been telling the truth. But I don't like to do that. It'd mean I don't trust you. I don't want anybody on the ship I can't trust one hundred percent."

Jill felt like running over to him and throwing her arms around him. Her eyes filmed, and she almost sobbed with joy. But she stayed in her chair. An officer did not embrace the captain. Besides, he might misinterpret her behavior and try to take her into his bedroom.

She felt ashamed of herself. Firebrass would never take advantage of any woman. He would scorn using his influence. At least, she thought he would.

"I don't understand about this hypnosis," she said. "How could you make all the others go through with it but omit me? That's discrimination which the others . . ."

"I've changed my mind about that."

He got up and walked to a rolltop desk, bent over it to write on a piece of paper, and then gave it to her.

"Here. Take this down to Doc Graves. He'll take an X-ray of you."

She was bewildered. "Whatever on earth for?"

"As your captain I could tell you to shut up and obey my order. I won't because you'd be resentful. Let's just say it's something the psychologists learned in 2000 A.D. It would defeat the purpose of the test if I told you what it was all about.

"Everybody else will have to be X-rayed, too. You have the honor of being the first."

"I don't understand," she murmured. "But I'll do it, of course."

She rose. "Thank you."

"No thanks necessary. Now get your tail down to Doc Graves."

When she arrived at the doctor's office, she found him talking on the phone. He was frowning and chewing his cigar savagely.

"All right, Milt. I'll do it. But I don't like it that you won't confide in me."

He hung the phone up and turned to her. "Hello, Jill. You'll have to wait until Ensign Smithers gets here. He'll pick up the X-ray photos as soon as they're made and run them up to Firebrass."

"He has a darkroom?"

"No. They don't need developing. Didn't you know? They're just like other photographs, electronically processed at the moment they're taken. Firebrass himself designed the equipment. It's a process developed about 1998, he said.''

Graves began striding back and forth, biting hard on the cigar.

''Damn it! He won't even let me see the X-rays! Why?''

''He said he didn't want anyone but himself to see the X-rays. It's part of the psychological evaluation tests.''

''How in hell could X-rays of the head tell you anything about a man's psyche? Is he nuts?''

''I suppose he'll tell us all about it when he's seen all the photos. By the way, speaking of a man's psyche, I'm not a man.''

''I was speaking in the abstract.''

He stopped and scowled even more fiercely. ''I won't be able to sleep nights worrying about this. Man, I wish I'd lived longer. I shuffled off this mortal coil in 1980, so I didn't get to see the later developments in medical science. Just as well, I suppose. I couldn't keep up with the deluge of new stuff as it was.''

Turning to Jill, and stabbing the cigar at her, he said, ''Something I'd like to ask you, Jill. Something that's been bothering me. Firebrass is the only one I've ever met who lived beyond 1983. Have you ever met anyone who did?''

She blinked with surprise. ''No-o-o. No, I haven't, now I think about it. Firebrass excepted.''

For a moment, she had been about to tell him about Stern. That was going to be a hard secret to keep.

''Neither have I. Damn peculiar.''

''Not really,'' she said. ''Of course, I haven't been all over The River, but I have traveled several hundred thousand kilometers and talked to thousands of people. The twentieth-century people seem to have been scattered thinly everywhere. If they were resurrected in clumps, as it were, I never heard of any. So that means that anywhere in the Valley you'll likely find a few, but most of the population segments will be from other centuries.''

''So there's nothing remarkable in the rarity of people born after 1983.''

''Yeah? Maybe so. Ah, here comes Smithers and two other thugs. Step into my X-rated parlor, my dear, as the spider said to the fly.''

36

Extracts from various editions of *The Daily Leak:*

Dmitri "Mitya" Ivanovitch Nikitin is *pro tempore* pilot third officer of the *Parseval*. He was born in 1885 in Gomel, Russia, of middle-class parents. His father was a harness-factory owner; his mother taught piano. His qualifications for candidacy were based on his experience as chief steersman of the *Russie*, a French airship built by the Lebaudy-Juillot Company in 1909 for the Russian government.

Ms. Jill Gulbirra, chief airship instructor, says that Mitya's experience was rather limited from her viewpoint, but he has shown excellent ability. However, according to rumors, he is too fond of skull-bloom. Take a tip from us, Mitya. Lay off the booze.

. . . Charges will not be brought by the editor against Pilot Nikitin. During a necessarily brief interview in the hospital, Mr. Bagg said, "I've been laid out by better men than that big slob. The next time he comes charging into my office, I'll be prepared. The reason I'm not having him arrested isn't just because I have a big heart, however. I just want a chance to personally knock his brains out. Speak softly and carry a big stick."

. . . Ettore Arduino is Italian (what else?), but he is blond and blue-eyed and can pass for a Swede as long as he keeps his mouth shut and doesn't eat garlic. As all but new citizens know, he entered Parolando two months ago and was immediately signed up for training. He has an illustrious though tragic history, having been chief motor engineer on the airship *Norge* and then on the *Italia* under Umberto Nobile. (See page 6 for a minibiogrpahy of this son of Rome.) The *Norge* accomplished its primary mission to fly over the North Pole on May 12, 1926. It also established that there was no large land mass between the North Pole and Alaska as reported by that great explorer, Commodore

Robert E. Peary (1856-1920), the first man to reach the North Pole (1909). (Though Peary was accompanied by a Negro, Matthew Henson, and four Eskimos whose names we don't remember, actually Henson was the first man to stand on the North Pole.)

The *Italia,* after passing over the Pole, found itself bucking a very strong headwind on its way to King's Bay. The controls jammed from heavy icing; a crash seemed assured. However, the ice melted, and the airship proceeded. Some time later, the vessel began to fall slowly. The helpless crew was forced to stand by while the queen of the skies struck the surface ice. The control gondola was torn off, a fortuitous event for those in it. These scrambled out and then looked up in shock as the dirigible, freed of the weight of the gondola, rose again.

Ettore Arduino was last seen standing on the gangway to the starboard engine gondola. As reported by a crew member, Dr. Francis Behounek of the Wireless Institute of Prague, Czechoslovakia, Arduino's face was a mask of utter disbelief. The *Italia* floated away, and nothing of it or the men still aboard was ever seen again. On Earth, that is.

Arduino relates that he perished of the cold after the *Italia* fell for the second and last time on the ice. His complete account of this horrendous experience will be printed in next Thursday's issue. After this blood-chilling event, no reasonable person could expect Ettore to volunteer again for airship travel. But he is undaunted by this and expresses eagerness for another polar expedition. We don't care what people say about Italians, and we have nothing but contempt for the attitude prevalent in Tombstone, where it was stated as a fact that all wops were yellow. We personally know that they have more guts than brains, and we are sure that Ettore will be a shining adornment to the crew.

. . . last seen paddling desperately toward the middle of The River while Mr. Arduino fired shots at him with the new Mark IV pistol. Either this weapon is not what it's cracked up to be, or Mr. Arduino's marksmanship was below normal that day.

. . . your new editor accepts the suggestion of President Firebrass that this journal temper the privilege of free speech with discretion.

. . . Mr. Arduino was released after promising that he would no longer settle grievances, justified or unjustified, by vio-

lent means. The newly created Board of Civil Disputes will
handle such matters from now on with President Firebrass as
the court of last appeal. Though we will miss S.C. Bagg, we
must confess that . . .

. . . Metzing had been chief of the Naval Airship Division
of Imperial Germany in 1913. He was Korvettenkapitan of
the Zeppelin L-1 when it went down on September 9, 1913,
during maneuvers. This was the first naval Zeppelin to be
lost. The crash was not due to any deficiency on the part of
crew or vessel but to the ignorance at that time of
meteorological conditions in the upper air. In other words,
weather forecasting was then a primitive science. A violent
line squall lifted the L-1 up past her pressure height and then
dashed her down. With propellers still spinning and ballast
ejecting, the ship smashed into the sea off Heligoland.
Metzing died with most of his crew . . . We welcome this
experienced officer and likable gentleman to Parolando but
hope he brings no bad luck with him.

. . . Flash! Just arrived! Another airship veteran, Anna
Karlovna Obrenova from up-River some 40,000 kilometers.
In the brief interview allowed before Ms. Obrenova was
taken to President Firebass' HQ, we learned that she had
been captain of the USSR freighter-dirigible *Lermontov,*
logging 8584 hours of flight time in this and other airships.
This exceeds Ms. Gulbirra's 8342 hours and Mr. Thorn's
8452 hours. A complete account of Obrenova should be in
tomorrow's issue. All we can say at the moment is that she is
a peach, a real pipperoo!

37

IT WAS FUNNY, THOUGH NOT LAUGHING-FUNNY.

She had been worried that a man with more airtime than herself would show up. One had, but he had not been aggressive. His only ambition was to be on the ship, and he did not seem to care what rank he got.

Somehow, she had never thought of being displaced by a woman. There were so few female airship officers in her time. And so few people who had lived past 1983 had come by—only one, in fact—that she had not worried about dirigibilists of that era. From what Firebrass said, post-1983 had been the great age of the large rigid airships. But the odds against aeronauts of that era showing were high.

Chance had thrown its dice, and so here was Obrenova, a woman who had 860 hours flight time as captain of a giant Soviet airship.

So far, the officers' positions had not been announced. No matter. Jill knew that the little blonde newcomer would be first mate. Realistically, she *should* be. If Jill were in Firebrass' place, she would have had to appoint Obrenova as first mate.

On the other hand, there were only two months left before the *Parseval* took off for the polar voyage. The Russian might need more retraining than that. After thirty-four years of ground life, she would be rusty. She would have a month reacquainting herself with gasbags in the *Minerva*. Then she would have a month of training in the big ship with everybody else.

Could she do it? Of course, she could. Jill would have been able to do it in that time.

She had been in the conference room with the officer candidates when Anna Obrenova was brought in by Agatha. On seeing her, Jill's heart had seemed to turn over like a sluggish motor. Before she heard Agatha's excited announcement of the newcomer's identity, she had known what it would be.

Anna Obrenova was short and slim but long legged and full breasted. She had long, shining yellow hair and large, dark blue eyes, a heart-shaped face, high cheekbones, a cupid's bow mouth, and a deep tan. She was, to quote another newspaper article, a "beaut."

Disgustingly delicate and feminine. Unfairly so.

Just the type that men simultaneously wanted to protect and to bed.

Firebrass was on his feet, advancing toward her, his face aglow, his eyes seeming to drip male hormones.

But it was Thorn's reaction that surprised Jill. On seeing Obrenova enter, he had jumped to his feet and opened his mouth, closed it, opened it, then closed it again. His ruddy skin was pale.

"Do you know her?" Jill said softly.

He sat down and covered his face with his hands for a moment.

When he took them away, he said, "No! For a second I thought I did! She looks so much like my first wife! I still can't believe it."

Thorn remained shaking in his chair while others crowded around Obrenova. Not until the others had been introduced did he get up and shake her hand. He told her then how remarkably she resembled his wife. She smiled—"dazzlingly" was a cliché, but it was the only adverb appropriate—and she said, in heavily accented English, "Did you love your wife?"

That was a strange thing to say. Thorn stepped back a pace and said, "Yes, very much. But she left me."

"I am sorry," Obrenova said, and they did not exchange another word while in the room.

Firebrass sat her down and offered her food, cigarettes, and liquor. She accepted the former but declined the rest.

"Does that mean you have no vices?" Firebrass said. "I was hoping you'd have at least one."

Obrenova ignored this. Firebrass shrugged and began questioning her. Jill got depressed while listening to the account of her experience. She had been born in Smolensk in 1970, had been educated as an aeronautical engineer, and in 1984 had become an airship trainee. In 2001 she had been made captain of the passenger freighter *Lermontov.*

Finally, Firebrass said that she must be tired. She should go with Agatha, who'd find quarters for her.

"Preferably in this building," he said.

Agatha replied that no rooms were available. She would have to be satisfied with a hut near those of Ms. Gulbirra and Mr. Thorn.

Firebrass, looking disappointed, said, "Well, maybe we can find a place here for her later. Meantime, I'll go with you, Anna, and make sure you're not given a dump."

Jill felt even lower. How could she expect objectivity from him, when he was so obviously smitten by the Russian?

For a while, she indulged in some fantasies. How about abducting the little Russian and tying her up in a hidden place just before the *Parseval* was to take off? Firebrass would not hold up the flight until she was found. Jill Gulbirra would then become first mate.

If she could do that to Obrenova, why not to Firebrass? Then she would be the captain.

The images evoked were pleasing, but she could not do that to anyone, no matter how strongly she felt. To violate their human rights and dignities would be to violate, to destroy herself.

During the week that followed she sometimes beat her fists on the table or wept. Or both. The next week she told herself that she was being immature. Accept what was unavoidable and enjoy what was left. Was it so important that she should finally be captain of an airship?

To her, yes. To anyone else in the world, no.

So she swallowed her resentment and disgust.

Piscator must have known how she felt. Frequently, she caught him looking at her. He would smile or else just look away. But he knew, he knew!

Six months passed. Firebrass gave up trying to get Obrenova to move into his apartment. He made no secret of his desire nor did he hide the fact that she had finally rejected him.

"You win some, you lose some," he said to Jill with a wry smile. "Maybe she doesn't go for men. I know a score or more who've been panting for her, and she's as cool to them as if she were the Venus de Milo."

"I'm sure she isn't a lesbian," Jill said.

"Takes one to know one, heh? Haw, haw!"

"Damn it, you know I'm ambivalent," she said angrily, and she walked away.

"Indecisive is the right word!" he had shouted after her.

At that time Jill was living with Abel Park, a tall, muscular, handsome, and intelligent man. He was a Rivertad, one of the many millions of children who had died on Earth after the age of five. Abel did not remember what country he had been born in or what his native language had been. Though resurrected in an area the majority of whom were medieval Hindus, he had been adopted and raised by a Scots couple. These were eighteenth-century Lowlanders of peasant origin. Despite his poverty, the foster father had managed to become a medical doctor in Edinburgh.

Abel had left his area after his parents had been killed and had wandered down-River until he came to Parolando. Jill had liked him very much and had asked him to be her hutmate. The big fellow had gladly moved in, and they had had some idyllic months. But, though he was intelligent, he was ignorant. Jill taught him everything she could; history, philosophy, poetry, and even some arithmetic. He was eager to learn, but eventually he accused her of patronizing him.

Shocked, Jill had denied this.

"I just want to educate you, to give you knowledge denied you because you died so early."

"Yes, but you get so impatient. You keep forgetting that I don't have your background. Things which seem simple to you, because you were raised among them, are bewildering to me. I don't have your referents."

He had paused, then said, "You're a knowledge-chauvinist. In short, a . . . what's the word? . . . a snob."

Jill was even more shocked. She denied this, too, though reflection showed her that he was perhaps right. By then it was too late to make reparations. He had left her for another woman.

She consoled herself by telling herself that he was too used to the idea of the man being the boss. He found it difficult to accept her as an equal.

Later, she realized that that was only partly true. Actually, she had, deep down, a contempt for him because he was not, and never would be, her mental equal. That had been an unconscious attitude, and now that she was aware of it, she regretted having it. In fact, she felt ashamed of it.

After that, she made no effort to have anything but the most impermanent liaisons. Her partners were men and women who, like her, wanted only sexual satisfaction. Usually, she and they got it, but she always felt frustrated afterward. She needed a genuine affection and companionship.

Obrenova and Thorn, she observed, must be doing the same thing as she. At least, no one moved into their huts. For that matter, though, she never observed them taking any interest in anybody which could be interpreted as sexual. As far as she knew, they were not even having one-night stands.

Thorn did, however, seem to like Obrenova's company. Jill often saw them talking earnestly together. Perhaps Thorn was trying to get her to be his lover. And perhaps the Russian refused because she thought she would only be a substitute for his first wife.

Three days before the final liftoff, a holiday was declared. Jill left the plains area because it was so crowded and noisy with people from up and down The River. She estimated that there were already several hundred thousands camping in Parolando and that there would be over twice that number by the time the *Parseval* left. She retired to her hut, leaving it only for a little fishing. The second day, as she was sitting on the edge of the little lake, looking emptily into the water, she heard someone approaching.

Her irritation at the invasion died when she saw Piscator. He was carrying a fishing pole and a wickerwork basket. Silently, he sat down beside her and offered her a cigarette. She shook her head. For some time they stared at the surface, rippled by the wind, broken now and then by a leaping fish.

Finally, he said, "It won't be long before I must reluctantly say goodbye to my disciples and to my piscatorial pursuits."

"Is it worth it to you?"

"You mean, giving up this pleasant life for an expedition that may end in death? I won't know until it happens, will I?"

After another silence, he said, "How have you been? Any more experiences such as *that* night?"

"No, I'm fine."

"But you have been carrying a knife in your heart."

"What do you mean?" she said, turning her head to look at him. She hoped her puzzlement did not look as faked as it felt to her.

"I should have said three knives. The captaincy, the Russian, and most of all, yourself."

"Yes, I have problems. Don't we all? Or are you an exception? Are you even human?"

He smiled and said, "Very much so. More than most, I can say with seeming immodesty. Why is that? Because I have realized my human potentiality almost to its fullest. I can't expect you to credit that. Nor will you, unless, some day . . . but that day may never come.

"However, regarding your question of my humanity. I have sometimes wondered if some people we have met are human. I mean, do they belong to *Homo sapiens?*

"Isn't it possible, even highly probable, that the Whoevers responsible for all this have agents among us? For what purpose, I don't know. But they could be catalysts to cause some kind of action among us. By action, I do not mean physical action, such as the building of the Riverboats and airships, though that may be part of it. I refer to psychic action. To a, shall we say, channeling of humanity? Toward what? Perhaps toward a goal somewhat similar to that which the Church of the Second Chance postulates. A spiritual goal, of refinement of the human spirit. Or perhaps, to use a Christian-Muslim metaphor, to separate the sheep from the goats."

He paused and drew on his cigarette.

"To continue the religious metaphor, there may be two forces at work here, one for evil, one for good. One is working against the fulfillment of that goal."

"What?" she said. Then, "Do you have any evidence for that?"

"No, only speculation. Don't get me wrong. I don't think that Shaitan, Lucifer if you will, is actually conducting a cold war against Allah, or God, whom we Sufis prefer to name The Real. But I sometimes wonder if there isn't a parallel to that in some sense . . . well, it is all speculation. If there are agents, then they look like human beings."

"Do you know something I don't?"

"I have probably observed certain things. You have, too, the difference being that you have not put them into a pattern. A rather dark pattern it is. Though it is possible that I am looking at the wrong side of the pattern. If it were turned over, the other side might be blazing with light."

"I wish I knew what you were talking about. Would you mind letting me in on this . . . pattern?"

He rose and tossed the cigarette stub into the lake. A fish rose, swallowed it, and splashed back.

"There are all sorts of activity going on beneath that mirror of water," he said, pointing to the lake. "We can't see them because water is a different element from the air. The fish know what's going on down there, but that doesn't do us much good. All we can do is to lower our hooks into the darkness and hope we catch something.

"I read a story once in which a fish sat down on the bottom of a deep, dark lake and extended his fishing pole into the air over the bank. And he caught men with his bait."

"Is that all you're going to say about that?"

He nodded, and said, "I presume you are coming to Firebrass' farewell party tonight."

"It's a command invitation. But I hate going. It'll be a drunken brawl."

"You don't have to soil yourself by joining the pigs in their swinishness. Be *with* but not *of* them. That will enable you to enjoy the thought of how superior you are to them."

"You're an ass," she said. Then, quickly, "I'm sorry, Piscator. I'm the ass. You read me correctly, of course."

"I think that Firebrass is going to announce tonight the ranking of the officers and pilots."

She held her breath for a moment. "I think so, too, but I am not looking forward with pleasure to that."

"You prize rank too highly. What is worse, you know it but will do nothing about it. In any event, I think you have an excellent chance."

"I hope so."

"Meanwhile, would you care to go out in the boat with me and participate in the angling?"

"No, thanks."

She rose stiffly and pulled in the line. The bait was gone off the hook.

"I think I'll go home and brood a while."

"Don't lay any eggs," he said, grinning.

Jill snorted feebly and walked away. Before she reached her hut, she passed Thorn's. Loud, angry voices were issuing from it. Thorn's and Obrenova's.

So, the two had finally gotten together. But they did not seem happy about it.

Jill hesitated a moment, almost overcome with the desire to eavesdrop. Then she plunged on ahead, but she could not help hearing Thorn shout in a language unknown to her. So—it would have done her no good to listen in. But what was that language? It certainly did not sound like Russian to her.

Obrenova, in a softer voice, but still loud enough for Jill to hear her, said something in the same language. Evidently, it was a request to lower his voice.

Silence followed. Jill walked away swiftly, hoping they would not look outside and think she had been doing what she had almost done. Now she had something to think about. As far as she knew, Thorn could speak only English, French, German, and Esperanto. Of course, he could have picked up a score of languages during his wanderings along The River. Even the least proficient of linguists could not avoid doing that.

Still, why would the two talk in anything but their native languages or in Esperanto? Did both know a language which they used while quarreling so that nobody would understand them?

She would mention this to Piscator. He might have an illuminating viewpoint on the matter.

As it turned out, however, she had no chance to do so, and by the time the *Parseval* took off, she had forgotten about the matter.

38

Discoveries in Dis

Jan. 26, 20 A.R.D.

Peter Jairus Frigate
Aboard the *Razzle Dazzle*
South Temperate Zone
Riverworld

Robert F. Rohrig
Down-River (hopefully)

DEAR BOB:

In thirteen years on this ship I've sent out twenty-one of these missives. Letter from a Lazarus. Cable from Charon. Missive from Mictlan. Palaver in Po. Tirades from Tír na nOc. Tunes from Tuonela. Allegories from al-Sirat. Sticklers from the Styx. Issues from Issus. Etc.

All that sophomoric alliterative jazz.

Three years ago I dropped into the water my Telegram from Tartarus. I wrote just about everything significant that'd happened to me since you died in St. Louis of too much living. Of course, you won't get either letter except by the wildest chance.

Here I am today in the bright afternoon, sitting on the deck of a two-masted schooner, writing with a fishbone pen and carbonblack ink on bamboo paper. When I'm done, I'll roll the pages up, wrap them in fish membrane, insert them in a bamboo cylinder. I'll hammer down a disc of bamboo into the open end. I'll say a prayer to whatever gods there be. And I'll toss the container over the side. May it reach you via Rivermail.

The captain, Martin Farrington, the Frisco Kid, is at the tiller right now. His reddish-brown hair shines in the sun and whips with the wind. He looks half-Polynesian, half-Celtic, but is neither. He's an American of English and Welsh descent, born in Oakland, California in 1976. He hasn't told me that, but I know that because I know who he really is. I've seen too many pictures of him not to recognize him. I can't name him because he has some reason for going under a pseudonym. (Which, by the way, is taken from two of his fictional characters.) Yes, he was a famous writer. Maybe you'll be able to figure it out, though I doubt it. You once told me that you had read only one of his works, *Tales of the Fish Patrol,* and you thought it was lousy. I was distressed that you'd refuse to read his major works, many of which were classics.

He and his first mate, Tom Rider, "Tex," and an Arab named Nur are the only members of the original crew left. The others dropped out for one reason or another: death, ennui, incompatibility, etc. Tex and the Kid are the only two people I've met on The River who could come anywhere near being famous people. I did come close to meeting Georg Simon Ohm (you've heard of "ohms") and James Nasmyth, inventor of the steamhammer. And lo and behold! Rider and Farrington are near the top of the list of the twenty people I'd most like to meet. It's a peculiar list, but, being human, I'm peculiar.

The first mate's real surname isn't Rider. His face isn't one I'd forget, though the absence of the white ten-gallon hat makes it seem less familiar. He was the great film hero of my childhood, right up there with my book heroes: Tarzan, John Carter of Barsoom, Sherlock Holmes, Dorothy of Oz, and Odysseus. Out of the 260 western movies he made, I saw at least forty. These were second or third runs in the second-class Grand, Princess, Columbia, and Apollo theaters in Peoria. (All vanished long before I was fifty.) His movies gave me some of my most golden hours. I don't remember the details or the scenes of a single one—they all blur into a sort of glittering montage with Rider as a giant figure in the center.

When I was about fifty-two years old, I became interested in writing biographies. You know that I had planned for many years to write a massive life of Sir Richard Francis Burton, the famous or infamous nineteenth-century explorer, author, translator, swordsman, anthropologist, etc.

But financial exigencies kept me too busy to do much on *A Rough Knight for the Queen.* Finally, just as I was ready to start full time on *Knight,* Byron Farwell came out with an excellent biography of Burton. So I decided to wait a few years, until the market could take another Burton bio. And just as I was about to start again, Fawn Brodie's life of Burton— probably the best—was published.

So I put off the project for ten years. Meanwhile, I decided to write a biography of my favorite childhood film hero (though I ranked Douglas Fairbanks, Senior, as my other top favorite).

I'd read a lot of articles about my hero in movie and western magazines and newspaper clippings. These depicted him as having led a life more adventurous and flamboyant than those of the heroes he played in films.

But I still did not have the money to quit writing fiction long enough to travel around the country interviewing people who'd known him—even if I could have found them. There were some who could have given me details of his careers as a Texas Ranger, a U.S. Marshal in New Mexico, a deputy sheriff in the Oklahoma Territory, a Rough Rider with Roosevelt at San Juan Hill, a soldier in the Philippine Insurrection and the Boxer Rebellion, a horse breaker for the British and possibly as a mercenary for both sides in the Boer War, as a mercenary for Madero in Mexico, as a Wild West show performer, and as the highest-paid movie actor of his time.

The articles about him couldn't be trusted. Even those who claimed to have known him well gave differing accounts of his life. His obituaries were full of contradictions. And I knew that Fox and Universal had put out a lot of publicity stories about him, most of which had to be checked out for exaggeration or downright lies.

The woman who thought she was his first wife had written a biography of him. You'd never know from it that he had divorced her and married twice thereafter. Or had two daughters by another woman. Or that he had a "drinking problem." Or an illegitimate son who was a jeweler in London.

She thought she was his first wife, but, as it turned out, she was his second or third. Nobody's too sure about that.

That he was still a flawless hero to her even after all this says much about the man, though. It says even more about her.

A good friend of mine, Coryell Varoll (you remember him, a circus acrobat, juggler, tightrope walker, gargantuan beer drinker, a Tarzan fan) wrote me about him. In 1964, I think.

"I remember the first time I met him I thought I was meeting God . . . over the years, being on the same lot with him many times" (in the circus, he means) "the awe fell apart but he was always liked by most people and always idolized by the kids even after he quit making pix . . . I know that sober he was a swell guy, drunk he'd fight at the least excuse and do some of the damnedest things (don't we all?) . . . I've a few dozen stories about him that never made the publications. I'll tell them the next time we get together."

But somehow Cory never did.

Even his birthdate was in doubt. His studios and his wife claimed he was born in 1880. The monument near Florence, Arizona (where he died doing 80 mph on a dirt road), says 1880. But there was contrary evidence that it was 1870. Whether he was sixty or seventy, though, he looked like a young fifty. He always kept himself in great shape.

Also, a friend who saw him off on his fatal trip said he was driving a yellow Ford convertible. His wife said it was white. So much for eyewitnesses. The studio publicity departments claimed he was born and raised in Texas. I found out myself that that was a lie. He was born near Mix Run, Pennsylvania, and he left there when he was eighteen to enter the Army.

Just as I was about to write to the War Department to get a copy of his military record—and find out for myself just what he had done in the Army—a novel by Darryl Ponicsan came out. I was stymied again; again, too late. Though the book was semifictional, its author had done the job of research that I'd been planning to do.

So—my hero wasn't the grandson of a Cherokee chief. Nor was he born in El Paso, Texas. And, though he was in the Army, he hadn't been severely wounded at San Juan Hill nor wounded in the Philippines.

Actually, he'd enlisted the day after the Spanish-American War started. I'm sure—as was Ponicsan—that he hoped to get into action. There is no doubt that he had great courage and that he desired to be where the bullets were the thickest.

Instead, he was kept at the fort, then honorably discharged. He thereupon reenlisted. But still, no action. So he deserted in 1902.

He did not go to South Africa, as the studios claimed. Instead, he married a young schoolteacher and went with her to the Oklahoma Territory. Either her father got the marriage annulled or she just left him and a divorce was never filed. Nobody's sure.

While working as a bartender, shortly before he went to work for the 101 Ranch in Oklahoma, he married another woman. This didn't work out, and he apparently failed to divorce her, too.

Most of what the studio publicity departments—and Rider himself—claimed was false. These tales were made up to glamorize a man who did not need it. Rider went along with these tales, maybe made up some himself for the studios. After a while he got to believing them himself. I mean, really believing them. I should know. I've heard him relate almost all of the prevarications, and it's evident that by now the fiction is as genuine as the reality to him.

This blurring of distinction between reality and fantasy in no way interfered with his competency in real life, of course.

He did, however, reject Fox's wish to advertise him as the illegitimate son of Buffalo Bill. That might have started inquiries which would have exposed the whole truth.

And he never says a word about having been a great movie star. He does tell stories about his film experiences, but in these he's always an extra.

Why is he using a pseudonym? I don't know.

His third wife described him as tall, slender, and dark. I suppose that in the early 1900's he would have been considered a tall man, though he's shorter than I am. His slim body does contain steelwire muscles. Farrington is shorter than he but very muscular. He's always after Tom to Indian wrestle him, especially when he (Farrington) has been drinking. Tom obliges. They put an elbow on the table, lock raised hands, and then try to force each other's hand down to the table. It's a long struggle, but Tom usually wins. Farrington laughs, but I think he's really chagrined.

I've wrestled with both of them, coming out about fifty percent winner (or loser). I can beat both of them in the dashes and the long jump. But when it comes to boxing or stick fighting, I usually get licked. I don't have their "killer instinct." Besides, this macho thing never was important to me. Though that may be because I suppressed it from some unconscious fear of competition.

It's important to Farrington. If it is to Tom, he never shows it.

Anyway, it was a thrill to be with these two. It still is, though familiarity breeds, if not contempt, familiarity.

Tom Rider has been up and down The River for hundreds of thousands of kilometers and has three times been killed. Once he was resurrected near the mouth of The River. By near I mean he was only about 20,000 kilometers distant. This was in the arctic region. The River's mouth is, like its headwaters, near the North Pole. However, the two seem to be diametrically opposite, the waters issuing from the mountains in one hemisphere and emptying into the mountains in the other hemisphere.

From what I've heard, there's a sea around the North Pole, and it's walled by a circular mountain which would make Mount Everest look like a wart. The sea pours out of a hole at the base of the mountains, winds back and forth in one hemisphere, finally curving around the South Pole to the other hemisphere. There it wriggles like a snake up and down from the antarctic to the arctic and back again a thousand or so times, and finally empties into the north polar mountains. (Actually, it's one mountain—like a volcanic cone.)

If I drew a sketch of The River, it'd look like the Midgard Serpent of Norse myth, a world-girdling snake with its tail in its mouth.

Tom said that the areas near the mouth are populated chiefly by Ice Agers, ancient Siberians, and Eskimos. There's a scattering of modern Alaskans, upper Canadians, and Russians, though. And some others from everywhere and every time.

Tom, being the adventurer that he is, decided to travel to the mouth. He and six others made some kayaks and paddled downstream from the land of the living into the wasteland of the fog shrouds. Surprisingly, vegetation grew in the mists and the darkness all the way to the mouth. Also, the grailstones extended for a thousand kilometers into the fog. The expedition had its last grail meal at the last stone and then, laden with dried fish and acorn bread and what they'd saved from the grails, they paddled on, the ever increasing current speeding them toward their goal.

The last hundred kilometers was in a current against which there was no turning back. They couldn't even try for the shore; sheer canyon walls soared up from the edge of the water. The voyageurs were forced to eat and sleep sitting up in their kayaks.

It looked like curtains, *finit,* for them, and it was. They plunged into a great cave the ceiling and walls of which were so far away that Tom's torchlight could not reach them. Then, with a horrible roaring, The River entered a tunnel. By then the ceiling was so low that Tom's head was knocked against it. That's all he remembers. Undoubtedly, the kayak was torn to pieces against the ceiling.

Tom woke up the next day somewhere near the south polar region.

39

(Frigate's letter continued)

"There's a tower in the middle of a sea surrounded by the polar mountains," Tom said.

"A *tower?*" I said. "What do you mean?"

"Haven't you heard about that? I thought everybody knew about the tower."

"Nobody ever mentioned it to me."

"Well," he said, looking somewhat peculiar, "It *is* a hell of a long River. I suppose there are plenty of areas where nobody's heard the tale."

And he proceeded to tell me that that was just what it was, a tale. No proof. The man who told Tom about it may have been a liar, and God knows there are just as many here as there were on Earth. But this wasn't an account heard from a man who'd heard it from another who'd heard it from still another and so on and so on. Tom himself had actually talked to a man who claimed to have seen the tower.

Tom had known this man for a long time, but he'd never said a word about it until he got stumbling drunk with Tom one night. After he sobered up, he refused to talk about it. He was too scared.

He was an ancient Egyptian, one of a party led by the Pharaoh Akhenaten or Ikhnaton, as some pronounced it. You know, the one who tried to found a monotheist religion about the thirteenth century B.C. Apparently, Akhenaten was resurrected in an area of people from his own time. The teller of the tale, Paheri, a nobleman, was recruited by Akhenaten along with forty others. They built a boat and started off, not knowing how far they had to go. Or, indeed, what their goal was, except the source of The River. Akhenaten believed that Aton, God, the sun, would live there and that he would receive any pilgrim with great honor. Would, in fact, pass him on to paradise, a place better than The Riverworld.

Paheri, unlike the Pharaoh, was a conservative polytheist. He believed in the "true" gods; Ra, Horus, Isis, all the Old Bunch. He went along with his Pharaoh, thinking that he would lead them to the seat of the gods and would then get his just deserts for having abandoned the old religion on Earth. Poetic justice. But he, Paheri, would be suitably rewarded for his faith.

Fortunately for their quest, the area in which they'd been first resurrected was in the northern hemisphere, far up The River. Also fortunately, they passed through areas mainly inhabited by late-twentieth-century Scandinavians. These were comparatively peaceful, so the boat's crew wasn't enslaved, and there was no problem using the grailstones.

As they got closer to the polar mountains, they came into an area populated by giant subhumans. These seem to have been a species the fossils of which were never found on Earth. Eight to ten feet high (2.45 to 3.048 meters), believe it or not. With noses like proboscis monkeys. Language users, though their speech was simple.

Any one of these behemoths could have wiped out the whole crew singlehanded, but the boat frightened them. They thought it was a living monster, a dragon. Apparently, their area, which extended for several thousand kilometers, was cut off from the area below them by a very narrow valley. The River boiled through it at great pressure, making a current against which a boat could not be rowed.

The Egyptians weren't stopped by this. It took them six months, but they made it. Using flint tools and some iron tools—there was some iron in this area for which they traded booze and tobacco from their grails—they chopped out a narrow ledge about 3 meters above the water. They disassembled the boat and, carrying the parts on their backs, they crawled the kilometer or so to the end of the narrow part.

In the land of the giants, the Egyptians recruited an individual whose name they couldn't pronounce. They called him Djehuti (the Greek form of this name was Thoth) because his long nose reminded them of that god. Thoth had the head of an ibis, a long-beaked bird.

The boat proceeded up The River, to where the grailstones ceased. This area was in perpetual fog. Though The River had given up much of its heat while going through the sea behind the polar mountains, it still had enough left to form clouds when it encountered the colder air.

They came to a cataract that was wide enough to float the moon on, or so said Paheri. The boat had to be left behind then, and for all anybody knows it is still on a platform in a sheltered cove. Rotten by now, what with all that moisture.

Now, here comes one of the strangest parts of the tale. The expedition came to a cliff which seemed insurmountable. But they found a tunnel which someone had cut through the cliff. And then, later, at the bottom of another insurmountable cliff, they found the end of a rope made from cloths. Up it they went, and though their path was anything but smooth from then on, they did get to the polar sea beyond the mountains.

Who made the tunnel and who left the rope? And why? It seems obvious to me that someone prepared the way for us Earthlings. I doubt that it was Riverdwellers who cut the tunnel and who planted the rope. The mountain which contained the tunnel was made of hard quartz. The tunnel would have worn out a large number of steel tools, which would not in any event have been available in large numbers. Moreover, Paheri said that there was no debris, no cuttings and shavings which would have to be piled outside the tunnel. Even with iron tools, a party would not have time enough to cut the tunnel. They couldn't possibly have brought along enough food for the time it would take to do the job.

In addition, how could anyone have gotten up the aforementioned cliff without a rope? Maybe some mysterious party preceding the Egyptians fired a rocket trailing a rope? But there was only one projection, a tall, thin spire of rock, for the hypothetical rope with hypothetical grapnels to catch on. The chances of the rocket hitting it (especially when it's invisible from below) and the grapnels catching on it are highly remote. Also, there was no empty rocket case around. Whoever had lowered the rope had tied the end of the rope around the projection. And Paheri said that it looked as if the projection had been cut out of a larger spire.

Anyway, after crawling on a ledge through a dark cave through which a cold wind howled, they came out onto the sea. Clouds covered the sea from rim to rim of the unbroken range circling the sea. Only it wasn't really unbroken. On the other side there must have been a great gap between two mountains. Djehuti saw it first; he went around a corner just as the sun broke through for a moment. Those behind him heard a cry, then a bellow, and then a long, dwindling wail. They inched around the corner and got to the edge of the ledge just in time to see Djehuti's body disappear in the clouds below.

Afterward, they reconstructed what had happened. He had rounded the corner and seen a grail a few paces before him. Yes, a grail. Someone had *preceded* them. Apparently, Djehuti saw it, too, and then the sun shone through the gap in the mountain. Blinded, or startled, he had stepped backward and tripped over the grail.

There was just enough light from the passing sun to give a glimpse of something in the middle of the sea. It looked like the upper end of a colossal grail sticking from the clouds. Then the sun passed the gap and the clouds rolled back up and covered the big grail.

You're probably asking, how could the Egyptians see the sun? Even if the break in the mountains extended to the horizon, wouldn't the clouds still cover it? The answer is, yes, the clouds would cover it under normal circumstances. But there was a combination of wind which cleared the clouds away momentarily just as the sun passed the gap. An unhappy combination of circumstances, for Djehuti, anyway.

The winds are peculiar in that region. Twice, they cleared the clouds away so that the Egyptians could see, briefly, the upper portion of the tower. Without the direct rays of the sun, in the gloomy twilight of reflection from the skies, they could see only a dark bulk. But it was enough. There was an object out there, a vast object. Not necessarily a manmade object, since we don't know if the owners and operators of this planet are human. But it was an artifact; it was too smoothly cylindrical to be anything else. Though, at that distance, it could have been a spire of rock, I suppose.

But here's another clincher. Several hours later the Egyptians saw an object rise up from the clouds around the tower. It was round, and for them to see it from where they stood, it must have been enormous. When it got far up, it reflected light from the never setting sun. Then it rose so high it became invisible.

That really excited me. I said, "That tower could be the head-quarters, the home base, of Whomever is behind all this?"

"That's what Frisco and I think."

The Egyptians had become fond of Djehuti. Despite his ogreish appearance, he had a good heart, and he liked to joke. He wasn't above making puns in Egyptian, which shows a considerable intelligence on his part. Humankind is unique in the animal kingdom; it's the only species that can pun. *Homo agnominatio?* I don't know. My Latin gets weaker by the day. If I could find an ancient Roman or a Latin scholar I'd take a refresher course.

Back to Paheri's tale. And Djehuti. If it hadn't been for his gorillan strength, the Egyptians wouldn't have gotten as far as they did. So they said some prayers over him and pushed on down the path.

The narrow ledge inclined, generally, at a 45-degree angle and was slippery with moisture. It was just wide enough for one man to walk along, his shoulder brushing the cliff. There were several narrowings where they had to face the cliff and slide along it, their chests against the rock, their heels hanging over the edge, their fingers clutching every tiny roughness.

Halfway down, Akhenaten almost fell off. He'd stumbled in the fog over a skeleton. Yes, a skeleton, undoubtedly the one who'd abandoned the grail. None of his bones seemed to be broken, so they guessed that he had died of starvation. The Pharaoh said a prayer over the bones and cast them into the sea. After a while they came to the end of the path. This was at sea level. They despaired then, but Akhenaten grabbed hold of an outcropping with one hand and with a torch in his other hand looked around the projection.

On the other side was an opening, the mouth of a cave. He eased around the outcropping, the sea up to his knees, his feet on the underwater continuation of the ledge. His torch showed him a smooth rock floor that slanted upward at a 30-degree angle. The others followed him without mishap.

Akhenaten in the lead, they walked up the slope. Their hearts beat hard, their skins were cold, their teeth chattered. One man—our Paheri—was so scared that he had nervous diarrhoea.

Was this the entrance to the hall of the gods? Was jackal-headed Anubis waiting to conduct them to the great judge who would balance their good deeds against the bad?

It was then that Paheri got to thinking about the mean and unjust things he'd done, his pettinesses and cruelties, his greed and treachery. For a moment he refused to go on. But when the others kept walking, and the darkness began to press in on him, he resumed walking—though at a distance behind them.

The cave became a tunnel, the rock walls evidently worked by tools. It began curving gently and then, after a hundred meters, it entered a very large circular chamber. This was lit by nine black metal lamps on tall tripods. The lamps were ball shaped, and they burned with a cold, steady light.

There were several things in the chamber to astonish them. The nearest, though, was another skeleton. Like the other, it was still clothed. The right arm was fully extended as if it had been reaching out for something. Beside it was a grail. At the moment, they didn't examine the bones, but I'll describe it now. It was the skeleton of a female, and the skull and some still unrotted patches of hair showed that it was a Negress's.

She had probably died of starvation. That was tragically ironic, since she had died a few meters from food.

After her companion had died, she'd gone on, probably crawling part of the way, summoning enough strength to stand up and edge around the very narrow places. Then, with salvation in sight, she had died.

I wonder who she was? What drove her to take that perilous journey? How many of her party died or turned back before they got through the vast cave through which the waves of the polar sea rush out? How did they get past the hairy, big-nosed colossi? What was her name, and why was she so fiercely determined to drive on into the heart of darkness?

Perhaps she may have left a message inside her grail. However, its lid was closed, and so only she could open it. Anyway, it's very unlikely that the Egyptians could have read her writing. This was before the Chancers spread Esperanto around the world. Furthermore, billions who can speak this language don't know how to read it.

The Egyptians said a prayer over the bones and then silently inspected the largest objects in the chamber, metal boats. There were eleven, some large, some small, all in low, metal V-shaped supports open at both ends.

There were also supplies of food. They didn't know that at first, since they'd never seen plastic cans. But diagrams on plastic sheets indicated how to open them, which they did. They contained beef, bread, and vegetables. They ate heartily, and then they slept for a long time, being very fatigued from their journey.

But they felt that the gods (in Akhenaten's view, The God) had provided for them. A path had been prepared for them, though it had not been an easy one. The road to immortality had never been easy, and only the virtuous and hardy would traverse it. Perhaps Djehuti had sinned in some way and so had been hurled from the ledge by the gods.

There were diagrams, how-to-do-it sketches using signs, in the boats. They studied these and then carried one of the large boats through the tunnel. It could hold thirty people, but four people could lift it easily or one strong man could drag it. It was shoved under the ledge into the sea, which was moderately rough, and the party got into it. There was a small control board by the wheel. Though he was a Pharaoh and so above work of any kind, Akhenaten nevertheless took over the controls. Following the diagrammed instructions, he punched a button on the board. A screen lit up, and a bright orange outline of the tower appeared on it. He punched another button, and the boat moved of its own accord outward into the sea.

Everybody was scared, of course, though their leader did not show it. Yet they felt that they were in the right place and were welcome—in a sense. The boat they likened to the barge in which, in their religion, the dead journeyed across the waters of the Other World, Amenti.

(Amenti comes from Ament, a goddess whose name meant "the Westerner." She wore a feather, as did the Libyans, the people to the west of Egypt. She may have been a Libyan goddess borrowed by the Egyptians. A feather was also the sign or hieroglyph for the word "Western." In later times, "the West" meant the Land of the Dead, and Ament became the goddess of the country of the dead. She it was who welcomed them at the gate of the Other World. She proffered them bread and water and, if they ate it, they became "friends of the gods.")

Naturally, the food they'd found in the cave reminded them of this, just as the boat was an analog of the barge used by the dead in the Other World. The Egyptians, like many people, had been upset, not to mention outraged, when they woke from death upon The Riverworld. This was not what the priests had said would happen to them after death. Yet, there were parallels here, physical analogs, to the promised land. Also, that there was a River was comforting. They had always been a riparian folk, living close to the Nile. And now they had been guided by a divine being to the heart of the Other World.

They wondered if they should have named the giant subhuman Anubis instead of Djehuti. Anubis was the jackal-headed god who conducted the dead in the Underworld to the Double Palace of Osiris, the Judger, the Weigher of Souls. Still, Djehuti was the spokesman of the gods and the keeper of their records. Sometimes, he took the shape of a dog-headed ape. Considering their companion's features and his hairiness, he did look like that avatar of Djehuti.

Note: These two aspects of Thoth (Djehuti) indicate that there may have been a fusion of two different gods in early times.

This world did have some similarities to the Other World. Now that they were in the Abode of Osiris, the similarities were even more striking. The Riverworld could be that country between the world of the living and the dead vaguely described by the Priests. The priests had told confusing, contradictory stories. Only the gods knew the full truth.

Whatever the truth was, it would soon be found. The tower didn't look like their picture of the Double Hall of Justice, but perhaps the gods had changed things. The Riverworld was a place of constant change, a reflection of the state of mind of the gods themselves.

Akhenaten turned the wheel so that the orange tower was bisected by the vertical line splitting the screen. At times, just to reassure himself that he had control of the speed, he would squeeze the bulb fixed to the right side of the steering wheel. The boat's speed would increase or decrease according to the force of the squeezing.

The boat headed straight through the choppy, fog-shrouded sea for the tower at a speed frightening to its passengers. Within two hours the image on the screen had become enormous. Then the image burst into a flame which covered the entire screen, and Akhenaten let the boat proceed very slowly. He punched a button, and they all cried out in fright and wonder as two round objects on the prow of the boat shot forth two bright beams of light.

Ahead lay a vast bulk—the tower.

Akhenaten punched a button indicated by the diagram. Slowly, a large, round door, a port, swung open from what had been a smooth, seamless surface. Light sprang into being. Inside was a wide hall, its walls of the same grey metal.

Akehnaten brought the boat alongside the entrance. Some of the crew grabbed the threshold. The Pharaoh pressed the button which shut off the invisible power that moved the boat. He stepped onto the side of the boat, which was just below the threshold. After jumping inside the hall, he took the ropes attached to the inside of the hull and secured them around hooks set into the hall. Apprehensively, silently, the others followed him.

All, that is, except for Paheri. The terror was now almost unendurable. His teeth clicked uncontrollably. His knees shook. His heart beat in his frozen flesh like a frightened bird's wings. His mind moved sluggishly, like winter mud flowing down a hillside warmed by the sun.

He was too weak to get up from the seat and step into the corridor. He was sure that if he could go on, he'd face his judge and be found wanting.

I'll say one thing for Paheri. Two. He did have a conscience, and he wasn't afraid to admit to Tom Rider that he'd been a coward. That takes courage.

Akhenaten, as if he had nothing to fear from The One God, walked steadily toward the end of the corridor. The others were bunched behind him at a dozen paces. One looked back and was surprised that Paheri was still in the boat. He gestured for him to come on. Paheri shook his head and hung on to the gunwale.

Then, without a single cry from anyone, those in the corridor slumped to their knees, fell forward on their hands, tried to rise, failed, and sagged onto their faces. They lay as still and limp as putty models.

The door swung slowly shut. It closed silently, leaving no evidence that there was a door, not even a thin seamline, and Paheri was alone in the dark fog and the cold sea.

Paheri wasted no time in getting the boat turned around. It moved at its former speed, but now there was no signal on the scope, no bright image, to direct it. He could not find the cave, and so he went up and down the base of the cliff until he gave up trying to locate the cave. Finally, he directed it alongside the cliff until he came to the archway through which the sea rams into the mountains. He got through the long and giant cave there, but when he came to the great cataract, he could find no place to beach the boat. It was carried over the falls. Paheri remembered the bellowing of the waters, being turned over and over, and then . . . unconsciousness.

When he awoke from his translation, he was lying naked in the dark fog under the overhang of a grailstone. His grail—a new one, of course—and a pile of cloths lay by him. Presently he heard voices. The dim figures of people coming to place their grails on the stone approached. He was safe and sound—except for the terrible memory of the hall of the gods.

Tom Rider was translated to Paheri's area after he'd been killed by some fanatical medieval Christians. He became a soldier, met Paheri, who was in the same squad, and heard his story. Rider worked up to a captaincy and then he was killed again. He awoke the next day in an area where Farrington lived.

Several months later they went up-River together in a dugout. Then they settled down for a while to build the *Razzle Dazzle*.

What's my reaction to all this? Well, Paheri's story makes me want to go see for myself if it's true or not. If he wasn't making it up, and Tom says Paheri was as stolid and as unimaginative as a wooden cigarstore Indian, then this world, unlike Earth, may have answers to the Big Questions, a mirror to the Ultimate Reality.

Towerward ho!

40

(Frigate's letter continued)

There's more to the story than what Rider told me. I chanced to overhear Frisco and Tex several days ago. They were in the main cabin, and the hatch was open. I had sat down, my back against the cabin, and had lit up a cigar. (Yes, for the nonce, I've fallen into the clutches of Ole Devil Nicotine.) I really wasn't paying much attention to their voices, since I was occupied with thoughts resulting from a conversation with Nur el-Musafir.

Then I heard the captain, who has a loud voice, say, "Yes, but how do we know he isn't using us for some reason of his own? Some reason beneficial to him but not so good for us? And how do we know we can get into the tower? That Egyptian couldn't. Is there another entrance? If there is, why didn't he tell us? He did say he'd tell us more about the tower later on. But that was sixteen years ago! Sixteen! We ain't seen him since!

"I mean, you ain't seen him. Of course, I never did see him. Anyway, maybe something happened to him. Maybe he got caught. Or maybe he doesn't need us anymore!"

Rider said something I couldn't catch. Farrington said, "Sure, but you know what I think? I think he didn't have the slightest idea those Egyptians got to the tower. Or that one got away. At least, not when he talked to you."

Rider said something. Farrington replied, "The tunnel and the rope and the boats and probably the path must have been prepared for us. But others got there first."

The wind strengthened then, and I couldn't hear anything for a minute or two. I moved closer to the companionway well. Farrington said, "You really think some of them, one, anyway, might be on this ship? Well, it's possible, Tex, but so what if it is?

"Why weren't we told who the others were so we could recognize each other and get together? When are we going to be told? Where do we all meet? At River's end? What if we get there and nobody shows up? Do we wait a hundred years or so there? What if . . ."

Rider broke in once more. He must have talked a long time. I was straining my ears, so lit up with curiosity that I almost shone with a sort of St. Elmo's fire. Mustafa, at the wheel, was looking at me with a strange expression. He must have known, or guessed, that I was eavesdropping. This made me uneasy. I wanted desperately to hear the rest. But if the Turk told those two I'd been listening to them, I might get tossed off the ship. On the other hand, he couldn't know that they were discussing anything I shouldn't be hearing. So I puffed on my cigar, and when it was out, I pretended to fall asleep.

The situation reminded me of Jim Hawkins' experience in the apple barrel in *Treasure Island,* when he overheard Long John Silver plotting with his pirate cronies to take over the *Hispaniola* after the treasure was found. Only, in this case, Farrington and Rider weren't planning anything evil against anybody at all. They seemed to be more plotted against.

Farrington said, "What I'd like to know is why he needs us? Here's a man with more power than a dozen gods, and if he's going against his buddies, what help can he get from mere mortals like us? And if he wants us in the tower, why doesn't he just ferry us to it?"

There was another interruption, followed by the clink of grail cups against each other. Then Rider spoke loudly. ". . . must have damn good reasons. Anyway, we'll find out in time. And what else do we have to do?"

Farrington bellowed laughter, then said, "That's right! What else? Might as well use our time for some end, good or bad. But I still feel like we're being exploited, and I'm fed up with that. I was exploited by the rich and the middle class when I was young, and then when I became famous and rich, I was exploited by editors and publishers and then by my relatives and friends. I ain't going to let anybody exploit me here on this world, use me like I was a dumb beast fit for nothing but shoveling coal or canning fish!"

"You did some self-exploiting, too," Rider said. "Didn't we all? I made plenty of money and so did you. And what happened? We spent more'n we made on big houses and fast cars and bad investments and booze and whores and putting on a big front. We could've played it smart and tight and saved our money and taken it easy and lived to ripe old ages in ease and plenty. But . . ."

Farrington exploded into laughter again. "But we didn't, did we? That wasn't our nature, Tex, and it ain't now. Live it up, burn the candle at both ends, spin off fire and beauty like a St. Catherine's wheel instead of trudging along like a steer turning a mill wheel! So the deballed beast gets turned out to pasture instead of going to the glue factory? So what? What does he have to think about while he's munching grass? A long, grey life and a short, grey future?"

More clinking. Then Farrington started to tell Rider about a train trip he'd taken from San Francisco to Chicago. He had introduced himself to a beautiful woman who was accompanied by her child and a maid. It wasn't more than an hour after meeting her that he and the woman went to his compartment, where they coupled like crazed minks for three days and nights.

I decided that then was a good time to leave. I got up and strolled to the foremast where Abigail Rice and Nur were talking. Mustafa apparently never suspected me of eavesdropping.

Since then, I've been wondering. Who was the *he* referred to? It's obvious that he must be one of Those who have made this world for us and then raised us from the dead. Could it really be? The idea seemed so tremendous, so difficult to grasp. Yet—Somebody has to have done this, Somebodies, I should say. And they are truly gods, in many senses, anyway.

If Rider is telling the truth, there is a tower in the north polar sea. And by implication it's a base for Whomever made this world, our secret masters. Yes, I know this sounds paranoid. Or like a science fiction tale, most of which were paranoid, anyway. But, except for the very few who got rich, science fiction writers were convinced that their secret (or not so secret) masters were the publishers. Even the rich ones questioned their royalty statements. Maybe the tower is inhabited by the cabal of super-publishers. (Just kidding, Bob. I think.)

Maybe Rider is lying. Or his informant, Paheri, was lying. I don't believe so. It's obvious that Rider and Farrington have been approached by one of these Whomevers. They weren't just making up this story to fool an eavesdropper.

Or were they?

How paranoid can you get?

No, they were discussing something that had really happened. If they were careless, left the hatch open, didn't talk subduedly, it was only natural. After all those years, who wouldn't get careless? As far as that goes, why shouldn't they tell everybody?

Somebody might be looking for them. Who? Why?

My mind yaws, pitches, and rolls. So many speculations, so many possibilities. And I think, wow! What a story! Too bad I hadn't thought of something like this when I was writing science fiction. But the concept of a planet consisting of a many-millions-kilometer-long river along which all of humanity that ever lived had been resurrected (a good part of it, anyway) would have been too big to put in one book. It would have taken at least twelve books to do it anywhere near justice. No, I'm glad I didn't think of it.

In light of those developments, what do I do now? Should I mail this letter or tear it up? It won't fall into your hands, of course, not a chance of that. Into whose, then?

Probably it'll be picked up by someone who can't even read English.

Why am I afraid it might fall into the wrong hands? I really don't know. But there is a dark, secret struggle going on under the seemingly simple life of this Valley. I intend to find out just what it is. I'll have to proceed cautiously though. A small voice tells me that I might be better off if I don't know anything about this.

Anyway, to whom am I really writing these missives? To myself, probably, though I hope hopelessly that just possibly impossibly one might drift into the hands of someone I knew and loved or at least was fond of.

And yet, this very moment, as I stare across the water at the many people on the bank, I might be looking directly at the person to whom I've written one of these letters. But the ship is in the middle of The River just now, and I'm too far away to recognize anyone recognizable.

Great God, the faces I've seen in twenty years! Millions, far more than I ever saw on Earth. Some of the faces came into being three hundred thousand years ago or more. Undoubtedly, the faces of many of my ancestors, some of them Neanderthals. A certain number of *Homo neanderthalis* was absorbed by miscegenation into *Homo sapiens,* you know. And considering the flux and reflux of large groups through prehistory and history, migrations, invasions, slavery, individual travel, some, maybe many, of the Mongolian, Amerindian, Australoid, and Negro faces I've seen belong to my ancestors.

Consider this. Each generation of your ancestors, going back in time, doubles its number. You were born in 1925. You had two parents, born in 1900. (Yes, I know you were born in 1923 and your mother was forty when she bore you. But this is an ideal case, an average.)

Your parents' parents were born in 1875. That makes four. Double your ancestors every twenty-five years. By 1800, you have thirty-two ancestors. Most of them didn't even know each other, but they were "destined" to be your great-great-great-grandparents.

In 1700 A.D., you have five hundred twelve ancestors. In 1600 A.D. 8192 ancestors. In 1500 A.D., 131,072 ancestors. In 1400, 2,097,152. In 1300, 33,554,432. By 1200 A.D., you have 536,870,912 ancestors.

So do I. So does everybody. If the world population was, say, two billion in 1925 (I don't remember what it was), then multiply that by the number of your ancestors in 1200 A.D. You get over one quadrillion. Impossible? Right.

I just happen to remember that in 1600 the estimated world population was five hundred million. In 1 A.D., it was an estimated 138,000,000. So, the conclusion is obvious. There was a hell of a lot of incest, close and remote, going on in the past. Not to mention the present. Probably from the dawn of humankind. So, you and I are related. And, in fact, it may be possible that we're all related, many times over. How many Chinese and black Africans born in 1925 were distant cousins of you and me? Plenty, I'd say.

So, the faces I see on both banks as I sail along are my cousins'. Hello, Hang Chow. Yiya, Bulabula. What's happening, Hiawatha? Hail, Og, Son of Fire! But even if they knew this, they wouldn't feel any more friendly toward me. Or vice versa. The most intense quarreling and the most vicious bloodletting take place in families. Civil wars are the worst wars. But then, since we're all cousins, all wars are civil. Mighty uncivil, at the same time. The paradox of human relations. I'll shoot your ass off, brother.

Mark Twain was right. Did you ever read his *Extract from Captain Stormfield's Visit to Heaven?* Old Stormfield was shocked when he got past the Pearly Gates because there were so many dark people. Like all of us pale Caucasians, he had envisioned Heaven as being full of white faces with here and there a few yellow, brown, and black ones. But it wasn't that way. He'd forgotten that the dark-skinned peoples had always outnumbered the whites. In fact, for every white face he saw there were two dark ones. And that's the way it is here. My hat is off to you, Mr. Twain. You told it like it was gonna be.

So, here we are in the Rivervalley, knowing not why and whence. Just like on Eath.

Of course, there are plenty of people who say they know. There are the two dominant churches, the Chancers and the Nichirenites, and a thousand sects of reformed Christians, Moslems, Jews, Buddhists, Hindus, and God knows what all. The former Taoists and Confucianists say they don't give a damn; this is a better life, on the whole, than the last one. The totemists are in a bit of a bind, since there are no animals here. But that doesn't mean the totem spirits aren't here. Many's the savage I've run into who sees his totem in dreams or visions. The majority of them, though, have been converted to one of the "higher" religions.

There's also Nur el-Musafir. He's a Sufi. He was just as shocked as anybody to wake up here. He wasn't outraged, however, and he reordered his thinking *tout de suite.* He says that whatever beings have made this world have done so with only our eventual good in mind. Otherwise, why go to all this great expense and trouble? (In this, he sounds like a barker for a circus. But he's sincere. Which doesn't mean he knows what he's talking about.)

We shouldn't concern ourselves with the Who or the How, he says. Just with the Why. In this respect, he sounds like a Chancer. But I see I'm about to run out of my quota of paper. So, adiau, adios, selah, amen, salaam, shalom, and so long. (The English *so long* is from *selang,* the Moslem Malayan's pronunciation of the Arabic *salaam.*)

Amicably and didactically yours in the bowels of Whomever,
                                    PETER JAIRUS FRIGATE

P.S. I still don't know if I'll mail this *in toto,* censor it, or use it for toilet paper.

41

ON THE AVERAGE, THE RIVER WAS 2.4135 KILOMETERS OR A MILE
and a half wide. Sometimes it narrowed into channels always lined
by high hills; sometimes it widened into a lake. Whatever its
breadth, its depth was everywhere about 305 meters or a trifle over
1000 feet.

Nowhere along The River was there water erosion of the banks.
The grass on the plains merged into an aquatic grass at the water
level, and the latter flourished on the sides and bottom of the
channel. The roots of this fused with the roots of the surface grass to
form an interconnected mass. The grass was not separate blades; it
was one vast vegetable entity.

The water plants were eaten by a multitude of fish life from
surface to bottom. Many species cruised about in the upper stratum,
where the sunlight penetrated. Others, paler creatures but no less
voracious, swarmed in the middle layer. In the darkness of the
bottom many weird forms scuttled, crawled, wriggled, jetted,
swam.

Some ate the leprous-white rooted things that looked like flowers
or were in turn enfolded and digested by them. Others, large and
small, slid steadily along, mouths gaping, collecting the microscop-
ic life that also lived in the fluid strata.

The largest of all, vaster than the blue whale of Earth, was a
carnivorous fish called the river dragon. It shared with a much
smaller water dweller the ability to roam the bottom or skim the
surface without harm from change in pressure.

The other creature had many names, but in English it was generally called "croaker." It was the size of a German police dog, as
slow as a sloth, and as undiscriminating in appetite as a hog. The
chief sanitation engineer of The River, it ate anything that did not
resist it. The greater part of its diet, however, was the human turd.

A lungfish, it also foraged ashore at night. Many a human had
been frightened on seeing its huge goggle eyes in the fog or when
stumbling over its slimy body as it crawled around seeking garbage
and crap. Almost as scary as its appearance was its loud croak,
evoking images of monsters and ghosts.

On this day of year 25 A.R.D., one of these vilely stinking

scavengers was near a bank. Here the current was weaker than in the middle. Even so, its fin-legs were going at near top speed to keep it from being moved backward. Presently, its nose detected a dead fish floating toward it. It moved out a little and waited for the carcass to drift into its mouth.

Along came the fish and another object immediately behind it. Both went into the croaker's mouth, the fish sliding down the gullet easily, the large object sticking for a moment before a convulsive swallow drew it in.

For five years, the watertight bamboo jar containing Frigate's letter to Rohrig had been carried downstream. Considering the vast numbers of fishers and voyagers, it should have been picked up and opened long before. However, it was ignored by all creatures except for the fish whose primary object had been the delectable rotting chub.

Five days before the container came to journey's end, it had drifted past the area in which its intended recipient lived. But Rohrig was in a hut, surrounded by the stone and wood sculptures he fashioned for trade in booze and cigarettes, snoring off the effects of a big party.

Perhaps it was just coincidence, perhaps some psychic principle was responsible, a vibratory link between the addresser and the addressee. Whatever the cause, Rohrig was dreaming of Frigate that early morning. He was back in 1950 when he had been a graduate student supported by the G.I. Bill and a working wife.

It was a warm, late-May day (Mayday! Mayday!). He was sitting in a small room, facing three Ph.D.s. This was the day of reckoning. After five years of labor and stress in the halls of learning he would gain or lose the prize, a Master of Arts in English literature. If he passed his oral defense of his thesis, he would go out into the world as a teacher of high-school English. If he failed, he would have to study for six months and then try for a second and final chance.

Now the three inquisitors, though smiling, were shooting questions at him as if they were arrows and he was the target—which was the case. Rohrig was not nervous since his thesis was on medieval Welsh poetry, a subject he'd chosen because he believed that the professors knew very little about it.

He was right. But Ella Rutherford, a charming lady of forty-six, though prematurely white haired, had it in for him. Some time ago they'd been lovers, meeting twice a week in her apartment. Then one afternoon they had gotten into a furious drunken argument about the merits of Byron as a poet. Rohrig wasn't crazy about his verse, but he admired Byron's lifestyle, which he considered to be true poetry. Anyway, he liked to take the opposite side of an argument.

As a result, he had stormed out of the apartment after saying some very cruel things to her. He had also shouted at her that he never wanted to see her in private again.

Rutherford believed that he had seduced her just to get a high grade in her course, that he was using the argument as an excuse to quit making love to a middle-aged woman. She was wrong. He was compulsively attracted to older women. However, he was finding her demands too great a strain. He could no longer satisfy her, his wife, two female sophomores, two of his friends' wives, a female bartender who gave him free drinks, and the superintendent of the apartment building in which he lived.

Five, he could handle; eight, no. He was being drained of time, energy, and semen, and he was falling asleep in class. Thus, he had craftily started violent arguments with his professor, one of the sophomores (it was rumored that she had the clap), and the wife of a friend (she was too emotionally demanding, anyway).

Now, Rutherford, her watery blue eyes narrowed, said, "You've done very well in your defense, Mister Rohrig. So far."

She paused. He felt suddenly chilled. His anus tightened. Sweat poured down his face and from his armpits. He had visions of her sitting up late nights thinking of some way to get him, some horrible, peculiarly humiliating way.

Doctors Durham and Pur quit drumming their fingers. This was getting interesting. Their colleague was burning bright, like the eyes of a tiger about to spring on a tethered lamb. Lightning was going to strike, and the unfortunate candidate was without a grounding rod, unless it was up his ass.

Rohrig gripped the arms of his chair. Sweat popped out on his forehead like mice scared from a Swiss cheese; sweat, acid sweat, nibbled at the armpits of his shirt. What in hell was coming?

Rutherford said, "You seem to know your subject thoroughly. You've given a remarkable demonstration of knowledge of a rather obscure field of poetry. I'm sure we're all proud of you. We haven't wasted our time with you in the classroom."

The sly bitch was telling him that she had wasted her time outside of the classroom with him. But this was only a sideswipe, a remark meant to injure but not to kill. She was setting him up for the big fall. It was seldom, if ever, that the examining professors congratulated the candidate during the torture. Afterward, perhaps, when the board had voted that he be passed.

"Now . . . tell me," Rutherford drawled.

She paused.

Another turn of the crank of the rack.

"Tell me, Mister Rohrig. Just where *is* Wales?"

Something in him lost its hold and slid bumping down to the bottom of his stomach. He clapped his hand on his forehead, and he groaned.

"Mother of mercy! Trapped! Holy shit!"

Doctor Pur, dean of women, turned pale. This was the first time in her life she had ever heard that vile word.

Doctor Durham, who wept when reciting poetry to his students, looked as if he was about to swoon.

Doctor Rutherford, having hurled her thunderbolt, smiled without pity or compassion upon the remains of her victim.

Rohrig rallied. He refused to go down without his flags flying, the band playing *Nearer My God to Thee*. He smiled as if the gold in the pot at rainbow's end had not suddenly been transmuted into turds.

"I don't know how you did it, but you *got* me! O.K. I never said I was perfect. What happens now?"

Verdict: failed. Sentence: six months of probation with another and final inquisition at its end.

Later, when he and Rutherford were alone in the hall, she said, "I suggest you study geography, too, Rohrig. I'll give you a clue. Wales is near England. But I doubt my advice will help you. You couldn't find your ass if it was handed to you on a silver platter."

His friend, Pete Frigate, was waiting at the end of the hall for him. Pete was one of the group of older students dubbed "The Bearded Ones" by a sophomore girl who liked to hang around them. They were all veterans whose college education had been interupted by the war. They and their wives or mistresses led a life which was then called "Bohemian." They were the unknown forerunners of the beatniks and the hippies.

As Rohrig drew near, Frigate looked questioningly at him. Though Rohrig was near tears, he put on a big smile and then began laughing uproariously.

"You won't believe this, Pete!"

Frigate did find it difficult to believe that anyone past the sixth grade of grammar school did not know where Wales was. When he was finally convinced, he too laughed.

Rohrig shouted, "How in hell could that white-haired fox have found out my weak spot?"

Frigate said, "I don't know, but she's magnificent. Listen, Bob. Don't feel so bad. I know a distinguished surgeon who doesn't remember if the sun goes around the earth or the earth goes around the sun. He says it's not necessary to know that when you're digging into people's bodies.

"But an English major . . . he ought at least to know . . . ooh, haw, haw!"

In one of those non sequiturs the Dream Scripter so often writes, Rohrig found himself elsewhere. Now he was in fog and chasing a butterfly. It was beautiful, and what made it so valuable was that it was the only one of its kind and only Rohrig knew that it existed. It was striped with azure and gold, its antennae were scarlet, its eyes were green emeralds. The king of the dwarfs had fashioned it in his cave in the Black Mountains, and the Wizard of Oz had dunked it in the waters of life.

Fluttering only an inch beyond his outstretched hand, it led him through the mists.

"Hold still, you son of a bitch! Hold still!"

He plunged after it for what seemed like miles. Dimly, out of the corner of his eye, he could see shapes in the clouds, things standing as motionless and quietly as if they were carved from bone. Twice he distinguished a figure; one wore a crown, the other had a horse's head.

Suddenly, he was confronted by one of the objects. He stopped since it seemed impossible for some reason to go around it. The butterfly hung for a moment above the top of the thing, then settled down upon it. Its green eyes glowed, and its front legs shook the antennae mockingly.

Moving forward slowly, Rohrig saw that it was Frigate who was blocking his path.

"Don't you dare touch it!" Rohrig whispered fiercely. "It's mine!"

Frigate's face was as expressionless as a knight's visor. It always looked deadpan when Rohrig was in one of his many furies and chewing out everybody in sight. That had made Rohrig even more angry, and now it rocketed him to the point of utter madness.

"Out of the way, Frigate! Step aside or get knocked down!"

The butterfly, startled by the outburst, flew off into the fog.

"I can't," Frigate said.

"Why not?" Rohrig thundered as he hopped up and down in frustration.

Frigate pointed downward. He was standing on a large red square. Adjoining it were other squares, some red, some black.

"I got misplaced. I don't know what's going to happen now. It's against the rules to put me on a red square. But then, who cares about rules? Besides the pieces, I mean."

"Can I help you?" Rohrig said.

"How could you do that? You can't help yourself."

Frigate pointed over Rohrig's shoulder.

"It's going to catch you now. While you've been chasing the butterfly, it's been chasing you."

Rohrig suddenly felt utterly terrified. There was something after him, something which would do something horrible to him.

Desperately, he tried to move forward, to go over or around Frigate. But the red square held him as it held Frigate.

"Trapped!"

He could still see the butterfly, a dot, a dust mote, gone. Forever.

The fog had thickened. Frigate was only a blur.

"I make my own rules!" Rohrig shouted.

A whisper came from the mists before him. "Quiet! It'll hear you!"

He awoke briefly. His hutmate stirred.

"What's wrong, Bob?"

"I'm drowning in a surf of uncease."

"What?"

"Surcease."

He sank bank into the primal ocean down to where drowned gods leaned in the ooze at crazy angles, staring with fish-cold eyes under barnacled crowns.

Neither he nor Frigate knew that he could have answered one of the questions in the letter. Rohrig had awakened on Resurrection Day in the far north. His neighbors were prehistoric Scandinavians, Patagonian Indians, Ice Age Mongolians, and late-twentieth-century Siberians. Rohrig was quick at learning new languages and was soon fluent in a dozen, though he never mastered the pronunciation and he murdered the syntax. As he always did, he made himself at home, and he was soon friends with many. For a while, he even set himself up as a sort of shaman. Shamans, however, must take themselves seriously if they would succeed, and Rohrig was only serious about his sculpturing. Also, he began to tire of the cold. He was a sun worshipper; his happiest days had been in Mexico where he was the first mate on a small coastal ship transporting frozen shrimp from Yucatan to Brownsville, Texas. He had been briefly involved in gun-smuggling there but had quit it before spending a few days in a Mexican jail. He had also quit Mexico. The authorities could not prove his guilt, but they suggested that he leave the country.

He was just about to take a dugout down-River for a warm climate when along came Agatha Croomes. Agatha was a black woman, born 1713, died 1783, a freed slave, a backwoods Baptist preacher, a holy roller, four times married, mother of ten children, and a pipe smoker. She had been resurrected a hundred thousand grailstones away, but here she was. A vision had come to her, a vision in which God told her to come to His dwelling at the North Pole, where He would hand her the keys to kingdom come, to glory and salvation forever, to understanding of time and eternity, space and infinity, creation and destruction, death and life. She would also be the one to cast the devil into the pit, lock him up, and throw the key away.

Rohrig thought she was crazy, but she intrigued him. Also, he wasn't so sure that the solution to the mystery of this world did not lie at the beginning of The River.

He knew that no one had ventured into the fog-laden land further north. If he accompanied her party of eleven, he would be among the first to reach the North Pole. If he had anything to do with it, he would be the very first person to get there. When their goal was in sight he was going to sprint ahead and plant on the site of the North Pole a stone statuette of himself, his name incised at the base.

From then on, anybody who got there would know that he'd been beat out for first place by Robert F. Rohrig. Agatha wouldn't take him, however, unless he believed in the Lord and the Holy Book. He hated to lie, but he told himself that he wasn't really deceiving her. Deep down, he did believe in a god, though he wasn't sure whether its name was Jehovah or Rohrig. As for the Bible, it was a book, and all books told the truth in the sense that their authors believed they were writing a kind of truth.

Before the expedition reached the end of the grailstones, five had turned back. When they got to the enormous cave out of which The River fell, four decided that they would starve to death if they kept on going. Rohrig went on with Agatha Croomes and Winglat, a member of an Amerind tribe that had crossed from Siberia to Alaska sometime in the Old Stone Age. Rohrig would have liked to turn back, but he wasn't going to admit that a crazy black woman and a paleolithic savage had more courage than he.

Besides, Agatha's preachings had almost convinced him that she had had a true vision. Maybe Almighty God and sweet Jesus *were* waiting for him. It wouldn't do to hold up the schedule.

After they had crawled along the ledge in the cave and Winglat had slipped and fallen into The River, Rohrig told himself that he was as crazy as Agatha. But he went on.

When they came to the place where the ledge sloped downward into the fog, the fog that covered a sea the sounds of which faintly reached them, they were very weak from hunger. There was no turning back now. If they did not find food within the day, they would die. Agatha, however, said that all they could eat was close at hand. She knew it was so because she had had a vision while they slept on the ledge within the cave. She had seen a place where meat and vegetables were in abundance.

Rohrig watched her crawl away from him. After a while, he followed. But he left his grail behind because he was too weak to drag it. If he survived, he could always come back for it. The statuette was in the grail, and for a few seconds he considered removing it and taking it with him. To hell with it, he thought, and he went down the path.

He never made it. Weakness overcame him; his legs and arms just would not obey his will.

Thirst killed him before starvation did its job. It was ironic that The River had rushed by him, and he could not drink because he had no rope with which to lower his grail and collect the precious fluid.

A sea was booming against the rocks at the base of the cliffs, and he could not descend it it.

"Coleridge would appreciate this," he thought. "I wish I did."

He muttered, "Now I'll never get the answers to my questions. Maybe it's just as well. I probably wouldn't have liked them anyway."

Now Rohrig was sleeping uneasily in a hut by The River in the equatorial zone. And Frigate, standing watch on the deck of a cutter, was chuckling. He was recalling Rohrig's ordeal while defending his thesis.

Perhaps it was telepathy that evoked the incident in their minds at the same time. It's preferable to use Occam's razor, that never dull but seldom used blade. Call it coincidence.

The croaker placed itself directly in the path of the floating dead fish. The body went into the wide mouth of the amphibian. Frigate's letter and its container, only a centimeter behind the carcass, were also engulfed, and both slid into the gullet and became lodged in the croaker's belly.

Its stomach could easily handle garbage, excrement, and rotting flesh. But the cellulose fibers of the bamboo case were too tough for it to convert into absorbable form. After feeling sharp pain for a long time, the croaker died trying to pass the container.

The letter often kills the spirit. Sometimes, the envelope does it.

42

ALMOST EVERYBODY WAS CHEERING. PEOPLE WERE CROWDING around Jill and hugging and kissing her, and for once she did not mind. Most of the display of affection was due to booziness, she knew, but she still felt a warm glow within herself. If they had not been pleased, their very drunkenness could have resulted in open hostility. Perhaps she was not as disliked as she had thought. Here was David Schwartz, whom she had once overheard calling her "Old Frozen Face," patting her on the back and congratulating her.

Anna Obrenova was standing by Barry Thorn, though neither had spoken much to the other all evening. She was smiling as if she were pleased that Jill Gulbirra had been chosen over her. Perhaps she really did not care. Jill preferred to believe that the little blonde was seething with hate, though she could be wrong. Anna might have a rational attitude toward her. After all, she was a Johnny-come-lately, and Jill had devoted thousands of hours to the construction of the ship and the training of the crew.

Firebrass had shouted for silence. The loud chatter and singing had finally stopped. Then he had said that he was announcing the roster of officers, and he had grinned at her. She had felt sick. His grin was malicious, she was sure of that. He was going to pay her back for all the cutting remarks she had made to him. Justified remarks, because she was not going to allow anyone to run over her just because she was a woman. But he was in a position to get revenge.

Yet, he had done the right thing, and he seemed to be happy about doing it.

Jill, smiling, made her way through the crowd, threw her arms around Firebrass and burst into tears. He thrust his tongue deep into her mouth and then patted her fanny. This time, she did not resent unasked-for familiarities. He wasn't taking advantage of her emotions or being condescending. He was, after all, fond of her, and perhaps he was sexually attracted to her. Or perhaps he was just being ornery.

Anna, still smiling, held out her hand and said, "My sincerest congratulations, Jill." Jill took the delicate and cool hand, felt an irrational, almost overpowering impulse to yank her arm out of its socket, and said, ''Thank you very much, Anna.''

Thorn waved to her and shouted something, congratulations, probably. He did, however, make no effort to come to her.

A moment later, she stumbled weeping out of the ballroom. Before she had gotten home, she hated herself for having shown how strongly she felt. She had never cried in public, not even at the funerals of her parents.

The tears dried as she thought of her father and mother. Where were they? What were they doing? It would be nice if she could see them. That was all: nice. She did not want to live in the same area with them. They were not her old mother and father, grey haired, wrinkling, and fat, their main concerns their grandchildren. They would look as young as she, and they would have little in common with her except some shared experiences. They would bore her and vice versa. It would be a strain to pretend that the child-parent relationship had not died.

Besides, she thought of her mother as a cipher, a passive appendage to her father, who was a violent, loud, domineering man. She did not really like him, though she had grieved somewhat when he had died. But that was because of what might have been, not because of what had been.

For all she knew, they might be dead again.

What did it matter now?

It did not matter. Then why the second flood of tears?

43

"WELL, FOLKS, HERE WE ARE AGAIN. THIS TIME IT'S THE BIG ONE. The final take-off. Heigh-ho for the Big Grail, the Misty Tower, the house of the Santa Claus at the North Pole, the Saint Nick who gave us the gifts of resurrection, eternal youth, free food, booze, and tobacco.

"There must be at least a million people here. The stands are full, the hills are crowded, people are falling out of the trees. The police are having a hell of a time keeping order. It's a beautiful day, isn't it always? The uproar is really something, and I don't think you can hear a word I'm saying even through this PA system. So, folks, up yours!

"Aha! Some of you heard that. Just kidding, folks, just trying to get your attention. Let me tell you again about the *Parseval.* I know that you have pamphlets describing this colossal airship, but most of you are illiterates. Not that it's your fault. You speak Esperanto, but you've never had an opportunity to learn to read it. So here goes. Only, wait a moment while I moisten my parched throat with some skull-bloom.

"Ah! That was smoo-oo-ooth! The only trouble is that I've been quenching my thirst since before dawn, and I'm having trouble seeing straight. I hate to think of tomorrow morning, but what the hell. You have to pay for everything good in this world, not to mention the others.

"There she is, folks, though it's hardly necessary to point her out to you. The *Parseval.* Named by Firebrass for the man who first suggested that the airship be built though there was a lot of argument at first about what name'd be painted on her silver sides.

"Third mate Metzing wanted to name her the *Graf Zeppelin III,* after the man who was responsible for the first airship commercial line and chiefly responsible for the military Zeppelins.

"First Mate Gulbirra thought that she ought to be called *Adam and Eve,* after the whole human race, since she represents all of us. She also suggested *Queen of the Skies* and *Titania.* A little bit of female chauvinism there. *Titania* sounds too much like *Titanic,* anyway, and you know what happened to that ship.

"No, you don't. I forgot most of you never heard of her.

"One of the engineers, I forget his name at the moment, he was a crewman on the ill-fated *Shenandoah,* wanted to name her *Silver Cloud.* That was the name of the airship in a book called *Tom Swift and His Big Dirigible.*

"Another wanted to name her the *Henri Giffard* after the Frenchman who flew the first self-propelled lighter-than-air craft. Too bad old Henri couldn't be here to see the culmination of the airship, the acme of dirigible art, the last and the best and the greatest of all aerial vessels. Too bad the whole human race can't be here to witness this challenge to the gods, the flying gauntlet flung against the face of the powers on high!

"Pardon me a moment, folks. Time for another libation to the gods to be poured down this dry throat instead of being wasted by pouring on the ground.

"Aaah! Mighty good, folks! Drink up! The liquor's free, compliments of the house, which is the nation of Parolando.

"So, folks, our esteemed ex-president, Milton Firebrass, ex-American, ex-astronaut, decided to call this colossus the *Parseval.* Since he's the chief honcho, the big enchilada, the boss, that's what she's titled.

"So . . . oh, yeah, I started to give you her statistics. Captain Firebrass wanted to build the biggest dirigible ever built, and he did. She's also the biggest that will ever be built, since there won't be any more. Maybe he should have called her *The Last Is the Best.*

"Anyway, the *Parseval* is 2680 feet or 820 meters long. Its widest diameter is 1112 feet or 328 meters. Its gas capacity is 120,000,000 cubic feet or 6,360,000 cubic meters.

"The skin is of stressed duraluminum| and it contains eight large gas cells with smaller cells in the nose and tail fairings. Originally, she was to have thirteen gondolas suspended outside the hull, the control gondola and twelve motor gondolas, each containing two motors. This exterior mounting was required because of danger from the highly flammable hydrogen. But tests of the gas-cell material, the Riverdragon intestinal layers, showed that it did pass some gas—that's a joke, folks!—and so Firebrass ordered his scientists to make a plastic material that wouldn't—in a manner of speaking—break wind.

"They did so—when Firebrass says jump, everybody sets a new record—and . . . ? What? My assistant, Randy, says everybody can't set a record at once. Who cares? Anyway, the hydrogen leakage is nil.

"So, the control room and all the motors are inside the hull except for those in the nose and tail gondolas.

"The hydrogen, by the way, is 99.999 percent pure.

"In addition to the crew of ninety-eight men and two women, the

Parseval will carry two helicopters, each with a thirty-two person capacity, and a two-man glider.

"But there won't be any parachutes. One hundred parachutes makes a heavy load, so it was decided not to carry any. That's sheer confidence for you. More than I have.

"Look at her, folks! Ain't she something! The sun shines on her as if she's the glory of God herself! Beautiful, beautiful, and magnificent!

"A great day for mankind! There goes the orchestra, playing *The Lone Ranger Overture*. Ha! Ha! Just a little joke that'd take too long to explain to you folks. It's really the *William Tell Overture* by Rossini, I believe. Chosen by Firebrass as the take-off music, since he's hung up on that fiery piece. Not to mention a few others, some of whom I see in the crowd.

"Hand me up another glass of ambrosia, Randy. Randy's my assistant M.C., folks, a writer of fantasies on Earth and now Parolando's chief quality-control inspector for the alcohol works. Which is like appointing a wolf to guard a steak.

"Aah! Great stuff! And here comes the *Parseval* now, moving out of the hangar! Her nose is locked into the only mobile mooring mast in the world. The take-off will occur in just a few minutes. I can see through the windscreen of the control room or bridge, which is set in the nose.

"The man in the middle, sitting at the control panel—you can see his head, I'm sure—is chief pilot Cyrano de Bergerac. In his day he was an author, too, wrote novels about travel to the moon and the sun. Now he's in an aerial machine the likes of which he never dreamed of, just as he never envisioned himself on such a voyage. Flying to the North Pole of a planet which nobody, not a single soul on Earth, as far as I know, had described in the wildest of tales. Soaring in the wild blue yonder in the greatest zeppelin ever built, the greatest that will ever be built. Headed for a fabled tower in a cold, foggy sea. An aerial knight, a post-Terrestrial Galahad, questing for a giant grail!

"Cyrano's running the whole operation all by himself. The ship's completely automated; its motors and rudder and elevators are tied into the control panel with electromechanical devices. There's no need to have ruddermen and elevator men and telegraph signals to the motor engineers as they did in the old dirigibles. One man could pilot the ship all the way to the North Pole, if he could stay awake three and a half days, the estimated flight time. In fact, theoretically, the ship could fly itself there without a soul aboard.

"And there by Cyrano's right is the captain, our own Milton Firebrass. He's waving now to the man who's succeeded him as president, the ever popular Judah P. Benjamin, late of Louisiana and ex-attorney general of the late but not necessarily lamented Confederate States of America.

"What? Get your hands off me, friend! No offense intended to any ex-citizen of the C.S.A. Take the drunken bum away, officers!

"And there, standing at the extreme left, is pilot third officer Mitya Nikitin. He promised to be sober during the flight and not hide any booze behind the gas cells, ha! ha!

"To Nikitin's right is first mate Jill Gulbirra. You've given some of us a hard time, Ms. Gulbirra, but we admire . . .

"There go the trumpets again. What a blast! There's Captain Firebrass, waving at us. So long, *mon capitaine, bon voyage!* Keep us informed by radio.

"And there go the cables from the tail. The ship is bobbing a little, but she's settling down. I saw the balancing done a couple of hours ago. The ship's so equili-bub-bub-rated that one man standing on the ground under that mighty mass could lift it with one hand.

"Now her nose is uncoupled from the mobile mooring mast. There goes a little of the water ballast. Sorry about that, folks. We told you to stand back, not that some of you couldn't stand a shower.

"Now she's rising a little. The wind's carrying her backward, southward. But the propellers have already been swivelled at an angle to drive the ship up and northward.

"There she goes! Bigger than a mountain, lighter than a feather! Off to the North Pole and the dark tower!

"My God, I'm crying! Must have had too much of the cup that cheers!"

44

UP ABOVE THE WORLD SO HIGH, THE AIRSHIP TWINKLED, THREADING the needle eye of the blue.

At an altitude of 6.1 kilometers or a little over 20,000 feet, the crew of the *Parseval* had a broad view of The Riverworld. Jill, standing at the front windscreen, saw the twisting parallels of the valleys, running north and south directly below her but taking a great bend to the east about 20 kilometers ahead. Then the lines ran for 100 kilometers like thin Malayan krises, wavy blades, side by side, before turning northeastward.

Now and then, The River bounced back a ray of the sun. The millions along its banks and on its surface were invisible from this height, and even the biggest vessels resembled the backs of surface-cruising dragonfish. The Riverworld looked as it was just before Resurrection Day.

A photographer in the nose dome was making the first aerial survey of this planet. And the last. The photographs would be matched against the course of The River as reported via radio by the *Mark Twain.* However, there would be large gaps in the map made by the *Parseval's* cartographer. The paddlewheeler had traveled far south, to the edge of the south polar regions, several times. So the airship's cartographer could only compare his pictures with the maps transmitted by the surface vessels in the northern hemisphere.

But he could make one sweep of his camera and cover areas where the *Mark Twain* would travel some day.

The radar was also making altitude measurements of the mountain walls. So far, the highest point was 4564 meters or 15,000 feet. At most points, the mountains were only 3048 meters or 10,000 feet. Sometimes the walls dipped as low as 1524 meters or 5000 feet.

Before coming to Parolando, Jill had assumed, along with everybody else she knew, that the mountains were from 4564 to 6096 meters high. These were eyeball estimates, of course, and no one she had known had ever tried to make a scientific measurement. Not until she was in Parolando, where late-twentieth-century devices were available, did she learn the true altitude of the mountains.

Perhaps it was the comparative closeness of the walls that deceived people. They reared straight up, sheer, so smooth after the first 305 meters that they were unscalable. Often they were thicker at the top than at the bottom, presenting an overhang that would daunt any would-be climber even if he had steel pitons. And these were available only at Parolando, as far as she knew.

At the top, the width of the mountains averaged 403 meters or a little more than a quarter of a mile. Yet that relatively small thickness of hard rock was impenetrable without steel tools and dynamite. It would be possible to sail north up The River until it curved for one of its southward travels. There, with enough drilling and blasting equipment, a hole could be bored through the mountain wall. But who knew what invulnerable ranges lay behind that?

The *Parseval* had bucked the northeasterly surface winds of the equatorial zone. Passing through the horse latitudes, it had picked up the tailwinds of the temperate latitudes. In twenty-four hours it had traveled approximately a distance equal to that from Mexico City to the lower end of Hudson Bay, Canada. Before the second day was over, it would run into headwinds from the arctic region. Just how strong these would be was not known. However, the winds here seldom matched the winds of Earth because of the lack of differential between land and water masses.

A difference in mountain altitude and valley width between the equatorial and temperate zones was apparent. The mountains were generally higher and the valleys narrower in the hotter region.

The narrowness of the valleys and the height of the mountains made for conditions comparable to those in the glens of Scotland. Generally, it rained every day about 15:00 hours or 3 P.M. in the temperate areas. Usually, a thunderstorm accompanied by rain occurred about 03:00 hours or 3 A.M. in the equatorial zone. This was not a natural phenomenon in the tropics or at least it was believed that it was not. The Parolando scientists suspected that some sort of rain-making machines concealed in the mountains caused this on-schedule precipitation. The energy requirements for this would be enormous, colossal, in fact. But beings who could remake this planet into one Rivervalley, who could provide an estimated thirty-six billion people with three meals a day through energy-matter conversion, could undoubtedly shape the daily weather.

What was the energy source? No one knew, but the best suspect was the heat of the planet's core.

There was speculation that some kind of metal shield lay between the crust of the earth and the deeper layers. That there was no volcanic activity or earthquakes tended to strengthen this hypothesis.

Since there were no vast ice or water masses making a temperature differential comparable to that of Earth, the wind conditions could have been different. But, so far, the pattern seemed to be Terrestrial.

Firebrass decided to take the ship down to 3600 meters altitude, a little over 12,000 feet. Perhaps the wind there might be weaker. The mountain tops were only 610 meters or about 2000 feet below the vessel, and the effect of the up- and downdrafts were strong at this time of the day. But the ability to change the angle of the propellers swiftly compensated somewhat for this roller-coaster motion. The ground speed increased.

Before 15:00, Firebrass ordered that the vessel be taken up above the rainclouds. He brought it back down at 16:00, and the *Parseval* rode majestically above the valleys. As the sun descended, both the horizontal and vertical winds would weaken, and the ship could plow through the air more evenly.

When night came, the hydrogen in the cells would cool, and the vessel would have to lift its nose even higher to give it more dynamic lift to compensate for the loss of buoyancy.

The pressurized control room was warmed by electric heaters. Its occupants were, however, in heavy cloths. Firebrass and Piscator were smoking cigars; most of the others, cigarettes. The fans sucked the smoke away but not quickly enough to remove the cigar odor which Jill so detested.

Hydrogen-emission detectors placed by the gas cells would transmit a warning if there were any leaks. Nevertheless, smoking was permitted only in five areas: the control gondola or bridge, a room halfway along the vessel's axis, the auxiliary control room in the lower tail fin, and rooms attached to the quarters of the crew fore and aft.

Barry Thorn, first officer of the tail section, reported some magnetic readings. According to this, the North Pole of The Riverworld coincided with the north magnetic pole. The magnetic force itself was much weaker than that of Earth's, so slight, in fact, that it would have been undetectable without the use of instruments known only in the late 1970's.

"Which means," Firebrass said, laughing, "that there are three poles on one spot. The North Pole, the magnetic pole, and the tower. Now, if only one of our crew was a Pole, we could have four on the same place."

Radio reception was excellent today. The ship was high above the mountains, and the transceiver of the *Mark Twain* was carried by a balloon towed by the boat.

Aukuso said, "You can talk now, sir."

Firebrass sat down by the Samoan's side and said, "Firebrass here, Sam. We just got word from Greystock. He's on the way, heading northeastward, ready to alter course the moment he gets wind of the location of the *Rex.*"

"In some ways I hope you don't find Rotten John," Sam said. "I'd like to catch up with him and so have the pleasure of sinking him myself. That's not a very practical attitude, though it's mighty satisfying. I'm not a vindictive man, Milt, but that hyena would make St. Francis himself long to kick him off a cliff."

"The *Minerva*'s carrying four forty-six-kilogram bombs and six rockets with nine-kilogram warheads," Firebrass said. "If only two of the bombs make a direct hit, they could sink the boat."

"Even so, that royal thief might get away safe and sound to shore," Clemens said. "He has all the good luck of the wicked. How would I ever find him then? No, I want to see his body. Or if he's taken alive, I want to wring his neck myself."

De Bergerac spoke softly to Jill. "Clemens talks big for a man who's appalled by violence. It's easy to do as long as the enemy's sixty thousand kilometers away."

Firebrass laughed and said, "Well, if you can't twist his head off, Sam, Joe's the man to do the job."

An unhumanly deep voice rumbled, "No, I'll tear off hith armth and legth. Then Tham can turn hith head around tho he can thee vhere he'th been. He von't like where he'th going."

"Tear off an ear for me," Firebrass said. "Old John almost hit me when he shot at me."

Jill presumed that he was referring to the fight aboard the *Not For Hire* when John had seized it.

Firebrass said, "According to calculations, the *Rex* should be in the area we'll be over in about an hour. You should be in the same area but about one hundred forty kilometers to the west of the *Rex*. Of course, we could be way off. For all we know, the *Rex* may not be traveling as fast as it could, or King John could've decided to dock for repairs or a very long shore leave."

An hour's conversation followed. Clemens talked to some of the crew, mostly those he had known before he'd left Parolando. She noticed that he did not ask to speak to de Bergerac.

Just as Sam was about to sign off, the radar operator reported that the *Rex Grandissimus* was on the scope.

45

STAYING AT 452 METERS ALTITUDE, THE *Parseval* CIRCLED THE boat. From that height it looked like a toy, but photographs, quickly enlarged, showed that it was indeed King John's vessel. It was magnificent. Jill thought that it would be a shame to destroy such a beautiful craft, but she did not say so. Firebrass and de Bergerac felt very strongly about the man who had hijacked their fabulous River-boat.

Aukuso transmitted the location to Greystock, who said that the *Minerva* should reach the *Rex* the following day. He also checked the location of the *Mark Twain*.

"I'd like to fly over her so that Sam can get a good look at the ship that's going to sink the *Rex*," Greystock said.

"It won't take you out of your way to do that," Firebrass said. "And it'll give Sam a big thrill."

After he had quit talking to Clemens, Firebrass said, "I really think Greystock's on a suicide mission. The *Rex* is loaded with rockets, and it carries two planes armed with rockets and machine guns. It all depends on whether or not Greystock can catch the *Rex* by surprise. Not much chance of that if John's radar detects the *Minerva*. Of course, it might be off. Why should it be on? The sonar is good enough for daytime navigation."

"Yes," Piscator said. "But the people on the *Rex* must have seen us. They'll be wondering about us, though they won't know who we are, and they might start using the radar because they'll be suspicious."

"I think so, too," Jill said. "They can figure out easily enough that only Parolando could build a dirigible."

"Well, we'll see. Maybe. By the time the *Minerva* gets to the *Rex*, we'll be behind the polar mountains. I don't think we can expect good radio reception there. We'll have to wait until we come back over them."

Firebrass looked thoughtful, as if he were wondering if the *Parseval* would return.

The sun sank behind the ground horizon, though at this altitude the sky remained bright for a long time. Finally, night came with its blazing star clouds and gas sheets. Jill talked for a few minutes with

Anna Obrenova before going to her cabin. The little Russian seemed warm enough, but there was something in her manner which indicated that she was not at ease. Was she really resentful because she had not been given the first mate's position?

Before going to her quarters, Jill took a long walk through the semipressurized passageway to the tail section. Here she drank some coffee and chatted briefly with some of the officers. Barry Thorn was present, but he, too, seemed a little nervous, even more reticent than usual. Perhaps, she thought, he was still unhappy at being rejected by Obrenova. If, indeed, that had been the cause of their argument.

At that moment, she was reminded that the two had spoken in a language unknown to her. Now was not the time to ask him about that. It was possible she might never be able to bring up the subject. To do so would be to admit that she had been eavesdropping.

On the other hand, she was very curious. Some day, when there were not more pressing things to consider, she would ask him about it. She could claim that she just happened to walk by—which was the truth—and had heard a few words of the dialog. After all, if she did not understand what they were saying, she could not be eavesdropping, could she?

She went to her cabin, where she crawled into the bunk and went to sleep almost at once. At 04:00 hours a whistle from the intercom awoke her. She went to the control room to relieve Metzing, the third mate. He stood around a while, talking about his experiences as commander of the LZ-1, then left. Jill did not have much to do, since Piscator was a very competent pilot and the atmospheric conditions were normal. In fact, the Japanese had set the automatic controls on, though he kept a close watch on the indicator panel.

There were two others present, the radio and the radar operators.

"We should see the mountains at about 23:00," she said.

Piscator wondered aloud if they were as high as Joe Miller had estimated. The titanthrop had guessed them to be about 6096 meters or 20,000 feet. Joe, however, was not a good judge of distances, or, at least, not good at converting distances into metrics or the English system.

"We'll know when we get there," Jill said.

"I wonder if the mysterious occupants of the tower will allow us to return?" he said. "Or even to enter the tower?"

That question had the same answer as the previous ones. Jill did not comment.

"Perhaps, though," Piscator said, "they may allow us to survey it."

Jill lit a cigarette. She did not feel nervous now, but she knew that, when they were close to the mountains, she was going to be at least a little spooked. They would be entering the forbidden, the tabu, the area of the Castle Perilous.

Piscator, smiling, his black eyes shining, said, "Have you ever considered the possibility that some of Them might be on this ship?"

Jill almost strangled as she sharply drew in cigarette smoke. When she was through coughing, she said, wheezing, "What in hell do you mean?"

"They could have agents among us."

"What makes you think that?"

"It's just an idea," he said. "After all, isn't it reasonable to believe that They would be watching us?"

"I think you have seen more than you're admitting. What makes you think this? It won't hurt to tell me."

"It's just an idle speculation."

"In this idle speculation, as you call it, is there someone you think could be one of Them?"

"It wouldn't be discreet to say so, even if there was someone. I wouldn't want to point the finger at a possibly innocent party."

"You don't suspect *me*?"

"Would I be stupid enough to tell you if I did? No, I am just thinking aloud. A most regrettable habit, one which I should rid myself of."

"I don't remember you ever thinking aloud before."

She did not pursue the subject, since Piscator made it evident he was not going to add anything. The rest of the watch she tried to think of what he might have observed and then put together to make a pattern. The effort left her head buzzing, and she went back to bed feeling very frustrated. Perhaps he had just been putting her on.

In the afternoon, only two minutes short of the time she had predicted, the tops of the polar mountains were sighted. They looked like clouds, but radar gave a true picture. They were mountains. Rather, it was one continuous mountain wall circling the sea. Firebrass, reading its indicated height, groaned.

"It's 9753 meters high! That's taller than Mount Everest!"

There was good reason for him to groan and the others to look disturbed. The airship could not go higher than 9144 meters, and Firebrass would hesitate to take it to that altitude. Theoretically, that was the pressure height of the gas cells. To go above that meant that the automatic valves on top of the cells would release hydrogen. If they did not do so, the cells would explode, having reached their inflation limit.

Firebrass would not like to take the vessel near the pressure height. An unexpectedly warm layer of air could cause the hydrogen in the cells to expand even more, thus making the ship more buoyant than was safe. Under those conditions, the *Parseval* would rise swiftly. The pilot would have to act swiftly, pointing the vessel's nose down and also tilting the propellers to give a downward drive. If this maneuver failed, the gas, expanding under the lessened atmospheric pressure, would stretch the cell walls to the rupture point.

Even if the ship got through this situation, its loss of valved-off gas would mean that it would become heavy. The only way to lighten the ship would be to discharge ballast. If too much ballast was dropped, the *Parseval* would be too buoyant.

Firebrass said, "If it's like this all the way around, we're screwed. But Joe said . . ."

He stood for a moment, thinking, watching the dark, ominous mass gradually swell. Below them the Valley wriggled snakily, eternally covered with fog in this cold area. They had long ago passed the last of the double line of grailstones. Yet the radar and the infrared equipment showed that thick, high vegetation grew on the hills. One more mystery. How could trees flourish in the cold mists?

Firebrass said, "Take her down to 3050 meters, Cyrano. I want to get a good look at the headwaters."

By "look" he meant a radar view. No one could see through the massive, boiling clouds covering the mighty hole at the base of the mountains. But radar showed a colossal exit for The River, an opening 4.9 kilometers or a little over 3 miles wide. The highest point of the arch was 3.5 kilometers.

The mighty flood rushed straight for 3 kilometers, then tumbled over the edge of a cliff and fell straight for 915 meters, over 3000 feet.

"Joe may have been exaggerating when he said you could float the moon on The River where it comes out of the cave," Firebrass said, "but it is impressive!"

"Yes," Cyrano said, "it is indeed grand. But the air here is almighty rough."

Firebrass ordered the *Parseval* to a higher altitude and on a course which would parallel the mountain at a distance of 12 kilometers. Cyrano had to crab the dirigible and swivel the propellers to keep from being blown south, and it crept alongside the towering range.

Meanwhile, the radio operator tried to get into contact with the *Mark Twain*.

"Keep it up," Firebrass said. "Sam'll want to know how we're doing. And I'm interested in finding out how the *Minerva* made out."

To the others he said, "I'm looking for that gap in the mountains. There has to be one. Joe said the sun momentarily flashed through a hole or what he thought was a hole. He couldn't see the break, but since the sun never gets more than halfway up the horizon here, it couldn't shine inside the sea unless there's a break that starts at ground level.

Jill wondered why They would have erected such a mighty barrier only to leave an opening.

At 15:05, radar reported that there was a break in the verticality. Now the airship was over mountains outside the main wall. These mountains were not the continuous process surrounding the sea but were peaks, some of which reached 3040 meters. Then, as they came closer to the break, they saw that between the lesser mountains and the wall was an immense valley.

"A veritable Grand Canyon, as you have described it to me," Cyrano said. "A colossal chasm. No one could get down its walls unless he used a rope 610 meters long. Nor could he ever get up the other wall. It is of the same altitude and its sides are as smooth as my mistress' bottom."

On the other side of the lesser mountains reared the mountain that walled The River. If a man could get over the nearer height and out of the Valley, he would then have to cross a rugged precipitous range for 81 kilometers or over 50 miles. After which, he would be confronted by the uncrossable valley.

"Ginnungagap," Jill said.

"What?" Firebrass said.

"From Norse mythology. The primal abyss in which Ymir, the first of created life, the ancestor of the evil race of giants, was born."

Firebrass snorted, and said, "Next you'll be telling me that the sea is populated by demons."

Firebrass looked cool enough, but she thought that this was a facade. Unless he had superhuman nerves, his body was under stress, the juices of the adrenals pouring out, his blood pressure up. Was he also thinking, as she was, that a much more experienced pilot should be at the controls? The Frenchman's judgment and reflexes were probalby swifter than anybody else's. They had been tested scores of times in simulated emergencies during training. But—he just did not have thousands of hours of airship travel under Terrestrial, that is, swiftly changing, conditions. So far, the voyage had been uneventful. But the polar environment was unknown, and passing over these mountains might bring the ship into sudden unexpected forces. Not might. Would.

Here at the top of the world, the sun's rays were weaker and thus it was colder. The River emptied into the polar sea on the other side of the circular range where it gave up the heat remaining after thousands of kilometers of wandering through the arctic region. The contact of cold air with warm waters caused the fog reported by Joe Miller. Even so, the air was relatively colder than that outside the mountains. The high-pressure cold air inside the ring of mountains would flow outward. Joe had described the wind that howled through the passes.

She wanted desperately to ask Firebrass to replace Cyrano with her. Or with Anna or Barry Thorn, the only other persons with much experience. Both were, objectively considered, as good as she. But she wanted to be in control. Only then would she feel at ease. Or as much at ease as the situation allowed.

Firebrass might have been of the same opinion. If so, he was not going to act on it, just as she was not going to express it. An unwritten, in fact, unspoken, code prevented that. It was Cyrano's watch. To order him to give it up for a more qualified pilot would humiliate him. It would show a lack of confidence, make him seem to be less a "man."

Ridiculous. Absolutely ridiculous. The entire mission and one hundred lives were at stake.

Despite which, she would have said nothing even if she had thought she might be needed. Like the others, she was bound by the code. Never mind how antisurvival it was. She could not shame Cyrano. Besides, for her to suggest that he be replaced would shame her, too.

Now they were opposite the gap. It was not the V-shaped notch they had expected. It was a perfect circle cut into the mountain wall, a hole 3 kilometers across and 1000 meters above the base. From it sped clouds, driven by a wind which, if they could have heard it, would be "howling." Cyrano was forced to point the dirigible directly into the hole to keep it from being blown southward. Even so, with motors operating at top speed, the *Parseval* could advance into it at only 16 km/ph or less than 10 mph.

"What a wind!" Firebrass said. He hesitated. The air flowing down from the top of the mountain would add its force to that streaming through the hole. And the pilot would have to rely on radar to sense the nearness of the sides of the hole.

"If the mountains aren't any thicker than they are along The River," Firebrass said, "we can get through the hole faster than a dog through a hoop. However . . ."

He bit down on his cigar, then said through clenched teeth, "Let's take her through the gates of hell!"

46

Convergence of paths through chance fascinated Peter Frigate.

Pure chance had brought his *in potentio* into *essems*.

His father was born and brought up in Terre Haute, Indiana; his mother, in Galena, Kansas. Not much chance for them to get together and beget Peter Jairus Frigate, right? Especially in 1918 when people did not travel much. But his grandfather, the handsome, affluent, gambling, womanizing, boozing William Frigate, was forced to take a business trip to Kansas City, Missouri. He thought his eldest son, James, should learn the details of handling his various interests throughout the Midwest. So he took the twenty-year-old along. Instead of driving in the new Packard, they took the train.

Peter's mother was in Kansas City, living with her German relatives while she attended a business school. The Hoosier and the Jayhawk had never heard of each other. They had nothing in common except being human and living in the Midwest, an area larger than many European countries.

And so, one hot afternoon, his mother-to-be had gone to a drugstore for a sandwich and a milkshake. His father-to-be had gotten bored listening to a business conference between his father and a farm machinery manufacturer. When lunch hour came, the two older men had headed for a saloon. James, not wanting to start boozing so early, had gone into the drugstore. Here he was greeted by the pleasant odors of ice cream and vanilla extract and chocolate, the swishing of two big overhead fans, a view of the long marble counter, magazines on a rack, and three pretty girls sitting on wire chairs around a small marble-topped table. He eyed them, as would any man, young or old. He sat down and ordered a chocolate soda and a ham sandwich, then he decided he'd look the magazine rack over. He leafed through some magazines and a paperback fantasy about time travel. He didn't care much about such romances. He'd tried H.G. Wells, Jules Verne, H. Rider Haggard, and Frank Reade, Jr. but his hard Hoosier head rejected such implausibilities.

On the way back, just as he passed the table at which the three giggling girls sat, he had to leap to one side to avoid a glassful of

Coke. One of the girls, waving her hand while telling a story, had knocked it off. If he hadn't been so agile, his pants leg would have been soaked. As it was, his shoe was stained.

The girl apologized. James told her that there was nothing to be concerned about. He introduced himself and asked if he could sit with them. The girls were eager to talk to a good-looking young man from the faraway state of Indiana. One thing led to another. Before the girls had gone back to the nearby school, he had arranged a date with "Teddy" Griffiths. She was the quietest of the trio and not quite the best looking, but there was something about the slim girl with the Teutonic features, the Indian-straight, Indian-black hair, and large dark-brown eyes that attracted him.

Elective affinity, Peter Frigate called it, not above borrowing a phrase from Goethe.

Courting in those days was not as free and easy as in Peter's day. James had to go to the Kaiser residence on Locust Street, a long trip by streetcar, and be introduced to her uncle and aunt. Then they sat on the front porch with the old folks, eating homemade ice cream and cookies. About eight o'clock, he and Teddy went for a walk around the block, talking of this and that. On returning, he thanked her relatives for their hospitality and said goodbye to Teddy without kissing her. But they corresponded, and, two months later, James made another trip, this time in one of his father's cars. And this time they did a little spooning, mostly in the back row of the local movie house.

On his third trip, he married Teddy. They left immediately after the wedding to take the train to Terre Haute. James was fond of telling his eldest son that he should have named him Pullman. "You were conceived on a train, Pete, so I thought it would be nice if your name commemorated that event, but your mother wouldn't have it."

Peter didn't know whether or not to believe his father. He was such a kidder. Besides, he couldn't see his mother arguing with his father. James was a little man, but he was a bantam rooster who ruled the roost, a domestic Napoleon.

This was the concatenation of events that had slid Peter Jairus Frigate from potentiality into existence. If old William had not decided to take his son along to Kansas City, if James had not been more tempted by a soda than by beer, if the girl hadn't happened to knock over the Coke, there would have been no Peter Jairus Frigate. At least, not the individual now bearing that name. And if his father had had a wet dream the night before or had used a contraceptive on the wedding night, he, Peter, would not have been born. Or if there had been no mating, if it had been put off for some reason, the egg would have drifted off and out and into a menstruation pad.

What was there about that one spermatozoan, one in

300,000,000, that had enabled it to beat all the others out in the race to the egg?

May the best wriggler win. And so it had been. But it had been close, too close for comfort when he thought about it.

And then there was the horde of his brothers and sisters *in potentio,* unhoarded. They had died, arriving too late or not at all. A waste of flesh and spirit. Had any of the sperm had the potentiality for his imagination and writing talent? Or were those in the egg? Or were they in the fusion of sperm and egg, a combination of genes only possible in that one sperm and that one egg? His three brothers had no creative and little passive imagination; his sister had a passive imagination, she liked fantasy and science fiction, but she had no inclination to write. What had made the difference?

Environment couldn't explain it. The others had been exposed to the same influences as he. His father had purchased that library of little red pseudoleather-bound books, what in hell was its name? It was a very popular home library in his childhood. But they hadn't been fascinated by the stories in them. They hadn't fallen in love with Sherlock Holmes and Irene Adler in *A Scandal in Bohemia,* or sympathized with the monster in *Frankenstein,* or battled before the walls of Troy with Achilles, or suffered with Odysseus in his wanderings, or descended the icy depths to seek out Grendel with Beowulf, or journeyed with the Time Traveller of Wells, or visited those wild weird stars of Olive Schneider, or escaped from the Mohegans with Natty Bumppo. Nor had they been interested in the other books his parents bought him, *Pilgrim's Progress, Tom Sawyer* and *Huckleberry Finn, Treasure Island, The Arabian Nights,* and *Gulliver's Travels.* Nor had they prospected at the little library branch, where he first dug the gold of Frank Baum, Hans Andersen, Andrew Lang, Jack London, A. Conan Doyle, Edgar Rice Burroughs, Rudyard Kipling, and H. Rider Haggard. And don't forget the lesser, the silver, ore: Irving Crump, A.G. Henty, Roy Rockwood, Oliver Curwood, Jeffrey Farnol, Robert Service, Anthony Hope, and A. Hyatt Verrill. After all, in his personal pantheon, the Neanderthal, Og, and Rudolph Rassendyll ranked almost with Tarzan, John Carter of Barsoom, Dorothy Gale of Oz, Odysseus, Holmes and Challenger, Jim Hawkins, Ayesha, Allan Quartermain and Umslopogaas.

It tickled Peter at this moment to think that he was on the same boat with the man who had furnished the model for the fictional Umslopogaas. And he was also a deckhand for the man who had created Buck and White Fang, Wolf Larsen, the nameless subhuman narrator of *Beyond Adam,* and Smoke Bellew. It delighted him also that he talked daily with the great Tom Mix, unequaled in cinema flair and fantastic adventure except by Douglas Fairbanks, Senior. If only Fairbanks were aboard. But then it would also be delightful to have Doyle and Twain and Cervantes and Burton, especially Burton, aboard. And . . . The boat sure was getting crowded. Be satisfied. But then he never was.

What had he drifted off from? Oh, yes. Chance, another word for destiny.

He didn't believe, as Mark Twain did, that all events, all characters, were rigidly predetermined. "From the time when the first atom of the great Laurentian sea bumped into the second atom, our fates were fixed." Twain had said something like that, probably in his depressing *What Is Man?* That philosophy was an excuse for escaping guilt. Ducking responsibility.

Nor did he believe, as had Kurt Vonnegut, the late-twentieth-century avatar of Mark Twain, that we were governed entirely by the chemical makeup of our bodies. God wasn't the Great Garage Mechanic in the Sky or the Divine Pill Pusher. If there was a God. Frigate didn't know what God was and often doubted that He existed.

God might not exist, but free will did. True, it was a limited force, repressed or influenced by environmental conditioning, chemicals, brain injuries, neural diseases, lobotomy. But a human being was not just a protein robot. No robot could change its mind, decide on its own to reprogram itself, lift itself by its mental bootstraps.

Still, we were born with different genetic combinations, and these did determine to some extent our intellect, aptitudes, leanings, reactions, in short, our characters. Character determines destiny, according to the old Greek, Heraclitus. But a person could change his/her character. Somewhere in there was a force, an entity, that said, "I won't do it!" Or—"Nobody's going to stop me from doing it!" Or—"I've been a coward but this time I'm a raging lion!"

Sometimes you needed an outside stimulus or stimulator, as had the Tin Woodsman and the Scarecrow and the Cowardly Lion. But the Wizard only gave them what they had had all the time. The brains of mixed sawdust, bran, pins and needles, the silk sawdust-stuffed heart, and the liquid from the square green bottle marked *Courage* were only antiplacebos.

By thought you could change your emotional attitudes. Frigate believed that, though his practice had never matched his theory.

He'd been reared in a Christian Scientist family. But when he was about eleven his parents had sent him to a Presbyterian church, since they were having a fit of religious apathy then. His mother cleaned up the kitchen and took care of the babies Sunday mornings while his father read *The Chicago Tribune*. Like it or not, he went off to Sunday School and then the sermon.

So, he had gotten two contrary religious educations.

One believed in free will, in evil and matter as illusion, in Spirit as the only reality.

The other believed in predestination. God picked out a few here and there for salvation and let the others go to hell. No rhyme or reason to this. You couldn't do a thing to change that. Once the divine choice had been made, it was done. You could live purely, agonizedly praying and hoping all your life. But when the end of life on Earth came, you went to your appointed place. The sheep, those whom God for some unexplainable reason had marked with His grace, went up to sit on His right side. The goats, rejected for the same mysterious reasons, slid down the prearranged chute into the fire, sinner and saint alike.

When he was twelve, he had had many nightmares in which Mary Baker Eddy and John Calvin had fought for his soul.

It was no wonder, when he was fourteen, that he had decided to blazes with both faiths. With all faiths. Still, he had been the epitome of the prudish puritan. No foul words escaped his lips; he blushed if told a dirty joke. He couldn't stand the odors of beer or whiskey, and even if he'd liked them, he would have rejected them with scorn. And he'd have luxuriated in a feeling of moral superiority for doing so.

His early puberty was a torment. In the seventh grade he would be called on to stand up and recite, his face red, his penis thrusting against his fly, having risen at the trumpet call of his teacher's large breasts. Nobody seemed to notice, but he was sure every time he stood up that he would be disgraced. And when he accompanied his parents to a movie in which the heroine wore a low-cut dress or displayed a flash of garter, he put his hand on his pants to hide the swelling.

The flickering light from the screen would reveal his sin. His parents would know what his thoughts were, and they would be horrified. He'd be ashamed to look in their faces forever after.

Twice, his father talked to him about sex. Once, when he was twelve. Apparently, his mother had noticed some blood on his bath towel and spoken to his father, James Frigate, had asked him if he was masturbating. Peter was both horrified and indignant. He had denied it, though his father acted as if he really did not believe him.

Investigation revealed, however, that, when bathing, Peter had not been peeling back his foreskin to wash under it. He had not wanted to touch his penis. As a result, the smegma had built up under the skin. How this could cause a bleeding neither he nor his father knew. But he was advised to wash thoroughly every time he took a bath. Also, he was told that jacking-off rotted the brain, and he was given the example of the village idiot of North Terre Haute, a boy who publicly masturbated. With a grave face, his father told him that anybody who jerked off would become a drooling imbecile. Maybe his father believed that. So many of his generation did. Or maybe he'd just passed on that horrifying tale, purveyed for only God knew how many centuries or even millennia to scare his son.

Peter would find out that that was superstition, a reasoning from effect to cause, totally invalid. It was in a class with the belief that if you ate a peanut butter and jelly sandwich while you were sitting in the outhouse, the devil would get you.

Peter hadn't lied. He had not been indulging in the sin of Onan. Though why it was called Onanism he didn't know, since Onan hadn't masturbated. Onan had just used what Peter overheard his father refer to as the IC (Illinois Central) railroad technique. Pulling out in time.

Some of his junior high school acquaintances—the "racy" ones—bragged about beating their meat. One of these low-lifers, a wild kid named Vernon (died in a crash in 1942 while training to be an Air Force bombardier) had actually masturbated in the rear of a streetcar on the way home from a basketball game. Peter, watching, had been fascinated and sickened at the same time. The other kids had just giggled.

Once he and a friend, Bob Allwood, as puritanical as he, had been going home on a streetcar after a late movie. There was no one else aboard except the operator and a hard-looking peroxide blonde in the front seat. As the trolley came up toward the end of the line on Elizabeth Street, the operator had closed the curtain around himself and the blonde and turned the overhead light off. Bob and Pete, watching from the back of the car, saw the woman's legs disappear. It wasn't until a few minutes later that Peter understood what was happening. The woman had to be sitting on the ledge in front of him, or on the control post itself, facing the operator, while he screwed her. Peter didn't say a thing about it to Bob until after they'd gotten off the car. Bob had refused to believe it.

Peter was surprised at his own reaction. He'd been more amused than anything. Or perhaps envious was more appropriate. The "proper" reaction came later. That man and his doxy would go to hell for sure.

47

THAT WAS A LONG TIME AGO. THE TIME HAD COME WHEN PETER HAD laid a woman in front of the altar of an empty church, though he was drunk when he did it. This was in a Roman Catholic cathedral in Syracuse, and the woman had been Jewish. It had been her idea. She hated the religion because the tough Polish Catholic kids in the Boston high school she attended had roughed her up several times because she was a Jew. The idea of defiling the church had seemed like a good idea at the time, though next morning he sweated thinking of what would have happened if they'd been caught. But doing it in a Protestant church wouldn't have appealed to him so much. Protestant churches had always seemed barren places to him. God wouldn't be caught dead there, but He did like to hang around Catholic places of worship. Peter had always had a leaning toward Romanism and had twice been on the verge of converting. You could only blaspheme where God was.

Which was a curious attitude. If you didn't believe in God, why bother to blaspheme?

As if that wasn't bad enough, he and Sarah had entered a number of apartment houses on a street whose name he couldn't recall now. It had once been a very posh district where the rich had built huge, gingerbreaded, many-cupolaed houses. Then they'd moved out, and the houses had been made into apartments. Mostly affluent old people, widows and aged couples, lived there. The two of them had wandered through the halls of three buildings where all the doors were locked tight and not a sound except the muffled voice of TV sets was heard. They'd been on the third floor of the fourth building, and Sarah was down on her knees before him, when a door opened. An old woman stuck her head out into the hall, screamed, and slammed the door shut. Laughing, he and Sarah had fled out into the street and up to her apartment.

Later, Peter had sweated thinking about what would have happened if they'd been caught by the police. Jail, public disgrace, the loss of his job at General Electric, the shame felt by his children, the wrath of his wife. And what if the old woman had had a heart attack? He searched the obituary columns and was relieved to find that no one on that street had died that night. This in itself was a rarity, since

Sarah said that she couldn't look out of the window from her apartment without seeing a funeral procession going down that street.

He also looked for a report of the incident in the papers. If the old lady had called the police, however, there was nothing in the papers about it.

A thirty-eight-year-old man shouldn't be doing stupid childish things like that, he had told himself. Especially if innocent people might be hurt. Never again. But as the years passed, he chuckled when he thought of it.

Though an atheist at fifteen, Frigate had never been able to rid himself of doubts. When he was nineteen, he had attended a revival meeting with Bob Allwood. Allwood had been raised in a devout fundamentalist family. He, too, had become an atheist, but this lasted one year. In that time, Bob's parents had died of cancer. The shock had set him thinking about immortality. Unable to endure the idea that his father and mother were dead forever, that he'd never see them again, he had begun visiting revival meetings. His conversion had taken place when he was eighteen.

Peter and Bob used to see much of each other, since they had been playmates in grade school and had gone to the same high school. They argued much about religion and the authenticity of the Bible. Finally, Peter agreed to go with Bob to a mass meeting at which the famous Reverend Robert Ransom was preaching.

Much to Peter's astonishment, he found himself deeply stirred, though he had come to ridicule. He was even more amazed when he found himself on his knees before the reverend, promising to accept Jesus Christ as his Lord.

That promise was broken within a month. Peter just could not hold fast to his convictions. In Allwood's parlance, he had "backslid," "fallen from grace."

Peter told Bob that his early religious conditioning and the passionate exhortations of the converts had been responsible for putting him in a fine frenzy of faith.

Allwood continued to argue with him, to "wrestle with his soul." Peter remained adamant.

Peter approached the age of sixty. His schoolmates and friends were dying off; he himself was not in good health. Death was no longer a long way off. When he was young, he had thought much about the billions who had preceded him, been born, suffered, laughed, loved, wept, and died. And he thought of the billions who would come after him, who would be hurt, be hated, be loved, and be gone. At the end of Earth, all, caveman and astronaut, would be dust and less than dust.

What did it all mean? Without immortality, it meant nothing.

There were people who said that life was the excuse for life, its only reason.

These were fools, self-deluded. No matter how intelligent they might be in other matters, they were fools in this. Self-blinkered, emotional idiots.

On the other hand, why should human beings have another chance at an afterlife? They were such miserable, conniving, self-deceiving, hypocritical wretches. Even the best were. He knew no saints, though he admitted that there might have been and might be some. It seemed to him that only saints would be worthy of immortality. Even so, he doubted the claims of some of those who had been awarded halos.

Take Saint Augustine, for instance. "Asshole" was the only word that fitted him. A monster of ego and selfishness.

St. Francis was about as saintly as a person could be. But he was undoubtedly psychotic. Kissing a leper's sores to demonstrate humility, indeed!

Still, as Peter's wife had pointed out, no one was perfect.

Then there was Jesus, though there was no proof that he was a saint. In fact, it was evident from the New Testament that he had restricted salvation to the Jews. But they had rejected him. And so, St. Paul, finding that the Jews were not about to give up the religion for which they had fought so hard and suffered so much, had turned to the Gentiles. He made certain compromises, and Christianity, better named Paulism, was launched. But St. Paul was a sexual pervert, since total sexual abstinence was a perversion.

That made Jesus a pervert, too.

However, some people just did not have much sex drive. Perhaps Jesus and Paul had been such. Or they had sublimated their drive in something more important, their desire to have people see the Truth.

Buddha was perhaps a saint. Heir to a throne, to riches and power, married to a lovely princess who had borne him children, he had given all these up. The miseries and wretchedness of the poor, the stark unavoidability of death, had sent him wandering through India, seeking the Truth. And so he had founded Buddhism, eventually rejected by the very people, the Hindus, whom he had tried to help. His disciples had taken it elsewhere, however, and there it had thrived. Just as St. Paul had taken the teachings of Jesus from his native land and planted its seeds among foreigners.

The religions of Jesus, Paul, and Buddha had started to degenerate before their founders were cold in their graves. Just as St. Francis' order had begun corrupting before its founder's body was rotten.

48

ON AN AFTERNOON WHILE THE *Razzle Dazzle* WAS SAILING ALONG, A good breeze behind its sails, Frigate told Nur el-Musafir these thoughts. They were sitting against the bulkhead of the forecastle, smoking cigars and looking idly at the people on the bank. The Frisco Kid was at the wheel, and the others were talking or playing chess.

"The trouble with you, Pete—one of the troubles—is you worry too much about other people's behavior. And you have too high ideals for them, ideals which you yourself don't try to live up to."

"I know I can't live up to them, so I make no pretense," Frigate said.

"But it bothers me that others claim to have these ideals and to be living up to them. If I point out that they aren't, they get angry."

The little Moor chuckled. "Naturally. Your criticism threatens their self-image. If that were to be destroyed, they, too, would be destroyed. At least, they think so."

"I know that," Frigate said. "That's why I quit doing that long ago. I learned on Earth to keep quiet about such matters. Besides, people got very angry and some even threatened violence. I can't stand anger or violence."

"Yet you are a very angry person. And I think your abhorrence of violence stems from fear of being violent yourself. You were—are—afraid that you'd hurt someone else. Which is why you suppressed that violence in yourself.

"But as a writer, you could express it. It would be done impersonally, as it were. You wouldn't be doing it in a face-to-face situation."

"I know all that."

"Then why haven't you done something about it?"

"I have. I tried various therapies, disciplines, and religions. Psychoanalysis, dianetics, scientology, Zen, transcendental meditation, Nichirenism, group therapy, Christian Science, and fundamental Christianity. And I was strongly tempted to become a Roman Catholic."

"I never heard of most of those, of course," Nur said. "Nor do I need to know what they were. The fault lies in yourself, regardless of the validity of these. By your own admission, you never stuck to any of them long. You didn't give them a chance."

"That," Frigate said, "was because, once in them, I could see their flaws. And I had a chance to study the people practicing them. Most of these religions and disciplines were having some beneficial effect on their practitioners. But not nearly what was claimed for them. And the practitioners were fooling themselves about much of the benefits claimed."

"Besides, you didn't have the stick-to-itiveness needed," Nur said. "I think that comes from fear of being changed. You desire change, yet dread it. And the fear wins out."

"I know that, too," Frigate said.

"Yet you have done nothing to overcome that fear."

"Not nothing. A little."

"But not enough."

"Yes. However, as I got older, I did make some progress. And here I have made even more."

"But not nearly enough?"

"No."

"What good is self-knowledge if the will to act on it is lacking?"

"Not much," Frigate said.

"Then you must find a way to make your will to act overcome your will not to act."

Nur paused, smiling, his little black eyes bright.

"Of course, you will tell me you know all that. Next, you will ask me if I can show you the way. And I will reply that you must first be willing to let me show you the way. You are not as yet ready, though you think you are. And you may never be, which is a pity. You have potentiality."

"Everybody has potentiality."

Nur looked up at Frigate. "In a sense, yes. In another sense, no."

"Mind explaining that?"

Nur rubbed his huge nose with a small, thin hand and then pitched his cigar across over the deck and over the railing. He picked up his bamboo flute and looked at it but laid it down.

"When the time comes, if it ever does."

He looked sideways at Frigate.

"You feel rejected? Yes. I know that you react too strongly to rejection. Which is one reason that you have always tried to avoid situations in which you might be rejected. Though why you should then have become a fiction writer is a mystery to me. Or is it? You did persist in your intended profession despite initial rejections. Though, according to your own story, you often let long periods of time elapse before you tried again. But you persisted.

"Be that as it may, it is up to you to decide if you will be disheartened by my refusing you at this time. Try me later. When you know that you are at least a fit candidate.''

Frigate was silent for a long while. Nur put the flute to his lips and presently a weird wailing, rising and falling, issued. Nur was never without the instrument when off duty. Sometimes he would content himself with short pieces, lyrics, presumably. Other times, he would sit cross-legged on top of the forecastle for hours, the flute silent, his eyes closed. At such time, his request that he not be interrupted was honored. Frigate knew that Nur was putting himself into some sort of trance then. But so far he had not asked him more than one question about it.

Nur had said, ''You need not know. As yet.''

Nur-ed-din ibn Ali el-Hallaq (Light-of-the-faith, son of Ali the barber) fascinated Frigate. Nur had been born in 1164 A.D. in Córdoba, held by the Moslems since 711 A.D. Moorish Iberia was then near the apotheosis of Saracenic civilization, which Nur had beheld in all its glory. Christian Europe, compared to the brilliant culture of the Moslems, was still in the Dark Ages. Art, science, philosophy, medicine, literature, poetry flourished in the great centers of population of Islam. The Western cities: Iberian Córdoba, Seville, and Granada, and the Eastern cities: Baghdad and Alexandria, had no rivals, except in faraway China.

The wealthy Christians sent their sons to the Iberian universities to get an education unobtainable in London, Paris, and Rome. The sons of the poor went there to beg for bread while they learned. And from these schools the Christians went back to transmit what they had imbibed at the feet of the robed masters.

Moorish Iberia was a strange and splendid country, ruled by men who differed in degree of faith and dogmatism. Some were intolerant and harsh. Others were broadminded, tolerant enough to appoint Christians and Jews as their viziers, inclined to the arts and the sciences, welcoming all foreigners, eager to learn from them, soft on matters of religion.

Nur's father plied his trade in the vast palace outside Córdoba, the near city of Medinat az-Zahra. In Nur's time this had been fabled throughout the world, but in Frigate's there was scarcely a trace left. Nur was born there and learned his father's craft. He desired to be something else, and, since he was bright, his father used his connections with his wealthy patrons to advance his son. Having demonstrated his aptitude for literature, music, mathematics, alchemy, and theology, Nur went to the best school in Córdoba. There he mingled with the rich and the poor, the important and the insignificant, the Northern Christian and the Nubian black.

It was also there that he met Muyid-ed-din ibn el-Arabi. This young man was to become the greatest love poet of his times, and echoes of his songs would be found in those of the Provencal and

German troubadors. The rich and handsome youth, liking the poor and ugly son of a barber, invited him in 1202 to accompany him to a pilgrimage to Mecca. During the journey through North Africa, they met a group of Persian immigrants, Sufis. Nur had encountered this discipline before, but talking to the Persians decided him to be a disciple. However, at the moment, he found no master who would accept his petition for candidacy. Nur continued with el-Arabi to Egypt, where both were accused of heresy by fanatics and narrowly escaped being murdered.

After completing their *hajj* in Mecca, they journeyed to Palestine, Syria, Persia, and India. This took four years, at the end of which they returned to their native city, spending a year on the voyage. In Córdoba both were, for a time, the pupils of the Sufi woman, Fatima bint Waliyya. The Sufis regarded men and women as being equal and so scandalized the orthodox. These were sure that if men and women mingled socially, it could only be for sexual purposes.

Fatima sent Nur to Baghdad to study under a famous master there. After some months, his master sent him back to Córdoba to another great teacher. But when the Christians took Córdoba after a savage war, Nur went with his master to Granada.

After several years there, Nur started on the series of wanderings that earned him his *lackab*, his nickname, el-Musafir, the Traveler. After Rome, where letters of introduction from el-Arabi and Fatima gave him safe conduct, he journeyed to Greece, to Turkey, Persia again, Afghanistan, India again, Ceylon, Indonesia, China, and Japan.

Settling down in holy Damascus, he earned his living as a musician and, as a tasawwuf or Sufi master, accepted a number of disciples. After seven years, he set out once more. He went up the Volga and across Finland and Sweden, then across the Baltic Sea to the land of the idol worshippers, the savage Prussians. Here, after escaping sacrifice to a wooden statue of a god, he made his way westward through Germany. Northern France and then England and Ireland became part of his itinerary.

At the time Nur was in London, Richard I, surnamed *Coeur de Lion,* was king. Richard was not in England then, being engaged in the siege of the Castle of Chalus in the Limousin, France. Richard was killed by an arrow from the castle the following month, and his brother John was crowned in May. Nur witnessed the ceremonies in the city. Some time after, he actually succeeded in gaining an audience with King John. He found him to be a charming and witty man, interested in Islam culture and in Sufism. John was especially fascinated by Nur's reports of far-off lands.

"Traveling in those days was at best arduous and dangerous," Frigate said. "Even the so-called civilized countries were no picnic.

Religious hatred was prevalent. How could you, a Moslem, alone, without protection or money, travel safely in the Christian lands? Especially when the Crusades were going on then and religious hatred was endemic?''

Nur had shrugged. "Usually I put myself under the protection of the dignitaries of the state religions of those countries. And these got me civil protection. The church leaders were more concerned with heretics in their own faith than in infidels. In their own provinces, anyway.

"At other times, my very poverty was my safeguard. Robbers were not interested in me. When I traveled in rural areas, I would earn my keep and provide amusement by my flute playing and by my skill as a juggler, acrobat, and magician. Also, I am a great linguist, and I could pick up the language or the dialect of a place very quickly. I also told stories and jokes. You see, people everywhere were crazy for novelty, for entertainment. They welcomed me most places, though I did have a number of hostile receptions here and there. What did they care if I was a Moslem? I was harmless, and I gave them joy.

"Besides, I radiated an assurance of friendliness. That is something that *we* can do.''

Returning to Granada, and finding the atmosphere there changed, not friendly to Sufis, he had gone to Khorasan. After teaching there for several years, he made another trip to Mecca. From southern Arabia he had traveled on a trading ship to the shores of Zanzibar and then to southeast Africa. Returning to Baghdad, he lived there until his death at the age of ninety-four.

The Mongols under Hulagu, Jenghiz Khan's grandson, stormed into Baghdad, slaughtering and plundering. Within forty days, hundreds of thousands of its citizens were slain. Nur was one of them. He was sitting in his little room playing on the flute when a squat, slant-eyed, blood-drenched soldier burst in. Nur continued his song until the Mongol brought his sword down upon his neck.

"The Mongols devastated the Mideast,'' Frigate had said. "Never in history has such desolation been wrought in such a short time. Before the Mongols left, they murdered half the population, and they had destroyed everything from canals to buildings. In my time, six hundred years later, the Mideast still had not recovered.''

"They were indeed the Scourge of Allah,'' Nur had said. "Yet there were good men and women among them.''

Now, sitting by the little man, watching the dark-skinned betel-nut chewers on shore, Frigate was thinking about chance. What destiny had crossed the paths of a man born in midwestern America in 1918 and of one born in Moslem Spain in 1164? Was destiny anything but chance? Probably. But the odds against this happening on Earth were infinity to one. Then the Riverworld had changed the odds, and here they were.

It was that evening, after his conversation with Nur, that all sat in the captain's cabin. The ship was anchored near the shore, and fish-oil lamps lit their poker game. After Tom Rider had cleaned up the final big pot—cigarettes were the stakes—they had a bull session. Nur told them two tales of the Mullah Nasruddin. Nasruddin (Eagle-of-the-Faith) was a figure of Moslem folktales, a mad dervish, a simpleton whose adventures were really lessons in wisdom.

Nur sipped on his scotch whiskey—he never drank more than two ounces a day—and said, "Captain, you've told the tale about Pat and Mike, the priest, rabbi, and minister. It's a funny story, but it does tell a person something about patterns of thinking. Pat and Mike are figures of Western folklore. Let me tell you about one from the East. .

"One day a man came by the house of the Mullah Nasruddin and observed him walking around it, throwing bread crumbs on the ground.

" 'Why in the world are you doing that, Mullah?' the man said.

" 'I'm keeping the tigers away.'

" 'But,' the man said, 'there are no tigers around here.'

" 'Exactly. It works, doesn't it?' "

They laughed, and then Frigate said, "Nur, how old is that story?"

"It was at least two thousand years old when I was born. It originated among the Sufis as a teaching tale. Why?"

"Because," Frigate said, "I heard the same story, in a different form, in the 1950's or thereabouts. There was this Englishman, and he was kneeling in the street, chalking a line on the curb. A friend, coming along, said, 'Why are you doing that?'

" 'To keep the lions away.'

" 'But there are no lions in England.'

" 'See?' "

"By God, I heard the same story when I was a kid in Frisco," Farrington bellowed. "Only it was an Irishman then."

"Many of the instructive Nasruddin stories have become mere jokes," Nur said. "The populace tells them for fun, but they were originally meant to be taken seriously. Here's another.

"Nasruddin crossed the border from Persia to India on his donkey many times. Each time, the donkey carried large bundles of straw on his back. But when Nasruddin returned, the donkey carried nothing. Each time, the customs guard searched Nasruddin, but he could not find any contraband.

"The guard would always ask Nasruddin what he was carrying. The Mullah would always reply, 'I am smuggling,' and he would smile.

"After many years, Nasruddin retired to Egypt. The customs man went to him and said, 'Very well, Nasruddin. Tell me, now it's safe for you. What were you smuggling?'

" 'Donkeys.' "

They laughed again, and Frigate said, "I heard the same story in Arizona. Only this time the smuggler was Pancho, and he was crossing the border from Mexico to the United States."

"I suppose every story is an old one," Tom Rider drawled. "Probably started with the cave man."

"Perhaps," Nur said. "But it is a tradition that these stories were originated by the Sufis long before Mohammed was born. They are designed to teach people how to change their patterns of thinking, though they are amusing in themselves. Of course, they are used in the simplest, the first, stage of teaching by the masters.

"However, since then these tales have spread throughout East and West. I was amused to find some of them, in altered form, told in Ireland in Gaelic. By word of mouth, over thousands of leagues and two millennia of time, Nasruddin had passed from Persia to Hibernia."

"If the Sufis originated them before Mohammed," Frigate said, "then the Sufis must have been Zoroastrians in the beginning."

"Sufism is not a monopoly of Islamism," Nur said. "It was highly developed by the Moslems, but anyone who believes in God can be a Sufi candidate. However, the Sufis modify their method of teaching to conform to the local cultures. What will work for Persian Moslems in Khorasan won't necessarily work for black Moslems in the Sudan. And the difference in effective methods would be even greater for Parisian Christians. The place and the time determine the teaching."

Later, Nur and Frigate stretched their legs on land, walking around a huge bonfire through a crowd of chattering Dravidians. Frigate said, "How can you adapt your medieval Iberian-Moorish methods to teaching in this world? The people are so mixed, from everywhere and every time. There are no monolithic cultures. Besides, those that do exist are always changing."

"I am working on that," Nur said.

"Then, one of the reasons you won't take me as a disciple is that you are not ready as a teacher?"

"You can console yourself with that," Nur said, and he laughed. "But, yes, that is one reason. You see, the teacher must always be teaching himself."

49

THE GREY CLOUDS MOVED THROUGH THE BOAT, FILLING EVERY room.

Sam Clemens said, "Oh, no, not again!" though he did not know why he said that. The fog not only pressed against the bulkheads and seeped into everything that could absorb moisture, it rolled down his throat and enveloped his heart. The water soaked it, and drops fell off of it, dripping into his belly, gurgling down inside his groin, running over, spilling down into his legs, waterlogging his feet.

He was sodden with a nameless fear which he had experienced before.

He was alone in the pilothouse. Alone in the boat. He stood by the control panel, looking out of the window. Fog shoved against it. He could see no more than an arm's length through the plastic. Yet, somehow, he knew that the banks of The River were empty of life. There was no one out there. And here he was in this gigantic vessel, the only one aboard. It didn't even need him, since the controls were set for automatic navigation.

Alone and lonely as he was, he at least could not be stopped from reaching the headwaters of The River. There was no one left in the world to oppose him.

He turned and began pacing back and forth from bulkhead to bulkhead of the pilothouse. How long was this journey going to take? When would the fog lift and the sun shine brightly and the mountains surrounding the polar sea be revealed? And when would he hear another human voice, see another face?

"Now!" someone bellowed.

Sam jumped straight up as if springs had been unsnapped beneath his feet. His heart opened and closed as swiftly as the beating of a hummingbird's wings. It pumped out water and fear, forming a puddle around his feet. Somehow, without being aware of it, he had spun around and was facing the owner of the voice. It was a shadowy figure in the clouds swirling in the pilothouse. It moved toward him, stopped, and reached out a vague arm. A pseudopod flicked a switch on the panel.

Sam tried to cry out, "No! No!" The words ran into each other in his throat and shattered as if they were made of thin glass.

Though it was too dim to see which control the figure had touched, he knew that the boat was now set on a course which would send it full speed into the left bank.

Finally, the words came . . . screeching.

"You can't do that!"

Silently, the shadowy mass advanced. Now he could see that it was a man. It was the same height as he, but its shoulders were much broader. And on one shoulder was a long wooden shaft. At its end was a truncated triangle of steel.

"Erik Bloodaxe!" he cried.

Now began the terrible chase. He fled through the boat, through every room of the three-tiered pilothouse, across the flight deck, down the ladder into the hangar deck and through every one of its rooms, down a ladder and through every room of the hurricane deck, down a ladder and through every room of the main deck, down a ladder and into the vast boiler deck.

Here, aware of the waters pressing against the hull, aware that he was below the surface of The River, he ran through the many rooms, large and small. He passed between the giant electric motors turning the paddlewheels which were driving the vessel toward destruction. Desperately, he tried to get into the large compartment holding the two launches. He would rip the wires out of the motor of one and take the other out into The River and so leave his sinister pursuer behind. But someone had locked the door.

Now he was crouching in a tiny compartment, trying to slow his rasping breath. Then, the hatch opened. Erik Bloodaxe's figure loomed in the greyness. It moved slowly toward him, the great axe held in both hands.

"I told you," Erik said, and he lifted the axe. Sam was powerless to move, to protest. After all, this was his own fault. He deserved it.

50

HE AWOKE MOANING. THE CABIN LIGHTS WERE ON, AND GWENA-fra's beautiful face and long honey-blonde hair were above him.

"Sam! Wake up! You've been having another nightmare!"

"He almost got me that time," he mumbled.

He sat up. Whistles were shrilling on the decks. A minute later, the intercom unit shrilled. The boat would soon be heading for a grailstone and breakfast. Sam liked to sleep late, and he would just as soon have missed breakfast. But as captain it was his duty to rise with the others.

He got out of bed and shambled into the head. After a shower and tooth-brushing, he came out. Gwenafra was already in her early-morning outfit, looking like an eskimo who had traded her furs for towels. Sam got into a similar suit but left his hood down to put on his captain's cap. He lit a corona and blew smoke while he paced back and forth.

Gwenafra said, "Did you have another nightmare about Bloodaxe?"

"Yes," he said. "Give me some coffee, will you?"

Gwenafra dropped a teaspoonful of dark crystals into a grey metal cup. The water boiled as the crystals released both heat and caffeine. He took the cup, saying, "Thanks."

She sipped her coffee, then said, "There's no reason to feel guilty about him."

"That's what I've told myself a thousand times," Sam said. "It's irrational, but when did knowing that ever make a fellow feel better? It's the irrational in us that drives us. The Master of Dreams has about as much brains as a hedgehog. But he's a great artist, witless though he is, like many an artist I've known. Perhaps including yours truly."

"There isn't a chance that Bloodaxe will ever find you."

"I know that. Try telling the Dream Master that."

A light flashed; a whistle blew from a panel on a bulkhead. Sam flicked its switch.

"Captain? Detweiller here. Arrival time at designated grailstone will be five minutes from now."

"Okay, Hank," Sam said. "I'll be right out."

Followed by Gwenafra, he left the stateroom. They passed down a narrow corridor and went through a hatch into the control room or bridge. This was on the top deck of the pilothouse; the other senior officers were quartered in the cabins on the second and third decks.

There were three persons in the control room: Detweiller, who had once been a river pilot, then a captain, then owner of an Illinois-Mississippi River steamboat company; the chief executive officer, John Byron, ex-admiral, Royal Navy; the brigadier of the boat's Marines, Jean Baptiste Antoine Marcellin de Marbot, ex-general for Napoleon.

The latter was a short, slim, merry-looking fellow with dark-brown hair, snub nose, and bright blue eyes. He saluted Clemens and reported in Esperanto.

"All ready for duty, my captain."

Sam said, "Fine, Marc. You can take your post now."

The little Frenchman saluted and left the pilothouse, sliding down the pole behind it to the flight deck. Lights flooded this, showing the Marines in battle array lined up in its middle. The standard bearer held a pole on top of which was the boat's flag, a light-blue square bearing a scarlet phoenix. Near him were rows of pistoleers, men and women in grey duraluminum coal-scuttle helmets topped by roaches of human hair stiff with grease, plastic cuirasses, knee-length leather boots, their broad belts holding holstered Mark IV revolvers.

Behind them were the spearmen; behind them, the archers. To one side was a group of bazookateers.

Off to one side stood a colossus clad in armor, holding an oaken club which Sam could lift with two hands only with difficulty. Officially, Joe Miller was Sam's bodyguard, but he always accompanied the Marines at these times. His chief function was to awe the locals.

"But as usual," Sam often said, "Joe goes too far. He scares the hell out of them just by standing around."

This day started out like every other day. It was destined to be, however, quite different. Some time during the day, the *Minerva* would attack the *Rex Grandissimus*. Sam should have felt jubilant. He wasn't. He hated the idea of destroying such a beautiful boat, one he had designed and built. Moreover, he'd been deprived of the joy of wreaking a personal revenge on John.

On the other hand, it was a lot safer this way.

There was a bonfire on the right side about half a kilometer away. It revealed a mushroom-shaped grailstone and gleamed on white cloths covering bodies. The fog over The River was lower and thinner here than that usually encountered. It would clear away quickly once the sun got over the peaks. The sky was brightening, washing out the flaming giant stars and gas clouds.

Per usual procedure, the *Firedragon III,* an armored amphibian launch, preceded the mother boat. When it got to an area where the boat would have to recharge its batacitor, its commander parleyed with the locals for the use of two grailstones. Most areas were pleased to do this, their remuneration being the thrill of observing the mammoth vessel at close range.

Those locals who objected found their grailstones temporarily confiscated. They could do nothing about it except to protest. The boat had overwhelming firepower, though Clemens was always reluctant to use it. When forced to resort to violence, Clemens refrained from massacre. A few spurts of .80-caliber plastic bullets from the big steam machine guns on the boat and from the armored steam-spurting amphibian tearing around on shore, usually sufficed. It wasn't even necessary to kill anybody in most cases.

After all, what did the locals lose if two grailstones were used by somebody else for one time only? Nobody had to miss a meal. There were always enough unused spots on nearby stones to take up the slack. In fact, most of those who surrendered their meal did not even bother to travel to the next stone. They preferred to stay there so they could ooh and ah at the magnificent beauty of the boat.

The four enormous electrical motors of the boat required tremendous energy. Once a day, a giant metal cap was placed over the grailstone by which the boat was stationed. A launch would carry the boat's grails to the next stone for filling. A crane extended from another launch would lift the cap and place it over the head of the stone. When the stone discharged, its energy flashed via thick cables into the batacitor. This was a huge metal box which rose from the boiler deck into the main deck. It stored the energy instantly in its function of capacitor. As demanded, it would release the energy in its function of battery.

Sam Clemens went ashore and talked briefly with the local chief officials, who understood Esperanto. This universal language had degraded here into a form which was difficult but not impossible for Sam to understand. He gravely thanked them for their courtesy, and he returned to the boat on his small private launch. Ten minutes later, *Firedragon IV* returned with a cargo of full grails.

Whistles blowing and bells clanging to give the locals a thrill, the boat headed on up-River. Sam and Gwenafra sat at the head of the great nine-sided table in the dining room in the main deck salon. The chief officers, except those on duty, sat with him. After some orders for the day, Sam retired to the billiards table, where he played against the titanthrop. Joe was not very good with a cue or with cards because of his huge hands. Sam almost always beat him. Then Sam would play against a more skilled person.

At 07:00, Sam would make an inspection of the boat. He hated to walk, but he insisted on this because he needed the exercise. Also, it helped keep up the appearance of a naval vessel. Without the drills and the inspections, the crew were likely to become sloppy civilians. They would get too off-hand, too familiar with their superiors when on duty.

"I run a tight boat," Sam had often boasted. "At least, the crew is tight, though no one has ever been found drunk on duty."

The inspection did not take place that morning. Sam was called to the pilothouse because the radio operator had gotten a message from the *Minerva*. Before Sam could get off the elevator, the radar scope had blipped an object coming over the mountain to portside.

51

THE BLIMP CAME DOWN OUT OF THE BRIGHTNESS AS IF IT WERE A silver egg just laid by the sun. To the startled people on the ground, few of whom had ever seen or even heard of an airship before, it was a frightening monster. No doubt some believed that it was a vessel carrying the mysterious beings who had raised them from the dead. A few may even have hailed it with a mixture of dread and joy, sure that a revelation was at hand.

How had the *Minerva* found the *Mark Twain* so easily? The great boat was towing a large kite-shaped balloon which was above the top of the mountains and which carried a transmitter sending powerful dots and dashes. Hardy, the *Minerva's* navigator, knew the boat's general location from the map of The River on his table. During the years of its voyaging, the *Mark Twain* had sent out data by radio which had enabled the Parolanders to trace its route. Furthermore, on spotting the boat, the navigator of the *Parseval* had sent a message which gave the *Minerva* a rough location.

Having also been given the location of the *Rex,* the captain of the *Minerva* knew that John Lackland's boat was almost on a straight line with Sam's due east. The *Rex* was only 140 kilometers away if a line as straight as a Prussian officer's back was followed. To follow The River, however, Sam's boat would have to go perhaps 571,195 kilometers or 355,000 miles before it arrived where the *Rex* was now.

Greystock, speaking over the transceiver in the control nacelle, asked permission to pass over the *Mark Twain.*

Sam's voice was flat over the transceiver. "Why?"

"To salute you," the Englishman said. "Also, I think that you and your crew might like to get a close look at the vessel that is going to destroy King John. And, to tell the truth, my men and I would like to see your splendid boat at close range."

He paused, and then said, "It may be our last chance."

It was Sam who paused this time. Then, sounding as if he were choking back tears, he said, "Okay, Greystock. You may pass by us, but not over us. Call me paranoid. But it makes me uneasy to have an airship carrying four big bombs directly over me. What if they were accidentally released?"

Greystock rolled his eyes in disgust and grinned savagely at the other men in the nacelle.

"Nothing could possibly go wrong," he said.

"Yeah? That's what the commander of the *Maine* said just before he went to bed. No, Greystock, you do as I say."

Greystock, obviously unhappy, replied that he would obey.

"We'll circle you once and then get to the job."

"Good luck on that," Sam's voice said. "I know that you fine fellows might not be . . ."

He seemed unable to complete his sentence.

"We know we might not get back," Greystock said. "But I think we have an excellent chance of taking the *Rex* by surprise."

"I hope so. But remember that the *Rex* has two airplanes. You'll have to hit the flight deck first so they can't get off."

"I don't need advice," Greystock said coldly.

There was another pause, longer than the others.

Sam's voice came over the speaker loudly. "Lothar von Richthofen is coming up to greet you. He wants to fly alongside and give you his personal blessing. That's the least I can do for him. I've had a hell of a time keeping him from convoying you. He'd like to be in on the attack, too.

"But our planes have a flight ceiling of only 3660 meters. That makes them too susceptible to downdrafts over those mountains. Anyway, they'd have to carry an extra fuel tank to get back."

Lothar's voice cut in. "I told him you could spare enough fuel from your ship, Greystock. We could fly back."

"Nothing doing!"

Greystock looked down through the forward port. The balloon was being reeled in, but it would be twenty minutes before it was landed.

The giant boat was a beauty, a fourth longer than the *Rex* and much taller. Jill Gulbirra had claimed that the *Parseval* was the most beautiful and the grandest artifact on The Riverworld. Earth had never had anything to equal it. But Greystock thought that this vessel, to use Clemens' phrase, "won the blue ribbon by a mile."

As Greystock watched, an airplane rose on an elevator to the landing deck while a crew readied a catapult.

The stocky man looked with arctic-grey eyes around the control gondola. The pilot, Newton, a World War II aviator, was at his post. Hardy, the navigator, and Samhradh, the Irish first mate, were at the port screen. Six others were aboard, stationed in the three engine gondolas.

Greystock walked to the weapons cabin, opened it, and took out two of the heavy Mark IV pistols. These were steel four-shooter revolvers using duraluminum cartridges holding .69-caliber plastic bullets. He held one by the grip in his left hand; the other, he reversed. Keeping an eye on the two at the port screen, he walked over to a position behind Newton. He brought the butt end of the gun in his right hand against the top of Newton's head. The pilot fell off his chair onto the floor.

He quickly reached over with his left hand and flicked the transceiver switch off with his thumb. The two men turned at the crack of the impact of metal against bone. They froze, staring at a totally unexpected scene.

Greystock said, "Don't move. Now . . . put your hands up behind your neck."

Hardy, goggling, said, "What be this, man?"

"Just keep quiet."

He waved a pistol at a cabinet. "Put on your parachutes. And don't try to jump me. I can shoot both of you easily."

Samhradh stuttered, his face going from pale to red. "Y . . . y . . . you bastard! You're a traitor!"

"No," Greystock said, "a loyal subject of King John of England." He smiled. "Though I have been promised that I will be second-in-command of the *Rex* when I bring this airship to His Majesty. That ensured my loyalty."

Samhradh looked out the stern port. The action in the control gondola was visible from the engine gondolas.

Greystock said, "I was gone for half an hour, checking with the engineers, remember? They're all tied up, so they won't be of any help to you."

The two men crossed the gondola, opened the cabinet and began to put on their parachutes. Hardy said, "What about him?"

"You can put Newton's chute on and throw him out before you go."

"And what about the engineers?"

"They'll have to take their chances."

"They'll die if you're shot down!" Samhradh said.

"Too bad."

When the two men had strapped on their packs, they dragged Newton to the middle of the gondola. Greystock, holding pistols on them, backed away while they did this. He then pushed the button which lowered the port plexiglas screen. Newton, groaning, half-conscious, was pushed over the ledge. Samhradh pulled Newton's ripcord as he fell out. A moment later, the Irishman leaped. Hardy paused with one leg outside the port.

"If I ever run across you, Greystock, I'll kill you."

"No, you won't," Greystock said. "Jump before I decide to make sure you won't ever have a chance."

He turned the transceiver on.

Clemens bellowed, "What in blue blazes is going on?"

"Three of my men drew lots to see who leaves the ship,"

Greystock said smoothly. "We decided that the ship should be lightened. It's better that way; we need all the speed we can get."

"Why in hell didn't you tell me?" Clemens said. "Now I'll have to put about and fish them out of the water."

"I know," Greystock said under his breath.

He looked out the port screen. The *Minerva* was past the *Mark Twain* now. Its decks were crowded with people looking up at the dirigible. The airplane, a low-wing single-seater monoplane, was on the catapult, which was being swung around to face the wind. The balloon was still being reeled in.

Greystock seated himself before the control panel. Within a few minutes he had brought the ship down to about 91 meters or 300 feet from The River. He turned it then and headed toward the boat.

The vast white vessel was stopped in The River, its four paddlewheels spinning just enough to hold it steady. A big launch had put out from its port in the stern and was going around the boat to pick up the parachutists, now struggling in the water.

Both banks were crowded with sightseers, and at least a hundred watercraft were sailing or being paddled toward the three chutists.

Steam spurted from the catapult, and the monoplane shot out from the deck. Its silvery fuselage and wings shone greyly as it began to climb toward the airship.

Clemens' voice yammered from the receiver. "What the damnation-to-hell-and-gone are you doing; John?"

"Just coming back to make sure that my men are safe," Greystock said.

"Of all the numbskulls!" Clemens screeched. "If your brains were expanded tenfold, they would still rattle around in a gnat's ass! This is what comes from trying to make a mink cap from a pig's anus! I told Firebrass that he shouldn't let a medieval baron near a dirigible!

" 'Greystock's from the dumbest, most arrogant, most untrustworthy class you could find!' I told him. 'A medieval nobleman!'

"Jumping Jesus H. Christ! But no, he argued that you had the potentiality, and it would be a nice experiment to see if you could adjust to the Industrial Age!"

Joe Miller's voice rumbled. "Take it eathy, Tham. If you pithth him off, he'll refuthe to attack Chohn'th boat."

"Thyove it up your athth!" Clemens said mockingly. "When I need advice from a paleoanthropus, I'll ask for it."

"You don't need to get inthulting chutht becauthe you're mad, Tham," Miller said. "Thay! Did it occur to Your Machethty that maybe Greythock ith up to thomething rotten? Maybe he thold out to that aththhole, King Chohn?"

Greystock cursed. That hairy, comical-looking colossus of an apeman was much shrewder than he looked. However, Clemens, in his towering fury, might ignore him.

By then the airship, her nose down at ten degrees to the horizontal, was heading straight for the boat. Her altitude was now 31 meters and dropping.

Von Richthofen's plane zoomed by within 15 meters. He waved at Greystock, but he looked puzzled. He would have been listening in on the radio conversation, of course.

Greystock punched a button. A rocket sprang from its launch under the port fore engine gondola. The dirigible gained altitude as it was relieved of the weight of the missile. Spurting tailfire, the long, slim tube swerved toward the silver plane, the heat locater in its nose sniffing the craft's exhausts. Richthofen's face wasn't visible, but Greystock could imagine his expression of horror. He had about six seconds to get out of the cockpit and take to his parachute. Even if he escaped, he'd be lucky at this altitude if it opened in time.

No, he was not going to jump. Instead, he had wing-overed the plane and sent it diving at the water. Now it was straightening out just above the surface. There flashed the rocket. And now the missile and the aircraft disappeared in a ball of flame.

By then, the flight crew was frantically running another plane to the catapult. The balloon crew, distracted by the sirens and horns and the sudden frenzied activity, had stopped hauling their charge down. Greystock hoped they would not have the presence of mind to cut it loose. The huge aerostat would be a drag when the boat tried to maneuver swiftly.

Through the transceiver, the wail of sirens and Clemens' voice, almost as high pitched as the alarms, came faintly.

The boat began to pick up speed and to turn at the same time. Greystock smiled. He had hoped that the *Mark Twain* would present her broadside. He punched a button, and the airship, relieved of the weight of two heavy torpedoes, soared. Greystock raised the elevators to depress the ship's nose even further, and he pushed the throttles in to full-speed position.

The torpedoes struck the water with a splash. Two wakes foamed from behind them. The transceiver yelped with Clemens' voice. The giant boat quit turning and sped at an angle toward the bank to the left. Rockets spurted up from its decks. Some of them arced down toward the torpedoes and exploded immediately after plunging below the surface. Others headed toward the dirigible.

Greystock swore in Norman French. He hadn't been quick enough. But the torpedoes would surely hit the boat, and if they did, King John's orders would have been carried out.

But he did not want to die. He had his own mission.

Perhaps he should have dropped the bombs while he was passing over the boat. She had veered off when he had tried to get directly over her, and he had not wanted to change course too abruptly. He should have neutralized the crew earlier and then told Clemens he was bringing the airship in close so everybody could have a good look at her.

During these thoughts, he had automatically punched the button which released all his rockets. They headed toward the boats' missiles, their heat detectors locked into the tailflames of the boat's, just as the boats' rockets were locked into the tailflames of his missiles.

The explosions from rockets meeting rockets shook the airship. Smoke spread before him, veiling the boat. Then he was through the dark clouds and almost on the *Mark Twain*.

By God's wounds! One torpedo had just missed the starboard corner of the stern, and the second was going to hit it! No, it wasn't! Its side had touched the corner, and it had veered off! The boat had somehow escaped both!

Now Clemens' voice, yammering, told him that no more rockets would be released. Clemens was afraid that the airship would explode and, carried by the wind, would fall flaming onto the boat.

The balloon, trailing its plastic cable, was floating down-River, rising at the same time.

Clemens had forgotten that the airship's bombs had not yet been released.

The second airplane, a two-seater amphibian, shot below him. Its pilot looked upward in frustration at him. They were too close to each other and he was going too fast to swing up to the right and shoot the nose machine guns. But the gunner in the cockpit behind the pilot was swinging his twin machine guns around. Every tenth bullet would be a tracer, phosphorous coated. Only one in a gas cell was needed to ignite the hydrogen. The *Minerva* was only 152 meters from the *Mark Twain* and was closing fast. Its motors were going at top speed. This, plus a 16-km/ph tailwind, meant that the boat could not possibly get away in time.

If only he could drop the bombs before the tracer bullets struck. Perhaps the gunner would miss. By the time he got his guns around, the airplane would be past the airship.

The side of the boat loomed up. Even if the dirigible wasn't hit by the tracers, she was so near the boat that the bombs would blow up both vessels.

Estimating the arrival time of the *Minerva* over the paddlewheeler, he set the release mechanism of the bombs with a twist of his wrist. Then he got out of the seat and dived through the open port. No time to put on a parachute. Besides, he was too near the water for it to open in time. As he fell, he was struck by a wave of air like a colossal winnowing fan. He spun, unconscious, unable even to think fleetingly of how he had lost his second-in-command under John Lackland. Or his plans to get rid of John and take over the captainship of the *Rex Grandissimus* for himself.

52

PETER FRIGATE HAD BOARDED THE *Razzle Dazzle* A WEEK AFTER
New Year's Day of year 7 A.R.D. Twenty-six years later, he was still
on the schooner. But he was getting sailweary and discouraged.
Would the ship ever arrive at the headwaters?

Since he had first stepped aboard, he had passed, to starboard,
810,000 grailstones. That meant he'd traveled about 1,303,390
kilometers or 810,000 miles.

He had started in the equatorial zone, and it had taken a year and a
half to get into the arctic regions, going not as the crow flies but as
the snake wriggles. If The River had been as straight as a ruler, it
would have taken the ship there in less than six months, maybe five.
Instead, it was as twisted as a politician's campaign promises after
election.

The first time the ship was in the arctic, just after The River had
definitely turned for its southward journey, Frigate had proposed
that they proceed northward on foot. The polar mountains could not
be seen, yet they must be relatively near. Tantalizingly so.

Farrington had said, "And just how in blue blazes can we get
over those?"

He had gestured at the unbroken stone verticality to the north.
Here it rose to an estimated 3650 meters or a little less than 12,000
feet.

"In a balloon."

"Are you nuts? The wind blows south here. It'd take us *away*
from the polar mountains."

"The surface wind would. But if the meteorological patterns are
the same here as on Earth, the upper polar winds should be flowing
northeastward. Once the balloon got high enough to get in their
stream, it'd reverse direction, get blown toward the pole.

"Then, when we got near mountains that're supposed to ring the
supposed sea, we'd come down. We'd have no chance of getting
over those mountains in the balloon, if they're as high as they are
said to be."

Farrington had actually turned pale when he'd heard Frigate's
proposal.

Rider, grinning, said, "Didn't you know that the Frisco Kid
doesn't even like the *idea* of air travel?"

"That isn't it!" Martin said, glaring. "If a balloon *could* get us there, I'd be the first to board it. But it won't! Anyway, how by the high muckamuck are we going to make a balloon even if we could travel on one?"

Frigate had to admit that it couldn't be done. At least, not in this area. To make a balloon and fill it with hydrogen was impossible. There were no necessary materials here. Or anywhere else, as far as he knew.

However, there was another method they might consider. How about a hot-air balloon to carry a rope up to the top of the mountain?

Even as he spoke, he had to laugh. How could they make a rope 3650 meters long, one strong enough not to break under its own weight? What size of balloon would be needed to lift the enormous weight of the rope? One as big as the *Hindenburg?*

And how could they anchor the rope at the top of the mountain?

Grinning, Frigate proposed sending a man up in the rope-carrying aerostat. He could get off at the top and secure the balloon.

"Forget it!" Farrington said.

Frigate was happy to do this.

The *Razzle Dazzle* continued to sail southward, the wind behind it, its crew glad to get away from this gloomy, chilly area. There were some Old Stone Age people living here, but they had dwelt in the arctic regions on Earth. They did not know any better.

Since then, the schooner had crossed the equator and entered the south polar region nine times. At the moment, they were in the equatorial zone again.

Peter Frigate was sick of shipboard life. Nor was he the only one. Shore leave had been getting longer and longer for some time.

One day, while eating lunch on the bank, Frigate experienced two thrills in rapid sequence. One was the offering of his grail. For years he had been hoping to get peanut butter and a banana at the same time. Now, as he opened the lid of his grail, he saw the realization of his dream.

A grey metal cup in a rack was filled with smooth, delicious-odored peanut butter. Across another rack was the yellow-brown-spotted form of a banana.

Grinning, slavering, chortling, he unpeeled the fruit and smeared one end with the peanut butter. Close to crooning with delight, he bit off the combination.

It was worth being resurrected if only for the food.

A moment later, he saw a woman walking by. She was very attractive, but it was what she wore that widened his eyes. He got to his feet and, speaking Esperanto, approached her.

"*Pardonu min, sinjorino.* I couldn't help observing that unusual armlet. It looks like brass!"

She looked down, smiling, and said, "*Estas brazo.*"

She accepted his proffered cigarette with a murmured, *"Dank-on,"* and lit it. She seemed to be very amiable. Too much so, one person thought. Scowling, a tall, dark man strode up to them.

Frigate hastily assured him that his interest was not in her but in the armlet. The man looked relieved; the woman, disappointed. But she shrugged and made the best of it.

"It comes from up-River," she said. "It cost one hundred cigarettes and two hornfish horns."

"Not to mention some personal favors on her part," the man said.

The woman said, "Oh, Emil, that was before I moved in with you."

"Do you know where it came from?" Frigate said. "I mean, where it was made?"

"The man who sold it to me came from Nova Bohemujo."

Frigate gave the man a cigarette, and this seemed to ease the tension. Emil said that New Bohemia was a rather large state about nine hundred grailstones up The River. Twentieth-century Czechs made up its majority. The minority was composed of some ancient Gaulish tribe with, of course, the usual one or two percent of peoples from everywhere and every time.

Until three years ago New Bohemia had been small, just one of the mingled Slavic-Gaulish peoples in this area.

"But its chief, a man named Ladislas Podebrad, launched a project about six years ago. He thought there might be mineral treasures, especially iron, buried deep under the soil. His people started digging at the base of the mountain, and they made an enormous and deep hole. They wore out much flint and bone. You know how tough the grass is."

Frigate nodded. The grass seemed designed to resist erosion. Its roots were very deep and intertwined. In fact, he wasn't sure that it was not one plant, a single organism extending on both sides of The River and perhaps beneath it. And its roots were tough silicon bearers.

"It took a long time to get below the grass, and when it was done, there was nothing but dirt beneath that. They kept on, and after going sixty meters, they came to rock. I believe it was limestone. They almost gave up then. But Podebrad, who's something of a mystic, told them he'd had a dream that there were great quantities of iron below the rock."

"Of course," the woman said, "I can't see you working like that."

"You're not so dedicated yourself."

Frigate did not give them long to stay together, but he said nothing. He could be wrong. He'd known couples like this on Earth who had verbally stung and stabbed each other from marriage to death. For some sick reason, they needed each other.

Three years ago, Podebrad's dream and the hard work of his people had paid off.

They had come across an immense store of minerals: iron ore, zinc sulfide, sand, coal, salt, lead, sulfur, and even some platinum and vanadium.

Frigate blinked and said, "You mean, in layers, strata? But they wouldn't occur naturally in that fashion."

"No," Emil said. "At least, the man told Marie that they shouldn't. What he said, and I've heard others from New Bohemia say this, too, it looked as if a gigantic truck had just dumped the ores there.

"Whoever made this world had pushed the stuff there, you know, as if by a gigantic bulldozer. Then the rock had been put over it, then the soil, then the grass."

Podebrad had gotten the minerals out, was, in fact, still bringing them up. All his people were armed with steel weapons now. And New Bohemia had expanded from its 12-kilometer-long boundaries to 60 kilometers on both sides of The River.

However, this had not been done by conquest. Neighboring states had asked to be absorbed, and Podebrad had welcomed them. There was wealth enough for all.

Meanwhile, other states along here had launched their own digging projects. They had been at it about three years but had gained only sweat, worn-out tools, and disappointment.

Podebrad's original site seemed to be the only one to contain minerals. Or else other dumpheaps—as Emil called them—were buried even deeper.

Emil pointed at the hills.

"Our own country has a hole sixty meters deep. But it's being filled up now. The caprock is dolomite. Podebrad was lucky. His was soft limestone."

Frigate thanked them and excitedly hurried off. As a result, the *Razzle Dazzle* anchored off the bank of Podebrad's capital eleven days later.

The crew smelled New Bohemia half a day before arriving at its southern limits. The fumes of sulfur and coal stank throughout the area.

High earth walls had been erected along the banks. Steel weapons, including flintlock firearms, were everywhere. The River was patrolled by four large steam-powered paddlewheeled boats, each carrying two cannons, and a large number of smaller boats with machine guns.

The crew of the *Razzle Dazzle* were astonished. Also, somewhat depressed. The fair valley was blighted. For too long, they had taken the clean air and pure blue skies, the green plains and hills, for granted.

Nur asked a local why it was necessary to foul the land and make all those weapons.

"We had to do so," the man said. "If we hadn't, then other states would have tried to take our ores away from us. And they would have embarked on conquest by arms. We made the weapons for self-defense.

"Of course, we make other artifacts, too. We trade these, and we get more tobacco, liquor, food, and ornaments than we can use."

The man patted his fat paunch.

Nur smiled and said, "The grails provide enough for any person's needs and some luxuries, too. Why tear up the land and make a stench to get far more than you need?"

"I just told you why."

"It would have been best to have filled up the hole again," Nur said. "Or never to have dug it in the first place."

The man shrugged. Then, looking surprised, he walked up to Rider.

"Say, aren't you the movie star Tom Mix?"

Tom smiled and said, "Not me, *amiko*. People have told me I look a little like him, though."

"I saw you . . . him . . . when he came to Paris during his European tour. I was on a business trip then, and I stood in the crowds and cheered you . . . him . . . as he rode along on Tony. It was a great thrill for me. He was my favorite cowboy actor."

"Mine, too," Tom said, and he turned away.

Frigate called the captain and first mate to one side.

"You look excited, Pete," Martin Farrington said. "You must be thinking of the same thing Tom and I were discussing just a minute ago."

Frigate said, "Now, how could you do that? What is it?"

Martin looked sidewise at Tom and smiled. "Sure, what else could it be? We were talking about, just speculating, mind you, about how nice it would be if we had one of those small steamboats."

Frigate was astonished. "That wasn't what I was thinking of! What do you mean, you'd steal it?"

"Sort of," Tom drawled. "They could always make another one. We were thinking of how much faster we could get up-River on one of those handy-dandy paddlewheelers."

"Aside from the ethics of the thing," Frigate said, "it'd be dangerous. I assume they guard them at night."

"Look who's talking of ethics," Martin said. "You stole your spear and bow and arrows, remember?"

Frigate's face became red.

"Not really. I had made them myself. They were mine."

"It was stealing," Martin said. He gave one of his wonderfully charming smiles and slapped Frigate on the shoulder. "No need to get huffy. Your need was greater than the state's, and you took something that could be easily replaced. We're in the same situation. We need to get up-River a lot faster."

"Not to mention a lot more comfortably," Tom said.

"You want us to risk getting killed?"

"Would you volunteer? I wouldn't order anybody to do this. If you don't care to do it, you won't peach on us, will you?"

"Of course not!" Frigate said, getting red in the face again. "I'm not objecting because I'm afraid! Listen, I'd do it, if it was necessary. But what I have in mind is not that. It's something that would get us far north a hell of a lot faster than a steamboat."

"You mean have this Podebrad build us a speedboat?" Martin said. "A steam yacht?"

"No, I don't. I mean something that won't go *up* The River. It'll go *over* it!"

"Rub me for a saddlesore," Tom said. "You mean an airplane?"

Tom looked eager. Martin turned pale.

"No, that wouldn't work. I mean, a plane could get us a lot farther faster. But we'd have to land several times and make more fuel, and there's no way of making more.

"No, I'm thinking about another type of air travel."

"You can't be thinking of a balloon?"

"Sure, why not? A balloon, or, better yet, a blimp."

53

Tom Rider liked the idea.

Farrington said, "No! It's too dangerous! I don't trust those fragile gasbags. Besides, you'd have to use hydrogen, right? Hydrogen can catch fire like that!"

He snapped his fingers.

"In addition, they're easy prey for strong winds and storms. Also, where are you going to dredge up a blimp pilot? Airplane pilots should be easy to find, though personally I've only run into two. Furthermore, we'd have to be its crew, and that means we'd have to be trained. What if we don't have the knack for it? There's another reason . . ."

"A yellow streak?" Tom said, smiling.

Martin reddened, and his hands balled. "How'd you like a few teeth knocked out?"

"It wouldn't be the first time," Tom Rider said. "But take it easy, Frisco, I was just trying to think of more reasons why we can't do it. Help you along, sort of."

Frigate knew that Jack London had never taken any interest in flying. Yet a man who had lived so adventurously, who had always been pugnaciously courageous, and who was also very curious, should have been eager to go up in the newfangled machine.

Was it possible that he was afraid of the air?

It could be. Many a person who seemed to be afraid of nothing on earth was scared of leaving it. It was one of those quirks of human character, nothing to be ashamed of.

Nevertheless, Martin might be ashamed to show fear.

Frigate admitted to himself that he had some of that brand of shame. He had gotten rid of some, but there was too much residue left. He was not afraid to admit a fear if there was a rational reason to do so. To reveal fear if it had an irrational basis was still difficult for him.

Farrington's reaction did have some logic. It could be dangerous, perhaps even foolish, to go in a blimp in the unavoidably uncertain conditions.

Nur and Pogaas were called in to hear Frigate's new idea. Frigate proceeded to tell them what the perils might be.

"Nevertheless, considering the time saved, it's more efficient, more economical, to go in a blimp. Actually, considering the time a blimp would take as against the time a boat would take, you'll encounter many more dangers in a boat."

"Damn it, I'm not afraid of danger! You know better than that! It's just that . . ."

Martin's voice trailed off.

Tom smiled.

Farrington said, "What are you grinning about? You look like a skunk eating shit!"

Pogaas grinned also.

"There's no need to get all fired up about this just now," Tom said. "First we have to find out what the Big Cheese, Podebrad, will do for us. More than likely, he won't build us a gasbag. Why should he? But let's mosey on up to his house and see what he has to say about this."

Nur and Pogaas had more pressing business, so the captain, first mate, and deckhand walked toward a large limestone building pointed out to them by a passerby.

"You aren't serious about stealing one of the steamboats?" Frigate said.

"That depends," Tom said.

"Nur will never go along with that," Frigate said. "Nor some of the others, either."

"Then we might do without them," Tom said.

They halted at Podebrad's house, which stood on top of a hill, its peaked roof of bamboo almost touching the lower branches of a tall pine tree. The guards passed them on into a reception room. A secretary listened to them, then disappeared for a minute. Returning, he told them that Podebrad would see them just after lunch two days from now.

They decided to go fishing the rest of the day. Rider and Farrington caught a few striped "bass," but they spent most of their time planning how to capture a steamboat.

Ladislas Podebrad was red headed and of medium height, very broad and muscular, bull necked, thin lipped, massively chinned. Though he had formidable features and an icy demeanor, he permitted the meeting to last longer than the three had expected. It even went well, though not entirely as hoped for.

"Why are you in such a hurry to get to the North Pole? I have heard of this tower that is supposed to be in the middle of a sea behind impassable mountains. I do not know that I believe the story. But it seems possible. Perhaps, even probable.

"This world may have been fashioned originally by God. But it is evident that human beings, or something similar, have remade the surface of this planet. It is also evident to me, a scientist, that our resurrection is caused by physical means, by science, not by a supernatural agency.

"Why, I do not know. But the Church of the Second Chance has an explanation that sounds somewhat logical. Though they lack much data and even more certainty.

"In fact, the Church seems to me to know more than anyone else about this business, if I may put it that way."

He drummed long, slim fingers on the table as they all fell silent. Frigate, watching them, thought how ill matched they were to his husky physique and broad, thick hands.

Podebrad rose and walked to a cabinet, opened it, and withdrew an object.

He held in his fingers a spiral bone taken from a hornfish.

"You all know what this is. The Chancers wear it as a symbol of their faith, though I wish they had more knowledge to back their faith. But if they had more knowledge, they wouldn't need faith, would they? In this respect they're like all other religions, Terrestrial or Riverworld.

"However, we do know that there is an afterlife.

"Or perhaps I should say, there *was* an afterlife. Now that people no longer are resurrected after death, we don't know what to expect. Even the Church has no answer to the question of why translation has suddenly ceased. It speculates that, perhaps, people have been given enough time to save themselves, and there is no longer a reason to continue the resurrections.

"Either you are saved by now or you are not.

"I really don't know what the truth is.

"Gentlemen, I was an atheist on Earth, a member of the Czechoslovakian Communist Party. But here I met a man who convinced me that religion has nothing to do with rationality. At least, its foundation, the basis for its existence, does not.

"After the act of faith comes, of course, the rationalization for the faith, its pseudological justification. However, neither Jesus nor Marx, Buddha nor Mohammed, Hindu nor Confucian, Taoist nor Jew were right about the afterworld. They were even more mistaken about this world than the one we were born in."

He walked to the desk, sat down behind it, and placed the spiral bone on it.

"*Sinjoroj,* I was going to announce today my conversion to the Church of the Second Chance. And also announce my resignation as head of the state of Nova Bohemujo. Several days afterward, I would embark up The River to journey to Virolando, which, I am assured, does indeed exist. And there I would ask the leader and the founder of the Church, La Viro, some questions. If he answered them satisfactorily, or even if he admitted that he did not know all the answers, I would place myself under his jurisdiction. Go where he said, do what he said.

"But if my information is correct, and I have no reason to believe my informants are liars, Virolando is millions of kilometers away. It would take me half an Earthly lifetime to get there.

"Now, you suddenly come to me with a proposal. One that I am astounded I did not think of myself. Perhaps because I was really more interested in the voyage than in its end.

"Voyages are always more rewarding in self-discovery than in anything else, are they not? Perhaps that is why the obvious escaped me.

"Yes, gentlemen, I can build a blimp for you.

"There is only one stipulation. You must take me with you."

54

AFTER A LONG SILENCE, FARRINGTON SAID, "I DON'T SEE HOW WE could say no, *Sinjoro* Podebrad. I think I speak for all of us."

Frigate and Rider nodded.

"You really got us by the short hairs. Not that I have anything against your coming along with us. In fact, I am delighted. Only . . . well, what if we can't find any experienced blimp men? We'd be crazy to go up there if we don't know how to handle the machine or what we might run into."

"Of course. But it will take a very long time to build the airship. Unless we can find some engineers who know how to design such a ship, or at least can calculate the specifications, we will have to do it from scratch.

"Meanwhile, we can look for a pilot. Though they're very rare, somewhere along The River, within two thousand kilometers either way, there must be the man we're looking for.

"Or perhaps I might say, there could be one. Actually, the odds are high against finding one."

"I was a balloonist," Frigate said. "And I read a great deal about lighter-than-air craft. I was up in a blimp for two short flights. That doesn't near make me an expert, of course."

"Perhaps we'll have to train ourselves, *Sinjoro* Frigate. In which case, any knowledge will be of help."

"Of course, that was a long time ago. I've forgotten a lot."

"You don't exactly inspire confidence, Pete," the Frisco Kid said fiercely.

"Confidence comes with experience," Podebrad said. "Now, gentlemen, I will start at once. I'll delay my announcement of my conversion until after the airship is ready to leave. No member of the Church, no one preaching total passive resistance, can be head of this state."

Frigate wondered how deep the man's conversion was. It seemed to him that anybody who really believed in the tenets of the Church would say so at once. No matter what the consequences would be.

"As soon as our conference is over, I'll get the facilities for making hydrogen underway. I think the best method, considering the minerals available, will be by the reaction of dilute sulfuric acid and zinc. Our sulfuric acid industry has been operating for some time. We were fortunate in finding both platinum and vanadium, though not in large quantities.

"I do wish we could make aluminum, but . . ."

"The Schütte-Lanz airships were made of wood," Frigate said. "A blimp wouldn't need much wood, anyway."

Farrington said, "Wood! You want me to go up in a wooden dirigible?"

"The only wood would be in the keel and the car," Frigate said. "The envelope could be made from the intestinal lining of the dragonfish."

"Which requires much fishing," Podebrad said. He stood up.

"I have much work to get done today. But I'll see you gentlemen tomorrow during lunch. We can discuss this in detail then. Meanwhile, good day."

Farrington, looking grave, spoke to Rider as they left the building.

"If you ask me, this is crazy!"

"It sounds great to me," Tom said. "To tell the truth, I'm getting pretty tired of sailing."

"Yeah, but we could get killed while we're bumbling around trying to learn how to fly that damned thing!

"And what if we find it won't work then? We'll have lost a lot of time!"

Frigate said, "That doesn't sound like the man who ferried people through the White Horse rapids in Alaska, time and again, just to pick up a few bucks. Or the man who pirated oysters . . ."

He turned pale. Rider and Farrington had stopped, and their faces were hard.

Farrington said slowly, "I've told a lot of stories about the Yukon, but I never said anything about the White Horse rapids. Not to you anyway. Have you been eavesdropping?"

Frigate drew a deep breath, and said, "Hell, I don't have to eavesdrop! I recognized you two the first time I saw you!"

Suddenly, Rider was behind him and Farrington had put his hand on the hilt of his flint knife.

Rider spoke in a low monotone. "Okay, whoever you are, just march on ahead of me. Right into the ship. And don't try anything funny."

"*I'm* not going incognito!" Frigate said. "You are!"

"Just do as I say."

Frigate shrugged, and he tried to grin. "It's evident you two are doing a lot more than just concealing your true identities. All right. I'll go. But you wouldn't kill me, would you?"

"That depends," Rider said.

They walked down the hill and across the plain. At the dock the only crew member present was Nur, who was talking to a woman. Rider said, "Not a word, Pete. And smile."

Frigate, looking straight at the little Moor, grimaced. He hoped that Nur would detect that something was wrong—he was so sensitive to expressions—but Nur only waved at them. When they were in the captain's cabin, Frisco shut the door and made Frigate sit on the edge of the bunk.

Frigate said, "I've been with you twenty-six years. Twenty-six! And I've never told anybody what your real names were."

Farrington sat down in the chair at his desk. Toying with his knife, he said, "That seems against human nature. How could you keep your mouth shut that long? And why?"

"Especially why?" Rider said. He stood near the door, a horn-fish stiletto in his hand.

"It was evident that you didn't want it known, for one thing. So, being your friend, I didn't say anything. Though I will admit I wondered why you were so secretive."

Farrington looked at Rider. "What do you think, Tom?"

Rider shrugged, and said, "We made a mistake. We should have just laughed it off. Admitted who we are and made up some tall tale to account for it."

Farrington put the knife down and lit a cigarette.

"Yeah. That's hindsight. What'll we do now?"

Rider said, "After all this mysterious folderol, Pete must know we got something to hide."

"He already said that."

Rider sheathed the stiletto and lit a cigarette. Frigate wondered if he should make a break for it now. His chances for success were small. Though both men were smaller, they were very strong and quick. Besides, trying to escape would make him look guilty.

Guilty of what?

Tom said, "That's better. Forget about getting away. Relax."

"With you two thinking of murder?"

Rider laughed and said, "After all these years you ought to know we can't kill in cold blood. Even a stranger, and we're sort of fond of you, Pete."

"Well, if I were what you think I am, whatever that is, what would you do?"

"Work up a passion so I wouldn't have to kill you in cold blood, I reckon."

"Why?"

"If you aren't really Peter Frigate, then you know."

"Who in hell else could I be?"

There was a long silence. Finally, Farrington ground out his cigarette in an ashtray clamped to the desk.

"The thing is, Tom," he said, "he has been with us longer than any of our wives. If he was one of Them, why would he stay around so long? Especially since he claims he recognized us the day he met us.

"We would have been scooped up that night, if he's one of Them."

"Maybe," Tom said. "We don't know more than one-quarter of what's going on. One-eightieth, maybe. And what we do know may be a lie. Maybe we've been played for suckers."

"Them? Scooped up?" Frigate said.

Martin Farrington looked at Tom, and he said, "What'll we do now? There isn't any way of identifying Them. We're fools, Tom. We should've just told him a big lie. Now we got to go all the way."

"If he's one of Them, then he already knows," Rider said. "So we wouldn't be telling him much he doesn't know. Except about the Ethical. And if he is an agent, then he wouldn't have been put on our trail unless They suspected we'd been contacted by Him."

"Yeah, we jumped the gun. And there isn't any gun in the first place. You know, if Pete's an agent, why would he have suggested the blimp? Would an agent want us to get to the tower?"

"That's right. Unless . . ."

"Don't keep me hanging."

"Unless there's something haywire, and he's as much in the dark now as we are."

"What do you mean?"

"Listen, Tom, lately I've been doing a lot of thinking when I should've been sleeping or screwing. I've been thinking that there's something mysterious going on. I don't mean what the Ethical told us. I mean this business of there suddenly being no more resurrections.

"Has it ever occurred to you that maybe stopping them wasn't the original plan—whatever that is?"

"You mean, somebody threw a monkey wrench in the machinery? And that blew the fuse and left everybody in the dark?"

"Yes. And the agents don't know what's going on any more than me and you."

"Which could mean that Pete here is an agent. He's just trying to get home."

"You mean he might've found us but couldn't do anything about it? So he went along for the ride? And he proposed this blimp idea because it'd help him, not us, get there faster?"

"Something like that."

"So that puts us back where we were. Pete could be one of Them."

"If he is, it's like I said. We won't be telling him anything he don't know."

"Yeah, but he could tell us plenty. Plenty!"

"You going to beat it out of him? What if he really is Frigate?"

"I wouldn't, anyway. Not unless I knew the stakes were really high. Oh, hell, not even then."

"We could just sail on and leave him behind," Farrington said.

Tom smiled crookedly and said, "Yeah? You'd like that, wouldn't you? You wouldn't have to trust your quivering flesh and beating heart to a skyboat."

"You're getting awful close to making me mad, Tom."

"Okay. I won't ever say another word about that subject. Besides, I know you ain't got a cowardly bone in your body.

"So, what'll we do? Remember, if we did sail on, by the time we got to the North Pole—if we ever did—Pete here would have the whole thing solved."

"Oh, hell," Farrington said. "How could he be one of Them? They're superior to human beings, right? And Pete sure isn't no superman. No offense, Pete."

Tom glanced narrow-eyed at Frigate.

"He could be pretending to be only human. But I don't think anybody could put up a front like that for twenty-six years."

"Let's tell him then. What do we have to lose? Besides, I'm tired of keeping a secret for twenty-nine years."

"You always did talk too much."

"Look who's talking, Old Chief Run-off-at-the-mouth himself."

Farrington lit another cigarette. Rider followed his example, then said, "You want to light up too, Pete?"

"You're trying to kill me with smoke," Frigate said. He drew a cigar out of his over-the-shoulderbag.

"I think I need a drink, too."

"We all do. Tom, you do the honors. Then we'll tell all. God, what a relief!"

55

" 'TWAS A DARK AND STORMY NIGHT," TOM SAID. HE SMILED TO acknowledge that he knew he was deliberately imitating the classical opening line of ghost stories.

"Jack and I . . ."

"Keep it Martin, Tom. Remember? Even when in private."

"Sure, but you were Jack then. Anyway, I knew the Kid here, but we weren't good friends yet. Our huts were close together, both of us were sailors on a patrol sloop in the navy of a local warlord.

"One night, when I was off duty, sleeping in my hut, I suddenly woke up. It wasn't the thunder and lightning that woke me up, either. It was a tap on my shoulder.

"At first, I thought it was Howardine, my woman. You remember her, Kid?"

"She was a beauty," Martin said to Frigate. "A red-headed Scotchwoman."

Frigate stirred, and he said, "I'm anxious to get to the heart of the matter."

"Okay, no frills then. It wasn't her, because she was sound asleep. Then a flash of lightning showed me a dark figure squatting by me. I started to rear up, my hand going under my pillow for my tomahawk. But I couldn't move.

"I guess I was drugged or under a spell of some kind. I thought, *Oh, oh! This guy has got it in for me, and he's paralyzed me somehow and now yours truly is going to get it.*

"Of course, I'd wake up some place else, but I didn't feel like leaving.

"Then a couple of flashes showed the outline of the guy in detail. I was startled. Not scared, you realize, just startled. His body was covered in a big black cloak. And the head! There wasn't any. I mean, it was covered by a big globe, like a fishbowl. It was all black so I couldn't see his face. But somehow he could see me.

"If I couldn't move, I could talk. I said, 'Who are you? What do you want?' I spoke loud enough to wake Howardine up, but she didn't stir during the whole parley. I figure she had been drugged, too, but worse than me.

"The stranger spoke in a deep voice, answering me in English.

" 'I don't have much time, so I won't go into much detail. My name doesn't matter. In any event, I couldn't tell you because they might find you and unreel your memory.'

"I wondered what that meant, unreeling my memory. The whole business was beginning to look bizarre. I knew I wasn't dreaming. I wished I was.

" 'If they should, they'll know everything that is said and done here,' the hombre said. 'It's like taking a movie of your mind. They can clip out what they don't want you to remember, and you won't. But if they should do that, I'll talk to you again.'

" 'Who's they?' I said.

" 'The people who restructured this planet and who resurrected you,' he said. 'Now, listen, and don't talk until I'm finished.'

"You know me, Kid. I don't take crap off nobody. But this guy spoke as if the whole world was a ranch he owned and I was just one of the hands. Anyway, what could I do?

" 'They,' he said, 'live in the tower set in the middle of the north polar sea. You may have heard rumors about this. Some men actually did get through the mountains that surround the sea.'

"Right there I would have asked him if he was the one who left that long rope so they could get up the cliff and bored that tunnel for them. But I didn't know about that story then.

"He continued, 'But they did not get into the tower. One of their party, however, died when he fell off a mountain into the sea. He was allowed to be translated back into the Valley.' "

Tom paused. "He must have had some way of knowing this.

"The stranger continued, 'But the others were not. They . . . never mind.'

"So," Tom said, grinning. "he did not know everything about the Egyptians. What he didn't know was that one of them escaped. Or, if he did, he wasn't telling me, for some reason. I don't think, however, he found out about it. Otherwise, he'd have never let him get away. Still . . . maybe he did.

"Anyway, the stranger said, 'The swiftness of verbal communication in the Valley is amazing. I believe you call it the grapevine. The man who fell off the mountain told his story after he was translated, and it has spread throughout the Valley. You may speak. Have you heard the story?'

" 'Not until now,' I said.

" 'Well, you will doubtless hear it in the future. You'll be going up-River and will surely encounter it in one distorted form or another. Its essence is true.

" 'Doubtless, you have wondered why you were raised from the dead and placed here?'

"I nodded, and he said, 'My people, the Ethicals, have done this purely as a scientific experiment. They have put all of you here, mixed the races and nations from different times, solely to study your reactions. To record them and to classify them.

"'Then!'—and here his voice rose to a pitch of great indignation—'after they have subjected you to this experiment, after they have filled you with hope for an eternal life, they will close the project! You will die, forever! There will be no more resurrections for you! You will go down into dust, be dust forever!'

"'That seems almighty cruel,' I said, forgetting he'd not given me permission to speak.

"'It is inhumanly cruel,' he said. 'They have the power to give you life everlasting! At least, it would last as long as your sun lasted. Longer even, since you could always be transported to another planet with a living sun.

"'But no! They won't do that! They say that you do not deserve immortality!'

"'That's downright unethical,' I said. 'In which case, how come they call themselves the Ethicals?'

"That seemed to stop him for a moment. Then he said, 'Because they think it would be unethical to permit such a miserable, undeserving species to live forever.'

"'They sure don't have a good opinion of us,' I said.

"'I don't either,'' the stranger said. 'But good or bad opinions of humanity, based on *en masse* consideration, have nothing to do with the ethical aspects.'

"'How can you love someone you despise?' I said.

"'It isn't easy,' he said. 'But nothing truly ethical is easy to do. However, this is wasting my time.'

"A bluish light glowed, and by its light I could see that he had taken his right hand out from under his cloak. Around its wrist was a device larger than a man's pocket watch, and it was emitting the bluish light. I couldn't see what was on its face, but it was also talking, softly, like a radio turned way down.

"I couldn't hear the words, but it all sounded to me like some foreign language I never heard before. And the blue light showed me the globe, which was black and looked glassy. His hand was a big one, broad, but with long, slim fingers.

"'My time is up,' he said, and he put his hand under the cloak, and the hut was dark again, except for a lightning bolt now and then.

"'I can't tell you now why I chose you,' he said, 'except to say that your aura shows you're a likely candidate for the job.'

"*What's an aura?* I thought. I knew what it meant according to the dictionary, but I had the feeling he meant something else. *And what job?* I thought.

"Suddenly, as if he'd been reading my thought, his hand came out from under the cloak again. The bluish light was bright, very bright, so bright I could hardly see him. But I could see both his hands now, and they lifted the globe off. I though I'd be able to see at least the outlines of his head, maybe something of his features if I squinted hard enough. But all I could see was the big globe above his head. Not the glass globe, because he held that to one side. The thing above his head was whirling, shot with many colors, and was so bright I could see only that. It put out feelers from time to time, feelers that shot out and then shrank back into the whirling thing.

"I don't mind admitting that I was scared then. Well, not really so much scared as awed. It was like seeing an angel face to face, and there's no shame in being afraid of an angel."

"Lucifer was an angel," Frigate said.

"Yeah, I know. I've read the Bible. Shakespeare, too. Maybe I didn't get through grammar school, but I'm self-educated."

"I wasn't intimating that you were ignorant," Frigate said.

Martin snorted, and he said, "You two don't really believe in angels, do you?"

"Not me," Tom said, "But he sure *seemed* like one. Anyway, I don't think that aura is ordinarily visible. I think he showed me it by means of that thing he wore on his wrist. It suddenly disappeared, and the bluish glow died immediately. Too soon for me to see his face. Another lightning flash silhouetted him then, and I saw he'd put the glass globe back over his head.

"Now I knew what he meant by an aura. I figured from what he said that I had one, too. And it was invisible."

"Next you'll be claiming to be an angel," Martin said.

" 'You can, you must, be of help to me,' the stranger said. 'I want you to start up-River, toward the tower. But first, you must tell this Jack London what has happened here tonight. And you must convince him that you are telling the truth. And get him to accompany you.

" 'But under no circumstances are you to tell anyone else that I have talked to you. No one. We Ethicals are few and seldom venture from the tower. But my enemies have agents among you. Not many, compared to you. But they are disguised as resurrectees, and they will be looking for me.

" 'Some day, they may even suspect that I have recruited help from you Riverdwellers. So they will be trying to find you. If they do, they will take you to the tower, unroll your memories, read them, and excise the parts relevant to me. And return you to the Valley.

" 'London has a tiger-aura, too. So you must convince him to go with you. Tell him that I will see both of you again, and then he will believe. And you two will learn more of what this is all about.'

"He rose, and he said, 'Until then.'

"I watched him as another flash of lightning outlined his dark figure, the cloak, and the globe. I was wondering if I was crazy. I tried to get up but couldn't. After about half an hour, the paralysis wore off, and I went outside. The storm was over then, the clouds were starting to break up. But I couldn't see any sign of him.''

Martin took up the story. Tom had come to him the next evening and made him promise to keep silent about what he was going to tell him. Martin did not know whether or not to believe him. What convinced him that he was not lying was that there was no reason for Tom to make up such a fantastic tale.

The incident *had* happened, but was it a hoax by some unknown party?

Tom thought about that and then wondered if perhaps London himself was the stranger, playing a joke on him. They soon realized that neither they nor anybody else they knew could have had the glass globe or the instrument he'd used. And how could anybody fake that blazing aura?

The Frisco Kid was getting itchy, anyway. He liked the idea of building a sailboat and going on. Whatever the story was, true or not, it gave him an incentive, a meaning to life. Tom felt the same way. The Tower became for them a sort of Holy Grail.

''I felt kind of lousy leaving Howardine without a word. The Kid wasn't getting along too well with his woman, a tall plain jane with a chip on her shoulder—I don't know what he ever saw in her—so he had no regrets about leaving.

''We scooted on up-River for a couple of hundred stones, and then we started to build our schooner. Nur came along and helped us build it. He's the only original member of the crew still with us.''

Tom, holding his finger to his lips, walked softly to the door. His ear against it, he listened for a moment. Then he yanked it open.

The little Moor, Nur el-Musafir, was standing by the door.

56

NUR DID NOT SEEM STARTLED OR AFRAID. HE SAID, IN ENGLISH, "May I come in?"

"Damn right you will!" Tom roared. He did not offer to drag him in, however. Something about the dark little man promised dire results if he were attacked.

Nur entered. Farrington, glowering, was on his feet.

"You were eavesdropping?"

"Obviously."

"Why?" Tom said.

"Because, when you three went to the ship, I could tell from your expressions that something was wrong. Peter was in danger."

"Thanks, Nur," Frigate said.

Tom Rider closed the door. Martin said, "I need another drink."

Nur sat down upon the top of a cabinet. Martin downed two shots of whiskey. Tom said, "You heard everything?"

Nur nodded.

Martin shouted, "We might as well stand on a deck with a megaphone and tell the whole world!"

Tom said, "For Chrissakes! Now we got another problem on our hands!"

"There's no more need to kill me than there was to kill Peter," Nur said. He removed a cigar from his shoulderbag and lit it.

"I overheard your women saying they'd be coming back soon. We don't have much time."

"He's a cool one, ain't he?" Tom said to Martin.

"Like an experienced agent."

Nur laughed, and he said, "No. More like one who's been *chosen* by an *Ethical!*"

Nur said, "You may well stare. But you should have wondered a long time ago why I joined you from the beginning and have stuck with you through such a wearying journey."

Martin and Tom both opened their mouths.

Nur said, "Yes, I know what you're thinking. If I were an agent, I'd pretend to be one of the Ethicals' recruits. Believe me, I am not an agent."

"How do we know you're not? Can you prove it?"

"How do I know you two aren't agents? Can you prove it?"

The captain and the first mate were flabbergasted.

Frigate said, "When did the mysterious stranger talk to you? And why didn't he tell Tom that you were in on this?"

Nur shrugged thin shoulders.

"He appeared shortly after his visit to Tom. I don't know exactly when. As for the second question, I don't know the answer.

"I do suspect that the Ethical may not be telling the truth. He may be lying in that he is telling us only a part of the real situation. Why, I don't know. But I am intrigued."

Martin said, "Maybe we should just leave these two behind."

"If you do," Nur said, "Peter and I will take the high road, and we'll be at the tower afore ye."

"He's paraphrasing Bobby Burns's song, the one you sing so often," Tom said to Martin.

Martin grunted, and he said, "They wouldn't be agents of the enemies of your visitor, Tom. Otherwise, we'd have been turned in long ago. So, we have to believe them. I still don't understand why the Ethical didn't tell us about Nur."

Tom proposed a toast to their newfound band, and they drank. By then, they heard the women on deck. The men were laughing at one of Martin's jokes when the women came into the cabin, but they had had time to arrange a meeting later in the hills.

The next day they met with Podebrad, who introduced them to his engineering staff. They launched at once into the specifications of the blimp.

Frigate pointed out that what they would build depended on their goal. If they just wished to get near the headwaters, they would need an airship large enough to carry enough fuel to take them there. It wouldn't have to have a ceiling of more than 4572 meters or 15,000 feet. If they wished to get over the mountains that ringed the polar sea, they'd have to build one which could rise 9144 meters.

That is, if the stories of their height were true. No one really knew.

It would take much longer to design and build a rigid dirigible for the longer, higher flight. It would require a much larger crew and, hence, more training. At higher altitudes, the engines would need supercharging. Besides, the winds there would probably be stronger than the lower winds. Too strong. The zeppelin would have to carry oxygen supplies for personnel and engines. That made the load heavier. And there was the problem of the engine freezing.

It would be nice if they could use jet engines. These, however, were inefficient at low altitudes and speeds. Airships couldn't use them unless they went to higher altitudes. Unfortunately, the metals needed for jet engines were lacking.

Podebrad coldly replied that a big rigid dirigible was out. He was interested only in the smaller nonrigid type. This would go over the mountains, keeping at a height of +3962.4 meters or 13,000 feet. He understood that the mountains sometimes rose to 6096 meters. The ship would just go along them until it came to those of lesser height.

"That would require more fuel, because it would make the trip longer," Frigate said.

"Obviously," Podebrad said. "The ship will have to be big enough to be prepared for that."

It was clear that *Sinjoro* Podebrad was the boss.

The next day Project Airship was started. It was completed in eight months, four less than estimated. Podebrad was a hard driver.

Nur asked Podebrad how he would find Virolando without charts.

The Czech replied that he'd talked to several missionaries who'd originated there. According to their accounts, Virolando was near the arctic region in which The River flowed downstream. It was an estimated 50,000 kilometers from the headwaters and shouldn't be too difficult to identify from the air. Since it was on the shores of a very large lake with a rough hourglass shape, and it contained exactly one hundred tall rock spires, it would be impossible to mistake it for another lake.

That is, it would be unless it had a duplicate somewhere else.

Afterward, Frigate said, "I got my doubts about his being a Chancer. Those I've met have been very warm, very compassionate. This guy could give a refrigerator lessons in freezing."

"Perhaps he is an agent," Nur said.

The others went numb at the thought.

"If he were, however," Nur said, "wouldn't he want to build a high-altitude zeppelin to get over the polar mountains?"

"I don't think an airship could get that high," Frigate said.

Whatever he was, Podebrad was efficient. Though he failed to find any airship pilots, he did have enough engineers to man a dozen vessels. And he decided that the pilots would train themselves.

Three crews were picked so that if any person dropped out for any reason, there would be enough replacements. It was during the ground training that Frigate, Nur, Farrington, Rider, and Pogaas began to have their doubts. None of them knew much about engines, which meant they'd have to be trained. Why should Podebrad use them when he had experienced engineers and mechanics?

He planned on a crew of only eight. But, true to his promise, the five from the *Razzle Dazzle* were assigned to the first crew. Podebrad went along on every trip, though ostensibly only as an observer.

Frigate was nervous when he took his first flight, but his experience as a balloonist helped him overcome his stage fright.

One after the other, the crews trained. Then the big, semirigid blimp took several shakedown flights of 600 kilometers roundtrip. It went over the four ranges of mountains, enabling them to see valleys they had never seen before though they were practically next door.

The night before the flight, the crews attended a big party given in their honor. The crew of the *Razzle Dazzle*, minus the women of the captain, first mate, and Frigate, were there. The women had gotten angry, understandably so, because they were being forsaken. Though they had already taken other lovers, they hadn't forgiven their former cabinmates.

Nur had arrived at New Bohemia without a woman, so he had nothing to feel bad about.

Shortly before midnight, Podebrad sent everybody home. The ascent was to be made just before dawn, and the crew had to be up even earlier. Farrington's party bedded down in a hut near the huge bamboo hangar, and, after some chatter, went to sleep. They had expected Podebrad to announce his resignation and departure at the party. But it was obvious now that he intended to wait until he was in the ship.

"Maybe he thought he'd be lynched," Martin said.

Frigate was the last to fall asleep, or, at least, he supposed he was. Martin might be faking slumber. Though he had not shown any fear, he still did not like being aloft.

Frigate tossed and turned, too high strung to relax. Sleep always came hard before important events, just as it had the nights before he played football or ran in a track meet. Too often, the insomnia had resulted in fatigue the next day, and so he had not been up to his full potential. The very worry about not being good enough had ensured that he would not be.

Besides, having flown airplanes in the U.S. Army Air Corps when young and balloons in his middle age, he knew the dangers they could encounter.

He awoke from a light sleep to hear motors roaring, propellers spinning.

He rolled out of bed and opened the door and looked out. Though he could see only fog, he knew that there could be only one source of the noise.

It took a minute to rouse the others. Clad only in kilts and wearing long, thick towels over their backs, they dashed toward the hangar. Several times, they ran headlong into huts, and many times stumbled. Finally, as they came up the slope of the plains, their heads were above the fog.

In the bright starlight, they saw what they had feared.

Men and women stood around on the ground, sleepily cheering. These had hauled out the big blimp on ropes. Now, their work done, they were watching the ship rise slowly. Suddenly, water ballast was discharged, drenching many of them. More swiftly now, the cigar shape rose, its nose turned up-River. Lights in the cabin, set below the long, triangular keel that ran beneath the vessel, blazed. They could see Podebrad's profile through a port.

Howling, cursing, they ran toward the dirigible. But they knew they could do nothing to prevent its departure.

Farrington grabbed a spear leaning against the side of the hangar and threw it. It fell far short and almost hit a woman. He threw himself on the ground and beat the grass with his fists.

Mix jumped and yelled and shook his fists.

Nur shook his head.

Pogaas howled curses in his native language.

Frigate wept. Because of him, the others had wasted nine months. If only he had not thought of the blimp, they would be 50,000 kilometers or so farther along on their voyage.

The worst of it was that the *Razzle Dazzle* had been sold. Not for a song. For five hundred cigarettes and much booze and some personal favors.

Later, they sat gloomily around near a grailstone, waiting for it to erupt and fill their grails. The New Bohemians around them were a noisy crowd, discussing and cursing their late chief. The ex-crew of the *Razzle Dazzle* and the airship were silent. Finally, Martin Farrington said, "Well, we can always steal my ship back."

"That wouldn't be honest," Nur said.

"What do you mean, not honest? I wasn't thinking of just taking it without paying for it. We'd leave them just what they paid for it."

"They'd never agree to the deal," Tom said.

"What could they do about it?"

There was a flurry of activity, silencing them for a moment. A man had announced that the council had elected a new head of state. He was Podebrad's second-in-command, Karel Novak. There was some cheering, but most people felt too depressed to work up much emotion.

"Why do you suppose he shafted us?" Martin said. "We were as good blimp men as anybody else, and he promised us."

Frigate said, his voice near breaking, "The truth is, I wasn't as good a pilot as Hronov and Zeleny. Podebrad knew that if he rejected me, you'd all raise hell. So he just took off without us."

"The dirty sneak!" Tom said. "Naw. That isn't it. Besides, you're good enough."

"We'll never know," Martin said. "Say, do you think Podebrad could be an agent? And he somehow found out about us and so left us behind, our thumbs up our tocuses?"

"I doubt it," Nur said. "He *could* be one. Perhaps he originally intended to build a fast steamboat to get up The River. Then we came along and put a bee in his bonnet: the blimp. But we're the ones who got stung."

"If he was an agent, how'd he find out about us?"

Frigate raised his head. "That's it! Maybe one of the women we sloughed off overheard you two talking. You did get pretty loud when you were talking in your cabin sometimes. Maybe Eloise or Nadja heard you talking in your sleep. For revenge, they told Podebrad all, and he decided he didn't want us along."

"Neither one of them could keep their mouths shut about it," Tom said. "They'd have spilled the beans to us long ago."

"We'll never know," Martin said, shaking his head.

"Yeah?" Tom said. "Well, if I ever catch up with Podebrad, I'll break his neck."

Farrington said, "First, I'll break his legs."

"No, I want to build a six-story house," Frigate said. "With only one window in it, in the top story. Then we'll execute him by a method peculiarly Czech. Defenestration."

"What?" Tom said.

"Throw him out the window."

Nur said, "Fantasy revenge is a good method of relieving anger. It's better, however, not to feel the need for revenge. What we must do is to act, not blow off steam."

Frigate got swiftly to his feet. "I got an idea! Nur, will you take care of my grail for me? I'm going off to see Novak."

"You and your ideas!" Farrington shouted. "They've got us in enough trouble! Come back here!"

Frigate kept on walking.

57

SLOWLY, MAJESTICALLY, THE *Parseval* MOVED ABOVE THE CHASM. Its nose was up, and its propellers were angled upward. The wind that ripped out of the hole dipped down when it hit the edge of the canyon top, and the dirigible had to keep from being gripped by the downdraft. Cyrano had to calculate the force exactly, keeping the airship at the same altitude, aimed at the center of the arch-shaped hole. A slight error could result in the great craft's being dashed down against the edge of the canyon and broken in two.

Jill thought that, if she were the captain, she would not have risked this entrance. It would be better to circle the mountain, to search for another gateway. However, that meant using much more fuel. Battling such strong winds, the motors could burn up so much that there would not be enough left to return to Parolando. Perhaps the ship could not even get to the *Mark Twain*.

Cyrano was sweating, but his eyes were bright and his expression eager. If he were scared, he did not look so. She had to admit to herself that he was, after all, the best one in this situation. His reflexes were the swiftest, and he would not freeze with panic. To him, this must be much like a duel with swords. The wind thrust; he parried; the wind riposted; he counterriposted.

Now they were in the thick clouds raging from the hole.

Suddenly, they were through.

Though still blinded by fog, they could read the radar-scopes. Before them was a sea, 1 kilometer below. Around it circled the mountain. And ahead, in the center of the sea, 48.5 kilometers away, a little over 30 miles, was an object which reared high above the water, though still dwarfed by the mountain.

Cyrano, looking at the CRT on the panel, said, "Behold the tower!"

The radarman, seated before his equipment on the port side, confirmed the sighting.

Firebrass ordered that the ship be taken to 3050 meters altitude, somewhat over 10,000 feet. The propellers could not be swiveled horizontally to lift the ship faster because it had to fight the wind.

However, as they rose, they found that the wind lessened. By the time the ship had reached the desired altitude, it could proceed straight ahead. Now its estimated ground speed was 80.50 km/ph, over 50 mph. As it neared the tower, it picked up more velocity.

The sky was brighter than at dusk, lit by both the weak sun and the clustered stellar masses.

Now the radars could sweep the entire sea and touch the top of the most distant wall. The nearly circular body of water was 97 kilometers across or somewhat over 60 miles in diameter. The opposite wall was the same height as the nearer one.

"The tower!" Firebrass exploded. "It's 1.7 kilometers tall! And 16 kilometers wide!"

In old-style measurements, that would have been slightly over a mile high and almost 10 miles in diameter.

There was an interruption. The chief engineer, Hakkonen, reported that the hull was collecting ice. It was not, however, on the windscreens of the control room, since they were made of an ice-resistant plastic.

Firebrass said, "Take her down to 1530 meters, Cyrano. The air's warmer there."

The River, entering the sea, still carried much heat even after its passage through the arctic regions. In this deep, cold cup the waters surrendered warmth, so much that the temperature at 1524 meters or 5000 feet was 2 degrees above Centigrade. But higher up, the moisture-heavy air was an ice trap.

While the dirigible was lowered, the radar operator reported that the interior of the mountain was not as smooth as the exterior. There were innumerable holes and bulges, as if the makers of the mountain had not thought it necessary to finish off the inside.

The narrow ledge described by Joe Miller had been detected by the radar. It led from the top of the mountain to the bottom. There was another narrow ledge leading along the base of the sea, ending at a hole about 3 meters wide and 2 meters high.

No one commented on this. But Jill did wonder aloud why the big hole through which the dirigible had entered had been made.

"Maybe it's for their aerial craft, if they have any," Firebrass said. "It could be used to keep from having to fly over the mountain."

That seemed as good a reason as any.

Piscator said, "Perhaps. However, the flash of light that startled Joe Miller so much could not have come from the sun's rays going through the hole. In the first place, the hole is darkened by that cloud stream. In the second place, even if the sun's rays had flashed through, they would not have illuminated the top of the tower. Joe did say that the fog was momentarily blown aside. But even so, the rays would not have reached the top of the tower. And if they had, he would have had to be in a straight line with the rays and the tower.

"He couldn't have been since the ledge on which he stood doesn't exist far enough to put him in the line of sight."

"Maybe that flash of light actually came from the aircraft he saw a minute later," Firebrass said. "It was coming down and perhaps its engines had to release some energy, in some fashion, to check its rate of descent. Joe thought it was the sun's rays."

Cyrano said, "It's possible. Or perhaps the light was a signal from the tower. However, if the tower is big enough to be seen by Joe, and he must have been standing high on that ledge to see 48.5 kilometers away, how could he see a much smaller object, the aerial machine?"

"Maybe it wasn't so small," Firebrass said.

They were silent for a moment. Jill tried to estimate the size of an aircraft that could be seen at that distance. She did not know what it should be, but she thought that it must be at least a kilometer wide.

"I do not like to think of it," Cyrano said.

Firebrass ordered him to send the ship in a circle around the sea. The radar indicated that the sides of the circular tower were smooth and unbroken, except for openings about 243 meters or slightly less than 800 feet below the top.

There was a difference in the height of the exterior top of the tower and the interior. Inside walls 243 meters tall was the smooth surface of a landing field almost 16 kilometers across.

"Those openings at the bottom of the wall are slightly lower than the center," Firebrass said. "That must be so the moisture can drain out through the holes."

What interested them most, however, was the only protuberance on the "landing field." This was located at one end, south—all directions from the tower's center were south—and it was a hemisphere with a diameter of 16 meters and a height of 8 meters.

"If that isn't an entrance, I'll eat my loincloth," Firebrass said. He shook his head. "Sam's going to be disappointed when he hears about this. There is no way that anybody can get into this tower except by air."

"We're not in yet," Piscator murmured.

"Yeah? I know. But we're sure as hell going to try. Listen, everybody. Sam ordered that we should make only a scouting trip. I think that trying to get into that tower comes under the definition of scouting."

Firebrass was almost always ebullient, but now his whole body seemed to quiver and his face was lit up as if all his nerves had suddenly become light transmitters. Even his voice shook with excitement.

"There may be defensive weapons, manned or automatic, down there. The only way to find out is to probe. But I don't want to endanger the ship any more than we have to.

"Jill, I'm going down with a small party in a chopper. You'll be in charge, which means you'll be captain, even if only for a short time. Whatever else happens, you've achieved that ambition.

"You keep the ship at about a thousand meters above the tower's top and a thousand meters away from it. If anything should happen to us, you take the ship back to Sam. That's an order.

"If I see anything suspicious, I'll holler. You take off then and let me worry about getting back. Got that?"

Jill said, "Yes, sir."

"If that dome has an entrance, it may take an electronic or mechanical Open Sesame to get in. Maybe not. They wouldn't think there'd be any chance of us ever getting to it. I don't think there's anybody home. Maybe there is, and they're just waiting to see what we do before they take action. Let's hope not."

Cyrano said, "I'd like to go with you, my captain."

"You stay here. You're our best pilot. I'll take you, Anna, and Haldorsson, he can fly a chopper, too, Metzing, Arduino, Chong, and Singh. That is, if they'll volunteer."

Obrenova phoned the others at their posts and then reported that they were more than willing.

Firebrass informed the crew of the radar findings over the general address system. He also told them that a party would be landing shortly.

He had no sooner finished than he got a call from Thorn. Firebrass listened for a minute, then said, "No, Barry, I have enough volunteers."

Turning away from the phone, he said, "Thorn was very eager to be with me. He sounded unhappy when I turned him down. I didn't know he was so fired up about this."

Jill phoned the hangar section and told Szentes, its chief petty officer, to prepare the No. 1 helicopter for flight.

Firebrass shook hands with everyone in the control room except Jill. He gave her a long hug. She was not sure that she liked that. It seemed unofficerly, and it was also too much like a farewell embrace. Did he have some doubts about being able to return? Or was she just projecting her own anxiety upon him?

Whatever the truth, she was having conflicting emotions. She resented his treating her differently from the others, yet she felt warmed because he was especially fond of her. It was a wonder that she did not have ulcers, she suffered so much and so frequently from opposing feelings. But then she had never heard of anybody having ulcers on this world. Mental and nervous tensions seemed to manifest themselves in psychic forms. Her hallucinations, for instance.

A moment later, she was no longer the exception. Cyrano had asked Piscator to take his post for a minute. Then he had risen and warmly embraced the captain while tears ran down his cheeks.

"My dear friend, you must not look so sad! There may be danger there, but do not fear! I, Savinien de Cyrano de Bergerac, will be at your side!"

Firebrass released himself, patted the Frenchman on the shoulder, and laughed, "Hey, I didn't mean to make everybody think something will go wrong! I wasn't saying goodbye, just so long! What the hell! Can't I . . . ? Oh, well! No, Cyrano, you get back to your post."

He smiled, his teeth very white in his dark face, and he waved at them. "So long!"

Anna Obrenova, looking very pensive, followed him. Metzing, looking very grim and Teutonic, walked out behind her.

Jill immediately gave orders that the ship be taken to the position Firebrass had commanded. The *Parseval* began to circle downward. When it had plunged into the fog, its searchlights were turned on. Though powerful, these could penetrate only 150 meters or somewhat less than 500 feet. The dirigible took its position, hovering in one place, its nose pointed into the wind, its speed exactly matching the force of the wind. Four tunnels of light were carved into the fog, but these showed nothing but dark-grey clouds. The tower was ahead and below, invisible, yet seeming to radiate a massive ominousness, extending feelers that gripped the ship.

No one spoke. Cyrano lit up a cigar. Piscator stood behind the radar operator and watched the sweeps on the scopes. The radio operator was intent on his dials, running the set through the frequency spectrum. Jill wondered just what he hoped to pick up.

After what seemed an hour but was only fifteen minutes, Szentes called the captain *pro tempore*. The belly hatch was open, the chopper was warmed up, and take-off would be in one minute.

Szentes sounded strained.

"There's a little problem, Ms. Gulbirra, which is why I called you before take-off. Thorn appeared, and he tried to argue the captain into taking him along. The captain told him to get back to his post."

"Did he do that?"

"Yes, sir. The captain told me to call you to make sure. Mr. Thorn won't have had time to get to the tail section yet, though, sir."

"Very well, Szentes. I'll take care of it."

She switched off, and she swore softly. Here she was, commander for only fifteen minutes, and she was confronted with a disciplinary problem. What had gotten into Thorn?

There was only one thing to do. If she ignored Thorn's behavior, she would lose control of the ship, the respect of the crew.

She phoned the auxiliary control room in the lower tail structure. Salomo Coppename, a Surinamese, the aft second mate, answered.

"Arrest Mr. Thorn. Have him conducted to his cabin by a guard detail, and make sure a guard is posted outside his cabin."

Coppename must have wondered what was going on, but he did not question her.

"And call me as soon as he shows."

"Yes, sir."

A red light on the control panel ceased blinking. The belly hatch had just been closed. The radar had picked up the No. 1 helicopter, heading downward for the top of the tower.

A voice suddenly came over the radio.

"Firebrass here."

"We read you loud and clear," the radio operator said.

"Fine. You're coming in L and C, too. I'm going to land about a hundred meters from the dome. Our radar's working A-OK and so we shouldn't have any problems. I expect that the wall will block off most of the wind when we land.

"Jill? You there?"

"Here, Captain."

"What did you do about Thorn?"

Jill told him, and Firebrass said, "That's what I would've done. I'll ask him why he was so hot to go with us when I get back. If . . . if I don't get back, for any reason, you question him. But keep him under guard until this tower business is finished."

Jill ordered Aukuso to tie in the radio with the general address system. There was no reason that everybody should not listen in.

"I'm coming down now. The wind is weaker now. Jill, I . . ."

Cyrano said, "The belly hatch is opening!"

He pointed at a blinking red light on the panel.

"Mon Dieu!"

He pointed out through the windscreen.

That was not necessary. Everybody in the control room was looking at the fiery ball suddenly born in the dark greyness.

Jill moaned.

Aukuso said loudly, "Captain! Come in, Captain!"

There was no answer.

58

THE INTERCOM WAS RINGING.

Moving slowly, as if the air was cotton candy, Jill pushed the switch to ON.

Szentes said, "Sir, Thorn just stole the other chopper! But I think I got the son of a bitch! I emptied my pistol at him!"

Cyrano said, "He's on the scope!"

"Szentes, what happened?"

She fought to get out of the thick element in which she was drowning. She had to shed this numbness, to recover quickness of analysis and decision.

"Officer Thorn left the hangar bay as the captain ordered. But he came back as soon as the chopper left, and he had a pistol with him. He made us get into the supply compartment, and he shot off the intercom unit. Then he locked us in. He forgot that arms are stored there, too. Or maybe he thought he'd be gone before we could get out.

"Anyway, we shot off the lock, and we rushed out. By then he was in the chopper and lifting it off the landing platform. I shot at him just as the chopper was going down out of the bay. The others shot, too.

"Sir, what's going on?"

"I'll notify the crew just as soon as I know myself," Jill said.

"Sir?"

"Yes."

"It was a funny thing. Thorn was weeping all the time he forced us into the supply room, even when he said he'd shoot us if we tried to stop him."

"Out," Jill said, and switched the intercom off.

The infrared equipment operator said, "The fire's still burning, sir."

The radar operator, pale under his dark pigmentation, said, "That fire is the helicopter, sir. It's on the landing deck of the tower."

She looked into the fog. She could see nothing except the swirling clouds.

"I've got the other chopper," the radarman said. "It's headed down. Toward the base of the tower."

A moment later, he added, "The chopper is on the surface of the sea."

"Aukuso, call Thorn."

The gluey feeling was receding now. She still felt confused, but now she was becoming capable of finding some order in the chaos.

After a minute, Aukuso said, "He doesn't answer."

According to the radar, the amphibious helicopter was now floating on the sea 30 meters from the tower.

"Keep trying, Aukuso."

Firebrass was probably dead. She was the captain now, her ambition achieved.

"God! I didn't want it this way!"

Dully, she called Coppename and told him to come to the control room to take over the duties of the first mate. Alexandros would be the aft first officer.

"Cyrano, we'll have to take care of Thorn later. As of now, we have to find out what happened to Firebrass . . . and the others."

She paused, and said, "We have to land on top of the tower."

"Certainly, why not?" Cyrano said.

He was pale, and his jaw set. But he seemed in perfect control of himself.

The *Parseval* moved through the clouds, its radar probing ahead and below. There was a powerful updraft around the tower, but it lost its force as soon as the dirigible was over the top.

The belly searchlights lanced downward, sweeping over the dull grey metal of the vast surface. The people in the control room could see the flames, but they could not distinguish the helicopter itself.

Slowly, the airship slid past the fire. Now its propellers were swiveled horizontally to pull the colossus down.

As gently as possible, its pilot brought it down. Under ideal conditions, there would have been no wind at all. However, the thousands of drainage holes along the base of the wall permitted a breeze of 8 km/ph. This, on the Beaufort scale, was a light breeze. Wind felt on the face. Leaves, if present, rustling. An ordinary wind vane moved by the wind.

A layman would consider it negligible. But the great surface of the buoyant ship was easily pushed by this breeze if no propulsive force countered it. It would be taken up hard against a wall unless something were done to stop it.

Unfortunately, there was no mooring mast. Also, the vessel could not be brought into direct contact with the landing field. Unlike the *Graf Zeppelin* and *Hindenburg,* the *Parseval* had no underslung control gondola with a wheel on its bottom to keep the lower tail structure from rubbing against the ground when landing. Since the control room of the *Parseval* was in the nose, the ship could not land without damaging the tail fin.

However, there were ropes stored aboard. These had been taken along in case a landing had to be made on a plain alongside The River. They were to be thrown down to the people on the ground, and these, hopefully, would volunteer as a ground crew.

Jill gave a few orders. Cyrano turned the craft broadside to the wind. For several kilometers, he allowed the wind, which was decreasing, to push the ship toward the wall. By then it was obvious that the wind was blowing the other way now, its source the nearest apertures.

When radar indicated that the nose was a half-kilometer from the wall, he reversed the propellers at slow speed. The airship halted, and the belly hatch opened.

Ropes were lowered, and, by fours, fifty men climbed down them. As each group touched the ground, the ship lost its weight and became more buoyant. Reluctantly, Jill ordered that hydrogen be released from the cells. This was the only way to balance the lift, and she hated to expend the gas. Ballast could be released later to regain the buoyancy.

Other ropes were thrown down from the nose and the tail. The men on the ground seized these and hung on, bringing their weight to bear.

Cyrano now let the airship sail toward the wall, the propellers unmoving. Before the nose touched the wall, the propellers started up again, and the airship stopped.

Two men ran to the wall and tested the wind at the apertures. Via walkie-talkie, they verified that the wind coming in through these would be strong enough to keep the ship from swinging broadside into the wall.

Other men were let down on ropes, and more hydrogen was valved. These added their weight to the crew holding the aft ropes.

Others hastened to help the men at the nose. After towing the *Parseval* slowly until its nose almost touched the wall, they passed the ropes through the three holes, using extended hooks to catch the ropes outside and then draw them in. These were tied, and the tail was swung around until the dirigible was parallel to the wall. Then the tail ropes were tied down.

The vessel was now floating about 20 meters away from the wall.

Jill did not expect any change in the wind. If there was, it could be exceedingly damaging. One rub of the ship against the wall could strip off the transmission gears and the propellers on the port side.

A ladder was let down from the belly hatch. Jill and Piscator hastened from the control room, walked swiftly down the passageway, and then went down the ladder. Doctor Graves was waiting for them, his black bag in his hand.

The helicopter had crashed about 30 meters from the dome. With its flames a beacon, they pressed through the fog toward it. Jill's

heart beat hard as they neared the wreckage. It seemed impossible
that vigorous, flamboyant Firebrass could be dead.

He lay a few meters from the flaming mass where the impact had
thrown him. The others were still in the machine, the blackened
body of one sitting up in its seat.

Graves handed his lamp to Piscator and bent down over the
figure. Smoke mingled with the fog and brought the sickening
stench of burning gasoline and flesh to them. Jill felt as if she were
going to vomit.

"Hold the light steady!" Graves said sharply.

Jill did so, forcing herself to look at the corpse. His clothes had
been blown off him; his skin was seared from top to bottom. Despite
the burning, his features were still recognizable. He must not have
been in the flames long. Perhaps he had been ejected by the explosion before the machine crashed. The fall would account for the
removal of the top of his head.

Jill could not see why the doctor had to examine the body. She
was about to tell him so when he stood up. His hand, its palm open,
was held out to her.

"Look at this."

She brought the lamp close to his hand. The object in it was a
sphere the size of a matchhead.

"It was on his forebrain. I don't know what the hell it is."

After he had wiped it clean of blood, he said, "It's black."

He wrapped the little ball in a cloth and dropped it into his bag.

"What do you want to do with the bodies?"

Jill looked at the blazing mass of crumpled metal. "There's no
use wasting foam to put the fire out now," she said in a dull voice.
She looked at the men who had followed them. "Peterson, you get
the body back to the ship. Wrap it up first. The rest of you follow
me."

A few minutes later, they halted before the dome. Searchlights
from the dirigible were turned on it, making it look like a ghost of an
Eskimo igloo. Using her lamp, Jill saw that the dome was made of
the same grey metal as the tower. It seemed to be continuous with
the metal of the tower. At least, there was no sign of welding, no
seams. It was as if it were a bubble blown from the surface.

The others stood back from its arched entrance, waiting for her to
decide what to do. Their lights revealed an opening like a cavern.
About 10 meters beyond, the walls curved in, forming a corridor
about 3 meters wide and 2.5 meters high. The walls were of the
same grey substance. At its end, about 30 meters away, the hall
curved abruptly. If there was an entrance down into the tower itself,
it had to be just beyond the curve.

Just above the opening were two symbols, both in altorelief. The
top one was a semicircle, and it bore the seven primary colors.

Below it was a circle inside of which was a looped cross, the Egyptian *ankh*.

"A rainbow above the emblem of life and resurrection," Jill said.

Piscator said, "Pardon me. The cross within the circle is also the astrological-astronomical symbol for Earth. However, in that symbol, the cross is a simple one, not the looped cross."

"A symbol of hope, that rainbow. And, if you remember the Old Testament, it's God's sign of covenant with His people. It also evokes the pot of gold at the end of the rainbow, the Emerald City of Oz, and many other things."

Piscator looked curiously at her.

She was silent for a minute, overcome with awe and a fear that she hoped would not become overwhelming.

Then she said, "I'm going in. You wait here, Piscator. When I get to the end of the hall, I'll signal you to come on in, too. If there's no trouble, that is.

"If anything should happen to me, I don't know what, you and the men get to hell back to the ship. And take off. That's an order.

"You'll be the captain. Coppename's a good man, but he doesn't have your experience, and you're the steadiest man I know."

Piscator smiled. "Firebrass ordered you not to land if something happened to him. Yet you *did* land. Could I allow you to be in a dangerous situation and just leave you?"

"I don't want you to endanger the ship. Or the lives of almost a hundred men."

"We shall see. I'll act as I feel the situation demands. You wouldn't do otherwise. And then there is Thorn."

"One thing at a time," she said.

She turned and walked toward the entrance. As she neared it, she gasped.

A low light had filled the hall.

After hesitating several seconds, she continued. As she passed beneath the arch, she was suddenly in a bright light.

59

Jill stopped. Piscator said, "Where is the light coming from?"

Jill turned and said, "I don't know. There doesn't seem to be any source. Look. I don't have a shadow."

She turned back and started to walk slowly. And then she stopped again.

"What's the matter? You . . . ."

"I don't bloody know. I feel as if I'm in a thick jelly! I can't breathe, but I have to struggle to take another step!"

Leaning into the palpable, invisible barrier as if she were going against a strong wind, she managed to force herself three more steps. Then, panting, she stopped.

"It must be a field of some sort. There's nothing material here, but I feel like a fly caught in a spider's web!"

"Could it be that the field is affecting the magnetic tabs in your cloths?" he called.

"I don't think so. If that was it, the tabs would be pulling the cloths, and that's not it. I'll try it, though."

Feeling some shyness at stripping in front of fifty men, she pulled the tabs loose. The air temperature was just above freezing. Shivering, teeth chattering, she again tried to force her way into the thick element. She could not go a centimeter beyond the limit of her original advance.

She bent down to pick up her cloths, noting that she could do so easily. The force acted only in a horizontal direction. After backing away two steps, and feeling the force diminish, she put her cloths back on.

Outside the entrance again, she said, "You try it, Piscator.

"You think I could succeed where you can't? Well, it is worth experimenting."

Naked, he walked in. To her surprise, she saw that he was not affected by the field. Not, at least, until he had gotten several meters from the curve. Then he called back that he was encountering difficulty.

He moved ever more slowly, struggling, his panting so loud that she could hear it.

But he did get to the curve, and there he paused to regain his breath.

He said, "There's an open elevator at the end. It seems to be the only way to get down."

"Can you get to it?" she called.

"I'll try."

Moving like an actor in a slow-motion film, he plowed ahead. And he was gone around the bend.

A minute passed. Two. Jill went into the corridor as far as she could. "Piscator! Piscator!"

Her voice rang strangely, as if the corridor had peculiar acoustical properties.

There was no answer, though if he were just around the curve, he would be able to hear her.

She shouted again and again. Silence replied.

There was nothing she could do except to return to the entrance and let others try.

The men went in by twos to save time. Some progressed a little further than she; some, not as much. All shed their cloths, but this did not help them at all.

Jill used the walkie-talkie to order the men in the ship to make the attempt. If one out of fifty-two could do it, perhaps one of the forty-one in the ship might succeed.

First, though, everybody except herself had to return to the vessel. They trooped off, phantom figures in the dimly lit fog. She had never felt so lonely in all her life, and she had known many hours of the blackest isolation. The mists pressed wet hands against her face, which seemed to be congealing into a mask of ice. The funeral pyre of Obrenova, Metzing, and the others burned fiercely. And there was Piscator, somewhere around the corner. What situation was he in? Was he unable either to go ahead or to go back? Returning had not been difficult for her or the other men. Why should he not be able to retreat?

But then she did not know what other obstacles there were beyond that grim grey hall.

She muttered to herself Virgil's line, *"Facilis descensus Averni."* ("It is easy to go down into Hell.")

What was the rest of it? After so many years, she found it difficult to remember. If only this world had books, reference materials.

Now it came back.

It is easy to go down into Hell. Night and day, the gates of Death stand wide. But to climb back again, to retrace one's steps to the upper air. There's the rub, the task.

The only real trouble with that quotation was that it was not appropriate. It had been very hard to get to the gates, impossible for all but one. And climbing back—except for one—had been easy.

She switched on the walkie-talkie.

''Cyrano. The captain here.''

''Yes, what is it, my captain?''

''Are you *crying*?''

''Yes, but of course. Did I not love Firebrass dearly? I am not ashamed of my grief. I am not a cold Anglo-Saxon.''

''Never mind that. Get hold of yourself. We have work to do.''

Cyrano sniffled, then said, ''I know that. And I am willing and able. You will find me no less a man. What are your orders?''

''You know you're to be relieved by Nikitin. I want you to bring along twenty-five kilograms of plastic explosive.''

''Yes. I hear you. But do you intend to blow up the tower?''

''No, just the entranceway.''

A half-hour passed. The men in the ship had to come out and those out had to go in. This was a long process, since, for every man that left, one had to go in immediately. Taking turns this way slowed the business but was necessary. Forty-eight leaving all at once would make the ship too buoyant. It would rise, leaving the end of the ladder above the reach of those on the ground.

Finally, she saw their lights and heard their voices. She told them what had happened, though they already knew. Then she told them what they were to do, which they expected.

The result was that no one got anywhere as far as Piscator.

''Very well,'' Jill said.

The plastic explosive was applied against the exterior of the dome opposite a point halfway down the corridor. She would have liked to have set it at the juncture of the back of the dome and the tower wall. She was afraid that the explosive might blow a hole in the dome. If it did so, it might also kill Piscator.

They retreated to the dirigible and the explosives expert pressed a switch on a transmitter. The blast was deafening, though the plastic had been applied to the side of the dome away from them. They ran to it, then stopped, coughing from the fumes. After the air was cleared, Jill looked at the dome.

It was undamaged.

''I thought so,'' she said to herself.

She had called in to Piscator that he should not come out until after the explosion. There had been no answer. She had a hunch that he was not in the vicinity, but hunches were not certainties.

Jill went back into the dome as far as she could. There was no force against the long-handled hook she thrust ahead of her. And she could throw a cloth weighted with metal to the end of the corridor. So, the field was no barrier to inanimate objects.

If they had a periscope long enough to reach to the end of the corridor, they could see around it. However, a periscope was not part of the ship's supplies.

She was not defeated by this. There was a very small machinist's shop on the *Parseval*. A wheeled device which would go to the end of the corridor could be built. A camera could be attached to its end, and the camera could be activated by a radio transmitter.

The chief machinist's mate thought he could construct the "contraption" in an hour. She told him to do so, and then she ordered three men to stand guard in the dome.

"If Piscator shows, radio me."

Having returned to the ship, she phoned the machinist's shop. "Can you do your work while we're aloft? The air might be rough."

"No sweat, sir. Well, only a little, anyway."

The process of untying the ship and getting it into the air took fifteen minutes. Nikitin took the *Parseval* up above the tower and then sent her down toward its base. Radar indicated that the helicopter was now against the base of the tower. Though the sea was not violent, its waves were short and choppy, and it had probably smashed the machine against the tower. However, if they were lucky, the damage could be minimal.

Aukuso radioed Thorn again without success.

Because of the updraft by the tower, it was impossible to bring the dirigible close to the helicopter. Nikitin piloted it down close to the surface and held her against the wind. The belly hatch was opened, and three men in an inflatable boat with an outboard motor were lowered. It headed for the tower, guided by the radarman on the ship.

Boynton, the officer in charge, gave a running report.

"We're alongside the chopper now. It's bumping into the tower, but its pontoons have kept the vanes from being damaged. The pontoons don't seem damaged, either. We're having a hell of a time with this pitching sea. Report back in a minute."

Two minutes later, his voice came back on.

"Propp and I are in the chopper now. Thorn's here! He's pretty bloody, looks as if he got a bullet in the left chest and some richocheting fragments got him in the face, too. He's alive, though."

"Is there an opening or entrance of any sort in the tower?"

"Just a minute. Have to light a flare. These lamps aren't strong enough . . . no, there's nothing there but smooth metal."

"I wonder why he landed there?" she said to Cyrano.

He shrugged and said, "I would guess that perhaps he had to land quickly before he passed out."

"But where was he going?"

"There are many mysteries here. We might be able to clear up some of them if we apply certain methods of persuasion to Thorn."

"Torture?"

Cyrano's long, bony face was grave.

"That would be inhumane, and, of course, the end never justifies the means. Or is that statement a false philosophy?"

"I could never torture anybody, and I wouldn't permit anyone else to do it for me."

"Perhaps Thorn will volunteer information when he realizes that he cannot be free until he does so. I do not really think so, however. That one looks very stubborn."

Boynton's voice came in again. "With your permission. Ms. Gulbirra, I'll fly the chopper out. Everything looks okay. My men can bring Thorn back in the raft."

"Permission granted," Jill said. "If it's operable, take it up to the top of the tower. We'll be along later."

Within ten minutes, the radar operator reported that the helicopter was lifting. Boynton added that everything was running smoothly.

Leaving Coppename in charge, Jill went down to the hangar bay. She arrived in time to see Thorn's cloth-wrapped body being lifted out of the raft. He was still unconscious. She followed the stretcher bearers to the sick bay, where Graves immediately took charge.

"He's in shock, but I think I can pull him through. You can't question him now, of course."

Jill posted two armed guards at the door and returned to the control room. By then the ship was lifting, headed for the tower. A half-hour later, the *Parseval* was again poised above the landing field. This time, it stayed 200 meters from the dome. Its nose was pointed against the slight wind, and its propellers spun lazily.

After a while, the little wagon made by the machinists was lowered onto the surface. After being pulled to the entrance, it was pushed as far as two men could get. Then long poles made by the machinists were used to push the wagon deeper. Extensions were added to the poles as needed. In a short time, the forward end of the wagon was against the far wall.

After six photographs were taken, the wagon was pulled back by a long rope. Jill eagerly removed the large plates, which had been developed electronically at the moment of exposure.

She looked at the first one.

"He's not there."

She handed it to Cyrano. He said, "What is this? A short hall and a doorway at its end. It looks like an elevator shaft beyond, yes? But . . . there is no cage and there are no cables."

"I don't think They would have to depend upon such primitive devices as cables," she said. "But it's evident that Piscator got through the field and that he took the elevator."

"But why does he not come back? He must know that we are concerned."

He paused, and then he said, "He must also know that we cannot stay here forever."

There was only one thing to do.

60

SHE GAVE THE ORDER TO TIE THE SHIP UP AGAIN. AFTER THIS WAS done, she summoned the entire crew to the hangar bay. The photographs were passed around while she told them in detail everything that had happened.

"We'll wait here a week if we have to. After that, we must leave. Piscator would not willingly stay down there so long. If he doesn't come back within twelve hours we can presume that he's being detained by . . . Them. Or perhaps he has had an accident and has been killed or hurt. There's no way of knowing. We can do nothing except wait for a reasonable period of time."

No one would think of deserting Piscator at this time. But it was evident that they did not like the idea of staying seven days in this cold, dark, wet, ominously silent place. It was too much like camping outside the gates of hell.

By then, helicopter No. 1 had quit burning. A work party went out to recover the bodies and to investigate the cause of the explosion. Mechanics began checking the other copter for pontoon damage and replacing the bullet-torn windshield and port door.

A three-man guard was posted just inside the dome. Just before Jill went to the messroom, she got a call from Doctor Graves.

"Thorn's still unconscious, but he's rallying. I've also looked at what's left of Firebrass' brain. I can't do much since I don't have a microscope. But I'd swear that that little black sphere was attached to the neural system of the forebrain. I considered the possibility that it was extraneous and had been injected by the force of explosion into his brain. But the mechanics tell me there wasn't any such thing in the copter's equipment."

"You mean that you think that sphere had been surgically implanted in his brain?"

Graves said, "There isn't enough frontal skull left to say for certain. But I'm going to cut the others open, too. In fact, I'm going to do a complete dissection on all the victims. That'll take time, especially since I have to keep an eye on Thorn."

Trying to keep her voice from trembling, she said, "You realize the implications of that sphere?"

"I've been doing some thinking about it. I don't know what the hell it means except that it's important. Now, Jill, I've been doing dissections for years, not because I had to but just to keep my hand in. And I've never found anything out of the ordinary in a thousand corpses.

"But I'll tell you this. I think I know why Firebrass insisted on X-raying the skulls of his crew. He was looking for people with black spheres on, or in, their forebrains."

"I'll tell you something else. I think he rushed Stern's corpse off to The River because he *knew* that Stern had a ball in his brain.

"It's like Alice said, 'Mysteriouser and mysteriouser,' isn't it?"

Her heart pounding hard and her hand shaking, Jill switched off the intercom.

Firebrass was one of Them.

A moment later she called Graves back.

"Firebrass said he'd tell us why he wanted us X-rayed. But he never did, not to me, anyway. Did he tell you?"

"No. I asked him to tell me, and he just put me off."

"Then you don't know whether or not Thorn has a sphere in his head. If he should die, open him up, Doc."

"I'll do that. Of course, I could expose the brain, anyway. But not now. He has to get well first."

"Wouldn't that kill him? I know that the top of the skull is removed in operations, but can you expose Thorn's forebrain?"

"It won't hurt me a bit."

Twenty-four hours passed. Jill tried to keep the crew busy, but there was very little to do except unnecessary cleaning and polishing. She wished that she had brought along some of the movies made in Parolando. Except for talking and playing checkers, chess, and card games and throwing darts, there was little to occupy them. She did organize exercise periods to tire them out, but only so much of this could be done, and it was almost as boring as doing nothing.

Meanwhile, the dark and the cold seemed to seep into their bones. And the thought that below them there might be those mysterious beings who had made this world for them was nerve stretching. What were They doing? Why had They not come out?

Above all, what had happened to Piscator?

Cyrano de Bergerac seemed to be especially affected. His long silences and obvious brooding could be caused by the death of Firebrass. It seemed to her, however, that something else was bothering him.

Doctor Graves asked her to come to his office. On entering it, she found him sitting on the edge of his desk. Silently, he held out his palm. In it was a tiny black sphere.

"They were all so badly burned that I couldn't even determine the sex by exterior observation. Obrenova was the smallest, though, so I dissected the smallest corpse first. I found this at once. I didn't say anything to you because I wanted to examine all of them first.

"She was the only one to have this."

"Two of them!"

"Yeah. And it makes me wonder about Thorn."

Jill sat down and lit a cigarette with trembling hands. Graves said, "Listen. The only liquor aboard is in my locker. It's for medical purposes, but I think you need some medicine. I know I do."

While he got a bottle out, she told him about overhearing the quarrel between Thorn and Obrenova.

He handed her a cup of the purplish fluid, saying, "So they weren't just nodding acquaintances?"

"I don't think so. But I don't know what all this means."

"Who does? Except maybe Thorn. Cheers!"

Jill downed the warming, fruity liquor, and she said, "We found nothing suspicious in the quarters of any of them, Firebrass', Obrenova's, or Thorn's."

She paused, then said, "There was one thing, significant not by its presence but by its absence. Like the dog in the Sherlock Holmes story who didn't bark. Thorn's grail wasn't in his chopper or in his cabin. I have, however, ordered a more thorough search of the chopper.

"You told me a few hours ago that Thorn's conscious now. Can he be questioned?"

"Not for very long. I'd advise waiting until he's stronger. Just now, if he doesn't want to talk, he can pretend to fall asleep."

The intercom rang. Graves flipped on the switch.

"Doctor? C.P.O. Cogswell here. I'd like to speak to the captain."

Jill said, "Captain here."

"Captain, we just found a bomb in the No. 2 chopper! It's plastic explosive. Looks like it weighs about two kilograms, and the fuse is connected to a radio receiver. It's on the underside of the arms locker in the rear."

"Don't do anything until I get down there. I want to see it before it's removed."

She stood up. "I don't think there's any doubt that Thorn set off a bomb in Firebrass' chopper. The investigating crew hasn't determined the cause of the explosion, but the chief said he thought it might have been a bomb."

"Yes," Graves said. "The question is why Thorn would want to do that."

Jill started to walk toward the door, then stopped. "My God! If Thorn planted bombs in both choppers, he could have hidden some on the ship, too!"

"You never found a transmitter when you searched his quarters," the doctor said. "Maybe he hid one, or several, on the ship."

Jill immediately alerted all personnel. After giving orders to Coppename to organize the search parties, she left for the hangar bay. The bomb was where the chief had said it was. She got down on her knees and looked at it with the aid of a flashlight. Then she left the machine.

"Remove the fuse and receiver. Put the plastic in the explosives hold. Call the electronics officer and tell him I'd like to know what frequency the receiver is set on.

"No, wait, I'll call him myself."

She wanted to make sure that his experimenting would be done in a shielded room. The various bombs—if any—would have been planted at the same time, but Thorn would set the receiver of each to respond to its own wavelength. Still, there was no use taking a chance.

After making sure that Deruyck, the electronics officer, understood why he should use a shielded room, she went to the control room. Coppename was at the intercom, listening to the reports of the search parties.

Cyrano was in the pilot's chair staring at the panel as if the ship were in flight. He looked up at her as she entered.

"Is it permitted to ask what Doctor Graves found?"

So far, she had not concealed anything from the crew. She felt that they had a right to know as much as she did.

Cyrano said nothing for some time after she had finished. His long fingers drummed on the panel while he looked upward as if something were written on the overhead. Finally, he stood up.

"I think we should have a little talk. In private. Now, if possible."

"With all this going on?"

"We can step into the chart room."

He followed her in and closed the door. She sat down and lit another cigarette. He began pacing back and forth, his hands locked behind him.

"It is evident that Firebrass, Thorn, and Obrenova were agents of Them. I find it hard to believe that Firebrass could have been. He was so human! Yet it is possible that They are human, too.

"Still, that being who called himself an Ethical said that neither he nor the agents were violent. They detested and abhorred violence. But Firebrass could be very violent; he certainly did not act like a pacifist. And then there's the incident of the newcomer Stern. It seems from what you tell me that Firebrass may have attacked him, instead of Stern assaulting Firebrass."

"I don't know what you're talking about," Jill said. "It would be better to begin at the beginning."

"Very well. I will tell you what I promised to keep secret. I do not easily break my word, in fact, this is the first time. But I may have given my word to someone who is my enemy, my secret enemy.

"It was seventeen years ago. How long ago that has been, yet how recently! I was at that time living in an area of which most of the people were of my country and time. On the right bank, you understand. The left was populated by brown-skinned savages. Indians who had lived on the island of Cuba before Columbus found it, though I believe its inhabitants were not aware that their country had been lost. They were fairly peaceful, and after some initial struggles and difficulties, our area had settled down.

"My own little state was, in fact, headed by the great Conti, under whom I had the honor to serve at the siege of Arras. Where I received a thrust through the throat, the second of the serious wounds that convinced me, along with all else I had seen of war's miseries and horrors, that Mars was the stupidest of the gods. Also, I was delighted to find there my good friend and mentor, the so justly famed Gassendi. He, as you no doubt know, opposed the infamous Descartes and revived Epicurus, whose physics and morals he so splendidly presented. Not to mention his influence on Molière, Chapelle, and Dehènault, all my good friends, by the way. He persuaded them to translate Lucretius, the divine Roman atomist . . ."

"Stick to the point. Give me only the undecorated truth."

"As for the truth, what is it, to paraphrase slightly another Roman . . ."

"Cyrano!"

61

"VERY WELL. TO THE BREACH. IT WAS LATE AT NIGHT. I WAS SLEEP-ing soundly next to my so lovely Livy, when I was suddenly awakened. The only illumination was the night light seeping in through the wooden bars of our open window. A huge figure was standing over me, a black mass with a tremendous round head like a burned-out moon. I sat up, but before I could bring up my spear, which always lay by my side, the figure spoke."

"In what language?"

"Eh? In the only one in which I was then fluent, my native speech, the most beautiful of all the tongues of Earth. The thing spoke not the most correct of French, but I understood him.

" 'Savinien de Cyrano II de Bergerac,' he said, giving me my full nomenclature.

" 'You have the advantage of me, sir,' I said. Though my heart was pounding hard and I felt the most intense need of pissing, I conducted myself most admirably. By then I could see, even in that faintly starlit darkness, that he was not overtly belligerent. If he had a weapon, he had concealed it under his huge cloak. Though I was somewhat distracted, I could not but wonder why Livy, a light sleeper, had not been awakened. But she slept on, snoring lightly and prettily.

" 'You may call me whatever you wish,' he said. 'My name is not important at this time. And if you wonder why your woman is not also awake, it is because I have made sure that she will not. Oh, no!' he said, as, furious, I tried to get up, 'she is not harmed in the least. She has been drugged and will awake in the morning without even a headache.'

"By that time, I discovered that I, or at least a part of me, had also been drugged. My legs would not function, though, strangely, they did not feel leaden or numb. They just wouldn't work. Naturally, I was furious at the liberties taken with my person, but there was little I could do about it.

"The stranger then pulled up a stool and sat down by me.

" 'Listen, and then determine for yourself if I am not worth listening to,' he said.

"And he told me a most amazing tale, Jill, the like of which it is evident that you have not heard. He said that he was one of the beings who had resurrected us. They called themselves Ethicals. He would not go into detail about their background or where they came from or anything like that. He did not have enough time for that. In fact, if he were caught—by his own people, mind you—it would be bad indeed for him.

"I had many questions, of course, but when I opened my mouth, he told me to keep quiet and listen. He would visit me again, he said, perhaps more than once. Then he would answer most of my questions. Meanwhile, I was to understand this! We had not been given life so that we could live forever. We were just subjects of scientific experiments, and when the experiments were finished, we would be finished. We'd die for the last time, forever."

"What kind of experiments?"

"Well, it was more than just experiments. It was also a historical project. His people wanted to collect data on history, on anthropology, and so forth. They were also interested in finding out what kind of societies we humans would form when we were so mixed together. How would people change under certain conditions?

"He said that many groups would be allowed to develop without any interference from his people at all. But some would be influenced, some subtly, some by more outright methods. The project would take a long time, perhaps several hundred years. Then it would be *finit* for the project and *finit* for us. Back to dust we would go—forever.

"I said, 'That does not sound so ethical to me, sir. Why do they deny to us what they have—eternal life?'

"He said, 'That is because they are not truly ethical. Despite their high opinions of themselves, they are cruel, as the scientist who tortures animals to advance science is cruel. But he has his justifications, his rationalization.

" 'You see, the scientist is doing some good, being ethical in one sense. It is true that as a result of this project, a few of you will become immortal. But only a few.'

" 'How is that?' I said.

"And then he told me about the entity which the Church of the Second Chance calls the *ka*. You know of this, Jill?"

Jill said, "I've attended many of their lectures."

"Then you know all about the *ka* and the *akh* and the other stuff. This person said that the Chancer's theology was partly true. Mainly because one of the Ethicals had visited the man called La Viro and had thus caused him to found the Church."

"I thought that was just one of the wild tales those visionaries had invented," Jill said. "I didn't put any more credence in it than I did in the ravings of Earth prophets. Moses, Jesus, Zoroaster, Mohammed, Buddha, Smith, Eddy, the whole sick crew.''

"No more did I," Cyrano said. "Though, when I was dying, I did repent. But that was to make my poor unhappy sister and my friend Le Bret happy. Besides, it couldn't hurt if I made a deathbed conversion. And, to tell the truth, I was scared of hellfire. After all . . ."

"Your childhood conditioning."

"Exactly. But here was a being who said that there was such a thing as a soul. And I had proof positive that there could be a life after death. Still, I could not help wondering if I was the butt of a joke. What if this man were just one of my neighbors, pretending to be a visitor from the gods, as it were? I would believe him, and then tomorrow I would be laughed at. What? De Bergerac, the rationalist, the atheist, to be taken in so completely by this fantastic tale?

"But . . . who would do this to me? I knew no one who would have the motive or the means for such a joke. And what about the drug which made Livy sleep and which paralyzed my legs? I had never heard of such a drug. Also, where would a practical joker get that sphere which enclosed his head? There was just enough light to see that it was black and opaque. Still . . .

"And then, as if he perceived my lack of belief, he handed me a lens of some material. 'Put this in front of your eye,' he said. 'Look at Livy.'

"I did so, and I gasped with astonishment. Just beyond the top of her head was a globe of many colors. It shone brightly, as if illuminated by itself. It spun and swelled and expanded and put out arms from time to time, six-sided tentacles, and these shrank back into the globe and then other arms came out.

"The being then reached out and told me to drop the lens into his hand. He did not say so, but it was evident that he did not want me to touch him. I obeyed, of course.

"The lens went back into his cloak, and he said, 'What you saw is the *wathan.* That is the immortal part of you.'

"Then he said, 'I have chosen a few of you to help me fight against this monstrous evil my people are committing. I picked you because of your *wathans.* You see, we can read *wathans* as easily as you can read a children's book. A person's character is reflected in his *wathan.* Perhaps I shouldn't say *reflected,* since the *wathan* is the character. But I don't have the time to explain that. The point is, only a minute fraction of humanity will reach the final, the desired ultimate stage, of *wathan*hood, unless humanity is given much more time.'

"He then went on to sketch what the Chancers expound in such detail. That the unfulfilled *wathan* of a dead person wanders through space forever, containing all that is human but unconscious. Only the complete evolved *wathan* has consciousness. And this stage is attained only by those who achieve an ethical perfection while alive. Or near perfection, anyway.

" 'What?' I said. 'The ultimate in attaining ethical perfection is to wander like a ghost through space, to bounce off the walls of the universe like a cosmic handball, back and forth, yet be conscious of this horrible state and unable to communicate with anyone but one's self? That is a desirable state?'

" 'You must not interrupt,' the stranger said. 'But I will tell you this. The being who attains perfect *wathan*hood or *akh*hood, *goes beyond.* He does not stay in this world. He *goes beyond!*'

" 'And where?' I said, 'is *beyond?*'

" 'To *go beyond* is to be absorbed into the Over*wathan.* To become one with the only Reality. Or God, if you wish to name the Reality that. To become one of God's cells and to experience the eternal and infinite ecstasy of being God.'

"I was more than half-convinced then that I was dealing with an insane pantheist. But I said, 'And this absorption means the loss of one's individuality?'

" 'Yes,' he said. 'But you then become the Over*wathan,* God. To trade your individuality, your self-consciousness, for that of the Supreme Being is surely no loss. It is the greatest gain possible, the ultimate.'

" 'It is horrible!' I cried. 'What kind of monstrous joke is this that God plays on His creatures? How is the afterlife, immortality, any better than death?

" 'No! It does not make sense! Speaking logically, why should the *wathan,* or the soul, be created in the first place? What sense is there to this creation when most *wathans* will be wasted, as if they were so many flies hatched only to be eaten or swatted? And those *wathans* who do survive, in a manner of speaking. What about those who achieve near perfection, sainthood, if you will, only to be cheated in the end? For surely to lose your self-consciousness, your individuality, your humanity, is to be cheated?

" 'No, I want to stand as myself, Savinien de Cyrano de Bergerac, if I am to be immortal. I do not want this spurious immortality, this beingness as an unknowing, brainless cell of God's body! Nameless and brainless!'

" 'Like most of your breed, you talk too much,' he said. 'However . . .'

"He hesitated, then said, 'There is a third alternative, one which you will like. I did not want to tell you . . . I won't, now. I do not have time, nor is this the best time. Perhaps the next time. I must leave shortly.

" 'First, though, is the matter of your loyalty and your aid. Are you with me?'

" 'How can I pledge my support when I do not know if you are worth supporting? For all I know, you may be Satan himself!'

"He chuckled hollowly, and he said, 'You are the one who denied both God and the Devil. I am not the Devil or any analog to him. I am in fact on your side, on the side of deluded, suffering humanity. I can't prove that to you. Not now. But think of this. Have my colleagues approached you? Have they done anything but bring you back from the dead for purposes they do not condescend to tell you? Have I not chosen you from many billions to help in this secret struggle? You and eleven others? Why have I honored you? I'll tell you. Because I know that you are one of the few who can aid me. Because your *wathan* tells me that you will be on my side.'

" 'It is, then, predetermined?' I said. 'I do not believe in predeterminism.'

" 'No. There's no such thing, except in a sense which you would not understand or would find difficult to accept.

" 'All I can tell you at the moment is that I am on your side. Without me, you and most of your kind are doomed. You must have faith in me.'

" 'But,' I cried. 'What can we pitiful few humans do? We are pitted against superhumans with superpowers.'

"He replied that we twelve could do nothing without a friend in court. He was that friend. We twelve must get together and journey to the North Pole, to the tower in the middle of the sea. We must get there on our own, however. He could not fly us there. He could not tell me at the moment why not.

" 'I must proceed slowly and cautiously,' he said. 'And you must promise not to reveal this conversation to anyone. To no one except one of the twelve I've picked.

" 'To do so might result in your being detected by an agent. That would mean that you would be stripped of all memory of your meetings with me. And I would be placed in even graver danger.'

" 'But how will I recognize these others?' I said. 'How will I get to where they are or they to me? Where are they?'

"While asking these questions, I felt awed and elated at the same time. That one of the beings who had raised us from the dead and made this world should be asking for my help! I, Savinien de Cyrano de Bergerac, who am just a human being, however great certain of my talents are. That he should pick me from many billions!

"He knew his man, knew I would not be able to resist his challenge. If I could have stood up, I'd have crossed swords with him—if swords were available—and I'd have pledged my loyalty with a toast—if wine had been handy.

" 'You'll do as I ask?' he said.

" 'But certainly!' I said. 'You have my word, and I never go back on that!'

"Jill, I won't go into any more detail about what else he said. Except . . . he did say that I was to tell Sam Clemens that he should be on the lookout for a man named Richard Francis Burton. He was one of those chosen. And we were to wait for a year in Virolando for all of us to get together. If some didn't show, then we were to go ahead. And we would be hearing from him—the Stranger—in the near future.

"He gave me directions to find Clemens, who was down-River about ten thousand leagues. Clemens would be building a great boat made of ore from a meteorite. I knew who Clemens was though I'd died one hundred and eighty-one years before he was born. After all, was not his Earthly wife sleeping in my bed? I told him that, and he chuckled and said, 'I know.'

" 'Is this not embarrassing for me?' I said. 'And especially for Livy? Would the great Clemens even admit me aboard his so grand boat in this situation?'

" 'Which is more important to you?' he said with some degree of impatience. 'A woman or the salvation of the world?'

" 'That would depend upon how I felt about the woman,' I said. 'Objectively and humanely, there is no argument. I am humane but I am not objective.'

" 'Go there and find out what happens,' he said. 'Perhaps this woman will prefer you.'

" 'When Cyrano is on fire with love,' I said, 'he does not cool off at command.'

"Then he stood up, and said, 'I will see you,' and he was gone. I dragged myself with my arms, my dead legs trailing uselessly, to the door, and pushed it open. There was no sign of him. The next morning, I announced to Livy that I was tired of this place. I wanted to travel, to see this brave new world. She said that she was tired of traveling. But if I went, she would go with me. So we set out. The rest you know."

Jill felt a sense of unreality. She believed Cyrano's story, but it nevertheless made her feel as if she were a player on a stage, the sets of which concealed something frightening. And she was also an actor who had not been given the script.

"No, I don't know the rest. What about you and Clemens? What did he know that you didn't? And did any of the others this Ethical had chosen show up?"

"Clemens was visited twice by the Ethical. Clemens calls him X or the Mysterious Stranger."

Jill said, "He wrote a book once titled *The Mysterious Stranger*. A very sad, bitter story, overwhelmingly pessimistic. The Stranger was Lucifer."

"He told me about it. However, he did not know much more than

I did. Except that this X had somehow deflected a meteorite so that it would fall where Clemens could find it.''

"Do you realize the energy that would take?''

"It was explained to me. Anyway, Sam broke his word to the Stranger. He told Joe Miller and Lothar von Richthofen about him. He said that he could not help telling them.

"Also, there were two more. A giant red-haired savage of a man named John Johnston. And . . . Firebrass!''

She almost dropped her cigarette. "Firebrass! But he . . . !''

Cyrano nodded. "Exactly. He would seem to be one of these agents whom the Ethical mentioned but did not explain. I never saw the Ethical again, so I did not get any answers to my many questions. But I think, though I can't be sure, that he would have been surprised to learn that Firebrass claimed to be one of the twelve. Perhaps Firebrass was an infiltrator. But that does not explain Thorn and Obrenova.''

"Did Johnston or Firebrass add anything to your knowledge?''

"Of the Ethical? No, Johnston was visited only once. Firebrass, of course, was not one of the twelve chosen. I doubt that the Ethical knew he was an agent. How could he unless he himself had been disguised and in our midst? Which perhaps he may have been. But if he knew that Firebrass was an agent, he had reasons not to tell us.

"What worries me, among many things, is that the Ethical hasn't visited us again.''

Jill sat upright.

"Could Piscator be an agent?''

Cyrano stopped walking, lifted his shoulders and eyebrows, and spread out his extended palms upward.

"Unless he returns, we may never know.''

"Purposes, cross-purposes, counter-cross-purposes. Wheels within wheels within wheels,'' Jill said. "Mâyâ lowers seven veils of illusion between us and them.''

"What? Oh, you are referring to the Hindu concept of illusion.''

"I don't think Piscator was an agent. If he had been, he wouldn't have said anything to me about his suspicions that something dark and secret was going on.''

A knocking on the door startled them.

"Captain! Greeson here, head of Search Group Three. All areas in this section except for the chart room have been searched. We *can* come back later.''

Jill, rising, said, "Come on in.''

To Cyrano she said, "I'll talk with you later. There's so much to puzzle out, so many questions.''

"I doubt I'll have any answers.''

62

THREE TWENTY-FOUR-HOUR PERIODS HAD PASSED.

The dead had been buried at sea, their cloth-wrapped bodies resembling Egyptian mummies as they were tilted outward through an aperture. As Jill stood in the klieg-lit fog and watched the corpses slide, one by one, through the arch at the base of the wall, she calculated the time of their fall. It was not callousness which made her indulge in the mental exercise. It was habit, and it was also a barrier against the horror of death.

Death was for real now; the hope of resurrection in this world was gone. Death seemed even more all-present and always threatening in this place with its cold, wet winds and dark, swirling clouds. She only had to walk a few paces into the mists, and she would be out of sight and sound of all living beings and their works. She could not see her feet or the metal on which she walked.

If she went to an aperture and stuck her head out, she could not even hear the cold, dead sea crashing against the tower. It was too far away. Everything was too far away, even if it was only a few meters distant.

It was truly a wasteland. She would be glad when she could leave it.

So far, Piscator had not come back. She did not think it likely that he would. Under no circumstances would he willingly have stayed so long in the tower. Either he was dead, hurt badly, or held prisoner. In any event, those on the outside could do nothing for him, and the proposed seven-day wait now seemed far too long. Therefore, Jill had announced to the crew that the airship would leave at the end of a five-day period.

They received the news with evident relief. Like her, their nerves were pulled tightly, overtightly, on a rack. So much so that she had been forced to change the four hours of guard duty at the dome to two. Some of the guards were hallucinating, seeing ghostly forms in the fog, hearing voices coming from the corridor. One man had even fired at what he thought was a huge form running at him from the mists.

The first search of the ship had found no bombs or transmitters. Fearing that the crew might not have covered every square centimeter, and also wanting to keep them busy, she ordered another search. This one was extended to the outside surface of the dirigible, too. Men went to the top and prowled the walkway, shining their lamps alongside it. Others swept their lights across the exteriors of the tail structures.

No bombs were located.

Jill was not relieved. If Thorn had planned from the beginning to hide explosives, he could have placed some inside a gas cell. If he had, he had thwarted them, since there was no way they could get into the cells without releasing the irreplaceable hydrogen. It was true he'd need a transmitter, but that was a small object. It could even be disguised as something else.

This thought set off a third search in which every small mechanical or electrical device aboard was inspected to make sure that it was indeed what it appeared to be. All were what they were supposed to be, but the idea that there could be a disguised transmitter added to the general nervousness.

Of course, as long as Thorn was kept inside the sick bay, he could not get to a hidden transmitter. A lock had been installed on the door to sick bay, and there were always two guards on the inside and two outside.

Jill talked to Cyrano about another problem.

"Sam's going to be bloody furious when he hears that he can't do anything if he ever does get here. There's no way he can get to the top of the tower from the surface of the sea. And if he did achieve the impossible, he still could do nothing to get in.

"It's possible that one or more of his crew might be able to enter the tower, if he could get to the top. But even then, what guarantee is there what happened to Piscator wouldn't happen to them?"

"Whatever that is," Cyrano said gloomily. He had been almost as fond of the Japanese as he was of Firebrass.

"Did Firebrass tell you, too, about the laser hidden on the *Mark Twain?*"

Cyrano came alive. "Aha! What a stupid man I am! The laser! Yes, Firebrass told me about it, of course. Would he tell you and not me? I should hope to kiss a pig under its tail he would not!"

"Well, it's possible that this metal might resist even a laser beam. But we won't know unless we try it, will we?"

The Frenchman swiftly lapsed into gloom.

"But what do we do about the fuel situation? We cannot fly to Clemens' boat and get the laser and return here and then get back to Parolando or the boat. We do not have enough oil for that."

"We'll get the laser from Sam and then go to Parolando and make some more oil and then come back here."

"That will take much time. But it is the only thing to do.

However, what if that hardheaded Clemens does not let us use the laser?''

"I don't see how he could refuse us," Jill said slowly. "That is the only means we have for getting into the tower."

"Ah, yes, true. But you are saying that logic will sway Clemens. He is human, which means that he is by no means always logical. But we will see."

Jill was so on fire with this idea that she saw no reason in waiting for Piscator any longer. If he were hurt or held prisoner by some mechanical device or by living beings, he wasn't going to be gotten free without the laser.

First, though, Thorn had to be questioned. After ordering Coppename to wait until she had returned, she walked down to sick bay with Cyrano. Thorn was sitting up in bed. His right leg was enclosed by a shackle attached to a chain, the other end of which was locked to the frame of the bed.

He said nothing as they entered, and Jill was also silent for a moment as she studied him. His thick jaw was locked; his chin, even more outthrust; his dark-blue eyes, half-lidded. He looked as stubborn as Lucifer himself.

She said, "Do you want to tell us what this is all about?"

Thorn did not reply.

She had made sure that he was to be left ignorant of the crash of the helicopter until she told him.

"We know that you set off that bomb. You murdered Firebrass and Obrenova, everybody on the chopper."

Thorn's eyes opened fully, but his expression did not change. Or was that a slight smile at the corners of his lips?

"You're guilty of premeditated murder. I can have you shot, and I may do it. Unless you tell me everything."

She waited. He glared steadily at her.

"We know about the little spheres on the forebrains of Firebrass and Obrenova."

That had pierced him, had struck something sensitive. His skin paled, and he grimaced.

"Is there a sphere on your brain?"

He groaned, and he said, "I was X-rayed. Do you think Firebrass would have taken me along if there had been one?"

"I don't know," Jill said. "He accepted Obrenova. Why would he have accepted her and rejected you?"

Thorn merely shook his head.

"Look. If it's necessary, I'll order that Graves remove the top of your skull and take a look at your brain."

"That would be a waste of time," he said. "I don't have any such thing inside me."

"I think you're lying. What is the purpose of that sphere?"

Silence.

"You do know, don't you?"

Cyrano said, "Where were you headed for when you stole the helicopter?"

Thorn bit his lip, then said, "I presume that you didn't get into the tower?"

Jill hesitated. Should she tell him about Piscator? Would that give him some sort of advantage? She could not imagine what it could be, but then she did not know the location of any piece in this jigsaw puzzle.

She said, "One man did get into it."

Thorn quivered, and he became even paler.

"One? Who was that?"

"I'll tell you if you'll tell me what this is all about."

Thorn's deep chest rose, and he let out air slowly.

"I won't say another word about this until we get to the *Mark Twain.* I'll talk to Sam Clemens. Until then, not a word. You can open my skull, if you will. But that would be cruel, and it might kill me, and it would be totally unnecessary."

Jill motioned to Cyrano to come with her into the next room. When they were out of Thorn's sight, she said, "Is there an X-ray machine aboard the *Mark Twain?*"

Cyrano shrugged and said, "I do not remember. But we can determine that as soon as we get into radio contact with the boat."

They returned to the foot of Thorn's bed. He stared at them for a minute. A struggle was obviously taking place in him. Finally, as if he hated himself for having to ask, he said, "Did that man come back?"

"What does that mean to you?"

Thorn looked as if he'd like to say something. Instead, he smiled.

"Very well," Jill said. "We are going to the boat. I'll talk to you when we get there, unless you change your mind before then."

The checkout tests of the equipment consumed an hour. The ropes were cast off and drawn into the dirigible. The guards and the rope handlers came aboard. With Cyrano in the pilot's seat, the *Parseval* rose, its propellers swiveled upward to give it additional lift. Water ballast was discharged to compensate for the loss of the valved-off hydrogen. The updraft around the tower lifted the ship higher than was desired, and so Cyrano sent it back down, headed toward the great hold through which they entered.

Jill stood at the windscreen and stared into the fog.

"So long, Piscator," she murmured. "We'll be back."

The wind hurled the vessel through the hole, spitting it out, as Cyrano said, as if it were a rotten piece of meat from the mouth of a giant. Or, he added, as if it were a baby overeager to be born, shot out from the womb of a mother who couldn't wait to get rid of her nine-months' burden.

The Frenchman sometimes overstrained his metaphors and similes.

The clear air and the bright sun and the green vegetation made them feel like bursting into song. Cyrano, grinning, said, "If I were not on duty, I would dance! I do not contemplate returning to that dismal place with any pleasure."

Aukuso had begun transmitting the ship's call letters as soon as it had gained a high altitude. Not until an hour had passed, however, did he report that he had made contact with the *Mark Twain*.

Jill started to report to Sam Clemens, but he interrupted her with a furious description of de Greystock's treacherous attack. She was shocked, but she became impatient with his overlong, overdetailed narrative. His boat was not badly damaged; her account was the important thing.

Finally, he ran down.

"I've discharged most of my bile, for the moment, anyway. Say, why are *you* talking to me? Where's Firebrass?"

"I didn't have a chance to say more than two words," she said. And she described in detail the events from the moment the airship had entered the hole in the mountain.

It was his turn to be shocked. Except, however, for some explosive curses, he did not comment until she had finished.

"So Firebrass is dead, and you think he was one of Them? Maybe he wasn't, Jill. Did it occur to you that the black sphere might have been implanted in a small number of us for some scientific purpose? That perhaps only one in a thousand or ten thousand has it? I don't know what its purpose could be. Maybe it transmits brain waves which They record for use in some sort of scientific experiment. Or it could be used by Them to keep tabs on certain preselected subjects."

"I hadn't thought of that," she said. "I'd like to think that you're right, because I hate to think that Firebrass could be one of Them."

"Me, too. However, the important thing just now is that a ground expedition is useless. I built those two boats for nothing. Well, not actually for nothing. There's something to be said for life on the boat. It affords luxuries you can't get elsewhere—except on the *Rex*—and it's the fastest way to travel, although I really have no definite place to go to anymore. But I haven't forgotten King John. I'm going to catch up with him and fix him for what he did to me."

"You're wrong about one thing, Sam," she said. "I think we can get into the tower. All I need is the laser."

It sounded to her as if Clemens was strangling.

"You mean that . . . that Firebrass told you about it? Why, that unjudicious, ungrateful, unprincipled . . . garrh! I told him not to say a word! He knew how important it was to keep it a secret! Now everybody in the wheelhouse knows it. They've heard every word you said. I'll have to get them to swear not to reveal it, and just how much chance is there they'll not let it slip? If Firebrass were here, I'd choke him with one hand and stick my cigar up his ass with the other!''

Sam went on, ''Besides, you should have waited until you got here before you said anything. For all I know, John's radiomen have been listening in to us for years! They might have figured out how our scramblers work and be taking in every word now, pleased as a hog that's just found a fresh pile of cow flop!''

''I'm sorry about that,'' she said. ''But it was necessary to mention it. We have to make arrangements for picking the laser up without landing.''

Jill added, ''I need the laser. It's the only means we have of getting into the tower. Without it all our long labors and the deaths of several people have been in vain.''

''And I need it to slice up John and his boat. It's a surefire thing, double-guaranteed to get a quick victory.''

Trying to keep the anger out of her voice, she said, ''Think on it, Sam. Which is more important, revenge on King John or solving the mystery of this world, finding out why we're here and who did this?

''Besides, there's no reason you can't have both. We'll return the laser to you after we use it.''

''Both be damned to hell and back! How do I know you will come back? The next time you may get caught by those people. They can sit inside, smug as mice behind a wall laughing at the cat, if you can't get to them. But when you start cutting with that laser, you think they'll just sit on their hands and allow you to waltz on in?

''They'll grab you, just as they did Piscator. And then what? Besides, for all you know, the metal of the tower could be resistant to a laser beam.''

''Too right. But we have to try. That's the only way we can find out.''

''All right, all right! You've got logic and right on your side, as if that ever won an argument! But I'm a reasonable man. So, you can have the laser!

''But, and this is a big but, as the queen of Spain said to Dan Sickles, you've got to get Rotten John for me first!''

''I don't know what you mean.''

''I mean that I want you to make a raid on the *Rex*. Send in a party in the chopper at night and grab John. I'd rather see him here alive, but if you can't get him alive and kicking, kill him!''

''That's stupid and vicious!'' Jill said. ''We could lose the chopper and all the raiding party in a useless, vainglorious venture.

Not to mention risking lives, we can't afford to lose the chopper. It's the only one we have.''

Sam had been breathing heavily, but he waited until he had regained his wind. Now he spoke smoothly, icily.

"It's you that's being stupid now. If John is gotten rid of, I won't have any reason to pit my boat against the *Rex*. Think of the lives that'll be saved. For all I care, his second-in-command, whoever he is, can take over and I'll wish him good luck. All I want is that John doesn't get away with all the crimes he committed and that he doesn't get to keep the beautiful boat I toiled and sweated and plotted and suffered agonies for. And don't forget that he tried to sink *this* boat, too!

"I want that miserable excuse for a human being standing in front of me so I can tell him exactly what he is. That's all. I promise I won't kill him or mistreat him, if that's bothering you. Thunderation! Why should it?

"And when I'm done chewing him out, the most glorious verbal reaming ever given anybody since the dawn of time—it'll make Jeremiah look tongue-tied—then I'll put him ashore and steam away. Of course, I may maroon him among cannibals or grail slavers.

"I promise you that, Jill.''

"What if he has to be killed?''

"I'll just have to endure my disappointment.''

"But I can't order my men to go on such a dangerous mission.''

"I won't ask you to. Just ask for volunteers. If you can't get enough, too bad. You can't have the laser. However, I don't anticipate any dearth of heroes. If there's one thing I know, Jill, it's human nature.''

Cyrano shouted, "I will be honored to enlist, Sam!''

"Is that you, Cyrano? Well, I have to admit you've not been one of my dearest friends. But if you do go, I wish you good luck. I mean it.''

Jill was so surprised she could not speak for a moment.

Here was the man who'd said he regarded Mars, the deity of war, as the most stupid of gods.

When she regained her voice, she said, "Why are you doing this, Cyrano?''

"Why? But you forget that I, too, was on the *Not For Hire* when John and his pirates seized it. I was almost killed. I would like to have my revenge, to see the expression on his face when he realizes that the trap is sprung on the trapper, the pirate pirated.

"This is not your vast, impersonal war initiated by greedy, glory-mad imbeciles who do not care how many thousands are slaughtered, mutilated, driven insane, frozen, starved, dying of disease;

how many children and woman blown up; how many women raped or left husbandless or sonless.

"No, this is personal. I know the man whom I would make my small, wholly justified war upon. So does Clemens, who abhors war as much as myself."

Jill did not argue with him. At that moment, he seemed like a little child to her. An idiot child. He still wanted to play at war, yet he had seen its miseries and horrors.

There was nothing for her to do but go along with Sam's proposal. She did not have to obey him, since he had no way of enforcing his orders. But if she wanted the laser, and she did, she could only carry out the raid.

Her last hope that there would not be enough volunteers died as soon as she called for them. There were enough to get into three helicopters if they had been available.

Perhaps, she thought, they had been so frustrated at the tower that they wanted violent action against a foe who could be seen, who would fight. But she did not really believe that.

Clemens was right. He did know human nature. Male nature, anyway. No, that wasn't fair. The nature of some males.

An hour's discussion followed. During this Cyrano said that he could draw accurate sketches of the layout of the *Rex*. Clemens finally signed off, but not before making sure that he would be notified of the results of the raid the moment the helicopter returned.

"*If* it returns," she said.

63

THE TORPEDOES SEEMED TO BE DEAD-ON, BUT SAM ORDERED THE boat swung away and full power applied. A minute later, an observer at the stern reported that the torpedoes had just missed. The dirigible loomed before him, coming swiftly, seeming about to collide with the pilothouse itself. Sam yelled an order to fire a second volley away. Before that order could be obeyed, the airship exploded.

Four bombs going off simultaneously should have blown in every port, should have caved in the hull of the boat. As it was, many ports were shattered or driven whole into the interior and people were knocked down. The boat, immense and heavy though it was, rocked. Sam was hurled to the deck along with everybody except the pilot, who was strapped in his chair. Byron was knocked unconscious as a windscreen slammed into his face.

Sam got to his feet as smoke roiled into the control room, blinding him, making him cough violently. An acrid stink surrounded him. He could not hear anything; he was totally deafened for a minute. He groped through the cloud and felt along the control panel. Knowing the location of every dial, gauge, and button, he ascertained that the ship was still on course—if the steering mechanism was still operating. Then he unstrapped Detweiller's bloody, unconscious form and eased him to the floor. By the time he had slipped into the chair, he could see again. The airship, or what was left of it, was in the water. Pieces were scattered over hundreds of square meters, burning. Smoke billowed out from them, but by then the boat was out of the clouds. He straightened her out and headed her up-River. After putting the automatic pilot on, and making sure that it still operated, he went to the starboard to survey the damage.

Joe was saying something, his mouth wide open and working furiously. Sam stabbed a finger at his ear, indicating that he couldn't hear. Joe kept on yelling. His skin was cut in a hundred places.

Later, after everybody had calmed down, Sam decided that just one of the bombs must have gone off. The force of its explosion should have set off the other three, but it surely had not done so.

Nobody had been killed, but several score had been severely

wounded. Luckily, the explosion had failed to set off the rockets aboard.

Detweiller was the worst casualty, but by the third day he was up and walking. The boat was still close to shore, anchored next to the stone that had provided breakfast. A wide gangplank was built so the crew could walk ashore. The damage was repaired, and the crew took turns on shore leave. Sam decided that now would be a good time to make more alcohol and gunpowder. Arrangements were made to trade tobacco and some of the whiskey and wine provided by the crew's grails for wood and lichen from the area.

Von Richthofen was dead. The only survivors of the *Minerva* were Samhradh and Hardy, Newton having drowned while still unconscious. Sam wept when the German's body, wrapped in a weighted bag, was dropped into The River. He had been very fond of the ebullient, happy-go-lucky fellow.

"I know why Greystock did this," Sam said. 'John Lackland made him an offer he couldn't resist. And the double-dealing swine almost did the job, too. I thought Greystock was a cruel man, like all of his kind, but I didn't think he'd be disloyal. Still, if you've read your history—you, Marc, not you, Joe—then you'll know that the medieval noblemen were notorious for treachery. Their god was Opportunity, no matter how many churches they built for the glory of Church and God. They all had the morals of a hyena."

"Not all of them," de Marbot said. "There was William Marshal of England. He never switched sides."

"Didn't he serve under King John?" Sam said. "He must've had a strong stomach to stick with him. Anyway, John has tried once and almost got away with it. What bothers me is, how many other saboteurs has he planted? You see now why I've insisted on double guards at every vulnerable point. And four outside the armory and ammunition hold.

"That's also why I've ordered that every man jack aboard, and jill, too, report any suspicious conduct they see. I know it's made some people jumpy. But I've had to be realistic."

"No vonder you got nightmareth. Me, I don't vorry about thuch thingth."

"That's why I'm captain and you're only a bodyguard. Say, don't you worry about protecting me?"

"I chuth do my duty and vorry only about the long time betveen mealth."

A few minutes later, the chief radio officer reported that she was in contact with the *Parseval*. By the time Sam was through talking to Gulbirra, he felt as if he were walking through a minefield. Treachery, lies, frustration, uncertainty, confusion, and misdirection were waiting to explode under his feet.

Smoking like a dragon though the cigar tasted bitter, he paced back and forth. So far, there were only two on the boat who shared the secret of X with him—Joe Miller and John Johnston. There were, or had been, eight who to his knowledge knew about the Stranger: Miller, Johnston, himself, Firebrass (now dead), de Bergerac, Odysseus (who'd disappeared long ago), von Richthofen (now dead), and Richard Francis Burton. The being whom Clemens called X or the Mysterious Stranger (when it wasn't son-of-a-bitch or bastard) had said he'd elected twelve to get to the polar tower. X was supposed to return in a few years and give Sam more information. So far he had not shown.

Perhaps the other Ethicals had finally caught him, and he was—where?

Sam had told Miller and von Richthofen about the Stranger. So that left six of those informed by X unknown to him. Though it was possible that they were all on this boat. Why had X not given each one a sign or a codeword of recognition? Maybe he meant to do so but had been delayed. X's schedule was about as uncertain as that of a Mexican railroad.

Cyrano had told him about Burton. Sam didn't know where Burton was, but he knew who he was. The newspapers had been full of his exploits during Sam's lifetime. And Sam had read his *Personal Narrative of a Pilgrimage to El-Medinah, First Footsteps in East Africa, The Lake Regions of Central Africa,* and his translation of the *Arabian Nights.*

Also, Gwenafra had known him personally, and she had told Sam all she remembered about him. She had been only seven or thereabouts when she had first been resurrected. Richard Burton had taken her under his wing, and she had traveled with him on a boat up-River for a year. Then she had been drowned, but she had never forgotten the fierce, dark man.

Greystock had also been with them. But neither he nor Gwen were aware of the Stranger. Or way Greystock an agent?

That fellow Burton. On Earth he'd led an expedition to find the source of the Nile. Here, he was as passionately involved in getting to the headwaters of the Nile, though for a different reason. De Bergerac had said that the Ethical had told him that, if he found Burton, Burton would pretend to have lost his memory of anything related to the Ethicals. Clemens should tell him that he knew better, and Burton would then explain why he was pretending to have amnesia. Very curious.

Then there were Stern, Obrenova, and Thorn. And Firebrass. Their roles were as clandestine as those of X and his colleagues. On which side were they?

He needed help in untangling the warp and woof of this crazy tapestry. Time for a conference.

Within five minutes, he was closeted in his cabin with Joe and

John Johnston. Johnston was a huge man, massively boned and muscled. His face was handsome though craggy; his eyes, a startling blue; his hair, bright red. Though he towered above other humans, he looked small beside the titanthrop.

Sam Clemens gave them the news. Johnston did not speak at first, but then the mountaineer was not one to talk unless there was extreme occasion to do so. Joe said, "Vhat doeth it all mean? I mean, the gateway through vich only Pithcator could pathth?"

"We'll find out from Thorn," Sam said. "For the time being, what worries me is Thorn and the rest of that filthy crew."

Johnston said, "Ye don't think Greystock was an agent for them Ethicals, do ye? I think the polecat was just one of King John's men."

"He could have been that and also an agent," Sam said.

"How?" Joe Miller rumbled.

"How do I know? Anyway, you mean *why*. That was really what the thief said to Jesus while he was being nailed to the cross. *Why*? That's what we should be asking. Why? Yes, I think Greystock could have been an agent. He just fell in with King John's purpose because it suited his own purpose."

"But them agents don't use violence," Johnston said. "At least, that's what ye told me X told ye. They not only hate violence, they don't even like to touch human beings."

"No, I didn't say that. I said violence was unethical for the Ethicals. At least, according to X. But I don't know that he wasn't lying. For all I know, he may be the Prince of Darkness, who was, if you remember your Bible, the Prince of Liars."

"Then what're we doing?" Johnston said. "Why're we following his orders?"

"Because I don't know he's lying. And his colleagues haven't had the courtesy or decency to speak to me. He's all I have to go on. Also, I said that X seemed rather reluctant to have me get too close. Like the abolitionist who aired out his house after he'd had a black to dinner. But I didn't say that the agents were Brahmins, too. Thorn and Firebrass certainly weren't. I don't know. Anyway, Joe has a nose for X. He came into my hut once right after X had left. And he said he smelled somebody not human."

"Hith thtink vath different from Tham'th," Joe said, grinning. "I didn't thay that Tham thmelled any better, though."

"You're a thly one, ain't you?" Sam said. "Anyway, Joe has never smelled anyone else like that. So I presumed that the agents are of human origin."

"Tham thmoketh thigarth all the time," Joe said. "I couldn't thmell a thkunk around thothe weedth."

"That'll be enough of that, Joe," Sam said. "Or I'll run you back up the banana tree."

"I never thaw a banana in my life! Not until I came here and my grail gave me vone for breakfatht. Even then I vathn't thyure it vathn't poithon."

"Stick," Johnston said.

Sam's eyebrows curved like the backs of recoiling caterpillars.

"Stick what? I hope . . ."

"To the point."

"Ah, yes. Anyway, I'm sure that there are agents around. The boat may be crawling with them. The question is, whose? X's or the others'? Or both?"

Johnston said, "They ain't seemed to interfere so far. Not with the boat, anyway. But when we get close to the headwaters . . ."

"I don't know about interference. Even though he never said so, it's safe to assume that X bored that tunnel and left that rope for Joe and his Egyptian friends. But there's no evidence that the others are particularly against us mere Earthlings getting to the tower. They just don't want to make it easy for us. Again, why not?

"Also, what about Odysseus? He showed up in the nick of time and saved us when we were fighting von Radowitz. I assumed at first that it was X who'd sent him. But no, Odysseus said it was a *female* Ethical. So, is there another one of them in on this? Another renegade who's X's ally? I asked him about her, and he just laughed. He wouldn't tell me.

"But maybe the woman wasn't X's pal. Maybe she was an Ethical who'd gotten wind somehow of what was going on. And she sent Odysseus, who may have been an agent posing as the historic Odysseus.

"I say that because I've run into two Mycenaeans who were actually at the siege of Troy. At least, they claimed to have been. There are so many phonies on The River, you know. Both said that Troy wasn't where Odysseus said it was. He had told me that Troy was much further down in Asia Minor than the archaeologists said it was. The two Greeks said that it was where everybody had always said it was. Near Hissarlik, Turkey. Well, they didn't identify the town and country under those names, of course. Neither was in existence in their day.

"But they did say that Troy was near the Hellespont, where Hissarlik was later built. Now, how about that mess?"

"If that Greek feller was an agent," Johnston said, "why would he make up a lie like that?"

"Maybe to convince me that he was the real stuff. That he was the dyed-in-the-wool original. He wasn't likely to encounter anyone who could call him a bald-faced liar. For one thing, he didn't stick around long enough to be challenged.

"Here's another thing. The scholars of my time had all said that the wooden horse of Troy was a myth. The story was about as credible as a politician's campaign promises. But Odysseus said that there was a wooden horse, and he himself proposed it, just as Homer said he did, and it did get the Greek soldiers into the city.

"But then maybe it was a double-ply lie. By telling me that the scholars were all wrong, he made it sound as if he'd really been there. Anybody who could stand there and look you in the eye and tell you the scholars were full of sawdust and mouse droppings, because he had been there and they hadn't, would convince me. The scholars are always sailing out, looking for a textural Northwest Passage, trying to navigate with a sextant in a snowstorm, not sure whether the bowsprit is on the fore or the stern.''

"At least, they tried,'' Johnston said.

"So did the eunuch in the sheik's harem. I wish I had some idea of what's going on. We are in deep waters, as Holmes said to Watson.''

"Who're thothe guyth?'' Joe said.

The giant mountaineer growled. Sam said, "Okay, John, sorry. I was hoping we could follow at least one thread through in this tangled warp and woof. Hell, we can't even find the end of one thread!''

"Maybe Gwenafra thyould be in thith,'' Joe said. "Thyee'th a voman, vhich you may have notithed, Tham. You thaid vomen can pertheive thingth men can't becauthe they got female intuithyon. Anyvay, thye doethn't like being left out in the cold. Thye ain't no dummy. Thye knowth there'th been thomething going on for a long time that you've been hiding from her. Right now, thye'th thulking in the main lounge. Thye hath the red athth every time you run her out tho ve can have a conferenthe about thith thubchect.''

"I don't believe in women's intuition,'' Sam said. "They're just culturally conditioned to observe different patterns of action and speech, different gestures and inflections from those men observe. They're more sensitive to certain subtleties because of this conditioning.''

"It'th the thame thing in the end,'' Joe said. "Vhat do ve care vhat ith'th called? I thay, ve been beating out our brainth on thith. It'th about time ve had a new dealer in on thith poker game.''

"Squaws talk too much,'' Johnston said.

"According to you, everybody talks too much,'' Sam said. "Anyway, Gwen is as smart as anyone here, maybe smarter.''

"It'll end up with the whole world knowing about it,'' Johnston said.

"Well, if you think on it,'' Sam said, "why shouldn't everybody know? Ain't it everybody's business?''

"The Stranger must have his reasons for wanting us to keep quiet.''

"But are they good reasons?" Sam said. "On the other hand, if we did blabber about this there'd be a mob trying to get to the North Pole. The '49 Gold Rush couldn't hold a candle to it. There'd be hundreds of thousands wanting to get to the tower. And a million hanging around to exploit them."

"Let'th take a vote on Gven."

"You ever heard of a woman at a council of war? The first thing you know, she'll be wanting to run us. Them petticoats take an inch if ye give 'em a mile."

"Women don't wear petticoats anymore," Sam said. "In fact, they don't wear much of anything, as you must've noticed."

The vote was two to one. Johnston said, "Okay. But you make her keep her legs crossed when she sits down, Sam."

"It's a strain just getting her to cover her breasts," Sam said. "She's a caution. But it ain't her fault. Anyway, just about everybody swims naked. So what's the difference if she is a little careless about how many square inches of flesh she exposes?"

"It ain't the flesh, it's the hair," Johnston said. "Don't it bother you none?"

"It used to. After all, I lived about the same time as you. But I didn't spend my life among the Rocky Mountain Indians. We've been here thirty-four years, John, on a planet where even Queen Victoria is traipsing around in an outfit that would've given her heart failure followed by diarrhoea if she'd seen it worn in front of Buckingham Palace. Now nudity seems as natural as sleeping in church."

64

GWENAFRA, FOREWARNED BY SAM, WAS WEARING A LOINCLOTH under her kilt. She sat in a chair and listened wide-eyed while Sam explained why she had been admitted to the council.

After she had heard Sam out, she sat silently for a while, sipping from a cup of tea. Then she said, "I knew more than you thought I did. You've talked a lot in your sleep. I knew you were keeping something very serious from me. That hurt me very much. In fact, I was going to tell you, Sam, that you must tell me what was going on. Otherwise, I was going to leave you."

"Why didn't you say so? I had no idea you felt that way."

"Because I supposed that you must have a very good reason for keeping it from me. But I was getting to the point where I couldn't stand it anymore. Haven't you noticed how cross I've been lately?"

"It hadn't escaped me. I thought you were just being moody. One of the mysteries of woman. But this is no place to discuss our personal affairs."

"What is the place, then? I know I would have said something if *you*'d been so irritable. Anyway, women are about as mysterious as a tin mine. All you have to do is carry a lantern into the dark places, and you see everything. But men like to think women are the eternally mysterious. That saves men the trouble of asking questions, taking a little time and effort."

"The eternally loquacious, then," Sam said. "You take as long to get to the point as a broken pencil."

"You're both gabby," Johnston said, scowling.

"There are other extremes," she said, glaring at Johnston. "But you're right. Maybe there's one thing that you could consider as a key to the mystery of the tower. That is, what kind of a person was Piscator?"

"Ah, hmmm," Sam said. "I see what you mean. Why was he able to enter the tower while the others couldn't? Well, for one thing, he could have been an agent. But if agents can get through the barrier, why couldn't Thorn?

"Besides, why should Thorn have to use the *Parseval* to get to the tower? The Ethicals and their agents have their own methods of transportation, some kind of flying machine."

"I don't know," Gwenafra said. "Let's concentrate on Piscator. How was he different from the others? It couldn't be a physical element—clothing, say—that was the key to entry. All tried to get in naked, yet only Piscator got in.

"Also, there was a difference in how far each was able to advance into the entrance. What were the elements in character that made some advance further than others?"

"We'd need a computer to figure that out," Sam said. "However, Gulbirra knows the men in the airship. She can describe them when she gets here. Anyway, to be scientific, the exact distance each person traveled would have to be known. And that would have to be compared to each person's character. Nobody was taking measurements there, so that's out."

"Just consider Piscator then."

"He was one of them samurai," Johnston said.

"I don't think race would have anything to do with it," Sam said. "So far we haven't uncovered any Mongolian agents, though I suppose there could be plenty. Consider this. Thorn did not want Firebrass and Obrenova to get into the tower. So he cold-bloodedly blew them up, not to mention the innocents with them. Maybe, though, Thorn didn't know Firebrass was an agent. If so, he got two for the price of one."

"Maybe there were more than two . . ." Gwen said. "No, only two had those black balls in their heads."

"Jumping catfish! Don't make it more complicated than it is!"

Gwen said, "If those two could've entered, then we should compare their characters with Piscator's."

"I vath around Firebrathth a lot, and he thmelled chutht like any human. Thith Ethical left a thmell behind him when he vithited Tham. It vathn't human. Pithcator, he vath human, though he did thmell Chapanethe. I can dithtinguith different typeth of people becauthe of their diet."

"But you never met a person who smelled nonhuman," Sam said. "So we don't know if the agents are nonhuman. They certainly look as if they are human."

"No, but they mutht've been around me," Joe said. "And thinthe I never thmelled anybody that didn't thmell human—though that ain't nothing to brag about—thmelling human, I mean, then the achentth mutht be human."

"That mought be," Johnston said. "It seems to this here child that if a non-Earthman cain look like a real person, then he cain smell like one."

Joe laughed and said, "Vhy don't ve chutht potht a notithe in the main lounge? *Any Ethicalth or achentth aboard pleathe report to Captain Clementh.*"

Gwenafra had been fidgeting about and frowning. She said,

"Why do all of you duck the question I brought up? What about Piscator?"

"Maybe we're like the circus midget who found the giant's shoes under his wife's bed," Sam said. "Afraid to ask.

"Very well. I wasn't too well acquainted with the gentleman from Cipango. He showed up about two months before the *Mark Twain* left. From all reports, he was a very quiet and likable person. Not withdrawn or aloof, just not aggressive. He seemed to get along with just about everybody. Which, in my book, makes him suspect. Yet he wasn't a yes-man. I remember he got into an argument with Firebrass about the size of the airship to be built. He thought that it would be better to build a smaller one. The end of the discussion was that Piscator said he still thought he was right. But since Firebrass, was the boss, he would do as he said."

"Did he have any peculiarities?" Gwenafra said.

"He was crazy about fishing, but I don't count that an eccentricity. Say, what're you asking me for? You knew him."

"I just wanted to get another viewpoint," she said. "When Gulbirra gets here, we'll ask her about him. She knew him better than we did."

"Don't forget Thyrano," Joe said. "He knew him."

"Joe loved Cyrano," Sam said. "The Frenchmen's got a bigger nose than his. Makes Joe feel right at home."

"That'th a crock of thyit. Ain't none of you pygmieth got a nothe to be proud of. I chuth like him even if you two get along like two male hyenath in mating theathon."

"I don't care for the simile," Sam said coolly. "Anyway, what do you think of Piscator, Gwen?"

"He radiated a sort of, what do you call it? Not animal magnetism, since there was nothing sexual about it. Just a warm attractiveness. You knew he liked you. Though, again, he wouldn't put up with fools. He'd go along with them, even when they were being stupid. But he got rid of them in a nice way.

"I don't think he was, what is the word? A fundamentalist or fanatic Moslem. He said the Koran was to be understood allegorically. He also said the Bible was not to be read literally. He could quote long passages of both, you know. I talked to him a number of times, and I was surprised when he told me that Jesus was the greatest prophet after Mohammed. He also said the Moslems believed that the first person to enter heaven will be Mary, the mother of Jesus. You told me Moslems hate Jesus, Sam."

"No, I said they hated Christians. And vice versa."

"No, you didn't. But that's not important. To sum it up, Piscator impressed me as a wise and good man. But there was more to him than that. I don't know how to describe it.

"Perhaps it was that he seemed to be in this world and yet not *of* it."

"I think you're saying this," Sam said. "He was somehow morally, or perhaps it's better to say spiritually, superior."

"He never said so or acted like he thought he was. But, yes, that might be it."

"I wish I'd known him better."

"You were too busy building your boat, Sam."

65

FRIGATE DID NOT COME INTO THE HUT UNTIL ABOUT AN HOUR BEFORE suppertime. When asked by Nur where he had been, he said that he had waited all day to see Novak. Finally, Novak's secretary had said Frigate would have to come back tomorrow. Novak could spare a minute or so for him in the morning.

Frigate looked disgruntled. Waiting in line made him very impatient. That he had done so for such a long time meant that he was deeply determined. But he refused to say what he had in mind until he had talked to Novak.

"If he says yes, then I'll tell you."

Farrington, Rider, and Pogaas paid him little attention. They were too busy discussing means for getting the *Razzle Dazzle* back. When asked if he would help them, Frigate said he did not know yet. Nur only smiled and said he would wait until they had made up their own minds about the ethics of the deed.

Nur, as usual, knew more about what was going on than the others. It was he who told them, just before they left the hut to eat breakfast, that the discussion was only academic. The *Razzle Dazzle* had been loaded with artifacts for trade by its new owners and would sail down-River just after breakfast.

Martin exploded. "Why didn't you tell us about this before?"

"I was afraid you three would do something rash such as trying to seize the ship in daylight before hundreds of witnesses. You would never have gotten away with it."

"We're not that stupid!"

"No, but you're that impulsive. Which is a form of stupidity."

"Thanks a lot," Tom said. "Well, maybe it's just as well. I'd much rather go off on one of those patrol steamboats. But we'd have to get the old crew together first and find some people to replace the women. This is going to take time and lots of planning."

There were some delays, however. A man from the government office told them they had to go to work for the state or clear out. Frigate was absent when this happened. He returned grinning broadly and did not seem at all upset by the news.

"I talked Novak into it!"

"Into what?" Farrington said.

Frigate sat down in a bamboo chair and lit up a cigarette.

"Well, first I asked him if he would build another blimp for us. I didn't expect him to agree, and he didn't. He said he meant to build two more blimps—but not for us. These would be used for patrols and for warfare, if war should come."

"You want us to steal their blimp!" Farrington said. Though he had been angry when Podebrad had deserted them, he had later been relieved. He had denied this, but it was obvious that he was glad that he did not have to fly in the airship.

"No. Neither Nur nor I believe that you would steal anybody's property, even if you like to talk about it. You two fantasize a lot. Anyway, Nur and I won't have anything to do with stealing."

"After my first proposal was turned down, I put forth my second. Novak hemmed and hawed, and then said that he would do what I suggested. It wouldn't require near the materials nor time that the blimp did. He felt bad because we'd been cheated, and he thought that helping us would compensate us."

"Besides, Novak is interested in balloons. His son was a balloonist."

"Balloons!" Martin said. "Are you still pushing that crazy idea?"

Tom looked interested, but he said, "We don't know anything about the winds above the mountains. We could be blown south."

"That's right. But we're a little north of the equator. If the upper winds are anything like they are on Earth, we could be driven north and east. Once past the horse latitudes it's a different matter. But I have in mind a type of balloon that could get us to the arctic zone."

"Crazy! Crazy!" Martin said, shaking his head.

"You refuse to do this?"

"I didn't say that. I've always been a little touched in the head myself. Besides, I don't think the winds will be going the right way for us. We should get down to business and build us a ship."

Farrington was wrong and probably knew he was just expressing a wish. The air, at the altitude at which they would float, flowed northeast.

However, when the others heard what type of balloon Frigate proposed making, all objected vehemently.

"Yes, I know it's never been tried out, except on paper," Frigate said. "But here's our chance to try something unique."

"Yes," Martin said. "But you say Jules Verne proposed that idea in 1862. If it was such a hot idea, why didn't anyone ever try it?"

"I don't know. I would have done it on Earth if I'd had the money. Look. It's the only way we can get a considerable distance. If we use a conventional balloon, we'll be lucky to get four hundred and eighty kilometers. That still might eliminate a million kilometers of surface travel. But with the *Jules Verne,* and a lot of luck, we could get all the way to the polar mountains.''

After much argument, the others finally agreed they should give his plan a try. But when the project began, Frigate became uneasy. As the time for lift-off neared, he became downright anxious. Several nightmares about balloons showed him just how deep his apprehension was. Nevertheless, he expressed only the greatest confidence in the project to the others.

Jules Verne had proposed in his novel *Five Weeks in a Balloon,* an idea which seemed feasible—though dangerous. It worked in his book, but Frigate knew that reality often failed to give diplomatic recognition to literature.

The balloon was made, and the crew took twelve practice flights. These, to everybody's amazement, especially Frigate's, suffered only minor mishaps. However, all the training runs were made at low altitudes which kept the aerostat below the top of the mountains walling the Valley. To rise above them was to be carried away from a reasonable distance of New Bohemia and so make it impossible to return before they were ready for the final flight.

The crew would have to get on-the-job training when they ventured into the stratosphere.

Doctor Fergusson, Verne's hero, had made a balloon based on the fact that hydrogen, when heated, expanded. This principle had been used in 1785 and 1810 with disastrous results. Verne's imaginary heating device was, however, much more scientific and powerful and worked—on paper. Frigate had available a more advanced technology than that in Verne's time, and he had made some modifications to the system. When the balloon was finished, he bragged that this was the first of its type in reality. They were making history.

Frisco said quite vehemently that nobody had tried Verne's concept because nobody had been crazy enough. Though he agreed with him, Frigate did not say so. This was the only type of aerostat that could go the immense distances to be traversed. He wasn't going to back out. Too many times, on both worlds, he had started something and then had failed to see it through. Even if this killed him, he was going all the way.

That it might also kill the others bothered him. However, they knew the dangers. No one was forcing them to go.

The final lift-off went according to schedule just before dawn. Arc lights and torches blazed on the immense crowd on the plain. The envelope of the balloon, painted with aluminum, floated like a wrinkled sausage skin hanging from an invisible hook.

The *Jules Verne,* at this stage of flight, did not correspond to the layman's idea of a balloon, a completely expanded sphere. But as it rose the bag would fill out from applied heat and decreasing air pressure around it.

The speeches had been made and the toasts drunk. Tom Rider noticed that Frisco was using a bumper twice as large as the others. He said something about "Dutch courage" but not loudly enough for Frisco to hear him. By the time Frisco entered the car, he was smiling and waving merrily to the onlookers.

Peter Frigate completed the weigh-off. Until now, this had always involved making sure that the weight—envelope, gas, net, cargo chute, load ring, car, ballast, equipment, supplies, aeronauts—was slightly less than the lift. The *Jules Verne* was the first aerostat in which the lift-off weight was slightly more than the upward pull of the gas.

The car hanging below the bag was pumpkin shaped, and its hull was a double-walled magnesium alloy. In the center of its deck was a vertical L-shape, the vernian. Two thin plastic pipes ran from the metal contraption holes in the overhead. These were tightly packed to prevent escape of air from the car.

From there, the plastic pipes extended upward and for some distance beyond the hermetically sealed neck of the envelope. Their ends were fitted to light alloy pipes which rose to varying heights inside. One was longer than the other; both were open-ended.

The crew had been talkative before boarding. Now they looked at Frigate.

"Close the main hatch," he said, and the lift-off ritual began.

Frigate checked a gauge and two stopcocks affixed to the vernian. He opened a little hatch on the side near the top of the L-shape. He adjusted another stopcock until he heard a slight hissing. This came from a narrow nozzle at the end of a steel pipe inside the highest compartment.

He stuck an energized electrical lighter at the end of an aluminum rod into the furnace. A tiny flame popped from the nozzle. He turned the stopcock to increase the flame, adjusted two more to regulate the mixture of oxygen and hydrogen feeding the torch. The flame began heating the base of the large platinum cone just above it.

The lower end of the longest pipe extending into the bag was fitted into the apex of the cone. As the heat was expanded in the cone, the hydrogen in it moved upward, flowing into the bag and causing it to expand. The cooler hydrogen in the lower half of the bag, aided by a suction effect, flowed into the open end of the shorter pipe inside the envelope. It went down this pipe into the side of the vernian and into the side of the cone. There it was heated and rose, completing the circuit.

One of the compartments at the base of the vernian was an

electrical battery. This was far lighter and much more powerful than the battery used by Fergusson in Verne's novel. It broke water into its elements, hydrogen and oxygen. These flowed into separate compartments, and then went to a mixing chamber, where the oxyhydrogen was piped to the torch.

One of Frigate's modifications to Verne's system was a pipe that led from the hydrogen storage chamber to the shorter pipe. By opening two stopcocks, the pilot could allow hydrogen from the storage chamber to flow into the balloon. This was an emergency measure used only to replace hydrogen valved off from the bag. When this was done, the torch was turned off, since hydrogen was highly inflammable.

Fifteen minutes passed. Then, with no motion noticeable, the car lifted off the ground. Frigate shut off the torch several seconds later.

The shouts of the spectators became less audible, then died out. The huge hangar shrank to a toy house. By then the sun had cleared the mountain, and the stones alongside The River thundered like artillery.

"That's our thousand-gun salute," Frigate said.

No one moved or spoke for a while after that. The silence was as intense as that at the bottom of a deep cave. However, the alloy walls of the hull had no sound-absorbing qualities. When Frisco's stomach rumbled, it sounded like distant thunder.

A slight wind sprang up now, carrying the vessel southward, away from their goal. Pogaas stuck his head out of an open port. He felt no sensation of movement since the balloon traveled at the same speed as the wind. The air around the hull was as still as if he was in a sealed room. The flame of a candle set on top of the vernian would have burned straight upward.

Though he'd gone up in aerostats many times, Frigate was always gripped by ecstasy during the first minutes of lift-off. No other form of flight—even gliding—could thrill him so. He felt as if he was a disembodied spirit, free of the shackles of gravity, of the cares and worries of flesh and mind.

This was a delusion, of course, since gravity had the balloon in its paws, was playing with it, and was likely to bat it around at any moment. Nor was there much respite from worries and cares. There was often work for both body and brain.

Frigate shook himself like a dog coming out of water, and he got down to the work that keeps a balloon pilot busy during much of the flight. He checked the altimeter. One thousand eight hundred and twenty-nine meters. A little over 6000 feet. The verimeter, or statoscope, indicated that the rate of ascent was increasing as the sun warmed the gas in the bag. After checking the O and H storage chambers were full, he disengaged the battery from the water. For the present, he had nothing to do except keep an eye on the altimeter and verimeter.

The Valley narrowed. The blue-black mountains, splotched with vast patches of grey-green and blue-green lichen, sank. The mists that ribboned the stream and the plains were disappearing as swiftly as mice that had gotten word a cat was in the neighborhood.

They were being carried southward increasingly swifter. "We're losing ground," Frisco muttered. However, he spoke only to release nervous tension. Test balloons had shown that the stratospheric wind would carry them northeast.

Frigate said, "Last chance for a cigarette." Everybody except Nur lit up. Though smoking had been forbidden on all hydrogen balloons previous to the *Jules Verne,* it was permitted on it at lower altitudes. There was no sense in worrying about burning tobacco while an operating torch was present.

Now the balloon had risen above the Valley, and they thrilled at the sight of more than one at a time. There they were, row on row. To their left were the valleys—broad, deep canyons actually—which they had passed in the *Razzle Dazzle.* And as they soared higher, the horizon rushed outward as if in a panic. Frigate and Rider had seen this phenomenon on Earth, but the others gazed in awe. Pogaas said something in Swazi. Nur murmured, "It's as if God were spreading out the world like a tablecloth."

Frigate had all the ports closed, and he turned on the oxygen supply and a little fan which sucked carbon dioxide into an absorbent material. At 16 kilometers or almost 10 miles altitude, the *Jules Verne* entered the tropopause, the boundary between troposphere and stratosphere. The temperature outside the cabin was −73 C.

Now the contrary wind seized the aerostat and in so doing slightly spun it. From then on, unless they encountered an opposing wind, they would have the view of a rider on a lazy merry-go-round.

Nur took over the pilot's post. Pogaas got the next, and Rider had the third watch. When Farrington became the pilot, he lost his nervousness. He was in control, and that made all the difference. Frigate was reminded of how Farrington had described in a book his fierce exultation when, at the age of seventeen, he'd been allowed to steer a sealing schooner in rough weather. After watching him for a few minutes at the wheel, the captain had gone below. Farrington was the only one above decks, the safety of the ship and its crew in his hands. It had been an ecstatic experience never surpassed in a life filled with perilous adventures.

However, as soon as Frigate relieved him, he lost his smile, and he looked as uneasy as before.

The sun continued to rise and with it the *Jules Verne.* The envelope was near its pressure height now, which meant that the joy ride was over. Since its neck was sealed, instead of being open as in most manned aerostats, it would keep rising until overexpanded. At this point the bag would rupture, and down would come everybody posthaste with a postmortem afterward. But provisions had been made for this.

Frigate checked the altimeter and then rotated a metal drum set in the overhead. This was attached by a rope to a wooden valve in the neck of the bag. It opened, releasing some gas. The balloon sank. It would shortly begin rising again, though, which meant more gas would have to be valved off. This called for operation of the torch at intervals, and also for shutting off the torch and feeding hydrogen into the balloon.

It required cool and accurate judgment to know just how much gas to valve and how much to replace. Too much valved off meant a too fast fall. Too much new gas meant that the craft could ascend beyond the pressure height. A safety valve on top of the bag would automatically release gas to prevent bursting of the bag—if the valve hadn't frozen—but the balloon would then become, possibly, too heavy.

In addition, the pilot had to watch out for unexpectedly warm layers of air. These could lift the *Jules Verne* too swiftly and carry it above the pressure height. A sudden cooling off could precipitate the craft downward.

The pilot could in the latter situation order ballast thrown out, but this might result in a yoyo motion. And if he lost all his ballast, he was in trouble. The only way to lose altitude quickly was to release more gas. Which meant that the burner might not be able to expand the hydrogen quickly enough.

Nobody Knows the Troubles I've Seen would be his swansong.

However, the day passed without any nerve-wracking emergencies. The sun sank, and the *Jules Verne,* its hydrogen cooling, did likewise. The pilot had to run the burner just enough to raise it now and then and keep the vessel above the tropopause. Those off-duty snuggled under heavy cloths and slept according to their natures.

Being the only one awake at night was eerie. The illumination was feeble. The starlight poured into the ports, but this, with some small lights above the gauges and dials, was not enough for comfort. The alloy hull amplified every noise: the impact of a hand on the deck as somebody turned over and flung out an arm; Pogaas muttering Swazi; Frisco grinding his teeth; Rider softly whinnying horselike; the fan whirring.

When Frigate ignited the torch, the sudden explosion and succeeding roar startled everybody from sleep. Then it was his turn to burrow under the cloths, to sleep, to be roused momentarily by the torch or a nightmare of falling.

Dawn came. The crewmen got up at different times, used the chemical toilet, drank hot instant coffee or tea, and ate food saved

from the grails, supplemented by acorn bread and dried fish. The
wastes from the toilet were not jettisoned. Opening a hatch at this
altitude meant a possibly fatal drop in air pressure, and any weight
loss increased the lift.

The Frisco Kid, whose eye was best at estimating ground speed,
though they were clipping along at 50 knots.

Before noon, the vessel was gripped by a wind that took them
backward for several hours before it curved the craft around northeast again. After three hours they were going southward again.

"If this keeps up we'll whirl around here forever," Frigate said
gloomily. "I don't understand this."

Late that afternoon they were back on the proper course. Frigate
said that they should descend to the surface winds and try their luck
there. They were far enough north to be where the winds generally
flowed toward the northeast.

By letting the burner stay off, the gas slowly cooled. The *Jules
Verne* sank at a minuscule rate at first, then began dropping swiftly.
Nur turned the burner on for a few minutes to check its descent. At
13 kilometers altitude, the wind lessened. It picked up again and in
an opposite direction, the wrong one for them. It also gave the craft
a counterspin. Nur allowed it to sink until it was about 2000 meters
above the mountaintops. Now they moved at an angle across the
valleys, which were running straight north and south in this area.

"We're going northeast again!" Frigate said happily.

At high noon of the third day they were sailing along at an
estimated 25 kmph or more than 15 mph. Only the *Jules Verne*
could have gotten this far. Any other type of balloon would not have
been able to ascend to the stratosphere or descend to the surface
winds without losing too much gas to go on.

They opened the ports to let the thin but fresh air in. The up- and
downdrafts caused them some discomfort, chiefly from the change
in air pressure. They had to keep swallowing and yawning to ease
their eardrums. As dusk approached, the drafts became less violent.

The next day, in the middle of the afternoon, they were surprised
by a thunderstorm. Farrington was pilot when the black clouds
beneath suddenly welled upward. At one moment, the storm
seemed to be safely below them. But tendrils reached upward like
the tentacles of an octopus. The next moment, the body of the
octopus seemed to shoot toward them, and they were enveloped in
darkness laced with lightning. At the same time, they whirled like
fleas on a spinning top.

"We're dropping like a brick," Frisco said calmly. He ordered
that some ballast be dropped, but the craft kept on falling. Lightning
cracking nearby flooded the car with a light in which their faces
looked green. Thunder bellowed in the echo chamber of the hull,

and their ears hurt. Rain shot into the open ports and covered the deck, adding to the weight.

"Close the ports! Tom and Nur, throw out a Number Three ballast bag!"

They leaped to obey him. Their bodies felt light, as if the car was dropping so quickly it would leave them floating.

Another nearby bolt cast light and fear. All saw a black rock below, the flat top of a mountain rushing at them.

"Two Number One bags!"

Nur, looking out a port, said loudly but calmly, "The bags're not falling much faster than we are."

"Two more Number Ones!"

Another fiery streak wrenched the air nearby.

"We ain't going to make it!" Frisco cried. "Two more Number Ones! Stand by to get rid of all ballast!"

The edge of the hull struck the edge of the mountaintop. The car bounced, throwing the entire crew to the deck. As the momentarily loosened net ropes tautened again, the crew, which had half-gotten to a standing position, were hurled down again. Fortunately, the savage strain had not snapped the ropes.

Ignoring their injuries, they got up and stared through the deck port. Darkness except for a small interior lights. Another bolt. They were too near the side of the mountain, and the downdraft was still gripping the balloon. The pointed tops of giant irontrees were coming at them like hurled javelins.

It was too late to turn the burner on. Its effect would be negligible in the little time left before impact. Besides, the collision with the mountain top might have loosened the junctions of the pipes. If that were so, one spark would turn the interior of the hull into a furnace.

"All the ballast!" Frisco shouted.

Suddenly they were out of the clouds, but the blackness was now a dark grey. They could see well enough to discern the treetops spinning just below them.

Frisco left his post to help the others throw the bags and the water containers out. Before anything could be cast overboard, before Nur could punch a button to release the ironshot ballast, the car crashed into the upper branches of an irontree. Again, they were knocked down. Helpless, they heard crashing noises. But the branches bent, then straightened out, hurling the car upward and into the envelope.

The car fell back, was caught once more by the almost unbreakable branches. Its occupants were rattled around as if they were dice shaken in a cup.

Frigate was battered, bruised, and stunned. Even so, he had wits enough left to envision the punishment the plastic pipes were taking. They were being violently bent between car and bag.

If . . . oh, God, make it not so! . . . if the pipes were torn loose from the bag . . . if the points of the branches gutted the bag . . . the car would fall to the ground . . . unless it was held among the branches or the net was tangled among them.

No. Now the car was rising.

But would the balloon go straight up? Outward toward The River? Or would it be hurled against the side of the mountain and the envelope ruptured against outcroppings?

66

WHILE THE RAINSTORM WAS AT ITS HEIGHT, THE AIRSHIP CAME OVER the mountain from the north. Lightning, the only illumination, tore the skies. The radar swept over the Valley, over the treetops, across the spires of rock, across the River, and zeroed in on the great boat. The passive radar detector indicated that the boat's own radars were not operating. After all, the boat was at anchor, and why use the radar when no enemy was expected?

The huge hatches in the belly of the ship opened. The helicopter, sitting on a platform, began rotating its vanes. Inside were thirty-one men, Boynton at the controls, de Bergerac by his side. Arms and boxes of plastic explosive were stacked in the rear.

As soon as the motors were warmed up, Boynton gave the high sign. Szentes, the C.P.O. in charge, listened to the phone on the bulkhead, getting the last-minute report on the wind. Then he whipped a little flag up and down. Go!

The copter lifted within the huge bay, moved sidewise off the platform, hovered over the opening, the bay lights glancing off its windshield and the tips of the whirling vanes. Then it dropped as a stone, and de Bergerac, looking up through the windshield, saw the colossal ship merge into the black clouds and disappear.

Cyrano knew that the two-man glider would be launched from it within a minute. Bob Winkelmeyer would be piloting it; James McParlan would be his passenger. Winkelmeyer was a West Point graduate, a flier who had been shot down by a Zero during a scouting flight over an island north of Austrailia. McParlan had been rather famous in the 1870's. A Pinkerton detective, he had infiltrated into the Mollie Maguires, a secret terrorist organization of Irish coalminers in Pennsylvania. Under the name of James McKenna, he had penetrated deep into the gang, narrowly escaping detection and death a number of times. As a result, the Maguires were arrested, nineteen of them were hung, and the mine owners continued to exploit their employees.

Winkelmeyer and McParlan would land in The River and there sink their glider. Later, if they got a chance, they would enlist aboard the *Rex*. There would be vacancies, since it was doubtful that the raiding party could pull off a coup without killing some of the crew of the *Rex*.

As Sam Clemens had said to the two, "Rotten John doesn't have a monopoly on double agents. Suck up to him, boys, get him in your confidence. That is, if the raid fails, do it. Maybe you won't have to. But I know that slippery character. He's the greased pole the monkey couldn't climb.

"So, if he gets out of it, you'll join his crew. And then, when Armageddon comes, you'll blow up his boat. It'll be as if Gabriel had planted two angels in the guise of devils in Hell."

The helicopter plunged into the clouds. Lightning cracked open the world, slicing like a flaming sword between earth and heaven. Thunder roared. Rain pelted the windscreens, dimming vision. The craft's radar, however, saw the boat, and, within two minutes, the lights of their target shone weakly.

Boynton took the chopper at a forty-five degree slant toward the boat, then dropped it until it was close to The River. At full speed, while lightning tore the fabric of the night, it sped a meter above the surface. Now the lights from the wheelhouse and along the decks grew bigger and brighter.

Abruptly, the copter lifted, shot over the edge of the flight deck, stopped, poised, and sank. Its wheels struck the surface, and it bounced a little. But it settled down, the vanes chirruped as they slowed, and its hatches burst open.

By the time de Bergerac was on the deck, the motors had been turned off. Boynton was helping men out on his side; Cyrano was ordering a man in the craft to hand out the boxes of bombs.

Cyrano glanced at the top deck of the pilothouse. So far, no one was looking out of its stern window, no alarms had been raised. Their luck was even better than they had expected. Incredibly, there were no sentinels. Or, if there were, they had noticed nothing untoward. Perhaps they felt very safe in this area. A large part of the crew might even be on shore leave. And the sentinels might be goofing off, sleeping, drinking, or making love.

De Bergerac took out the Mark IV pistol and patted the hilt of his épée. "Follow me!" Five men raced after him. Two other groups took off on their appointed duty. Boynton stayed in the copter, ready to start the motor at the necessary time.

The flight deck was an extension of the overhead of the Texas. The Frenchman ran down it toward the pilothouse, the feet of his men thudding on its oaken surface. Arriving at the entrance to the second deck of the pilothouse, he paused. Now someone was shouting from the open port of the wheelhouse above him. Cyrano ignored him and plunged through the doorway. The others followed him up the steep ladder. Before the last man had gotten through, a shot sounded. Cyrano looked back down. "Anybody hit?" he shouted.

The man behind him, Cogswell, said, "He missed me!"

Alarms were ringing above, and from a distance came the whooping of a siren. Within seconds, other sirens joined it.

The second deck was a brightly illuminated corridor lined by cabins in which the chief officers and their women would be quartered. Hopefully, John Lackland would be in the cabin on the left, just below the ladder leading up to the bridge or wheelhouse. Clemens had planned to use that cabin, since it was the largest, and it was not probable that John would take a smaller one.

There were four doors on each side of the passageway. One of these opened as de Bergerac plunged in. A man stuck his head out. De Bergerac aimed the pistol at him, and the man slammed the door shut.

Quickly, working as planned, each of the six pulled a device from his belt. These had been delivered from the machinist's shop only an hour before, and two men carried an extra. They were short bars of duraluminum with long, heavy steel nails in each end. Fitted over the side of the door and the bulkhead, they were driven by heavy hammers into the oak. A determined person in the cabin could batter them out in time, but by then, if all went as planned, John and his abductors would be gone.

There were shouts and screams coming from inside the cabin. One man tried to push a door open while Cogswell was hammering. He dropped the hammer and fired through the narrow opening, not attempting to shoot the man. The door closed, and he quickly finished his work.

By now, John would have been informed via intercom that the boat was under attack. But the noise in the corridor would have been enough to inform him that the invaders were there. He did not need the explosion of the pistol to tell him that.

Three men should also have rounded the pilothouse and be going up its fore ladder. However . . . ah, yes, here came one of the wheelhouse watch. He stuck a pale face around the corner of the entrance at the top of the ladder leading to the corridor. Now he was stepping out from it, a heavy .69-caliber pistol in two hands. He wore no armor.

"*Peste!*"

Though Cyrano hated to harm the man, whom he had never seen before, he aimed and fired.

"*Quelle merde!*"

Cyrano had missed, the plastic bullet shattering against the bulkhead beside the man. Some fragments must have struck him, for he screamed and staggered back, dropping his pistol and clutching his face.

Cyrano was not an excellent shot. This was just as well, he told himself. If the bullet removed the man without greatly harming him, instead of killing him, its effect was even more desirable.

Shots and yells came from the wheelhouse. That would mean that the three had gone up the aft ladder and were now keeping the watch busy.

He strode to the door of the cabin in which John must be. There was no use asking its occupant to come out with hands up. Whatever the ex monarch of England and half of France was, he was not a coward.

Of course, it was possible that he was not aboard tonight. He might be on shore, roistering and wenching.

Cyrano smiled as, reaching out from the side of the bulkhead, he tried the knob. The door was locked. So, the captain of the *Rex* was at home, though not receiving.

A man's voice cried out in Esperanto. "What is happening?"

Cyrano grinned. It was King John's baritone.

"Captain, we're being attacked!" Cyrano shouted.

He waited. Perhaps John would fall for this trick, thinking it was the voice of one of his men, and open the door.

An explosion sounded, followed by a bullet which would have hit him if he had been standing in front of the door. It was not one of your plastic missiles which would shatter against the oak. It was of the precious lead and made a respectably sized hole.

He gestured at one of his men, and the fellow removed a package of plastic explosive from a small box. Cyrano stood to one side while his colleague, Sheehan, crouching low, pressed the explosive around the lock and over the hinges.

Crafty John sent another bullet crashing through the wood. This was low, catching Sheehan in the skull just above his eyes. He fell back and lay staring, mouth open.

"Quel dommage!"

Sheehan had been a fine fellow. It was a pity that his funeral sermon was confined to, "What a pity!"

On the other hand, he should not have been so careless as to put himself in the line of fire.

Cogswell ran up to the corpse, retrieved the electrical line and battery, and walked swiftly backward, unreeling the line. Fortunately, Sheehan had inserted the fuse in the plastic, thus saving a few seconds. Everything was a matter of utmost speed, and seconds might mean the difference between success or failure.

Cyrano retreated to the corner, flattened himself against the bulkhead, turned his head away, and stuck his fingers in his ears, opening his mouth at the same time.

Though he could not see him, he could imagine Cogswell securing one end of the wire to a terminal of the battery, then touching the other with the other end of the wire.

The explosion rocked and half-deafened him. Clouds of acrid smoke filled the corridor. Coughing, he felt his way along the bulkhead, touched the now open doorframe, dimly saw the blasted door lying over Sheehan's body, and then he was inside the stateroom.

He had dived in and then rolled sidewise, a maneuver made clumsy by the sheathed sword attached to his belt.

Now he was up against something that felt like the legs of a bed. Almost directly above him, a woman was screaming. But where was John Lackland?

A pistol boomed. Cyrano saw its flash through the smoke and was up and flying across the corner of the bed. His arms enfolded a thick and naked waist, and the tackled man went over sideways. There was a grunt, a flailing arm that struck Cyrano's head without hurting him, and then the man went limp.

Cyrano had his dagger out and against the man's throat. "Make one move, and I'll cut your throat!"

There was no response. Was the fellow frozen with terror or was he faking?

Cyrano's other hand felt along the shoulder, up the neck, and along the head. The man did not move. Ah! A stickiness! John, if it was John, had struck his head and was indeed unconscious.

Cyrano got up, groped along the bulkhead, and found the switch. The light showed a large room, luxuriously decorated and furnished by Riverworld standards. The smoke was clearing away now, revealing a very pretty and quite naked woman on her knees in the center of the bed. She had stopped screaming and was staring at him with huge blue eyes.

"Get under the covers and stay there, and you won't be hurt, mademoiselle. De Bergerac does not make war upon women. Unless they try to kill him."

The man sprawled on the deck was short and muscularly built and tawny haired. His blue eyes were open, and he was mumbling something. In a few seconds, he would be recovering his wits.

Cyrano turned and saw why John had fired his pistol. Hoijes lay on his back on the floor, his chest torn open.

"Mordioux!"

He must have run in immediately after he had seen his colleague dive through the doorway. And John, seeing him outlined against the light from the corridor, had shot him. Doubtless, he, Cyrano, had not been fired at because the smoke was still too thick for him to be seen.

Two of his men were dead so far. Perhaps there were others elsewhere. They would be left there, since it had been agreed that carrying off bodies would slow the getaway.

Where were the others? Why had they not come in after him?

Ah, here were Cogswell and Propp!

Something hard struck him, lifted him up and backward, hurling him into a bulkhead. He fell down on his face, and lay there, while his ears rang and his head seemed to expand and collapse, expand and collapse, like an accordion. More heavy clouds of smoke filled the room, stinging his eyes and making him cough violently.

It was some time before he could get onto his knees and more time before he managed to stand. By then he understood that a bomb had gone off in the corridor. Had it been thrown down from the wheelhouse?

Whoever had done it, he had killed Cogswell and Propp. And he had come close to killing Savinien de Cyrano II de Bergerac.

John was on his knees now, swaying, staring ahead of him while he coughed. A pistol lay within reach of his hand, but he did not seem aware of it.

Ah, now the vile fellow had extended his hand to grasp its butt!

Having neither gun nor dagger, Cyrano unsheathed his épée. He stepped forward and brought its triangular blade down like a club against the back of John's head. John fell forward on his face and lay motionless.

The woman was on her face on the bed, her hands covering her ears and her shoulders shaking.

Cyrano staggered through the smoke, almost stumbling over Propp's body. He stopped when he reached the doorway. His sense of hearing was coming back, but the firing in the corridor sounded faint. He got down on his knees and dared to stick his head out. The smoke was being carried away by the draft from the doorway at the top of the ladder. A body lay at the foot of the ladder. Evidently someone from the wheelhouse, perhaps the bomb thrower. Down at the end of the corridor two men crouched, firing out through the entrance. They were raiders, Sturtevant and Velkas.

Now two men, smoke-grimed, were coming down the ladder. Reagan and Singh. They must have cleaned out the wheelhouse and were coming to help the abduction party. Their aid was indeed needed.

Cyrano got up and gestured at them. They said something, but he could not hear it. That bomb must have been a rather large one. It had certainly made a mess of the corridor.

Reagan and Singh entered the cabin and picked up the limp body of John. Cyrano followed them after sheathing his sword and reloading his pistols. The woman continued to hide her face in the mattress and to keep her hands over her ears. See no evil, hear no evil.

On stepping out of the cabin, he saw that Sturtevant and Velkas had left. So—whoever they had been shooting at had been eliminated. Reagan and the giant Sikh, dragging John, his head lolling, his feet trailing, were almost to the door.

Velkas reappeared, running by the three men, shouting something at them. They kept on while Velkas sped to Cyrano.

By putting his mouth against Cyrano's ear and yelling, Velkas made himself understood. Some of John's crew had gotten to a steam machine gun. But their backs would be exposed to fire from John's cabin.

They ran into the cabin and looked out a port. To the right was a platform which extended over the edge of the flight deck. On it was mounted the thick barrel of a steam gun. Two men were behind its shield, swinging the weapon around to bear on the helicopter.

To his left, below him, were Sturtevant and the two carrying John. They would also be in the line of fire of the gun.

Cyrano opened the wide, square port, braced his pistol on its ledge, and fired. A second later, Velkas' gun boomed in his ear, deafening him even more.

They emptied their pistols. At this distance accuracy was impossible. The Mark IV pistols were using precious lead bullets, but the charges required to propel .69-caliber missiles caused a powerful recoil. Moreover, the wind, though slight, had to be compensated for.

The first two volleys missed. Then the gunner fell sidewise and the other man, taking over, dropped a few seconds later. Neither may have been struck by a direct hit. The shield could have made the bullets ricochet. It did not matter. The effect was the same.

By then, Sturtevant and the man dragging John were halfway across the deck. The chopper's vanes were whirling, but Cyrano could not hear them. Even if his hearing had been regained, the alarm sirens would have drowned out their noise.

Cyrano grabbed Velkas' arm and pulled him close. Shouting in his ear, he told him to get to the machine gun and hold off anybody who tried to attack. He gestured at the armed men who had just emerged from a hatch at the far end of the deck.

Velkas nodded and ran out the door.

Cyrano looked again through the porthole. The parties sent to blow up the paddlewheel motors and the ammunition supply were not in sight. Either they were still working or they were cornered and trying to shoot their way out.

He ran up the ladder and into the wheelhouse. Bodies lay on the deck. One of his men, two of John's. The lights shone on their blue-grey faces, staring eyes, and open mouths.

He turned off the alarm sirens and looked out the front screens. There was no one on the fore decks except a body at the foot of the ladder leading down from the fore part of the pilothouse and several bodies near the prow.

The boat was alongside a well-lit dock far longer and more massive than those usually found along The River. Perhaps the crew of the *Rex* had built it, their captain having decided to give everybody a long liberty. Or perhaps extensive repairs were needed.

It did not matter. What did was that the raiders had had the luck to find the boat manned only by guards and a few officers. John had decided to spend the night aboard, another item of luck, though not for him.

However, the uproar had awakened those on shore. They were streaming out from the huts on the plain and the stockaded fortresses. The lights from the boat showed the forefront of the mob racing toward the dock. Many of these were crew members, since they carried metal weapons.

It had not been in the plan to move the boat from the dock, but it should have been. Cyrano, knowing that the boat would be invaded in overwhelming numbers within a minute or so, took action. He sat down in the pilot's seat, pressed the motor power switches, and grinned as he saw the ON lights illuminated. Until now, he had not been sure that the motor power was available. After all, to make sure that the vessel was not stolen, John could have had the switches disconnected.

He prayed that just now would not be the moment for the motors to be blown up. If they were, the boat would be immobilized, and he and his fellows might not get to the chopper in time.

There was no time to untie the mooring lines. Too bad, but the power of the great electrical motors was immense.

He pulled back on the long, knobbed metal rods, one on each side of him, and the paddlewheels began turning backward. They moved slowly at first, too slowly to tear the lines. He pulled the sticks as far back as they would go, thus causing the wheels to rotate at full speed.

The giant mooring ropes were stretched. But, instead of snapping, they pulled the ends of the vertical beams alongside the dock after the boat.

For a moment, the fastenings of the piles held. The people on the dock either threw themselves down or leaped across the space between dock and boat. With a rending noise that could be heard even above their shouts and the firing aft, the piles came loose.

Its supports removed, the near side of the dock tilted, precipitating most of those on it into the water. Only one man managed to jump onto the boat without falling in.

The *Rex* backed swiftly away, dragging the beams alongside it at the ends of the massive ropes. Cyrano, laughing, stabbed a panel button, and the steam whistles hooted derisively at those left ashore or in the water.

"How do you like that, John!" he yelled. "Not only you but your boat is stolen! It's only just!"

Now he pushed the starboard stick forward, and the great boat turned down-River. He steered it to the middle of the stream and set the automatic pilot on. Its sonars estimating the depth and the distance from both banks, it would now hold a course exactly in the middle unless it was on a collision course with a large object. Then it would turn to avoid it.

The man who had jumped onto the boat ran across the deck and disappeared from view. A half-minute later, he came up the ladder to the next deck. Evidently he was headed from the pilothouse.

At that moment, the rain ceased.

Cyrano leaned out of the door and emptied his pistol at the man as he ran across the deck. The man dived beneath an overhang, then stuck his head out and shot back at Cyrano. The only bullet that came near smashed itself halfway up the ladder.

Cyrano looked out the aft screen. The helicopter was still sitting on the flight deck. John and his three captors were now inside it. Four men were running across the deck toward the texas. He lowered the screen and leaned out, gesturing to them that it was he who had moved the boat. They stopped and waved at him, grinning, and then turned and ran to the copter.

At the far end of the deck some men were still shooting at the copter from a hatch. But their large-caliber plastic bullets were going against the wind, and most of them were falling on the deck or being blown over the deck. Cyrano could not determine how many were firing, but it seemed to him that there could not be more than three or four.

Of course, there might be others in the boiler deck fighting with the demolition men.

And then the boat shook and a great cloud of smoke rose from the deck near the port wheelhousing.

The blast was followed by another almost immediately. This one was from the starboard side, a much more powerful explosion than the other. Pieces of flight deck soared up through the smoke, falling on the deck, some being propelled near the helicopter. The clouds were quickly dissipated, however, revealing a great hole just beside the starboard wheel.

The lights went off, then burned again as the emergency system took over. The motors having stopped, the boat began to turn slowly, its nose moving toward the right bank. It would be drifting now, though it might be many kilometers before it rammed the bank.

Sturtevant was back of the chopper and waving at Cyrano to hurry.

Four men appeared on the starboard side of the flight deck. Two came up from the ladder on the port.

Cyrano cursed. Were these the only survivors of the explosives crews?

Now little clouds of smoke rose from the hatch where the defenders had been firing at the chopper. One of his men dropped. The others gave protective fire while two of them picked up the fallen man and began to carry him between them toward the copter. One of them fell and could not get back up. He was picked up by two men. The other wounded man was hoisted up onto the shoulders of a comrade, and that one carried him though he staggered under the burden.

Cyrano ran back to the other side of the wheelhouse. That damnable fellow who had gotten aboard appeared for a moment, running across the deck just below. He was not carrying his pistol, which meant that he must have discarded it after emptying it. He carried an épée in his right hand.

His eye caught the movement near the foot of the ladder leading from the wheelhouse to the deck below. One of the men whom he had thought dead was living. And he was motioning for help. He must have seen the face of his chief at the screen.

Cyrano did not hesitate. The orders were to leave the dead behind, but nothing had been said about abandoning the wounded. In any case, he would have disregarded such a command. There seemed to be no immediate grave danger to the chopper. The few defenders could not cross the flight deck without exposing themselves to the fire of those in the chopper. Of course, they could take another route, come up a ladder near the machine. But he, Cyrano, could get this poor wounded fellow to the copter before John's men got there.

He went down the ladder as swiftly as he could, skipping steps, sliding his hands along the railings. By then Tsoukas had gotten on his hands and knees. His head hung low, and he was shaking it.

Cyrano knelt by him. "Do not worry, my friend. I am here."

Tsoukas groaned and pitched forward into a puddle of blood.

"Mordioux!"

He felt Tsoukas' pulse.

"Merde!"

The fellow was dead.

But perhaps the other two were still alive.

A swift examination dispelled his hope.

He rose, and whirled, his hand going to the butt of his holstered pistol. Here came that lone man, a brave person but a nuisance. Why had he not fallen into the water and so saved Cyrano the trouble of killing him and himself the irreparable harm of being killed?

"Ayyy!"

The pistol was empty; he had forgotten to load it. And there was no time to pick up one from the deck, to use the gun dropped by a dead man. Indeed, there was scarcely time to unsheath his sword and so prevent this audacious fellow from running him through.

Boynton would have to wait for him a few seconds longer. That surely would be sufficient to dispose of this obstacle.

"En garde!"

The man was a trifle shorter than himself. But, whereas Cyrano was as thin as a rapier, this foolish person was as sturdy as the shaft of a war axe. His shoulders were broad, his chest was deep, and his arms were thick. He had a dark, Arabic-looking face of imposing structure, though his lips were too thick, and his blazing black eyes and white grin made him look like a pirate. He wore only a cloth fastened around the waist.

With those wrists, Cyrano thought, his antagonist would make an excellent saberman—if he had the skill to match his muscle.

But with a rapier, where speed, not strength, was most important, ah, that was a different matter.

After the first few seconds, Cyrano knew that, whatever the man's aptitude with the saber was, he had never crossed blades with the likes of such before.

Cyrano's parries, attacks, advances and retreats, lunges and recoveries were equally matched. Fortunately, the devil did not so far have the slightest superiority in quickness. If he had, he would have run his opponent through.

He must know, however, that he was fighting another master. Even so, he was still smiling, seemingly undaunted, but behind his savage mask must be a realization that he would die if he became a fraction of a second slower in reflex and judgment.

Time was on the side of the dark man. He had no place to go, nothing to do but fight, and Cyrano had to get to the machine soon. Boynton must know that Cyrano was still alive, since Sturtevant had seen him in the wheelhouse. He would be wondering what was keeping him.

Would he wait a few minutes longer, and then, his chief not showing, think that he was dead for some unaccountable reason? Would he then take off? Or would he send someone to investigate?

There was not time to think about such matters. This devil was countering every maneuver, just as Cyrano was countering his. It was a stalemate, though there was certainly nothing stale about this. The attacking and the defending blades flashed almost in rhythm with each other.

Ah! Knowing this, the fellow had broken the rhythm. Once the rhythm was well established a fencer had a tendency to continue the sequence of motion. This almost unparalleled swordsman had hesitated slightly, hoping that Cyrano would follow the rhythm himself and so be spitted.

He had underestimated his man. Cyrano adjusted in the split second needed and so saved himself from a bad wound. But the point did penetrate his upper right arm slightly.

Cyrano came out of the retreat with a lunge which was parried. Not quite well enough. The man's arm also bore a slight wound.

"You have the honor of the first blood," Cyrano said in Esperanto. "And that is indeed an honor. No other man has ever succeeded in doing that."

It was foolish to waste desperately needed breath in conversation. Cyrano, however, was as curious as the alley cat he resembled.

"What is your name?"

The man said nothing, though it could be stated that his blade spoke for him. Its point was quicker than the tongue of a fishwife.

"I am one whom you may have heard of. Savinien de Cyrano de Bergerac!"

The dark man only smiled more ferociously, and he pressed Cyrano even more. This fellow was not one to be shaken by a name, no matter how impressive. Nor did he intend to expend energy in talking. Of course, it was barely possible that he did not know the name of de Bergerac.

Someone shouted. It could have been this distraction or perhaps it was after all the shock of finding out whom he faced. Whatever the reason, the man's reaction was not quite what it should have been. Using the thrust invented by Jarnac, Cyrano drove his blade through the man's thigh.

Even so, his point went deep into Cyrano's right arm. His épée clattered on the deck.

The man fell then, but he tried to get up on one knee to defend himself. Blood flowed swiftly down his leg.

Cyrano, hearing the slap of feet, looked around. Here came Sturtevant and Cabell, pistols in their hands.

"Do not shoot him!" Cyrano cried.

The two halted, their weapons aimed at the dark man.

Cyrano picked up his sword with his left hand. His right arm hurt abominably; the blood was running like wine from a freshly broached cask.

Cyrano said, "Perhaps this match might have ended in another fashion if we had not been interrupted."

The fellow must be in great pain, but he was not showing it. Those black eyes burned as if they were those of Satan himself.

"Throw down your sword, sir, and I will bind your wound."

"Go to hell!"

"Very well, sir. But I wish you a speedy recovery."

"Come on, Cyrano," Cabell said.

For the first time, Cyrano heard the shots. They were coming from the port side, which meant that the defenders had worked their way around to a closer position to the helicopter.

Cabell continued, "The chopper's been hit several times. And we'll have to run through their fire to get to it."

"Very well, Richard," Cyrano said. He pointed at the walkie-talkie fastened to Sturtevant's belt.

"My dear fellow, why don't you summon Boynton to this side? Then we can board in comparative safety."

"Yeah. I should have thought of that."

Cabell bound a cloth ripped from a corpse around the wound in the Frenchman's arm. The dark man's skin was greyish, and his eyes had lost their fire. As the helicopter settled down near them, Cyrano stepped forward and, using his épée, knocked the other's from his grasp. He said nothing; he did not resist as Cyrano tied a cloth around the wound in his thigh.

"Your comrades can give you more than first aid when they arrive," Cyrano said.

He ran to the machine and climbed in. Boynton took it up before the door was closed, sending it at an angle up-River. John, still completely naked, was slumped in a seat in the second row. Cyrano, looking at him, said, "Get some cloths on him. Then tie his hands and his feet."

He looked down. There were about twenty men on the flight deck. Where had the others come from? They were shooting away, their guns flashing like sex-crazed fireflies. But they had no chance of hitting their target. Did they not know that their captain was aboard, that they might hit him? Apparently not.

Something hit him in the back of his head. He was floating somewhere in a dark greyness while faraway voices said peculiar things. The ugly face of his childhood schoolteacher, the village curé, loomed before him. The brutal fellow had often beaten his student, rapping him savagely with a stick on the body and on the head. At the age of twelve, Cyrano, desperate, mad with rage, had attacked the parish priest, knocked him down, kicked him, and beaten him with his own stick.

Now the apish features, growing ever larger, swept through him. And he began to regain his senses.

Boynton was yelling, "I can't believe it! He got away!"

Cabell was saying, "He rammed his elbow into my ribs, and he kicked Cyrano in the head!"

The chopper was tilted so that he could look down through the still unclosed door. A searchlight from the boat briefly caught the king's naked body. His arms were flailing in an effort to keep himself upright. Then John had disappeared into the darkness.

"He couldn't survive!" Boynton said. "It's at least a thirty-meter fall!"

They would not be able to go back down and make sure. Not only were some shooting at the chopper, others were running now to a rocket battery. Though there was no chance the pistol shots could hit the chopper, the heat-seeking rockets would be unavoidable unless Boynton got the machine to a safe distance.

However, Boynton was not the man to be so easily frightened. And he was undoubtedly infuriated that their prisoner had escaped.

Now he was flying the copter, not away, but toward the boat. He was bringing it to a point about 90 meters opposite the rockets. There went the four rockets the machine carried, flames spurting from their tails.

And there went the battery in a huge ball of flame and a cloud of smoke, bodies and pieces of deck and metal flying on all sides.

"That'll stop them!" Boynton said.

Sturtevant said, "How about strafing them?"

Cyrano was startled. "What? Oh, use the machine gun? No, let us depart with speed. If there's one survivor, he could get to another rocket battery, and we'd be done for. We have failed our mission and lost too many brave fellows to risk more casualties."

"I don't see how we've failed," Boynton said. "Sure, we didn't bring John back, but he *is* dead. And it'll be a long, long time before the boat is ready to operate."

"You think John is dead, eh?" Cyrano said. "I would like to believe that. But I will not say for certain that he is dead until I see his corpse."

67

GROANING WITH PAIN, THE CREW OF THE *Jules Verne* QUICKLY
checked themselves for injuries. Three had ribs that hurt so badly
they were not sure they were not cracked or broken. Frigate thought
that his neck muscles were either torn or severely strained. Tex and
Frisco had bloody noses, and the latter's knee was paining him.
Pogaas' forehead was skinned and bleeding. Only Nur was unhurt.

There was little time to worry about themselves. The balloon was
now rising but was drifting away from the mountain. The storm
clouds were disappearing as swiftly as burglars who hear a police
siren. Fortunately, the light system was still working. Frisco could
see the flight instruments. Nur got a flashlight, and he and Frisco
applied a thin liquid to the pipe connections. Nur, examining these
through a magnifying glass, reported that he could see no bubbles.
Apparently, no hydrogen was escaping.

Nur opened the top hatch, and he and Pogaas climbed out onto the
load ring. While the Swazi directed the beam of the flashlight, Nur
went up the ropes like a monkey. He could not get close enough to
the neck of the bag to apply a paste. But he did report that the
envelope seemed to be tight around the entrance of the pipes.

Frisco heard this with skepticism. "Yeah, they seem to be O.K.
But we can't really tell unless we land and deflate the bag."

Frigate said, "As long as we have positive buoyancy, we'll stay
aloft. I don't think we should land until we come up against the polar
winds. That ought to be tomorrow if we've estimated our travel
distance correctly. If we touch down, we might lose the balloon. For
one thing, we don't know how the locals will react to it. In the early
days of Terrestrial ballooning, a number were destroyed by ignorant
and superstitious peasants when the aeronauts landed in rural areas.
The peasants believed the balloon to be the devil's work or the
vehicle of evil magicians. We might run into such people."

Frigate admitted that it made him very uneasy to be without
ballast. However, if they must, they could always unbolt the chemical toilet and throw it out. Of course, the situation might be such
that there wouldn't be time to do this.

The *Jules Verne* lifted above the Valley, and the wind sent it
spanking along northeasterly. After an hour it lost much of its

strength, but the craft was still moving in the right direction. It was also steadily ascending. Frigate took over the pilot's post at 4877 meters or a little over 16,000 feet of altitude. To stop further ascension, he valved off hydrogen in driblets. When it began to sink, he turned the burner on. From then on, the pilot would be busy trying to maintain the vessel within a 2000-meter zone while losing as little gas as possible and running the burner at a minimum.

Frigate's neck and shoulder pained him very much. He would be glad when he was relieved and could get under the cloths and stretch out. One drink of booze wouldn't hurt him and it might ease the agony.

So far the voyage had been mostly hard and fast work, some stomach-squeezing danger, and much boredom. He'd be happy when the final landing was made. Then the events of the trip would start to take on the patina of amusing adventure. As time passed, it would gain a golden glow, and it would all seem wonderful. The crew would tell exaggerated stories, making their perils seem even more hairbreadth than they had actually been.

Imagination was the great cozener of the past.

Standing by the vernian, the only illumination the cold starlight and the instrument bulbs, all but himself asleep, Frigate felt lonely. Tempering the loneliness, however, was pride. The *Jules Verne* had broken the record for nonstop balloon flights. From lift-off to this point, it had floated approximately 4824 kilometers or 3000 miles. And it would cover much more distance—if all went well— before it was forced to land.

And it had been done by five amateurs. Except for himself, none had ever been in a balloon on Earth. His forty hours in hot-air balloons and thirty in gas balloons did not make him a veteran aeronaut. He'd logged more time on this flight than all his hours on Earth.

The crew had gone on a voyage which would have made history if it had been on the native planet. Their faces would have been on TV screens worldwide, they'd have been feted and banqueted, they could have written books which would become movies, the royalties would have rolled in.

Here, only a few would ever know what they had done. Even a smaller number would refuse to believe them. Not even a few would know if the voyage ended in the deaths of the crew.

He looked out a port. The world was bright starlight and dark shadows, the valleys like snakes crawling, serpents in march order. The stars were silent, the valleys were silent. As quiet as the mouths of the dead.

That was a gloomy simile.

As silent as the wings of a butterfly. It recalled the summers of Earth in his childhood and youth, the many-colored flowers of the backyard garden, especially the sunflowers, ah, the tall yellow sunflowers, the songs of birds, the savory odors of his mother's cooking drifting to his nose, roast beef, cherry pies, his father playing the piano . . .

He remembered one of his father's favorite songs, one of his own favorites. He'd often sung it softly while on night watch on the schooner. When he did so, he saw in his mind a small glow far ahead of him, a glow like a star, a light that seemed to travel before him, guiding him toward some unnamed but nevertheless desirable goal.

> "Shine, little glow-worm, glimmer, glimmer,
>   Shine little glow-worm, glimmer, glimmer.
> Lead us, lest too far we wander.
>   Love's sweet voice is calling yonder.

> "Shine, little glowworm, glimmer, glimmer,
>   Shine little glow-worm, glimmer, glimmer.
> Light the path below, above.
>   And lead us on to love!"

Suddenly, he was weeping. The tears were for the good things that had been or might have been, for the bad things that had been but should not have been.

Drying his tears, he made a final check and roused the little Moor for his watch. He crawled under the cloths, but his neck and shoulders drove sleep away. After trying vainly to sink into blessed oblivion, he got out to talk to Nur. They continued a conversation that had gone on, day and night, for many years.

68

"IN SEVERAL RESPECTS," NUR SAID, "THE CHURCH OF THE SECOND chance and the Sufis agree. The Chancers, however, have somewhat different technical terms which might lead you to think that each refers to different things.

"The final goal of the Chancers and the Sufis is the same. Ignoring the difference in terms, both claim that the individual self must be absorbed by the universal self. That is, by Allah, God, the Creator, the Rel, call Him what you will."

"And this means that the individual being is annihilated?"

"No. Absorbed. Annihilation is destruction. In absorption the individual soul, *ka,* or brahman, becomes part of the universal self."

"And that means that the individual loses his self-consciousness, his individuality? He is no longer aware of himself?"

"Yes, but he is part of the Great Self. What is the loss of self-consciousness as an individual compared to the gain of self-consciousness as God?"

"That strikes me with horror. You might as well be dead. Once you're no longer self-conscious, you *are* dead. No, I can't understand why the Chancers of Buddhists or Hindus or Sufis think this state desirable.

"Without self-consciousness, the individual is indeed dead."

"If you'd experienced that ecstasy which Sufis experience in one stage of development, the *passing-away*, you'd understand. Can a person blind from birth be filled with ecstasy while those with sight are looking at a glorious sunset?"

"That's just it," Frigate said. "I have had mystical experiences. Three.

"One was when I was twenty-six years old. I was working in a steel mill. In the soaking pits. There cranes strip large ingots from the molds into which molten steel was poured in the open hearths. After the stripping, the cooling ingots are lowered into gas-burning pits which reheat them. From there they're taken to the rolling mill.

"When I worked in the pits, I fancied that the ingots were souls. Lost souls in the flames of purgatory. They'd be soaked in the flames for a while, then carried off to the place where they'd be pressed down into shape for heaven. Just as the big rolls in the mill squeezed down on ingots, shaping them, pressing the impurities to the ends of the ingots, which were then chopped off, so the souls would be shaped and purified.

"However, this has little to do with the subject of conversation. Or does it?

"Anyway, one day I was standing at the huge open door of the soaking-pits building, resting a moment. I was looking out along the yards at the open hearth. I don't remember what I was thinking then. Probably that I was tired of working in this extremely hot place at hard labor for such low pay. I was also probably wondering if I was ever going to become a successful writer.

"All of my stories had been rejected, though I'd had a few encouraging notes from editors. Whit Burnett, for instance, the editor of a high-prestige if low-paying magazine, *Story*, twice came close to buying my stories, but both times his wife disagreed with him, and he bounced them.

"Anyway, there I was, staring at the mill's ugliness, not at all conducive to pleasant thoughts and especially not to a mystical state.

"I was in low spirits, very low. And the train tracks that filled the yard, the grey metal dust that covered the mud and every object on the yard, the huge, hideous sheet-iron building that housed the open hearths, the smoke that the wind brought down low to the ground, the acrid stink of the smoke, all made for a very depressing mood.

"And then suddenly, unaccountably, it all seemed to change. In a flash. I don't mean that the ugliness became beautiful. It was just as grey and unpleasant as before.

"But, somehow, I suddenly felt that the universe was *right*. And all was and would be *well*. There was a subtle shift in my perspective. Let me put it this way. It was as if the universe was composed of an infinity of glass bricks. These bricks were almost, but not quite, invisible. I could see their edges, though these were ghostly.

"The bricks had been piled so that their faces were not quite even. As if God was a drunken mason. But now, in this subtle shift, the bricks moved, and their faces were even. Order had been restored. Divine order and beauty. The cosmic building was no longer an ill-built structure, fit only to be condemned by the cosmic zoning inspectors.

"I felt exalted. For a moment, I was looking into the basic structure of the world. Past the plaster that has been smeared on to make the walls look smooth and even.

"I knew, I *knew*, that the universe was right. And that I was right. That is, my place in the world was right. I fitted. Though I was a living being, yet I was one of those bricks, and I'd been aligned in the proper place.

"Rather, I'd suddenly become aware that I *had* been aligned all along. Until that moment I had thought that I was out of place, not quite on a level with the other pieces. But how could I be? All the pieces, the bricks, were misaligned.

"That was my mistake. Everything was in its place. It was my eyesight, my comprehension, rather, that had been twisted. Aberrated, call it what you will."

Nur said, "And how long did that state last?"

"A few seconds. But I felt very good, even happy, afterward. The next day, though, I remembered the . . . revelation . . . but its effect was gone. I went on living as before. The universe was again a structure built by an incompetent or drunken builder. Or perhaps by a malicious, cheating contractor.

"Still, there were moments . . ."

"The other experiences?"

"The second should be thrown out. It came from marijuana, not from myself. You see, I've smoked perhaps half a dozen marijuana cigarettes in my life. This was during one year, 1955, some time before the younger generation took up drugs. At that time, marijuana and hash were mostly confined to bohemian groups in the big cities. And to the blacks and Mexicans of the ghetto.

"This particular incident took place, of all places, in Peoria, Illinois. My wife and I had met a couple from New York, Greenwich Village types . . . I'll explain what this means later . . . and they talked us into trying marijuana. It made me pretty uncomfortable, downright uneasy, to have the stuff around. I had visions of narcotics agents bursting in, arresting us, being in jail, the trial, the conviction, the penitentiary. The disgrace. And what would happen to our children?

"But alcohol had dissolved my inhibitions, and I tried a joint, as it was called, among other things.

"I had trouble getting the smoke into my lungs and holding it, since I had never even smoked tobacco though I was thirty-seven years old. But I did it, and nothing happened.

"Later that evening, I picked up what was left of the joint and finished it. And this time I suddenly felt that the universe was composed of crystals dissolved in a solution.

"But now I perceived a subtle shift. Suddenly, the crystals in the supersaturated solution were precipitated. And they were all in some kind of beautiful order, rank on rank, like angels drawn up in a parade.

"However, there was no accompanying sense, as on that other occasion, that the universe was right, that I had a place in it, and that the place was right. That it could be no other way."

"The third time?" Nur said.

"I was fifty-seven then, the sole passenger in a hot-air balloon soaring over the cornfields of Eureka, Illinois. The pilot had just turned off the burner, and so there was no noise except from a flock of pheasants the roar of the burner had disturbed in a field.

"The sun was setting. The bright summerlight was turning grey. I was floating as if on a magic carpet in a light breeze which I couldn't feel. You can light a candle in the open car in a strong wind, you know, and the flame will burn as steadily as if in an unventilated room.

"And suddenly, without warning, I felt as if the sun had come back up over the horizon. Everything was bathed in a bright light in which I should have had to squint my eyes to see anything.

"But I didn't. The light was coming from within. I was the flame, and the universe was receiving my light and my warmth.

"In a second, maybe longer, the light disappeared. It did not fade away. It just vanished. But for another second the feeling that the world was right, that no matter what happened, to me or to anybody or to the universe, it would be good, that feeling lasted for a second.

"The pilot noticed nothing. Apparently, I wasn't showing my feelings. And that was the last time I had any experience like that."

Nur said, "Apparently these mystical states had no influence on your behavior or your outlook?"

"Did I become better because of them? No."

Nur said, "The states you describe are akin to what we call *tajalli*. But your *tajalli* is a counterfeit. If it had resulted in a permanent state, by self-development in the right path, then it would have been a true *tajalli*. There are several forms of false or wasteful *tajalli*. You experienced one of these."

"Does that mean," Frigate said, "that I am incapable of experiencing the true form?"

"No. At least you felt some form of it."

They fell silent for a while. Frisco, hidden under a pile of cloths, muttered something in his sleep.

Suddenly, Frigate said, "Nur, for some time I've been wondering if you'd accept me as your disciple."

"And why didn't you ask me?"

"I was afraid of being rejected."

There was another silence. Nur checked the altimeter and turned on the vernian for a minute. Pogaas shook aside his blankets and stood up. He lit a cigarette, the glow of his lighter throwing strange lights and shadows on his face. It looked like the head of a sacred hawk cut from black diorite by ancient Egyptians.

"Well?" Frigate said.

"You've always thought of yourself as a seeker after truth, haven't you?" Nur said.

"Not a steady seeker. I've drifted too much, floated along like a balloon. Most of the time I've taken life as it was or seemed to be. Occasionally, I've made determined efforts to investigate and even practice this and that philosophy, discipline, or religion. But my enthusiasms would subside, and I'd forget about them. Well, not entirely. Sometimes an old enthusiasm would flare up, and I'd drive myself again toward the desired goal. Mostly, though, it's just been floating with the winds of laziness and indifference."

"You become detached?"

"I tried to be intellectually detached even when my emotions fired me up."

"To achieve true detachment, you must be free from both emotion and intellect. It's evident that, though you pride yourself on a lack of preconceptions, you have them. If I did take you as a disciple, you'd have to put yourself absolutely under my control. No matter what I ask, You must do it at once. Wholeheartedly."

Nur paused. "If I asked you to jump out of this car, would you do so?"

"Hell, no!"

"Nor would I do so. But what if I ask you to do something which is the intellectual or emotional equivalent of jumping out of the car? Something which you'd regard as intellectual or emotional suicide?"

"I won't know until you ask me."

"I wouldn't ask you until I thought you were ready. If indeed you ever will be."

Pogaas had been looking out of a port. He grunted and then said, "There's a light out there! It's moving!"

Frigate and el-Musafir joined him. Tex and Frisco, aroused by their excited voices, got up and stared sleepily out another port.

A long shape, at about the same altitude as the balloon, was silhouetted against a bright stellar cloud.

Frigate said, "It's a dirigible!"

Of all the things they'd seen on The Riverworld, this was the strangest and most unexpected.

"There're lights near its prow," Rider said.

"It can't be from New Bohemia," Frigate said.

"Then there is another place where metals have been found," Nur said.

"Unless it's one They built!" Farrington said. "It may not be an airship, it's just built like one."

One of the lights near the nose of the vessel began blinking. After looking at it for a minute, Frigate said, "It's Morse code!"

"What's it saying?" Rider said.

"I don't know Morse code."

"Then how do you know it's Morse?"

"By the length of the pulses. Long and short."

Nur left the port to return to the vernian. He shut it off, and now the only sound was the heavy breathing of the crew. They watched the great, sinister-looking shape turn and move directly toward them. The light continued blinking. Nur ignited the torch for about twenty seconds. When he turned it off, he started toward the port again. But he stopped suddenly, and he said sharply, "Don't anybody make a noise!"

They turned to stare at him. He took a few steps and turned off the fan which sucked in carbon dioxide.

Frisco said, "What're you doing that for?"

Nur went swiftly to the vernian, saying, "I thought I heard a hissing!"

He looked at Pogaas. "Put that cigarette out!"

Nur bent down to place his ear against the connection of the inlet pipe to the cone inside the case.

Pogaas dropped the cigarette and raised his foot to stamp it out.

69

Jill Gulbirra heard the report on the raid from Cyrano before the helicopter arrived in the hangar bay. She was appalled at the casualties and furious because the mission had even been considered. Part of her anger was at herself. Why hadn't she argued more firmly with Clemens?

Yet . . . what could she have done? The laser was the only means possible to get into the tower. Clemens would not release it unless the raid was carried out.

After the copter landed, she ordered the airship taken up out of the Valley. It turned its nose southwest, heading for the *Mark Twain*. Cyrano went to sick bay to have his wounds bandaged, then reported to the control room. Jill got a more complete report from him, after which she radioed the boat.

Clemens was not as happy as she had expected him to be.

"So you think Rotten John is dead? But you're not one hundred percent sure?"

"Yes, I'm afraid so. But we did everything you asked, so I assume you'll give us the LB."

LB was the code name for the laser.

"You can have the LB. The chopper can pick it up from the flight deck."

The radar officer said, "UFO portside, sir. At approximately our altitude."

Clemens must have heard her, since he said, "What's that? A UFO?"

Jill ignored the voice. For a moment she thought the radar-scope was showing two objects. Then recognition came.

"It's a balloon!"

Clemens said "A balloon? Then it's not Them!"

Cyrano said softly, "Perhaps it is another expedition to the tower. Our unknown colleagues?"

Jill gave orders to turn a searchlight toward it and use it as a Morse code transmitter.

"This is the airship *Parseval*. This is the airship *Parseval*. Identify yourself. Identify yourself."

She had also told the radio operator to send the same message. There was no reply by wireless or light.

She spoke to Nikitin. "Head directly for the balloon. We'll try to get a look at it close up."

"Jes, kapitano."

The Russian, however, started, and he pointed at a blinking red light on the control panel.

"The hangar-bay hatch! It's opening!"

The first officer sprang to the intercom. "Hangar bay! Hangar bay! Coppename here! Why are you opening the hatch?"

There was no answer.

Jill pressed the general-alarm button. Sirens began whooping throughout the ship.

"This is the captain! This is the captain! Central crew's quarters! Central crew's quarters!"

The voice of Katamura, an electronics officer, said, "Yes, Captain! I read you!"

"Get men down to the hangar bay fast. I think Officer Thorn has escaped!"

Cyrano said, "Do you really think it's he?"

"I don't know, but it seems likely. Unless . . . someone else . . ."

She called sick bay. No answer.

"It's Thorn! Damn! Why didn't I install a belly-hatch override switch?"

In rapid sequence, she ordered two groups to run to the hangar bay and one to the ship's hospital.

"But, Jill," Cyrano said, "how could he escape? He has not recovered from his wounds, he is guarded by four men, he is shackled to the bed, the door is locked, and the two men inside don't have the key!"

"He's no ordinary man! I should have chained his hands, too! But it seemed unnecessarily cruel!"

"Perhaps the helicopter was not refueled?"

"If it wasn't, Szentes was neglecting his duty. No chance of that!"

"The hatch is full-open now," Nikitin said.

Graves' voice came over the intercom. "Jill! Thorn . . ."

"How'd he get out?" Jill snapped.

"I'm not sure of the details. I was sitting in my office, sampling some of the medical alcohol. All of a sudden I heard a hell of a brouhaha. Shouts, somebody crashing into something. I got up, but there was Thorn at the door. A length of broken chain was trailing from his ankle shackle. He must have broken the links with his bare hands!

"He charged on in, shoving me to one side so hard I was knocked against the wall. For a minute I was stunned, I couldn't even stand up. He ripped the intercom off the bulkhead with his hands! His bare hands! I tried to get up, but I couldn't. He tied my hands behind me and my ankles together with belts he'd taken from the two guards. He could have killed me easily enough, snapped my neck. Man, I still hurt where he grabbed me. But he left me alive, I'll say that for him.

"I finally got loose and staggered out to the ward. All four guards were on the floor. Two are still alive but badly hurt. The intercoms were all wrecked. The door was locked, and the pistols and knives of the outside guards were gone. I'd still be there if I wasn't so handy at picking locks and the lock wasn't pickable. Then I ran to the nearest bulkhead phone . . ."

"How long ago was it that he broke loose?"

"Twenty-five minutes ago."

"Twenty-five?"

She was dismayed. What had Thorn been doing in all that time?

"Take care of those men," she said and switched him off.

"He must have had a transmitter hidden somehow, somewhere," she said to Cyrano.

"But how do you know that?"

"I can't be sure. What else would take so much of his time? Nikitin, take her down to ground level! As fast as possible!"

Katamura's voice came over the intercom.

"Captain, the chopper's gone."

Cyrano swore in French.

Nikitin flipped on the general address and informed the crew that the ship would be going into dangerous maneuver. All personnel should make themselves secure.

"Forty-five degrees, Nikitin," Jill said. "Full speed."

The radar operator reported that the helicopter was on his scope. It was going south and downward at a maximum velocity at a forty-five degree angle to the horizontal.

By then, the deck of the control room was tilted downward. The others hastened to strap themselves into chairs bolted to the deck. Jill took a seat by Nikitin. She would like to have taken over the pilot's chair, but even now protocol forbade that. However, it did not matter that she was not at the controls. The wild Russian would get the dirigible down as swiftly as she could. Her job would be to make sure that he did not overdo it.

"If Thorn has a transmitter," Cyrano said, "he can use it now. We'll never make it."

Though he was pale and wide-eyed, he smiled at her.

Jill looked from Cyrano to the control panel indicators. The ship was parallel to the Valley, so there was no problem about clearing the mountaintops. The Valley looked narrow, but it was rapidly broadening. There were some lights down there, bonfires around which would be sentinels or late-night revellers. The rain clouds had dissipated swiftly, as they almost always did. The star-packed skies cast a pale light into the space between the two mountains. Was anybody down there looking up at them? If so, they must wonder what this huge object was and why it was coming down so swiftly.

Not that it was going fast enough to suit her.

Cyrano was right. If Thorn did intend to set off a bomb, he would be doing it now. Unless . . . unless he would be willing to wait until the ship had landed. After all, he had spared Graves, and he could have killed the other two guards.

Keeping an eye on the panel radar-scopes, she called the hangar bay.

Szentes answered.

"We were all in our quarters," he said. "There's no guard posted in the bay."

"I know," she said. "Just tell me . . . quickly . . . what happened?"

"Thorn stuck his head in the door. He pointed a pistol at us. Then he ripped off the intercom, and he told us that he was going to close the door. He said he had a bomb rigged to explode if the door was opened. Then he shut it. We didn't know if we should believe him, but no one was willing to find out if he was lying or not. Then Officer Katamura opened the door. There wasn't any bomb; Thorn had lied. I'm sorry, Captain."

"You did what you should have done."

She told the radio operator to transmit their situation to the *Mark Twain.*

At 915 meters, a little over 3000 feet, she ordered Nikitin to tilt the propellers to give the ship an upward thrust. Also, to raise the nose by three degrees. The inertia would keep them diving despite the braking effect of the propellers. In a minute she would order the nose raised by ten degrees. This would flatten out the dive even more.

What to do when the ship straightened out at about 915 meters or somewhat over 3000 feet? *If* it leveled at that altitude. She was really cutting it close, though she knew the capabilities of the *Parseval* almost as well as she knew hers.

Should she land the ship? There was no way to moor it, and the hydrogen would have to be valved off so that it would not rise as the crew abandoned it. Otherwise, some of the men would not get off in time, and they would be carried away.

But what if Thorn had no transmitter, what if there was no bomb? The airship would be lost for no reason.

"Too fast! Too fast!" Nikitin said.

Jill was already leaning forward to set the ballast switch for a discharge of 1000 kilograms of water. She punched the button, and a few seconds later the ship rose abruptly.

"Sorry, Nikitin," she murmured. "There wasn't any time to waste."

Radar indicated that the helicopter was hovering north of them at 300 meters altitude. Was Thorn waiting to see what they would do? If so, he did not intend to set off the bomb if they crash-landed or abandoned the ship.

What was she to do? The thought of either alternative made her grind her teeth. She could not bear the idea of wrecking or losing this beauty. The last airship.

The safety of the crew, however, had to come first.

"One hundred and fifty-two meters altitude," Nikitin said.

The propellers were turned fully upward and biting into the air at full speed. The mountains loomed on both sides; The River sparkled in starlight on the port; the plains ran smoothly beneath them.

There were dwellings below, frail bamboo structures filled with people, most of whom would be sleeping. If the dirigible landed on the plain, it would crush hundreds. If it caught fire, it would burn many more.

Jill ordered Nikitin to steer it over The River.

What to do?

Of the people along The River who had to stay awake or who wanted to, a few had looked into the white-and-black-spangled sky. These saw two silhouetted objects, one much larger than the other. The smaller one was composed of two spheres, one below the other, the larger of the spheres above the other. The greater object was long and shaped like a fat cigar.

They were moving toward each other, the smaller emitting a faint light from the lower sphere, the other sending out bright beams. One of these beams began to go on and off in measured lengths of time.

Suddenly, the larger object dipped its nose, and it came down swiftly. As it neared the ground, it emitted a strange noise.

Many did not recognize the shape of either object. They had never seen a balloon or a dirigible. Some had lived when balloons were not unknown, though many of these had only seen illustrations or photographs of them. But most of this group had never seen or heard of an airship except in illustrations of what might be expected in the future.

A very small minority recognized the larger, now diving, object as a dirigible.

Whatever their knowledge, many ran to wake up their mates and friends or to sound a general alarm.

By then some had seen the helicopter, and this caused even more curiosity and apprehension.

Drums began to beat; people, to shout. Everybody was awake by then, and the dwellings were emptied. All looked up and wondered.

The questions and the shouts became one great cry as one of the flying objects burst into flame. They screamed as it plunged, bright orange fire trailing like the glory of a falling angel.

70

TAI-PENG WORE ONLY A GARMENT OF IRONTREE LEAVES AND VINE
blossoms. A cup of wine in his left hand, he paced back and forth,
extemporizing poems with the ease of water flowing down a hill. A
poem would tumble out in the court speech of the T'ang dynasty,
sounding to non-Chinese like dice clicking in a cup. Then he would
translate it into the local Esperanto dialect.

Much of the sublety and reference were lost in the mutation,
but enough was retained to move his listeners to laughter and
tears.

Tai-Peng's woman, Wen-Chün, softly played on a bamboo flute.
Though his voice was usually loud and screeching, it was subdued
for the occasion. In Esperanto it was almost as melodious as the
flute. He wore only a garment made for the occasion, red-green-
striped leaves and red-white-blue-striped blossoms. These fluttered
as he walked back and forth like a great cat in a cage.

He was tall for a man of his race and time, the eighth century A.D.,
lithe yet broad shouldered and heavily muscled. His long hair shone
in the late noon sun; it glittered like a dark jade mirror. His eyes
were large and pale green, blazing, a hungry—but wounded—
tiger's.

Though he was a descendant of an emperor by a concubine, he
was nine generations removed. His immediate family had been
thieves and murderers. Some of his grandparents were of the hill
tribes, and it was these wild people who had bequeathed him the
fierce green eyes.

He and his audience were on a high hill from which the plain, The
River, and the land and the mountain wall beyond could be seen.
His listeners, even drunker than he, though none had drunk so
much, formed a crescent. This left an opening for him to stride into
and out of. Tai-Peng did not like barriers of any kind. Walls made
him uneasy; prison bars, frenzied.

Though half of the audience was Chinese of the sixteenth century
A.D., the others were from here and there, now and then.

Now Tai-Peng stopped composing, and he recited a poem by
Chen Tzu-Ang. First, he stated that Chen had died a few years
before he, Tai-Peng, was born. Though Chen was wealthy, he had

died in a prison at the age of forty-two. A magistrate had put him there so he could cheat him out of his father's inheritance.

> *"Men of affairs are proud of their cunning and skill,*
> *But in the Tao they still have much to learn.*
> *They are proud of their exploitations,*
> *But they do not know what happens to the body.*
> *Why do they not learn from the Master of Dark Truth,*
> *Who saw the whole world in a little jade bottle?*
> *Whose bright soul was free of Earth and Heaven,*
> *For riding on Change he entered into Freedom."*

Tai-Peng paused to empty his cup and hold it out for a refill.

One of the group, a black man named Tom Turpin, said, "Ain't no more wine. What about some alky?"

"No more drink of the gods? I don't want your barbarians' juice! It stupifies where wine enlivens!"

He looked around, smiled like a tiger in mating season, and he lifted Wen-Chün and strode off to his hut with her in his arms.

"When the wine stops, it's time to begin with women!"

The brightly colored leaves and blossoms fluttered to the ground as Wen-Chün mock-struggled with him. He looked like a being from ancient myth, a plant man carrying off a human female.

The others laughed, and the group began to break up before Tai-Peng had shut the door of his hut. One of them walked around the hill to his own hut. After entering, he barred the door and drew down bamboo-and-skin blinds over the windows. In the twilight he sat down on a stool. He opened the lid of his grail and sat for a while staring at it.

A man and a woman passed near his door. They were talking of the mysterious event that had taken place less than a month ago down-River. A great noisy monster had flown from over the western mountain at night and had landed on The River. The braver, or more foolish, locals had boated out toward it. But it had sunk into the waters before they could get close to it, and it had not come up again.

Was it a dragon? Some people said there never had been any dragons. These, however, were skeptics from the degenerate nineteenth and twentieth centuries. Anybody but a fool knew that dragons did exist. On the other hand, it could have been a flying machine of the beings who had made this world.

It was said that some had seen or thought they'd seen—a manlike figure swimming away from where the dragon had sunk.

The man in the hut smiled.

He thought of Tai-Peng. That was not his true name. Only Tai-

Peng and a few others knew what it was. His adopted name meant "The Great Phoenix," a clue to his real name since he had often boasted in Terrestrial life that he was just such.

Tai-Peng had met him long ago, but he did not know this.

The man in the hut spoke a code word. Instantly, the exterior of the grail sprang into light. The light did not shine over the entire surface. Against the grey metal were two large circles, one on each side of the cylinder. Inside each circle, which represented a hemisphere of the planet, were thousands of very thin, glowing, twisted lines. These intersected many tiny flashing circles. All were empty except for one. This enclosed a flashing pentagram, a five-pointed star.

Each circle, except for that holding the star, emitted dots and dashes of light.

The display was a chart not made to scale. The lines were the valleys, and the circles indicated men and women. The pulse group of each was an identity code.

Clemens and Burton, among others, had been told by X that he had chosen only twelve to assist him. There were twelve times twelve symbols on the lines, not counting the circled star. One hundred and forty-four in all.

A number of circles were pulsing the same group. The man sighed, and he spoke a code phrase. Instantly, the symbols emitting dash-dash-dash-dots disappeared.

Another code phrase. Two glowing symbols appeared near the top of the grail.

Only seventy recruits were still alive. Less than half of the chosen.

How many would there be forty years from now?

Of these, how many would quit before then?

However, there were many nonrecruits who now knew about the tower. Some of these even knew about the person whom Clemens called the Mysterious Stranger or X. The secret was out, and some who'd learned it second-hand were as intensely motivated as the recruits.

Given the changed situation, it was inevitable that others would get in on the quest polarward. And it was possible that not one recruit would get to the tower whereas some nonrecruits might.

He spoke another code phrase. The circles were suddenly accompanied by other symbols. Triangles, an uncircled pentagram, and one hexagram, a six-pointed star. The triangles, which pulsed code groups, were the symbols of the second-order Ethicals, the agents.

The hexagram was the Operator's.

He spoke again. A square of light appeared in the center of the hemisphere facing him. Then the display outside the square faded away. Immediately, the square expanded. It was a blow-up of the area in which the three stars and a few circles were located.

Another phrase brought forth glowing digits above the square. So, the six-pointed star was down-River by many thousands of kilometers. The Operator had failed to board the *Rex*. But the second paddlewheeler would be coming along, though much later.

In the neighboring valley to the east was Richard Francis Burton. So near yet so far. Only a day's walk away—if flesh could pass like a ghost through stone.

Burton was undoubtedly on the *Rex Grandissimus*. His circle had moved too swiftly along his line for him to be traveling by sailboat.

The Operator . . . what action would the Operator take if he did get on the *Mark Twain?* Reveal a part of the truth to Clemens? All of it? Or keep silent?

There was no telling what would happen. The situation had been changed too drastically. Even the computer at HQ would not have been able to indicate more than a small percentage of the probabilities.

So far, there was only one agent on a boat, the *Rex*. At least ten could be picked up by the *Mark Twain,* but it was improbable that more than one would be. If that.

Fifty were in the line between the *Rex* and Virolando.

Of the total of sixty, he could identify only ten. These were upper echelon, heads of their sections.

The chances were that he would encounter none of the sixty.

But . . . what if he failed to get aboard either boat?

He felt sick.

Somehow, he would do it. He *must* do it.

To be realistic, he had to admit that he could fail.

At one time he had believed that he could do anything humanly possible and some things which no other humans could do. But his faith in himself had been somewhat shaken.

Perhaps this was because he had lived among the Riverpeople too long.

There were so many journeying up-River, driven by one great desire. By now most of them would have heard Joe Miller's story, though it was at hundredth-hand. They'd be expecting to find the towel rope up which they could climb the precipice. They'd also expect the tunnel which would permit them to detour an almost unscalable mountain. They would expect the path along the face of the mountain.

These were no more.

Neither was the tunnel at the end of the path, at the base of the mountain. It had melted into lava.

He looked again at the unencircled star. Close. Far too close by. As the situation now was, it represented the greatest danger.

Who knew how the situation would change?

Now the loud voice of Tai-Peng entered the hut. He was outside, having tumbled his woman, and he was shouting something unintelligible at the world. What a noise the man made in this world! What a blur of action!

If I cannot shake the gods on high, I will at least make an uproar in Acheron.

Now Tai-Peng was closer, and his speech could be heard clearly.

"I eat like a tiger! I crap like an elephant! I can drink three hundred cups of wine at a sitting! I have married three wives, made love to a thousand women! I outplay anyone on the lute and the flute! I write immortal poems by the thousands, but I throw them into the stream as soon as they're finished and watch the water, the wind, and the spirits carry them off to destruction!

"Water and flowers! Water and flowers! These I love the most!

"Change and impermanence! These wound, pain, torture me!

"Yet it is change and ephemerality that make for beauty! Without dying and death can there be beauty? Can there be perfection?

"Beauty is beautiful because it is doomed to perish!

"Or is it?

"I, Tai-Peng, once thought of myself as flowing water, as a blooming flower! As a dragon!

"Flowers and dragons! Dragons are flowers of the flesh! They live in beauty while generations of flowers bloom and die! Bloom and become dust! Yet even dragons die; they bloom and become dust! A white man, pale as a ghost, blue-eyed as a demon, once told me that dragons lived for eons! Eons, I say! For ages that make the mind turn upside down to think of them! Yet . . . they all perished millions of years ago, long before Nukua created men and women from yellow mud!

"In all their pride and beauty, they died!

"Water! Flowers! Dragons!"

Tai-Peng's voice became less loud as he went down the hill. But the man in the hut heard one especially clarion passage.

"What evil person brought us back to life and now wishes us to die forever again?"

The man in the hut said, "Hah!"

Though Tai-Peng's poems spoke much of the shortness of life of men and women and of flowers, they never mentioned death. Nor had he ever before referred to death in his conversation. Yet now he was speaking boldly of it, raging at it.

Until now he had seemed to be as happy as a man could be. He'd lived for six years in this little state and apparently had no desire to leave it.

Was he ready now?

A man like Tai-Peng would be a good companion for the voyage up-River. He was aggressive, quick witted, and a great swordsman. If he could be subtly urged to resume the course he had forsaken . . .

What was likely to happen in the decades to come?

All he could predict—for now he too was one of the webs in the dark design, no longer a weaver—all he could predict was that some would get to Virolando and some would not.

The more astute would discover a message there. Some of these would surely decipher it. Among these would be both recruits and agents.

Who would get to the tower first?

He *must* be the one who did.

And he must survive the perils of the journey. Probably the greatest of these would be the inevitable battle between the two great boats. Clemens was determined to catch up with King John and kill or capture him. It was possible, highly possible, that both vessels and their crews would be destroyed.

Savagery! The idiocy of the tiger!

All because of this frenzied desire for vengeance which had seized Clemens. Clemens, who was otherwise the most pacifistic of men.

Could Clemens be talked out of this childish passion for revenge?

Sometimes he agreed with what the Operator, in a depressed mood, had once said.

"Humankind sticks in the throat of God."

But . . . *Evil will bless, and ice will burn.*

And the Master of Dark Truth was riding on unpredictable Change.

"What . . . ?"

The glowing lines and symbols had disappeared.

For a few seconds he stared, his mouth open. Then he uttered a string of code phrases. But the surface of the grail remained grey.

He clenched his fists and his teeth.

So . . . what he had feared had at last happened.

Some element in the complex of the satellite had suddenly quit working. No wonder. After over a thousand years the circuits were due for a checking, but no one had been able to inspect them on schedule.

From now on, he would no longer know exactly where the other men and women were. Now he too was in the house of night, bounded by fog. The passing of the lights on the grail had left a deeper gloom behind. He felt like a tired and companionless pilgrim on a lonely shore, a shadow among shades.

What would go amiss next? What *could*? For one thing, no, surely not . . . But if it did, then he might not have all the time needed.

He stood up and straightened his shoulders.

Time to go.

A shadow among the shades and running out of time.

Like the recruits and the agents, like the Riverdwellers, like all sentient creatures, he would have to make his own light.

So be it.

SCIENCE FICTION BESTSELLERS
FROM BERKLEY

Frank Herbert

DUNE (03698-7—$2.25)

DUNE MESSIAH (03585-9—$1.75)

CHILDREN OF DUNE (03310-4—$1.95)

Philip José Farmer

THE FABULOUS RIVERBOAT (03378-3—$1.50)

NIGHT OF LIGHT (03366-X—$1.50)

TO YOUR SCATTERED
BODIES GO (03175-6—$1.75)

* * * * * * *

STRANGER IN
A STRANGE LAND (03782-7—$2.25)
  by Robert A. Heinlein

TAU ZERO (03909-9—$1.75)
  by Poul Anderson

THE WORD FOR
WORLD IS FOREST (03466-6—$1.75)
  by Ursula K. Le Guin

Send for a list of all our books in print.

These books are available at your local bookstore, or send price indicated plus 30¢ for postage and handling. If more than four books are ordered, only $1.00 is necessary for postage. Allow three weeks for delivery. Send orders to:

Berkley Book Mailing Service
P.O. Box 690
Rockville Centre, New York 11570